"A tightly crafted debut wrought with the measured voice of an expert craftsperson, Lucy Tan's *What We Were Promised* is an exquisite exploration of class, family, and self." —*Bookreporter*

"An intriguing debut novel. Set in Shanghai, made empathic with a multigenerational family saga, embellished with timeless class conflict, this story entertains and enlightens." —*Christian Science Monitor*

"The ultimate message of *What We Were Promised* is one all young millennial readers can relate to." —*Bustle*

"As the narrative jumps across decades and continents, it throws the rural villages and urban skylines, as well as the lives of the locals and aloof expatriates, into sharp relief...All the while, Tan asks what it means to belong—to a person or a place." —*Time*

"Tan's debut will be entertaining—and enlightening—to savvy cosmopolitan readers." —Smithsonian Asian Pacific American Center

"Fans of Kevin Kwan's Crazy Rich Asians series will especially enjoy *What We Were Promised,* which takes place among a similar social set." —*Refinery29*

"Tan's talent as a storyteller clearly shines through her strong plotlines and characterization; readers will want to know more about each well-crafted player in the story...A novel of class, culture, and expectations; readers who enjoyed works like Kevin Kwan's *Crazy Rich Asians* will likely find Tan's surprising and down-to-earth tale an entertaining read." —*Library Journal*

"I read *What We Were Promised* in a state of enchantment, immediately drawn into the longings, secrets, and very human foibles of its finely drawn cast of characters. Both intimate and panoramic, Lucy Tan's debut is a revealing consideration of modern China as well as a thrilling discovery of the generations-long secrets between two families. Compassionate and heartbreaking, funny and wise, local and universal, *What We Were Promised* marks the arrival of an inspiring new voice."

—Chloe Benjamin, author of *The Anatomy of Dreams* and *The Immortalists*

"Lucy Tan brings to vibrant life the self-made, newly cosmopolitan Zhens, who have gone from the tea fields and silk factories of small-town China to the luxury high-rises of Shanghai in one generation. Abounding in insight and deftly told, *What We Were Promised* is a story both sweeping and intimate, as this most modern of families discovers it must confront its past in order to find its future."

—Maggie Shipstead, author of *Seating Arrangements* and *Astonish Me*

"*What We Were Promised* is a big, beautiful novel. Lucy Tan's dazzling debut grapples with the persistence of the past, the inevitability of the present, and the difficulty of balancing individuality with community."

—Hannah Pittard, author of *Visible Empire* and *Listen to Me*

"In *What We Were Promised*, Tan skillfully brings to life the issues of modern-day China and Shanghai. It is an immigrant story but one that also delves into the subject of going back to one's homeland. Tan humanizes each and every one of her characters. There is also depth to how the stories of past and present are interwoven. As a reader, I felt that I was in good hands."
—Weike Wang, author of *Chemistry*

"Reading *What We Were Promised* is like being let into the heads of the characters in a C-drama...From its first page, the novel promises a mix of emotion and intellect, plot and cultural critique, and it delivers. These characters are deeply understood and deeply felt, and the conflicts they get themselves into will keep you up at night turning pages. By the end of *What We Were Promised* you will agree that the real promise belongs to its debut author. Put Lucy Tan on your literary radar now."

— Matthew Salesses, author of *The Hundred-Year Flood*

"A story that moves forward with such momentum—you can't look away."

— Danielle Evans, author of *Before You Suffocate Your Own Fool Self*

"A quietly brilliant book, and a truly singular debut."

— Arna Bontemps Hemenway, award-winning author of
Elegy on Kinderklavier

"A beautifully rendered debut with vivid characters who will stay with readers long after the last, satisfying page."

— Judith Claire Mitchell, author of *A Reunion of Ghosts*

WHAT WE WERE PROMISED

LUCY TAN

BACK BAY BOOKS
LITTLE, BROWN AND COMPANY

New York Boston London

Copyright © 2018 by Lucy Tan
"Questions and Topics for Discussion" copyright © 2019 by Lucy Tan and Little, Brown and Company

Hachette Book Group supports the right to free expression and the value of copyright. The purpose of copyright is to encourage writers and artists to produce the creative works that enrich our culture.

The scanning, uploading, and distribution of this book without permission is a theft of the author's intellectual property. If you would like permission to use material from the book (other than for review purposes), please contact permissions@hbgusa.com. Thank you for your support of the author's rights.

Back Bay Books / Little, Brown and Company
Hachette Book Group
1290 Avenue of the Americas, New York, NY 10104
littlebrown.com

Originally published in hardcover by Little, Brown and Company, July 2018
First Back Bay paperback edition, August 2019

Back Bay Books is an imprint of Little, Brown and Company, a division of Hachette Book Group, Inc. The Back Bay Books name and logo are trademarks of Hachette Book Group, Inc.

The publisher is not responsible for websites (or their content) that are not owned by the publisher.

The Hachette Speakers Bureau provides a wide range of authors for speaking events. To find out more, go to hachettespeakersbureau.com or call (866) 376-6591.

ISBN 978-0-316-43718-9 (hardcover) / 978-0-316-43719-6 (paperback)
LCCN 2017944470

10 9 8 7 6 5 4 3 2 1

LSC-C

Printed in the United States of America

For my parents,
and theirs

谭凌实
陈朝霞
谭明儒
杨稔年
陈恩泉
罗锡贞

Shanghai, 1988

It wasn't the plane Lina feared, but the sky above the airfield. Acres of space unbroken by trees or buildings made Lina nervous. They made her feel as though she would float away.

From where they stood in the Shanghai Hongqiao airport terminal, Lina and Wei watched the planes move around the tarmac. Men in reflective jumpsuits directed traffic with semaphores, but it seemed a miracle the huge machines weren't crashing into each other without physical barriers to stop them.

"What do you think?" Wei asked, pressing his fingers against the glass.

"It reminds me of a funeral," Lina said. "Like in American films. Those big, shiny cars. What do you call them?" It was an odd word; she had just learned it. "Hearses. The planes look like a fleet of hearses."

"That's no way to think of it," Wei said, his smile waning.

Lina hadn't meant to be gloomy, only meant to say that she was impressed by the carriers' power, their solemn elegance. They looked like the kind of vehicles that would take you someplace you would never come back from.

When they finally boarded the plane an hour later, the first thing Lina noticed was the smell of foreign cigarettes—a lighter, sweeter scent than

Chinese tobacco. She didn't know for sure what American cigarettes smelled like, but the scent matched her idea of America, the way long legs matched blond hair. She gripped her husband's hand as he led the way down the aisle.

"Let's just enjoy ourselves," he said. "Here, give me your bag."

They had lucked into a row of three empty seats. Wei helped Lina buckle into the middle one, but before he could return to his own by the window, she stopped him.

"Wait. Switch with me."

If she was going to leave, she would say a proper good-bye to her home country. It felt wrong that her final glimpse of China would be of Shanghai, a city to which she was a stranger, and not her little house in the suburbs of Suzhou or the warm, tree-lined campuses of Wuhan. Not looking down at the one person whom she had not truly been ready to leave. Lina felt calmer now that the evening was growing dark, the wash of blue like a safety net thrown across the sky.

Soon, the pilot's voice came over the PA system, and then the plane started to move. Wei took her hand. He wanted this to be an experience they shared together, but she could not share it with him. Would not. These last moments she'd save for herself, to grieve the passing of a future that would never play out. She couldn't help it; Qiang's face flashed across her mind, and instead of fighting it, as she had been for the past few days, she let herself hold on to it, even closed her eyes to help herself remember. A dusty room filled with sunshine. Her breathing heavy from climbing the stairs, and all around her, the sound of mulberry leaves being torn apart by tiny mouths. Qiang leaning in close, his hair in his eyes, lifting a silkworm to Lina's face.

"It's perfectly safe," Wei said. "I promise." His voice sounded as though it came from hundreds of meters away.

She focused on thoughts of the lake. The breeze coming in both cold and hot at the same time. The shadow of a boy leaping from the water's edge, his back shiny and curved like a blade.

The plane began to lift. As Lina's center of gravity changed, she was pressed flat against her chair. Outside, the ground slipped from view. They were gaining speed, and soon they would be far away. Far enough to cross time zones, the concept of which still made Lina's head spin. In China, a person's day might start with the sun a little higher or a little lower than that of his countrymen, but their lives were all marked by the same clock, no matter how far apart they lived. America had six time zones. Lina's father called it the land of dreams, and so it seemed. For what other country would aspire to occupy the past, present, and future, all at the same time?

SHANGHAI

2010

1

One day you'll walk into a suite and find doors closed to you—the second bedroom, the study, the many closets. *We had guests over,* Taitai will say. *We went ahead and tidied a little ourselves.* But that won't explain the jade missing from the display case or her designer shoes gone from the entryway. In the master bedroom, someone will have done your job, badly. A bureau cleared, its contents stuffed out of sight; the bed made so that the sheets still hang loose from the mattress. Taitai will stay in the next room with the baby. She will not come out until after you've gone, but for once, she'll be listening to you—listening for the sound of your feet. With fewer rooms to clean, you'll finish up quick and wheel the cart back through the service entrance to the laundry hall. That's when you'll take out your phone and text your loved ones the news: you're about to be accused.

When Sunny had heard this speech from Rose on her first day of work, five years ago, she hadn't thought much of it. She'd assumed it was just an old housekeeper's attempt to scare her new partner, a way of saying *I know what's what and you know nothing.* Sunny was expert at knowing nothing. Where she'd come from, she'd spent more than a year as a professional odd-jobber, a forever-apprentice hired out by her parents for gigs around her hometown. She'd fixed motors with the handyman and skinned vegetables for restaurant stews. She'd washed laundry and delivered cargo — rubber tires and concrete slabs and dead chickens in need of plucking — on a bicycle, her load sometimes a few hundred pounds more than her own weight. In every job, she had been trained by someone like Rose, a person too old to learn new skills and who craved recognition for the ones she already had. This kind of trainer expected Sunny to learn quickly and yet resented her for doing so. Sunny was tired of being a novice. She was determined to be great at something, and cleaning homes was as good as anything else. Na, it would be different here. Full-time job. No end date.

Rose had led Sunny down the hall to the changing room, listing the shortcomings of the hotel and serviced apartments. The guests and residents were wealthy and therefore very particular. Management was unfriendly, at best. They hired English speakers for the front desk, and those employees looked down on the rest of the staff. Worst of all, though, were the accusations of theft. They were easy to make and difficult to defend against. Any one of the maids could be replaced faster than you could fry up an egg for mei guo lao breakfast. There wasn't any shortage of migrant labor.

"Where is your hometown?" Rose asked, opening a locker and retrieving her uniform from its shelf.

"Hefei," Sunny replied. *The outskirts,* she didn't say. Rose looked Sunny up and down, her expression making it clear that she understood exactly where she was from — the distinction wasn't necessary.

"Another one from Anhui Province. You will find many friends in this city." As she spoke, Rose pulled on a khaki-colored tunic, black cotton trousers, and standard-issue cloth shoes. She was in her forties but looked older. Her hair was shot through with silver, and the skin on her face was pocked as an orange rind. With practiced twists of her wrists, she rolled up the sleeves of her tunic and adjusted her collar so that it sat comfortably on her shoulders.

Sunny had put on her own uniform before leaving the house that morning, but she had ridden from Hongkou to Lujiazui on her motorbike, and by the time she had arrived at the hotel the entire back of the tunic was drenched in sweat. In the air-conditioned changing room of Lanson Suites, she felt the polyester's damp weight. Sweat had stiffened her bangs in flat strokes across her forehead.

"Where are your stockings?" Rose asked when she caught Sunny pressing a swollen heel against the metal lockers. "Xiao gu niang," she called her, even though Sunny was nearing twenty-nine, had not been a girl for some time. "You're lucky to have been partnered with me. Some country girls learn quick; others are back on the job market within a week. We'll see which kind you are." From inside her cubby, Rose pulled out a pair of nude-colored hose and handed them over.

Each of the housekeeping supplies had its own place on the cart. The bottom shelf held cleaning fluids, towels, and toilet paper, which Western residents used with incredible speed. The top shelf was filled with boxed soaps, tissues, pouches full of needles and coils of colored thread, plastic combs with teeth too fine for thick Chinese hair like their own. With these, they stocked only the short-term hotel rooms—the permanent residents preferred toiletries imported from abroad. When the cart was ready and both women fully dressed, Rose reached into a cabinet and pulled out a plastic bin full of name tags. "Here," she said. "Pick one."

Sunny couldn't read English but did not want to ask Rose for help. This moment felt too important, too private. Years later, she would remember digging through the bin, not knowing what she was looking for, but knowing it was right the moment she found it: S-u-n-n-y. There was something balanced and generous about the shape of that S, and she liked the way the double n's looked like the u turned upside down. The letters reminded her of a row of children playing leapfrog. She especially liked that the tag was still in its plastic wrapping. It meant that no other maid had used it before, that she would be the first S-u-n-n-y to sweep Lanson Suites' floors. That was something she had been looking forward to when she arrived in Shanghai—an identity all her own.

In the five years since her first day at Lanson Suites, Sunny had developed a way of moving about the residents' homes that was quiet and deferential. She had learned each family's habits and customs—the direction in which they stacked the dishes on the drying rack, the stuffed toys that were loved enough to have a permanent spot on top of a child's bed—and by attending to these details, she had her own means of communicating with these families. She wanted them to see that she was a person who took pride in her work, who would go out of her way to make their lives run smoothly.

The housekeeping staff at Lanson Suites always went by their English names, even though none of them spoke English. Chinese names were too difficult for foreign residents to pronounce and carried too much meaning to be revealed to the Chinese speakers. When characters in a name were combined, they produced a complex of feelings and images. That was no good; the best thing for a housekeeper to be was forgettable. Better to take on the blankness of American names. Choose well—a flower, a tree, a month—and its prettiness might make you also seem faultless. They liked to think that giving themselves the right names could prevent them from being accused of stealing, but they knew it wasn't true. Having an English name would not improve a person's language skills, and without the language, they would always seem like intruders.

As a child, Sunny never imagined that she would end up in Shanghai. She was here because it gave her a life different from the one she *didn't* want, one that would have been a matter of course in Anhui: more odd jobs, a second marriage, children, and restless old age. She had gone to extra lengths to protect her position, which was why, on the day Sunny was finally accused of theft, it came to her as a shock.

"I'm just reading what I see here," the hotel manager had said, pointing to his clipboard. "Zhen Taitai told us there is no doubt the bracelet was taken by the cleaning staff. You and Rose were the only two with access to her bedroom these past four months, so until we find the bracelet, we'll have to run security checks on you. Nightly."

Sunny was glad that at least both of them were being accused; Rose had been accused before. At the end of their shift that evening, Sunny followed Rose to the back of the service hall, where they unzipped their bags and laid them on the table. The regular security guard wasn't in, so the hotel manager's son had taken his place. He was sixteen and seemed to be only pretending to know what he was doing. He picked open packets of tissue, unscrewed thermoses, and fingered the contents of their coin purses. When a text came through for Sunny, he even paused to read the message on the screen.

"Enough," Rose said. She had two sons of her own, could sharpen her voice to make boys listen. The hotel manager's son dropped the phone back into Sunny's purse, where it lay glowing mutely into the fabric lining. She had been worried, earlier, about the next part, the part where he touched them. But his hand strokes over their bodies were quick and embarrassed. Sixteen, after all. In a place like this, with its badges and uniforms, it was easy to forget that their greater age could still be an intimidating factor.

When it was over, they were the only housekeepers left on the premises. Their shift had ended just as the sun set on the compound, covering the grounds in rose and gold, stretching shadows back as far as they would go. The service hall opened onto a stone path that led around the back courtyard and through a small sculpture garden, where European conquerors stood dumbly on their stone foundations, trapped in the darkening green. Past Lanson Suites' painted iron fence, high-rises leaped up out of the ground, their glassy walls catching the last of the evening light. And though it wasn't visible from where she stood, northwest of these was the iconic Oriental Pearl TV Tower—two reddish-purple spheres, one above the other, held high in the sky by cylindrical stanchions.

The first time Sunny had seen an image of the Pearl Tower was six years ago, when she was still living at home. On an errand to Hefei's city center one day, she'd come across a trinket shop that carried postcards. As she was flipping through them, one postcard in particular caught her eye—a photo of the Bund at night. Sunny's eyes had immediately been drawn to the Pearl Tower's alien presence. How unlike the drab, boxy buildings in Hefei. In that evening shot, the tower was lit, and each of its two orbs shone like a disco ball.

It hadn't struck her as odd to see souvenirs of another city sold in Hefei. After all, Hefei was a city full of other cities' leftovers—overstocked furniture, *yuandan* bags, and name-brand watches that were too expensive for anyone but tourists to buy. It was a city full of people who did not have the connections, start-up costs, or the guts to move to Shanghai, Guangzhou, or Beijing. Even its pollution was secondhand. Smog blew in every May and June from the surrounding lands, where farmers burned their crops in preparation for the next harvest year. Third-tier city though it was, Hefei was where Sunny had been wanting to move before luck swung her way. A year or two after stumbling across that postcard, Sunny got word that a neighbor's cousin who had been working in Shanghai had gotten pregnant and was giving up her position at a luxury hotel. Sunny knew she had to act. She begged three months' salary from her parents and took it to the neighbor's doorstep. *Put me in touch,* she'd said. *Qiu ni—introduce me.* It had been out of character for Sunny to behave so rashly, to offer up all that money in the slim hope of landing a job. But never before had anything called to her the way that the Pearl Tower had. What she wanted most of all was to live in a place where she could look up at the sky every day and see something beautiful and more permanent than herself, the people she knew, and their own sorry circumstances.

Now the Pearl Tower was far from the flashiest building in the city. Over the past few years, Shanghai's skyline had become crowded with lights and spires, and each had been designed to look grander than the last. Right there in the center of the photos was Lanson Suites Hotel and Residences. In the evening, its towers were all lit up like neon keyboards laid on their sides.

"That little dog-fart kid isn't nearly as bad as any of the older guards," Rose said. "I hope they keep sending him."

The two of them ducked through the side gate, came out onto Binjiang Road, and turned in the direction of the riverbank. They had an evening ritual of strolling along the boardwalk before heading back to Lanson Suites, retrieving their scooters, and going home. The boardwalk had recently been built and few people knew of its existence, aside from the hotel residents, who never took advantage of it anyway.

"They think we envy them so much, those taitai," Rose said. "As if we'd wear their boring jewelry. With all that money, you'd think they could afford better style."

"Have you seen this bracelet?" Sunny asked. "What does it look like?"

"If it's the one I'm thinking of, it looks cheap. Beaded, not even a solid chunk of ivory. I don't see how it could be worth much."

When she first started working at the hotel, Sunny had shyly admired the women who lived inside it. Up close, they were even more exotic than they seemed from far away. Everything about them was smoother and more flawless, from their ironed blouses to their creamy skin. She'd watched these women sit at their vanity tables and apply layers of ointments with light pats into their cheeks and necks, as if molding their features into place. It was hard not to compare them to the other finery in the household that required polishing and preserving, and enough time had passed for Sunny's admiration to turn into contempt. These women were less useful than their furniture.

Zhen Taitai was one of the worst types of resident to work for. She herself was lazy but had ruthless requirements of her staff. There was usually a day's worth of dishes to be washed when Sunny arrived and Taitai would stand behind her to watch as she did them. She looked almost apologetic then, as if to say she couldn't help it, it was her job to guard the porcelain just as much as it was Sunny's to wash it.

The husband, Boss Zhen, was all right. He kept mainly to his study, a place so crammed with his personal and work items that it seemed against his nature to spread out. Sunny liked that he used cheap notebooks, a brand meant for students. They were filled with large, looping English words and the cross-hatchings of geometric shapes. There was a franticness to his handwriting that wasn't obvious in his person. His physical demeanor was measured and his speech economical. A few weeks ago, one of the clubhouse café servers claimed that he had seen Boss Zhen on TV and that in those few minutes on-screen, he had said more than the server had ever heard him say in all the years he'd been working at the hotel. But you didn't need to see him on TV to know he was important. He had a serious manner that even Zhen Taitai went out of her way to accommodate. When her husband was home, Taitai occupied herself by fussing around the kitchen, fixing snacks and dirtying dishes. But during the day, she was left alone to attend to the rest of her self-appointed duties—rearranging furniture according to whim and imagining scenarios in which her belongings were taken by the hotel staff.

Some girls did take things. They knocked lipsticks from vanity countertops into empty buckets, bundled loose cash up with the dirty bedsheets. But the things they stole were so minor. The worst Sunny had ever heard of was a woman who'd pinned little stud earrings to the band of her bra. The trick, the woman had said, was to take only one earring and then wait a month before taking the other. By then, the owner would have assumed she'd lost the first and not look too hard for the second.

Sunny had only done it once. A couple of years ago, a Polish woman had almost had Rose fired for scrubbing the toilet with the same brush she used to clean the sink. After Sunny heard, she stole a bag of brass buttons from the back of the woman's utility closet. That weekend, Sunny and Rose met on the Bund and pitched them into the river, one by one, until they had all found homes in the shit-silt of the Huangpu.

"So," Rose said now, turning to Sunny brightly as they walked along the river. "Have you thought anymore about my proposal?"

"I don't know," Sunny said. "Meeting a stranger—"

"He isn't a stranger! He's my husband's coworker's son. He's not from Anhui, but close enough nearby. I forgot where. Your ma will like him."

Sunny laughed. "I guess my ma's opinion is the only one that matters."

"Aiya, you know what I mean. You'll like him too. Hardworking. Over one point eight meters. Both legs the same length, feet in good working condition. What's not to like?"

"Give it up, Rose. I'm too old."

"If you're old, I'm a mountain." She yanked on the hem of her shirt in a way that settled the matter. "You know, my cousin had a child at thirty-five. Perfectly healthy. Big, fat boy. Head like a watermelon."

Sunny had been married once before. The match had been brief and loveless, arranged because both were past the usual marrying age. She had put marriage off as long as possible, telling her parents that she wasn't ready, that she hadn't met anyone she liked enough to spend an entire life with. But the truth was, she had never had any real intention to marry. She kept waiting for the *wanting* to begin as it had for her sister and her friends. She thought maybe the desire to be married would be released like a hormone within her once she reached a certain age. But it never happened. She still couldn't understand why anyone should want to move in with a near stranger, call his parents hers, and live so close to home while feeling a world away. All for what? To produce children neither family could afford? It simply didn't add up.

When Sunny reached twenty-seven, the people in her village began calling her unnatural, and this was a kind of talk her parents couldn't bear. They didn't openly say they would kick her out of the house if she did not marry, but they certainly implied it. *Your brother already has one baby,* they said. *When the next one comes, who knows if there will be room for you?*

By the time Sunny finally gave in, all the most promising men had been paired off with other women and there was little choice in husbands. The one her parents decided on was named Wang Jian. He was twenty years old with a sweet face and one leg half an inch shorter than the other. The limp didn't affect his capacity for fieldwork, his parents had assured hers — it had only affected his ego a little. Over the six months that Sunny had lived with him as his wife, she discovered other ways in which he was abbreviated. He had a habit of stopping midsentence when he was speaking to her, as if suddenly remembering that he barely knew Sunny at all. She couldn't get used to this guardedness, though she was guarded herself. In the small, single-room hut off the Wang family's farm that the two of them shared, he liked to sleep facing the wall, his shorter leg curled beneath him.

Wang Jian hadn't seemed any more enthusiastic about the idea of marriage than Sunny had, but he was filial and good-natured. Like Sunny, he had married to make his parents happy. This silent but mutual understanding that their relationship was forced allowed them to become used to each other. She didn't mind that one of his legs was shorter than the other. She liked his strong torso and the gentle way he responded to her in bed. Sex with him was unlike the two experiences she'd had before him — a whole lot of jostling with men who treated her body as nothing more than warm flesh.

What everyone was waiting for was a baby, but Sunny didn't want a baby. Raising one seemed too difficult a project for two people who still sometimes behaved like strangers. Her sister and cousins assured her that a child would give her marriage purpose and raise her position in the Wang household, but Sunny could not justify bringing a human being into the world simply to improve her own life. Before bed every night, she inserted into her body a diaphragm that she had picked up from one of the city hospitals. When, four months into their marriage, Sunny still had not conceived, Wang Jian's parents became worried that she was barren. They began asking about her menstrual cycle and feeding them both medicinal herbs. Whether Wang Jian could tell the difference between rubber and flesh, Sunny never knew, but if he did know the diaphragm was there, he said nothing about it.

One day, about six months into their marriage, Wang Jian took off from work to go to town in search of bike gears. On his way home, he was walking along an unmarked dirt path when a cargo truck came up behind him. He'd startled when he saw it coming so fast out of nowhere, tried to run, and fell. Onlookers said that the truck hit him with such force that it sent his body tumbling off the path. He continued to roll downhill until he was caught in a stand of trees, like a piece of driftwood. The truck hadn't stopped.

After Wang Jian's death, Sunny couldn't stop picturing the accident. What a way for a life to end, especially for a person who had seemed only half alive to begin with. Sunny wasn't an idealist, but she had always thought that each human life was due some measure of fulfillment or understanding before its end. Wang Jian was proof against that. She felt guilty for dreading the marriage as much as she had and guiltier still that the occasion of his death had ended up improving her own life. With Wang Jian gone, his parents had little use for Sunny, whom they had never truly been able to welcome into their family. Preferring to grieve alone, they let her go home.

Sunny's life before getting married had been no different than the lives of a million other girls raised in the countryside, but for her it had been enough. She was depended upon, and that was a powerful feeling. Though she'd been a budding spinster, no one could say that she hadn't made herself useful. Sunny had been a cook, a vegetable seller, a confidante to her siblings, and an interpreter of Nainai's demented babble. She'd found a way to get the cousins to school and the chickens fed en route. She'd also been the one to organize the books— to enter the li of grain they harvested into the ledger via shorthand only she could understand. And while she had no official say in family decisions, her parents trusted her opinion enough that it counted for something. More, in any case, than it could ever have counted for at her in-laws' house.

For a while, Sunny was welcomed back into their old routines. But one day, her mother pulled her aside. *Now that your brother has a little wife,* she said, *there's not enough work in the house to go around. I've arranged for you to help out at the Shao noodle shop instead. What do you think about that?* Sunny hadn't known what to think, but what she thought didn't matter. *Hao ba,* she'd replied, and her mother forced a smile. *People go in and out of that restaurant all the time. Maybe you'll catch someone's eye.*

It was only a matter of time before Sunny would be expected to remarry. And over the next year, during which she performed odd jobs in the surrounding villages, she became more and more resistant to the idea. She'd never thought of herself as headstrong or disobedient, but there it was: a decision growing in her day by day. She wouldn't remarry. She'd go away to the city to make money, as young people sometimes did. Without her in the house, her parents could forget about her failure to create her own family, and Sunny could atone for her failures by sending money home. Only then would she be free to remember home as the welcoming place it once was.

"I think one lap does it for me today," Sunny said to Rose.

"We're not leaving until you agree to meet him. Do it as a favor for my husband."

Rose was the closest thing to family that she had found in the city. When Sunny first arrived in Shanghai, her friendship had been a lifeline. In these streets, too many faces passed for anyone to look into anyone else's. Sunny eventually grew to like the freedom that came from disappearing into a crowd, but before that, Rose was there to confirm her continued existence. *Where are you from? What does your family do? How old are you? Where are you living?* Although Rose was a born-and-bred local and had never known any life but city life, Sunny felt close to her in a way she'd never felt about anyone outside of her family. Rose had assumed, immediately and wholeheartedly, the role of a guardian in her life; it was almost as difficult for Sunny to say no to her as it was for her to say no to her own mother. But unlike her mother, Rose wasn't trying to set Sunny up on dates for the sake of furthering a family line or escaping village gossip. Rose just wanted to know that she would be taken care of. She wanted her to be happy.

"All right," Sunny said, as Rose had known she would all along. "Set it up." Rose could be a mountain in more ways than one.

Sunny didn't usually go straight home—most nights she drove out to People's Square. After leaving her scooter parked on a side street, she joined the crowds at the Metro entrance, where an escalator funneled them into the brightly lit concourse below. The underground network of stores branched out in many directions, but her favorite route was south, toward electronics stalls full of things that buzzed and flickered— light-up toys, novelty cigarette cases, and cell phone charms. If she walked even farther in, there were girlie shops with photos of celebrities pinned to their walls. Bright red circles were drawn around items worn in the photos and corresponding arrows pointed to copycat items on racks.

"Mei nu," a shopkeeper said as she entered that night. "Welcome. Try on what you like." *Mei nü* meant "beautiful woman," but it was a standard greeting offered by retail personnel before they got a good look at you. Sunny wasn't much to look at. She was used to eyes landing on her only to flick away within seconds. Her nose was broad and her ears stuck out through her hair on either side of her head. It was a decidedly unbeautiful face. Her friends back home had called her *jia xiaozi,* because of the way she did nothing to improve her appearance. But it couldn't be helped; when she tried on makeup, her face looked like a territory under siege. In her thirty-four years, she had come to like this stubbornness, her body's unwillingness to be adorned. On days when she felt adrift, it had even become a comfort. All she had to do was catch a glimpse of her reflection in a window or in the mirror of a store like this one. *We are still here,* the face said. *Ugly or not.*

2

A film van pulled up to Plaza 66 and parked illegally for the third time that month, penning several cars into their spots. From his office on the eighth floor of the plaza, Wei Zhen watched one of the van's doors slide open and two men climb out, shouldering tripods and trailing wires behind them. They took their time gathering their equipment, then rounded the side of the vehicle and disappeared behind the glare of the sun. Wei could not make out which cars were blocked by the van but suspected that one of them was his own. "Ta ma de," he cursed under his breath.

"What was that? I didn't hear you."

With the time difference, it was one in the morning on Wednesday in New York. Wei could hear car horns coming through the speakerphone, which meant that his boss, Patricia, was in a cab on her way home.

"Nothing, never mind. I forgot about the film crew. They're here again. They're always on time. It's incredible. Nobody here has any concept of time except for the people you least want to see…"

June first would mark five years of Wei's tenure as general manager of the Medora Group's Shanghai office. On some afternoons, he looked up into the silver-green wash of light coming through the double-paned windows and was disoriented by the room's similarity to his old office back in New York. He felt an eerie certainty that if he were only to swivel his chair around so that his back was to the city, he would find himself on Fifty-Seventh Street again, and no time at all would have passed. A drowsiness came over him in those moments, an existential gloom. But today was not one of those days. Today, the very essence of what it meant to work in China was about to come rolling in through the marketing firm's doors. The lights, the cameras, the noise—Wei could feel his temples begin to tighten.

"Ah, the film crew," Patricia said. "I saw Sandrik's reports. It looks like the TV show is working. Are you filling the positions you need?"

"We're starting to get better candidates," Wei admitted. "It does seem like it."

When Wei got the Shanghai job, it had been the most exciting thing to come his way in a long time. Over the years working in the New York office, he had watched the Medora Group grow bloated and ineffectual. A new office meant a chance not only to build business in China but also to make the company lean again—to hire a team of young, local people with bilingual language and cultural proficiency, the set of highly educated Chinese who had grown up watching American movies.

Unfortunately, as Wei had explained in one of his early reports back to Patricia, the perception of the advertising industry in China had changed. The work used to seem more glamorous. On the one hand, drinking and schmoozing; on the other, distilling human insight into sexy, succinct messages. Things used to be simple. You'd create the ad, buy space for it—call up a magazine or a billboard, negotiate a price—and then the ad would run for however long it was supposed to run. But these days, advertising was about measurement, about whether sales upticks were due to banner ads or direct mail, about coming up with the right questions to ask the market rather than simply creating a campaign idea that pleased the CEO. They needed employees who were both analytical and smart, and top graduates didn't know enough about digital advertising to consider it a viable career option. Despite the company's efforts to recruit the best in the workforce, his employee base was a mix of unexceptional college graduates who had majored in English and the few bilingual expats who had come over with Wei from abroad.

Wei and his human resources manager, Sandrik, had puzzled over this hiring problem for the better part of four years before Sandrik had come up with the idea for the show. *Pitch 360*, it was called—an elimination-style reality-TV micro-series sponsored by Medora. Twenty contestants were put through a succession of tasks that ranged from designing consumer-research plans to developing viral marketing strategies to pitching to clients. Each week, two contestants were eliminated, and at the end, one victor was granted a cash prize and a salaried position at Medora. A TV show would give the company the right kind of visibility, Sandrik had said. It would show young people what it was like to work in digital advertising while also positioning Medora as an industry leader. They could air it online as well as on Shanghai's bilingual TV channel, thereby attracting their perfect demographic: people who were educated and who consumed media.

Wei was skeptical, but he didn't have any better ideas; he'd allowed it.

"I watched a clip of the show online," Patricia said now. "You looked uncomfortable."

"Thank you."

"I'm teasing. You were fine. Just not your *usual* superconfident camera-ready self."

"It's different with interviews and press conferences. I'm not good at reading off a script."

At the very start of the show, Wei Zhen himself had been a cast member. He'd hated every part of the experience: waiting around for the filming to start, wearing makeup, having his own face inches away from the flawless skin of the young makeup artist. "Don't do that weird thing with your lips," she had whispered to him just before the lights were aimed in his direction, leaving him with no chance to ask, *What? What am I doing with my lips?*

He'd been stupid to think that the reality show would resemble anything close to reality. The contestants were not the bright-eyed creative savants he'd imagined. They were more attractive than they were smart, and 40 percent of them came from performing arts schools. As each episode aired, Wei had become increasingly perturbed by the show's existence. Every time a neighbor stopped him at Lanson Suites to say, *I saw you on TV!* he'd grow red in the face. It was becoming clear to him, if not to them, if not to Patricia, that he was turning the business into a farce. Wei would have pulled the plug on the show long ago if what they were doing hadn't been working. But Sandrik was right; the show was attracting ten times the number of job applications, and many of these from *real* candidates, the sort of people they wanted.

"Look, I'm going to try to get out of the office before they start setting up to shoot," said Wei. "Do you have anything else for me?"

"No," Patricia said. "Except…Wei, take it easy over there."

On the way down, in the glass elevator, Wei caught sight of the TV show's director; his bleached hair was immediately recognizable in an adjacent car. The man was Chinese, but when they'd met three months ago, he'd introduced himself as Dash and insisted on speaking to Wei in Manchester-accented English. Dash embodied the type of Chinese-born expat Wei hated the most — those who believed they were better than the locals because they had once lived outside the country. Whenever Wei was in conversation with Dash, he had the distinct impression that the man was waiting for Wei to ask him where he was from. He had done everything he could to lessen the number of interactions with Dash. His first move had been to request that he be written off the show.

"But you're the general manager," Dash had said.

"So?"

"We need a figurehead character for the show. We need a boss."

"What about Sandrik?" he suggested.

"We can't just switch figureheads three episodes in."

"I don't care how you do it," Wei said. "Just leave me out."

The following week, Wei had arrived at work to find someone who looked exactly like him crouched on the sidewalk in front of Plaza 66, eating fried chicken out of a Styrofoam carton. It was uncanny. Wei had to look down at his own feet to be sure he was really standing there, that he wasn't having an out-of-body experience. This person had the same bullish nose, the same long arms. Even the set of his back as he leaned into his food—straight, but with a touch of stiffness in the shoulders—was Wei's. This was the actor they had hired to replace him on camera.

Wei's doppelgänger caused a sensation at the office. No one knew his real name, nor did they care to find out. They all called him Mr. Boss and clapped whenever he walked in, handed him briefs to sign, yelled requests for him to raise their bonuses. They begged for photos of the two of them side by side—Mr. Boss and the real Boss Zhen—striking a variety of poses. He had humored these requests for the first day or two, stood with his arms around his colleagues and the actor. He had also stood back to back with Mr. Boss with his arms crossed or with his hands in his pockets—everything short of the finger-gun James Bond pose that was so popular with the interns.

No longer. He wouldn't fuel the distraction anymore.

The moment he and Dash made eye contact through the glass partition, Wei saw the man begin to raise his arm in a gesture he'd come to know well—*Boss Zhen, can I get a word?* But then the elevator car rose out of view, and immediately, Wei felt the pressure at his temples begin to lift.

Shanghai humidity was unforgiving. It seeped into your lungs in early June and sometimes stayed until September, when fall winds pushed out the lingering heat. In the short walk from the plaza's steps to where the car had pulled up at the curb, Wei felt his neck begin to prickle with sweat. He got into the backseat, stripped off his tie, and inhaled a blast of air from the cooling system.

Little Cao turned around and grinned. "They're filming again, ah? I saw the van." He waved to the film crew's driver, who had moved his vehicle farther down the lot. Here was something Wei had learned since transferring to China: The value of a driver wasn't so much in his punctuality, or even in his sense of direction. What was important was that a driver had the ability to make friends with policemen, valet attendants, and other drivers. Little Cao had been able to get the film crew's driver to move the van out of his way before they had finished unloading, and that was the skill that kept him on the payroll.

"Next season you should put me on your show." Little Cao wiggled his eyebrows at Wei in the rearview mirror. "I'm full of advertising ideas, Boss. I'll split the prize money with you."

"If there ends up being a next season," Wei said darkly, "you can have my job."

The district of Jing'an was busy at any hour of the day, but the stretch of Nanjing West Road along which they traveled was particularly tricky around lunchtime. Office workers exited the Plaza 66 office tower and mixed with the retail shoppers heading to and from the mall next door. It was easy to distinguish the workforce from the *fu er dai* — the rich second generation, young men and women whose parents' money afforded them the leisure to stroll around during the day in designer couture. The workers carried tension in their shoulders and were prone to looking myopically up at the buildings around them — all of them sparkling, all erected within the last ten years. The trees lining either side of Nanjing West Road were too strong, too green for their natural environment, lush in a way that seemed purchased. Money; the whole avenue reeked of it.

It had been a sudden business decision, Medora's lunge for China. The fastest thing the slug of a company had accomplished in the ten years Wei had worked for it, and that was a kind of accomplishment in itself— although it meant that Wei, who was supposed to be in charge of it all, often didn't get clued in to his own operations until the last minute. The first time Medora sent him to Shanghai, he'd made the trip with three others: his chief of staff, Chris, a twenty-eight-year-old bilingual kid who had spent a couple years at Yelp; Sandrik, with whom he'd worked back in New York; and Katrina, a recent Yale graduate whose title wasn't quite clear to Wei, even now.

"We just got approved for the final head count," Sandrik said as he'd settled in next to Wei on that first plane ride over from New York. He'd lowered the back of his leather seat until it was practically horizontal within its pod. "Guess how many."

"Ten," Wei said. "First quarter."

"Think big," Sandrik said. "Think the whole year."

"Twenty-five?"

"A hundred and fifty."

"A hundred—" Wei blinked at Sandrik, who smiled and lowered his eye mask, as though the number indicated a grand coup instead of an irresponsible risk. Wei pulled the eye mask back up Sandrik's face.

"A hundred and fifty? We can't train people that fast. We're going to have new hires sitting around doing nothing for all of March."

"Well, we have to start off strong."

Even as he resented Sandrik's ignorance at what these numbers meant—how near impossible it would be to run an organization of that size right off the bat—Wei knew, deep down, that he was right. The bigger the employee base they started off with, the more money they could ask for to run the branch next year. He realized later that if anyone had been naive, it was him. What kind of midsize corporation like Medora approached softly? It had to come in strong, elbow its way in. Had to be American.

So instead of doing what he had wanted to do that initial year — fly through China to visit the different agencies, study the habits of the Chinese and how they engaged with media — Wei had spent it in the office processing paperwork. He had approved applications, interviewed candidates, and set up an organizational structure that he was not convinced would work. He'd been expected to blindly follow the orders of the executives above him, executives to whom he was indebted because they had promoted him so quickly. And suddenly, China didn't seem so different from New York.

They turned off Nanjing West and headed toward the elevated thruway on Yan'an Road. Seeing pedestrians sweat as they walked along the streets made Wei thirsty. He had a sudden craving for calamansi juice but didn't ask Little Cao to stop — didn't want to test the traffic. Instead, he grabbed a bottle of water from the pocket of the front seat, wrested it open, and drank half its contents at once. The greedy act of gulping, mixed with the afternoon sunshine, was delicious. It reminded him of how it felt to be young. What a treat, to be going home at this hour. He'd almost forgotten the pleasure of truancy.

The traffic let up as soon as they hit the bridge, and within minutes they were descending into Pudong New District. He could see Lanson Suites already, the serviced apartment in which he and his wife lived. They'd chosen it out of a catalog the company had sent to him when he'd taken the job in Shanghai. That night, Lina had sat on his lap and they'd flipped through the pages together. Each apartment's price was listed in the lower-right-hand corner — sums that made them gape at each other in surprise. *This is the monthly cost?* Lina had asked. *And the company will cover it?* He'd felt both happy and ashamed then. Happy that he could give her something nicer than she had expected, ashamed that he hadn't been doing so for years. His success at Medora had come upon him so quickly that they hadn't had the time for their lifestyle to catch up with his paycheck. He wasn't even sure if Lina knew how much money he'd made in the past year, with bonuses and stock options. Unlike his colleagues, he hadn't yet put his daughter in private school or bought a nicer car or moved the whole family to New York City. But this was his chance. *That's right,* he said. *Whichever one we pick. It's time to think big.*

And so they had settled on Lanson Suites. Lina liked it for its dark wood floors and the building's countless amenities: three pools, two gyms, four "relaxation rooms," two business lounges, a billiards room, a child-care center, a full-time staff including twenty-four-hour kitchen service, and more. These were nice to have, but Wei had rightly predicted that he would be too busy to take advantage of any of it. The only room that truly mattered to him was the office space, and of all the apartment photos they'd flipped through, this one had been just perfect: floor-to-ceiling windows, a good view of the river. It was just large enough for pacing. And sure enough, he'd done some of his best work walking from one end of the room to the other, looking down at the waterfront restaurants and, if there wasn't too much smog, at the buildings beyond. The visual distance gave way to mental distance, space for patterns to emerge and ideas to present themselves in ways that they couldn't when he was just staring at numbers and graphs at a desk.

When Wei walked into the apartment that afternoon, Lina was lying on the couch with a magazine covering her face. Hearing him come in, she sat up, alarmed. Her hair was mussed and mascara dust clung to the skin below her left eye.

"What happened?" she asked, her voice foggy.

"Nothing happened. I'm home early."

"Oh," she said. "I was just having a nap."

Wei often feared that life in Shanghai bored Lina, who had gone from working full-time teaching Chinese to grade-schoolers in America to not working at all. He had once suggested that she take up teaching again, but Lina pointed out that there was little need for Chinese-language teachers in China. Not true, Wei told her. The influx of expats meant that there were more international schools these days, and they were all looking for bilingual teachers to teach Western kids how to speak Chinese. Lina scoffed at the idea. *Our friends' kids go to Shanghai American. You want me to start working for our friends?* Privately, Wei believed that the real reason she didn't want to go back to work was that she had become too used to the lifestyle of a taitai. That's how they referred to them now, as *taitai*—ladies of luxury who could not be called housewives because, aside from cooking the occasional meal, they did no housework at all. Wei thought, watching her now, that it hardly seemed possible he'd once known her as a schoolgirl in Suzhou, her hair in braids.

"Do you want something to eat?" she asked.

"No," he said. "Where's Karen?"

"Swimming, I think." The balcony's sliding doors stood open and a warm wind beckoned him through. Outside, he rested his palms on the hot stone balustrade. As he leaned over it, a line of palm trees came into view, then water, and, at last, his twelve-year-old daughter. Wei rarely knew what to say to Karen, but her presence—her dark head bobbing on the pool's surface—was a stabilizing force. One of his favorite things to do when she was home for the summer was to open the door to her room and just look in on her.

He returned to the living room with an inspiration. "Let's go out for dinner tonight."

As his eyes were adjusting back to the low light, he almost tripped over a wine-colored urn that he could not remember having been there a moment before. "Is this new?"

"I got it yesterday," Lina said. "At a crafts show in Hongqiao."

It had to have been the third or fourth urn purchased this year. There was no telling where the others had gone.

"Did you put anything out to defrost?"

"Not yet," Lina said, rising and running her fingers over her blouse to catch stray wrinkles. "There's that new restaurant along the water we could try. Near the sushi place?"

"Perfect," Wei said.

"I'm going down for coffee. Do you want anything?"

"No, thanks. I still have some work to finish." He watched Lina slip her feet into sandals and clatter out into the hall.

Wei had just settled into his chair when the phone rang. Usually, he let the house line go to voice mail, but on impulse—chalk it up to a good mood—he answered.

"Hello?"

There was a crackling on the other end. And then: "Wei?"

"Yes. Who's calling?"

"It's me. Qiang."

"Who?" he said, even though he'd heard it clearly the first time, had felt his heart rise in his chest like a creature coming up for air.

"Qiang. Your little brother." The sound of something brushing across the speaker, and then the voice came back, clearer. "You don't remember me anymore?"

He said it loud enough that Wei could hear the old humor in his voice. Qiang had always had the most expressive of voices—somehow, even if he was in the other room, you could tell after just a word if he was smiling or scowling or about to tell a lie.

"No, of course—I—where are you?"

"I'm in Kunming. I saw you on TV last week, on some kind of reality show. What's your company called? Mei duo la? I didn't know you were even in China until I saw you on TV. And then I called up Auntie Pei from the old village. She tracked down your number for me..."

Wei began to sweat.

"Are you there?" Qiang asked. "Can you hear me?"

"Yes! Yes, I hear you. Can I come see you? Can we meet?"

"I thought I'd come up and visit you, if it's convenient. I haven't been to Shanghai in a very long time. Plus there's all the talk about the World Expo happening over there right now. I kind of want to see it."

Wei shifted forward in his seat. "Yes, of course, come. I'm looking forward to it. When can you be here?"

"Well, this weekend is probably too soon. Next Friday? Is that all right with you? I was thinking I could come for about a week or so."

Wei nodded fiercely into the phone.

"Hello?"

"Yes, yes. That's great."

"And Lina won't mind?"

"No, of course not," Wei said. "She'll be glad to see you. We'll be here. We'll both be here."

"Great. Take my number. Let's not lose touch again."

Later, Wei would think about those last few words—*Let's not lose touch again*—and wonder whether there was something accusatory in them. But in the moment, he had simply said good-bye and hung up. Before he could register any follow-up emotions, he heard his wife's voice behind him.

"Who was that?" Lina stood in the doorway of his study holding a paper cup of coffee.

"Ah," he said, coming back to himself. Already he could anticipate the dozen more questions this one answer would prompt. "That—that was Qiang."

3

When she had first moved into Lanson Suites, Lina found a stack of name cards in her mailbox. LINA ZHEN, they read. And underneath, in English: LANSON SUITES, 6221 MID YINCHENG ROAD, TOWER 8, APARTMENT 8202, LUJIAZUI, PUDONG NEW DISTRICT, 207290. Her name looked so small sandwiched there between the embossed logo of the hotel and her complicated new address. She put the cards back in their box and took them downstairs.

The first floor of Tower Eight resembled a spa more than it did the lobby of a hotel. When the elevator doors opened, soft music wafted through them. Three young women sitting behind the front desk spoke to one another in equally musical tones, pausing when they saw Lina approach.

"Excuse me. What are these for?" Lina placed the box of cards on the table, and the three of them leaned in to look. When they saw what it was, one of the women smiled—or was it a smirk?—and looked up at the others. Lina felt herself begin to blush.

"For you to make friends," another one of the women said cheerfully. "For all the foreign wives. You will find the Chinese address on the back. If you get lost, you can ask a local." She took a card out of the box and flipped it over. Sure enough, on the back was the same address printed in Chinese. There was also a small square map of the streets surrounding her new home, the apartment complex marked with a red star.

When Wei came home that night, Lina showed him the cards, described her confusion earlier that day in the lobby, and they shared a good laugh.

"It looks like I'm not the only one with a promotion," he said.

To go from a full-time job to unemployed with benefits—in other words, to adopt the lifestyle of a taitai—was no small upgrade. Wei pulled out one of his own business cards so they could compare. GENERAL MANAGER, SHANGHAI; VICE PRESIDENT OF STRATEGY, GLOBAL, read Lina's husband's double title. His cards were plainly printed and functional, unlike the raised ink on Lina's cards and their thick, cotton-bond construction.

"The girl downstairs didn't think I could speak Chinese," she told him. But as soon as she said it, she remembered that it hadn't been the girl at the front desk who'd started the conversation in English—it had been her. Why had she done that? Had being away from China for all these years made her nervous about speaking Mandarin? No, not even a lifetime in America could make a person forget her mother tongue. Lina had spoken English because she associated speaking English with the act of pretending she was someone she was not. Down there in the lobby, she had already felt that way—as though she were *putting on.*

After five years in Shanghai, Lina had come to terms with being neither American nor Chinese but an in-between: an expat. There were other families here like hers, other spouses who had quit their jobs and relocated so that their partners could claim Chinese business for foreign companies. And Lina was relieved to find that the expat community did not require its members to hold a common set of cultural values, as American families had seemed to do. Instead, it assumed a feeling of foreignness. There was no expectation for someone to understand, only to accept. One did this with a lot of smiling and nodding and polite questions. Meeting people from all over the world had made Lina aware of physical demeanors as she never had been before, and she'd become skilled at controlling her facial expressions, conveying joy or pain or exasperation in the Continental way or the Oriental way, depending on her audience. It was tiring, but it had also made Lina agile in how she presented herself. And that kind of agility was what saved her on the day that her husband received Qiang's phone call.

When she had walked past Wei's study that evening, there was something about the way his voice sounded on the phone that made her stop to listen. Though she could see only Wei's back, she could tell that every part of his body was under strain. He had the cord of his keyboard wrapped around his thumb, something he did only when he was nervous.

"Hao," he said finally. "Na, ni dao le women zai tan. Zaijian." He hung up the phone.

Lina gave him a few moments before stepping into the room. "Who was that?" she asked.

When Wei turned around, his face was flushed. "Ah," he said. "That was Qiang."

"Qiang," she repeated. The two of them stared at each other. His name sounded strange said out loud. For years, Lina had said it only in her head. "So he's alive, then."

"Of course he's alive."

"Is he all right?"

"He's fine. He's in Kunming. He says he wants to visit us in a week. He wants to see the World Expo."

Lina laughed. "The Expo? He wants to see the Expo?"

They hadn't heard from Qiang in twenty-two years. And now he was calling to say that he wanted to go to the World's Fair. Lina tried to meet her husband's gaze but he just sat blinking at a spot above her shoulder.

Wei opened his mouth and closed it again. "It will be strange," he finally murmured, "to see him again."

Qiang had disappeared from Lina and Wei's hometown in Suzhou shortly after the couple had married. At first, the word *disappeared* had seemed dramatic. It wasn't as though Qiang hadn't left home before. He had already been involved for some time with *hei shehui*, or "black society." In their small town, local criminals banded together to gamble and fight other gangs in neighboring communities. Sometimes they would travel to larger cities where operations were more lucrative and dangerous. Qiang would leave for months at a time, driving his parents and Wei into fits of panic. When he got back, he would claim that he'd been chasing "business opportunities," which, if legal, seemed unlikely for a boy his age with no university degree. But even in those instances, he had told them where he was going. On the day of Lina and Wei's wedding, Qiang had left without a word to anyone, and he had been missing ever since.

Wei told Lina about Qiang's disappearance as he shivered next to her in their new American bed. It had been a few weeks since their marriage, two since they'd moved to the States, and she still hadn't let him touch her at night. Good, generous, patient Wei was also a little clueless. He'd taken her silence for shyness and filled those first nights with conversation, hoping to bring her closer to him. *I know you were friends with Qiang,* he said. *But he had a life you never knew about.* He sighed and placed his hand on her stomach, where it lay cold as a starfish. Staring up at the ceiling she thought, *I knew more about his life than you ever did.* How little consequences had mattered to her in that moment. She might have told Wei everything then—that she was the reason his brother had disappeared, that her marriage to Wei had been a mistake—if forming the words had not felt so difficult.

Months later, they still hadn't heard from Qiang, and Wei's parents were becoming more and more worried. Wei dealt with it in the same straightforward manner he dealt with all business: he made it into a project. By then, he had started graduate school in engineering at Penn, so he was occupied during the days. But on weeknights, when the rates were cheaper, he placed calls back to China looking for information. He sat in a chair facing the window of their small Philadelphia studio apartment, a notebook balanced on the ledge, looking out at the iced-over gray and brown city streets. *Surely you remember somebody, Auntie. Surely you can give me the name of a province, at the very least.* He'd assigned Lina the job of drawing up a map of contacts and a chronology of the dates that people claimed to have heard from Qiang. They'd collected a list of phone numbers, twelve digits as opposed to the American ten, just past the limits of Lina's short-term memory. And Qiang had felt that way to Lina then too: a figure that existed just beyond her immediate grasp.

She talked through details of the investigation with Wei and helped keep notes, careful to be no more involved in the matter than one would expect a good sister-in-law to be. Amid all this activity, she had stayed in the background, showing no greater personal investment in Qiang's disappearance. Because it was too late to undo what had been done. Qiang was gone, and she and Wei were in America, and Lina was determined to forget about Qiang so she could make the best of her situation.

But during Lina's early years in America, his presence would come to her without warning. Not only reminders of their time together but memories of his physicality. The smell of him carried on a wind as she came out of a supermarket or a gesture of his made by a man on a bus. As the struggle and excitement and forward momentum of her time in the States with Wei finally forged into familiarity and, eventually, love, Lina's mental encounters with Qiang became less visceral. Until one day, she thought of him less as someone she had once loved and more as one of many figures in her youth. It reached the point where she wasn't sure if it was Qiang she missed; perhaps it was just China, or the home that it had once been.

There were times when she had considered telling Wei everything about her past with Qiang. She would begin casually: *Want to hear a funny story?* There had to be a way to frame it that wouldn't make her entire relationship with Wei seem like a lie. She had been young, after all, when she fell in love with Qiang. They both had. But she hadn't brought it up with Wei, and eventually she decided it was too late.

Because she couldn't speak truthfully about her feelings for Wei during the early years of their marriage — or, rather, the ways in which those feelings were complicated — she'd done her best to tell him everything else: her expectations and fears for their new life in America, what she delighted in and what made her curious, what she missed about home. She encouraged him to do the same and watched him struggle to answer. Despite being thoughtful and introverted, Wei was more interested in the workings of the world than he was in the workings of his own mind, which made it difficult for him to give Lina satisfactory answers.

But she came to know him deeply anyway, and to love him. The newness of their experience in America was a bonding force. Beginning in the late eighties and up through the aughts, they learned together how to thrive as immigrants in the U.S. Together, they had been duped by a landlord, assisted by neighbors, and baffled by the Internet. After finally getting work visas and citizenship, they turned their attention to buying a home. They researched mortgage rates and tax brackets and once, in a fit of panic, identity theft. When they had Karen, the final piece of the puzzle fell into place. Lina's life and love became inextricable from his and she finally knew what that word *union* meant. How wonderful it was to discover that happiness could exist in the everyday like that, so overwhelming and underwhelming at the same time.

And then ten, twenty years had passed. She had kept her secret about Qiang and never given Wei any reason to suspect that his brother had been more than a friend to her. And yet, after Wei told her about the phone call, there was a part of her that blamed him for not being able to see past the mask of control she'd put on to hide her true reaction. He should know her well enough by now, but comfort and habit had blinded him. Lina exchanged a few more words about it with Wei. She couldn't remember what was said. But this much she knew: Qiang wasn't coming to see the Expo. After all this time, he was coming to see her.

• • •

Lina's life in Shanghai had never been what her husband might call "productive." Often, it wasn't until the maid rang her doorbell that she would get out of bed and position herself at a desk or in front of a closet to appear busy. She would slip into a daze going through the motions of her day and begin moving around the apartment, unaware of where her feet were taking her. More often than not, she found herself leaning against the doorway of whichever room the maid was in. Maybe her body was guiding her there in the hopes that watching someone else work would break her out of her own slothfulness. Or maybe it was just because she was lonely.

There was a period in the beginning when she'd joined clubs and engaged in charity work. She'd spent an entire month knitting hundreds of tiny sweaters for stuffed bears to be donated to a children's hospital. Another time, she'd helped arrange a gardening project in Century Park. Shanghai Dolls, the Shanghai Women's Club, the Shanghai Expatriate Association — the names of these organizations had been difficult to tell apart. They hosted invitation-only dinner clubs, book clubs, and parties at museums. These events were flashy and fast-paced, full of well-groomed ladies from all over the world: Indian women with their chandelier earrings and jewel-colored saris, Continental women in their tweed Chanel jackets, Korean women with their sleek haircuts and perfect skin. Whether walking through carpeted banquet halls or on the dust-covered streets of Dongtai Road bargaining for antiques, these women seemed more at home in China than Lina ever could be.

Wei had been working a lot, so Lina had attended many of these events alone. It was pleasant enough, making conversation with acquaintances and going glassy-eyed from staring at the other women's jewelry. But one day, for no reason that she could remember, she had simply stopped going. For months after that, her focus had turned to exercise — badminton, swimming, and long, solitary strolls through luxury malls, bargain-hunting for haute couture. Her favorite pastime became buying discounted dresses for Karen at Miu Miu and Dolce and Gabbana. What a pleasure it was to watch the collection grow in her daughter's closet while Karen was away at school, each little bundle of tulle and silk still lightly perfumed from the shops, hanging there like a bouquet out to dry.

Nine months of the year, Lina was waiting for her daughter to come home for the summer. She and Wei had discussed whether to have Karen educated in Shanghai, and Lina had eventually yielded to her husband's logic. She should be culturally adapted to America and have an American education in the States. What had been the point of their immigrating if not to enjoy American privilege? Mostly, though, Lina had given in because she feared that selfishness was the real reason she wanted to keep Karen in Shanghai. It had taken years of trying before Karen came along. When she was born, Lina was thirty-one years old, and Karen had seemed like a miracle. She still seemed this way to Lina every time she saw her daughter moving and talking and forming her own ideas about the world — ideas that Lina had helped shape. The more time that Karen spent at Black Tree Academy and that Lina spent half a world away, missing her, the less sound Wei's logic seemed. Shanghai was not right back where they had started. Some of the international schools had reputations that rivaled the best private schools in the States. Why shouldn't they have kept Karen with them if the Americans themselves were sending their kids to school in Shanghai?

It was one of many disagreements she'd had with Wei lately that never truly manifested itself as an argument. Since moving to China, she and Wei had become careful with each other, avoiding small conflicts for fear of unearthing bigger, more complicated ones. It was hard to face the fact that they had turned into clichés—he, a husband who worked too much; she, a restless woman at home. In America, they had been equals, each helping the other understand how to work and live in a country that wasn't their home. Here, she was useless. There was little need for Chinese-language teachers when there were plenty of younger, cheaper Chinese locals with English degrees who were eager to tutor expats. All the time Lina spent by herself made her aware of her loneliness as something that had always been with her but that she had been able to distract herself from when they lived in America. She sought comfort in beautiful places—the tearoom at the Peace Hotel, the little cafés in Xuhui District, and the ground floor of the Waldorf Astoria. Once, because she had liked the look of rose-flavored *macarons* against the Waldorf's blue china, she'd convinced the manager to let her buy a set of plates to take home with her along with the desserts she'd ordered.

Sure, the spending was excessive, but it wasn't all for frivolity's sake. The members of the expat community in Shanghai were transient but well connected, and she had to keep up with the news. To hear the news, she needed to attend certain events. To attend these events, she needed the requisite attire. In the end, a Chinese-American had to work much harder at social upkeep in China than she did in the States. It would probably have been easier for her to make friends with some local Chinese women; at least they would have had their childhoods in common.

Everyone who grew up in the sixties and seventies in China knew the same card games and revolutionary music, had drunk from the same tin mugs. And though times had changed, there were things that hadn't. Recipes, for instance. Her mother had a special one for jiaozi that she made on the eve of each Lunar New Year. Lina thought of dumpling-making as a communal activity. When she was younger, the village women gathered in teams under different roofs. Some aunties made the meat filling, others rolled dough for the skins, and still others molded the dumplings into the shape of gold ingots, which symbolized wealth for the new year. There hadn't been very many Chinese aunties in Pennsylvania, and she had never attempted the project alone.

That wasn't the case here, and yet Lina couldn't bring herself to strike up friendships with any of the local women. She knew that their company would only make her feel lonelier in the end. After all, how could she explain to them what fifteen years of her life in America had been like? At first, it had meant learning rule after rule after rule. Garbage goes out between this hour at night and this hour in the morning. It's acceptable to take home leftovers from a restaurant but not the bread they give you at the start of the meal. You can't hang your laundry out of the window for others to see, but you also can't leave it in the apartment building's dryer for longer than a half an hour after the cycle ends unless you want it to wind up on the floor of the basement. The main problem, of course, was the language. Although Lina had studied English in college, those first few years she still jumbled up nouns and adjectives, leaving off the nuisance endings of words, like -*ing* and -*ily*. And those pesky articles—*a* and *the*—whose presence in sentences seemed completely arbitrary. On afternoons when Wei was at the university, Lina would sometimes lie on their little twin bed with a pillow to her face and scream in Chinese.

But things had gotten easier. In America, you could buy your own house on its own piece of land and disappear inside it forever. That neat little yard that Wei trimmed every other weekend, before he'd gotten too busy with work. The screen door that rattled in the wind. America was where she had fallen in love with the idea of ownership. Nowadays, she could spend tens of thousands of yuan a month on housewares, but nothing would ever compare to the way she felt when she and Wei had found a shiny red enamel kettle on sale at the Golden Eagle on Falcon Street. The neighbors might stare at them and her colleagues might talk about her behind her back, but paying money for American belongings made her feel that the space she occupied was really hers.

When they'd moved to Collegeville, Wei had bought a second car for Lina, and that was the moment she finally began to feel at home: when she was ferrying herself around in a vehicle customized just for her, a copper-colored Honda with air-conditioning and a radio, which she listened to while sitting at drive-through windows or waiting for the traffic lights to change from red to green. During her drive home from work, she passed a storage facility backlit by the sunset, the pink and tangerine teasing out shades of cobalt blue from the whitewashed building. She would never be able to explain to anyone the beauty of suburban Pennsylvania. Nor could she explain how sad it made her one day when she caught herself thinking in English, feeling her very mind switch nationalities. But how powerful it felt, too, to become fluent in another language, her mind opening fold by fold like a paper fan to reveal a fuller picture of the world around her. And that knowledge of its fullness was what Lina didn't want to give up.

As much as she didn't want to admit it, Wei was right. They had worked hard to be assimilated into American culture. What a waste it would be to relegate themselves to a social group that had never left China.

•   •   •

Lina watched her daughter step out of the closet with a scarf knotted once around her neck and once around her waist, a makeshift halter top that left her back bare. The words *Hermès Paris* were pulled taut across her chest in gold silk.

"Can I wear this to breakfast?" Karen asked.

On the floor between them were eight orange boxes of scarves, their lids discarded and their contents strewn across the floor.

"What about the dress we bought yesterday?"

"I can wear that whenever. I can wear it at school."

Karen collected her hair on one side of her neck, considered her image in the mirror, and then turned back to Lina. "Do you have any new jewelry?"

Going through Lina's jewelry box had become a ritual for the two of them every summer Karen was back from school. Each time Lina made a purchase of or received jewelry from Wei, she looked forward to showing it to her daughter.

"Nothing for little bones," Lina said slyly.

"That means you have something good. Show me."

It never took less than thirty minutes for Karen to go through all the items in her jewelry box. Lina checked her watch and saw that it was only eight o'clock. "All right," she said. "Come sit."

Lina kept the jewelry box in a safe and its key hidden above the door frame of the closet. She retrieved them both and joined Karen, who sat cross-legged on the bed. Together, they opened the lid and watched dust particles scatter as sunlight moved across the top tray. Here was mostly pearl jewelry; black, white, and peach-colored pearls made into drop earrings, long strands knotted together in a necklace, pearls on silver or platinum chains, and pearls strung on clear illusion cords, designed to float on collarbones. Scattered among them were also jade bracelets, brooches, and a small garnet ring. These were the items Karen was allowed to borrow.

Beneath those were the ones forbidden to her, and therefore more exciting. The ruby earrings Lina wore often around Christmas, a cushion-cut emerald ring wreathed in smaller diamonds, a string of sapphires on a choker, a watch that featured free-floating diamond stones trapped between the watch dial and its smooth crystal face, and Karen's favorite: a chrome-tourmaline pendant set in gold filigree. The yellow tones of the metal made the jewel shine like a tiny lime in the palm of her hand. She fastened the chain around her neck and lowered her head to examine the pendant better, sticking out her lower lip to aid the process.

"Are my bones big enough for this one yet?"

Lina laughed. "Not yet."

But she always let Karen wear the pendant while looking at the rest of her jewelry. Among the old boxes, Karen picked up the new addition. When she opened it, a violent blue flashed up at them, warmed by tones of red.

"Whoa. What is it?"

"It's called tanzanite. It comes from Tanzania."

"Where's that?"

"Africa."

Karen reached out to brush the face of the gemstone with her thumb. "When did you go to Tanzania?"

"I got it on a cruise with Daddy. I've never actually been there. Do you like it?"

She nodded and held it closer to her face.

Lina had spotted the necklace in one of the cruise ship's jewelry stores and Wei had seen her looking. *That would look beautiful on you,* he'd said encouragingly. It had been the weekend of their wedding anniversary, which happened to coincide with Medora's biannual management retreat. That was how they had ended up touring the Cayman Islands rather than lounging in a riad in Morocco, where Lina had wanted to go.

She accepted the bribe and let him think that the piece of jewelry could buy her happiness for the weekend.

"I wish I'd gotten to see the bracelet," Karen said, slipping the tanzanite ring all the way up to her first knuckle. "Now you only have one thing from Africa."

Lina felt a blush coming on. When she thought of the bracelet, she remembered a version of herself she'd rather forget. Lying in bed that first year in Philly, rolling the beads between her fingers as if the bracelet were a rosary. Following it down neural pathways to emotional exhaustion, putting it away upon the arrival of Wei, drifting through the rest of the day insensate.

"It wasn't much to look at. It was only special because I got it from my mother a long time ago. Sentimental."

Karen nodded gravely. "And then you could have given it to me. And it would have been like I'd known her."

Now she'd lied about her dead mother on top of everything else.

"Let's put everything back. It's time for breakfast."

"But I haven't even looked through it all yet."

Lina had experienced enough of her daughter's fake pouts to know when she was truly upset. Karen avoided eye contact by twisting the cocktail ring around her finger.

Usually, when school was out, Lina felt a spurt of energy. She would rise early, see Wei off to work, devise a mental list of activities to keep Karen entertained. While her daughter usually complained when taken to the zoo ("Mom, I'm pretty sure the animals are *balding*") and the cafés ("Why are there so many *people* everywhere?"), she loved visiting Xintiandi, watching the old women and men who ballroom-danced in People's Square, and seeing Chinese movies, where she learned colorful language that she would later use to upset her father. But Qiang's phone call had changed things. Instead of planning activities for Karen, Lina was distracted. Again and again she found herself thinking of how it had felt to be young. Her hometown came back to her more clearly than it had since she'd visited after her parents' death. She could see the wind dancing across the lake, the swaying trees, the road filled with dust and the rocks that could be skipped into the water. And then, of course, there was Qiang. What was she doing, exactly? The word *pining* occurred to her. How embarrassing, how irrational—but she couldn't deny it. She was existing simultaneously in the imaginary past and in the actual present, an effort so all-consuming that every other action seemed a chore. Funny how the theft of the bracelet had come just before Qiang's phone call. As if the loss of the first was meant to remind her of how it felt to lose the second.

Meanwhile, Karen had grown impatient. Often, Lina would look up from a daydream to see her daughter staring at her with an eyebrow raised—a facial expression likely picked up from one of her sassier classmates at Black Tree Academy. "Mom," she would say in a high, cartoonish voice. "Stop being weird." Now she was staring at Lina, waiting for her attention to wander back to the present.

"Hey," Lina said. "What if we hired an ayi?"

Karen frowned. "Why?"

"To help with the cooking. And grocery shopping." A half-truth was better than a lie. "If we had an ayi, I wouldn't have to make you come with me. You hate grocery shopping."

Karen narrowed her eyes. "Is this because the other Lanson ladies all have ayis?"

Lina had always known her daughter was smart, but these days she was becoming shrewd too. "Xiao shagua, ni yiwei you know everything. Well, fine, I guess we won't ask Sunny to come work for us, then."

"Sunny?" The jewelry box slid off Karen's lap. "You're going to ask Sunny?"

Lina nodded. "Daddy suggested her, actually."

"But Daddy never likes anyone."

"He likes her. He thinks she takes initiative."

As Karen digested this, a look of wonder crossed her face. Lina knew that her daughter had always liked the younger maid who cleaned their rooms, but this summer she seemed more attached to her than ever. At first, their relationship had made Lina uncomfortable—partly because she didn't know much about the woman; partly because it made her jealous—but then Lina resolved to make the situation work in her favor. If she hired Sunny as an ayi, at least she would feel less guilty about neglecting Karen while Qiang was in town.

"That's what I thought," Lina said. "So it's settled. Let's go to breakfast."

It had done the trick; Karen was smiling once again. "You go first," she said. "I have to finish getting dressed."

Lina was one of four women who met at eight thirty every morning at the back of the clubhouse breakfast room. The unstated agreement was that they—Maggie, Susan, Peng, and Lina—were not friends in the usual sense of the word. Aside from an occasional lunch in Puxi or trip to the fabric market, they did not see one another outside of the clubhouse restaurant. They did not phone one another at home to gossip. What information they came upon was shared when they met at breakfast each morning. It was the ritual of it that Lina liked. They sat in a booth near the windows so they could be the first to see who was coming in and going out. They noted which husbands were late to work and which might not have spent the night at home at all, which residents were feuding and which had just moved in. In truth, these three other women were solidly middle class. They had come to Shanghai via Wilmington, North Carolina (Maggie); St. Louis, Missouri (Susan); and a suburb of Holland (Peng). But in Shanghai, they could forget about the fact that their company sponsors supported a standard of living three or four times beyond their personal means. In Shanghai, they were expats; with no rent to pay, they could become the kind of frivolous women they'd always associated with wealth. They developed vivid recall for wardrobes and for where other people went on vacation. When certain loose-lipped ayis came downstairs with kids, they were not above apprehending them on their way to the yogurt station to ask for the latest news. Sometimes the women stayed so long in the clubhouse that the waitstaff had to sweep the floor around their feet.

Wei had once described these other women as "ridiculous," and as Lina slipped year by year through middle age, she could feel herself becoming ridiculous too. The "putting on" she'd felt when she'd arrived in Shanghai no longer seemed like putting on. And yet — so what if she enjoyed being a taitai? Wei had been the one to throw her into the expat life, after all, and couldn't expect her just to disengage from the community around her. Plus, she suspected that a part of him liked having a wife with the right kind of taste to build a nice home, to buy fashionable clothes and come down to breakfast looking put together.

No — looking good. Thirty-five rather than forty-three. Better, at least, than Maggie, who practically carried her entire home down with her to breakfast: PG Tips in a clay mug, the newspaper (which she never touched), a scarf in case she got cold, and the latest gadget or knickknack she'd picked up at a market and wanted to show the girls. Better than Susan, who, for all her worldliness, couldn't escape certain food phobias, and stuck to her heavy Midwestern diet. Lately, Lina had even turned it up a notch. No more tees or athletic wear, only silk blouses and dresses that fit her frame. She was more Western now than she'd ever been in the West. Some mornings, she put on Italian heels just to walk the few steps to the elevator, then the twenty-five meters from the lower-level lobby across the parking lot, and finally to the center of the complex, where the clubhouse sat. It was a solarium, glass-domed and sparkling. She knew that behind the glimmering windows, the Lanson ladies were watching her approach just as they watched the others, and so she made sure to do it well. And then they'd talk and eat. And then she'd walk the thirty meters back to her apartment, take off the heels, and get into bed.

But not today; today was a rare clear day in Shanghai. Late-May warmth turned the jasmine bushes encircling the clubhouse extra-fragrant. The Lanson ladies arrived at their usual booth within moments of one another, which meant that no one had to wait long for her caffeine to be brought out: green tea for Peng, lattes for Lina and Susan, and hot water for Maggie, which she promptly poured into her mug of PG Tips. Lina hadn't placed a drink order in years. As old staff left and new staff came on, their morning beverage preferences had been communicated from server to server. By now, she could tell which barista was behind the espresso bar by the way her latte tasted. It was just how she liked it today: heavy on the steamed milk and light on the foam.

Maggie leaned in to take a sip from her mug. "So, did she come clean?" she asked Lina in a hushed voice.

"What?"

"The maid who took your bracelet."

"Oh," Lina said. "No." For one nonsensical, panicked moment, Lina had taken *she* to mean herself. She smiled as neutrally as she could. If anyone could pick up the scent of imagined adultery, it was Maggie.

"What reason would she have to come clean?" Susan put in. "I wouldn't if I were her. That bracelet is as good as gone. You might as well go ahead and nudge Rose out so that this sort of thing doesn't happen again. To you or to the rest of us, you see what I mean? Especially if you're sure it was her, like you say you are."

Susan had a habit of fluttering her near-invisible eyelashes when she wanted to soften the tone of her opinions. She had so many opinions it was sometimes hard for her to keep them from becoming bodily reactions. Often while someone was talking and Susan was trying to stop herself from interrupting, she would shift her weight or touch her face in a way that Lina found extremely distracting.

"I'm positive," Lina said, even though *positive* was too strong a word. She hadn't seen the older maid take it, but Rose and Sunny were the only ones with regular access to the apartment besides the family, and Lina's gut told her that Sunny wasn't the type to steal.

Lina probably should have been storing the bracelet in the safe along with her other jewelry all these years, but she hadn't wanted to risk Karen seeing it and asking questions. Instead, she had kept it in her sock drawer, where she could see it every morning when she got dressed. That's how she knew that the bracelet was there one day and gone the next. She had told management that she thought one of the maids had taken the bracelet from her room, but she hadn't accused Rose outright. Doing so would almost definitely get her fired, and she didn't need that on her conscience. But to her friends, Lina nodded, indicating that she would do as they suggested. There was other news she needed to get to, news that wouldn't be smart to put off announcing. Better to tell them now instead of waiting for them to find out some other way.

"I'm going to ask the other maid who works in our unit, Sunny, to be our ayi," Lina began.

"Really?" Susan put down her fork. "I didn't know you were looking for one."

Lina resented the way these women felt entitled to the details of her life, as if her daily decisions were up for discussion.

"Just for the summer. We have a guest coming to town. Wei's brother."

She paused here, expecting someone to sense her guardedness. No one did.

"That's wonderful!" Peng said. "When is he coming?"

"Next week."

"That soon."

"It happened pretty suddenly." Lina made a face to suggest that it was all very annoying, and a couple of the others began to commiserate. To the extent that taitai could be said to have duties, their main one was to serve as tour guide and hostess to friends, family, and their husbands' business contacts from abroad. Between them, these women had enough experience to write two or three guidebooks on Shanghai.

"How long will he be here for?" Susan asked.

"A week. He's here for the Expo."

"A week, and you're hiring an ayi for the whole summer?"

There it was. Leave it to Susan to push Lina where she didn't want to be pushed. The truth, of course, was that Lina wasn't sure what Qiang had in mind for his visit, what kind of disturbance it would cause their family, and how long such a disturbance would last. And as much as she feared what his coming might mean, she also hoped that after so many years apart from them, he would stay for more than just a week.

"I thought Wei and I could take some time off and travel too. Later in the summer. I don't know, I just wanted to keep our options open."

"You want to travel without Karen?" Susan leaned back against the booth and respread the napkin on her lap.

Lina pictured droplets of milk sliding down around each one of her chins. She imagined stapling those blinking eyelids shut. *Accuse me of something, then,* she wanted to say. Instead, she shrugged and stirred her congee. "That's not the only reason. We have too much junk in the house. I need someone to help me pack for the move." There was no better way to distract these women from gossip than by reminding them of their own jealousy. At the end of summer, Lina and Wei were moving to the penthouse of Tower Eight, a suite of even larger apartments that had recently come on the market.

Just then, Lina looked up to see a flash of color — Karen, wearing double strands of pearls over the gold-and-black scarf/top, carrying a cereal bowl and scanning the room.

"Karen!" Lina called.

Karen turned at the sound of her mother's voice, and the center of her forehead relaxed. This was a reflex she had inherited from Wei, and in both the expression was so touching that it opened what felt like a fifth valve in Lina's heart. That expression said so clearly: *Oh, I've found you, and now all is well.* Karen walked over, the milk sloshing at the edges of her bowl. Lina motioned for the other women to scoot over.

She watched her daughter settle in and begin spooning cereal into her mouth without giving any thought to the adult conversation, stopping only to scratch at an eye with the back of her fingernail. It amazed Lina, the way a parent's presence could lead children to behave so comfortably around strangers. She tried to remember a time when her own world was not made up of individual people, each of whom judged her and sought validation from her, but a general mass grouped under "acquaintances of Ma" and "acquaintances of Ba." How nice it must be to view people as extensions of one's parents' goodwill toward you and to expect compassion and solicitude from each person you met.

Inside of forty seconds, Karen had finished eating her cereal and sat back with a sigh. Lina checked her watch — it was only 9:10 a.m. She had wanted to be done with breakfast a good while ago.

"Ready, sweetie?" she said to Karen.

One by one, the women slid out again to free Lina and Karen from the booth. Lina put her arm around her daughter's shoulders and together they walked to the back exit and out into the spring air.

4

The strange thing about being "under suspicion of theft"—as the hotel manager had written in Sunny's employment file—was that the Zhen family didn't seem to suspect her of stealing the bracelet at all. She knew this because their American daughter, home for the summer, told her so.

"There's no way Mom and Dad think you took it," said Karen. "They actually want to hire you as our ayi."

When Sunny had walked into the apartment that day, the scene wasn't at all what Rose had described in her warning speech. There was nothing suspiciously neat about it—the living room was a mess, as usual. A dish filled with orange peels was on the couch, and a hundred-yuan bill had been left sitting on the coffee table.

Karen lay on the bed while Sunny straightened the perfumes on her dresser. In the mirror, her preteen body was slumped against the headboard, thighs agape. She wore machine-frayed shorts, and her eyes were lined so that they looked as big as dates.

"*Hell-ooo?*" she said in English. "I said, you could be our ayi!"

Sunny liked Karen, even if she was spoiled. It was surprising that the Zhens didn't have more children, especially since their only child was a girl.

"I'm excited, even if you aren't. We don't get ayis in America. I mean, people have nannies, but it's not really the same."

"What's a nanny?"

"Someone who takes care of kids but doesn't cook or clean. Ayis can do everything, right? They're like the superheroes of caretakers. Zhen liao bu qi."

Aptitude for language was one thing that Karen did have. Most bilingual kids could talk in their second language about school, families, food, and not much else. But Karen was always a surprise. Idioms, proverbs, obscure nouns—Karen knew them all. Once, Sunny had even heard her recite a Tang dynasty poem, which she claimed to have learned from a Chinese-American librarian in her hometown.

After she had tidied the bedroom, Sunny moved on to the bathroom. There, she found one towel on the floor and two more hanging from the door.

"You want these changed?" she asked, nodding at the ones on the door.

Karen shrugged, crowding in behind her and taking a seat on the sink. "Do you think she took the bracelet?" Her legs were swinging so close to Sunny that she could almost feel them breeze past her face as she cleaned the toilet bowl.

"Who?"

"The other maid."

"No."

"Well, it's either you or her. And it's not you. So it has to be her."

Sunny looked up from her scrubbing. "Or maybe your ma just lost it."

But Karen's mind had already moved on from the question. "I never liked her anyway. Her phone is always going off and it's so loud. Plus she calls me *mei*."

Most of the maids acted chatty and familiar with the Chinese-speaking families, thinking that it helped to be friendly. They called the younger girls *mei,* for "little sister," and the younger boys *di,* for "little brother." They couldn't tell that this made foreigners nervous. Foreigners liked to keep their distance. If they decided that the distance was going to be crossed, they wanted to be the ones crossing it.

"Ma's really upset about the bracelet because it came from Africa. Yesterday she had the night manager in here crawling around looking for it. But I think they both know someone took it."

Sunny stood, picked up the cleaning caddy, and nodded at Karen to get out of the way.

"Living room next?" Karen asked.

"Yes."

The Zhens' apartment was one of the largest in Tower Eight. Karen's room and the guest room lay in the northern wing, while the master bed and study lay in the southern. The hallways met in a large living room and bar area that extended eastward into the dining room. It was too big for the Zhen family, especially when Karen was gone during the school year, and sometimes while inside the still, silent apartment, Sunny felt a great wave of sadness come over her. But other times, when she was out on the balcony watering the flowers, she could pretend that the whole apartment behind her was hers alone, that she was the owner of this prime city real estate.

"Watch it," she said to Karen, who was leaning so far over the balcony railing that a harsher word might have sent her headlong into the pool below.

"I see Mom coming out of the water."

Zhen Taitai never did any real swimming, just parted the water this way and that, aimless as a swan. But when she lifted her arms so that she could towel beneath them, her muscles looked alert, even sculpted. Sunny peered over the edge in time to see her gather her towel and disappear into the hotel lobby. *Ta ma de,* she cursed silently. She hadn't thought to make up the southern wing of the apartment first, and now it was too late. She'd have to tidy the master bedroom with Zhen Taitai inside it.

By the time Sunny finished the living room and kitchen, Taitai had already taken a shower and was sitting at her desk looking at letters. When she saw Sunny and Karen come in, she began a conversation with her daughter in English. Karen's last word — *Fine!* — followed by exaggerated stomping down the hallway was all that Sunny understood.

To exist alone in a room with Taitai was to be trapped in silence. No matter how softly Sunny moved, the sounds she made seemed amplified. She set about emptying the wastebaskets — the one in the bathroom, the one by the bed, the one in the walk-through closet that separated the bathroom from the bedroom. Boss Zhen had confused the wastebasket with the hamper again. Sunny fished out a pair of silk socks from the garbage, draped them over the edge of the actual hamper, and removed the plastic bag from the trash can's metal mouth. When she looked up, Taitai was leaning against the doorway of the closet, watching her. "Sunny, I want to ask you something." Under the sweep of her palm, a lock of hair fell from her widow's peak and arced softly toward her chin.

"What is it?" Sunny asked.

"How much do you get paid every month?"

"Twenty-five hundred," she said, instinctively upping the amount by five hundred. The twitch in Taitai's eyebrow seemed to indicate that the lie hadn't gone undetected.

"Maybe this goes without saying, but trust is very important to me. I think I'm good at knowing whom to trust."

"I —"

"I trust you."

It took a moment for Sunny to work out that Taitai wasn't talking about Sunny's fabricated salary — she was talking about the theft. When

Zhen Taitai wanted to, she could relax her demeanor and appear almost imploring. She had large, dark eyes with thick lashes that stood out against her fair skin. Though her jaw was a little long, there was refinement in the arc of her neck and the tilt of her head. She was a true fujianü, not one of those countryside wives who had stumbled into the role wearing skirts that were three inches too short.

"I can pay double your salary if you'll work for us as an ayi this summer."

"Double," Sunny repeated. "Five thousand?"

Taitai nodded. "My husband's brother is coming in a week or so, and it will be a busy time for our family. Have you done this kind of work before?"

Sunny thought about lying again and decided against it. "No."

"Do you cook?"

"I can."

"Good. We won't ask you for a trial meal. You won't be cooking too much anyway. The main thing will be for you to watch Karen while the adults are out—or take Karen out when the adults are here. How does that sound?"

Sunny hesitated.

"That sounds fine. Only—I wonder—if it's just for the summer, what will happen to me in the fall? If I give up my job here…"

"I have friends. I can make referrals."

This was the response she had been hoping for. "Can I think about it?"

"Of course," Taitai said, and she handed over a slip of paper. "You can call me when you decide."

What a funny feeling, to have the phone number of the Zhen residence. It felt more like a lottery number than a phone number. Sunny had wiped down that receiver once a week for the past five years. Now her voice would be coming through that very same device.

Not only had Sunny never been an ayi, but the possibility had never even crossed her mind. She was a good housekeeper. During her five years at Lanson Suites, she had learned how to read people; she knew to leave an extra bar of soap for soiled laundry if she saw maxi-pads in the trash can or sachets of green tea if someone seemed unable to hold his liquor. She didn't just clean, she anticipated. Move the bottles back beneath the bar and out of reach of the cat's paw. Part the curtains just far enough so that the sun won't fade the couch. Being an ayi, however, required a deeper commitment to her employers. She would have to dedicate herself totally to these residents — to breakfast with them, travel with them, swim in that infinity pool. It was one thing to work at the hotel for a set number of hours a day. When you were on the clock, you were an employee. When you went home, you were yourself again. She knew what happened to people who got used to living the ayi lifestyle. Some of the women she roomed with had stopped sending money home altogether. They spent it on Taobao and Starbucks coffee, fooled into thinking that acceptance into a rich household meant that they could adopt its habits and standards. But five thousand yuan — that number was enough to set her spine humming. When no one was looking, she took out her phone to calculate. Five thousand yuan was 178.5 Starbucks coffees a month!

That night in the service hall, Sunny met up with Rose. They unclipped their radios, signed them in, and threw them into the collection bin. The regular security guard still hadn't returned; this time it was Lao Huo, who was usually stationed at the back gate, performing the checks.

"My God," Rose whispered. "They really want every single man in this compound to have a feel, don't they? Next they'll be sending in Boss Zhen."

Lao Huo had never said a word to them. Each time they'd passed him when they exited the compound at night, his hat was positioned low on his forehead so that no one could tell if his tiny eyes were open.

His hands over Sunny were quick, but thorough — the movements of someone used to taking his share of pleasure before deciding whether he wanted it to begin with. Afterward, she could still smell Lao Huo's cigarette fingers on her uniform.

"What's the point of all this checking?" Sunny asked once they were outside again. "Even if we did take it, wouldn't we have sold it or hidden it by now?"

"This is just the way it goes," Rose said. "It's to scare us. They'll do this until the Zhen woman stops complaining."

"Let me ask you something," Sunny said suddenly. "Would you ever consider becoming an ayi?"

"For one of those ladies? It would be good money. But you'd have to deal with their personal lives. And if you think the security checks are bad, imagine what it would be like if the husband wanted you in bed. I've even heard of wives getting those kinds of ideas." Rose pursed her lips, the way she did when readying herself for a rant. But then she caught Sunny's expression. "Why, has someone asked you?"

"Zhen Taitai did. Just for this summer."

Rose stopped walking. "Zhen Taitai?" There was something babyish about the surprise on her face and the way her features stilled. Then came a long pause. "How much?"

"Five thousand."

"A month?"

"I haven't said yes."

Rose blinked. She turned to look back in the direction of the hotel.

All day, Sunny had been desperate to share this news. She had taken her urgency for excitement, but now she realized it was also because the offer had made her uneasy. A career change for Sunny would be a boost for her, but it would also put Rose further at risk of losing her job. If the Zhens hired Sunny, it would be as good as saying to management that Rose was the only maid the Zhens suspected.

"I don't know why she's so sure I didn't take the bracelet," Sunny said. *And that you did.* She turned to stand side by side with Rose to look up at the hotel and its dull neon glow. The tops of those towers felt as remote as the moon that was starting to appear behind them.

"Of course you should say yes," Rose said after a moment. "Congratulations."

"Don't congratulate me. We deal with enough of their shit as it is. I don't know what other kinds of accusations Zhen Taitai could come up with when it's just me in the house." She looked down at her feet and found that she'd been too distracted to change out of her work shoes. "Plus I don't want my taking this job to affect you."

"Aiya," Rose said. "Forget about it. I'll be fine. Really, this is too good to pass up. Once you become an ayi, you can tell all the other rich ladies about me."

They walked silently.

"Why do they need an ayi all of a sudden?" Rose asked. "Their girl is as good as grown."

"I don't know," Sunny said. "Boss Zhen's brother will be in town. He's coming to see the Expo."

"Do you think you'll get to go with them?"

The thought hadn't occurred to Sunny until that very moment. For months, she and Rose had talked about the World's Fair and how much they'd like to see it. All those nations traveling so far to set up exhibits, not only in the women's country but in their very city! It was a chance to experience the world without leaving home. But it would be difficult to scrape together the price of a ticket and even more difficult to get a day or two off.

"I don't know," she said. "If I took the job, then I guess — maybe." And suddenly she wished she hadn't said anything at all. Rose started walking again. After a moment, Sunny followed.

It had always been this way, Rose in front, Sunny behind. On the mornings when they worked the same shift, each servicing one of the two units on every floor, they filed down the service hall together. Rose pressed the button for the elevator and Sunny pushed their cart inside. Their cleaning routines had become so synchronized that they both finished their units with time to spare. They loitered in the laundry hall afterward, talking about the residents. *Could you hear what she was saying on the phone? No, but do you think she was talking with her doctor? Couldn't be — the conversation was in Chinese and her prescription bottles are in English. Have you seen that new Céline shopping bag on the nightstand? Ha! Her husband probably messed up big this time.*

When Sunny worked her shifts alone, she was less interested in the inhabitants than in their things. She loved dusting the little wooden cabinets full of porcelain figurines and straightening the silk ties that hung in rows, each dizzying pattern just barely touching the next. In the bathroom, Sunny unscrewed jars to smell their contents, held them up to the vanity light. Her favorite ones had the heft and feel of an abalone shell. Five thousand a month. If she could get a long-term gig like that, she could move out of her shared room. She could even buy a container of one of those ointments for herself, just once — just for the jar.

Sunny lived on the outskirts of Shanghai in a *qunzu fang* — a group-living facility — in the Hongkou District. She liked to get back as late as possible, when her five other roommates were already in their bunks. By then, the bathrooms were usually free and she could shower and get ready for bed without waiting in line for a stall or a sink.

The reek of incense masked the bathroom's usual smell of boiled cabbage, urine, and copper. Yang Zifei had posted a sign on a wall that said: INCENSE BOUGHT FOR PUBLIC USE BY YOURS TRULY, YANG ZIFEI. DON'T STEAL.

A few sticks of incense lay neatly on a window ledge, untouched, but the burner was nowhere to be found. Typical. Sunny stepped into the shower, undressed, laid her clothes on top of a chair just outside the stall, and turned the water on.

She probably should have been living someplace nicer. The money she sent home was more than acceptable coming from a single woman her age, and no one in her family would begrudge her funds for a little extra privacy, a little comfort. But living less than comfortably meant that Sunny was forced outside and into the streets, which was where she found herself truly at home in Shanghai anyway. She liked people-watching and tracking the progress of new architecture. She liked getting lost in crowds. Being a nobody here was still better than being nobody in Hefei. Here, there was camaraderie among the nobodies—although maybe that was just her imagination. At home, Sunny never felt lost in a crowd, but she did sometimes feel at risk of dissolving. Just one member of a family of people who studied, worked, married, birthed, parented, and grandparented, she took on everyone's daily grievances and victories, illnesses and successes, and they took on hers. When she was younger, she could sometimes forget that there was any difference at all between herself and her little sister, Yan. They both had hair so black it was almost blue, they both told the same jokes, and they both could eat more than their brothers. But then Yan had gotten married, and suddenly Sunny felt too old and too young at the same time. Too old to be living at home and, because she was unmarried, too young to be treated like an adult.

What did it mean to be an adult anyway? An adult was someone who took responsibility for her parents by sending money home. But not only that, it was someone who made her own decisions, who had come into her own self. *Ziji.* At home, the concept of "self" was not one she had really considered. But in the city, when a stranger's eyes landed on her, she knew that to this person, she could be anyone—and the possibilities of it excited her. If she often felt lonely around strangers, she also sometimes thought that her "self"—that unformed possibility—might be the best company she'd ever had.

Sunny could no longer be made happy by the things that made her sister happy, like telling stories and playing dice games when the kids were down for a nap. Earning a salary did something to you—it spun your whole world into sharper focus. She had grown up feeling sorry for the men in her family who went away to cities to work. But now that she knew what it felt like to hold those notes in her hand, to add them up at the end of the week, she understood that these men had taken the best jobs for themselves. She saw how work, if you had a salaried position, could become an addiction. It had led her uncles to labor on sore shins and miss coming home for New Year's to conserve cash. Working was a pleasure she couldn't imagine giving up now that she'd had a taste of it. And like any addiction, the pleasure of it seemed always on the move, always one step ahead of her. Who could say which she liked better, earning the money or bringing it home to her family? At times, Sunny felt that the only moments she was truly happy were when she was on the train rushing toward either Shanghai or Hefei. Her happiness could exist only in motion, in the thought of what lay ahead.

Back in Sunny's bedroom, the lights had already been turned off, and she used her cell phone to illuminate the few steps to her bottom bunk. Not that she had to bother—her roommates slept through everything. Their own phones chimed all night as they received messages from their friends. Occasionally, when these sounds woke Sunny, she liked to pretend they were coming from her sister's phone—that they were both back home for a visit, and if she were only to roll over, she'd feel human warmth.

Here's the calculation she had not done earlier on her phone, wanting to savor it by computing in her head: five thousand RMB meant three thousand extra a month; three thousand divided by two hundred RMB per train ticket came to fifteen round trips home. But if she were to become an ayi by trade, she would be working seven days a week. There would be no guarantee that she would have time for trips home.

And then there was the issue of Rose.

It was not something she could decide now. Sunny rolled over onto her stomach, which helped to quiet her mind. Before falling asleep, she always pictured the same scene from home. She was standing at the window of their house and could see the rape flowers leaning into the autumn air and the cornstalks reaching up into the sky. She could hear behind her, in the living room, the bright plastic footstools that cracked a little more each time a grandmother sat on one to get to toddler height. Domestic quarrels of aunts and uncles came from upper floors, and below them, there was the raucousness of ten people in front of the same TV set. Soon, this noise of home was enough to drown out all the other sounds in her head. Zhen Taitai's offer was reduced to the size of a fly, nothing more than a tiny distraction dodging in and out of Sunny's mind.

5

Lina had never minded being promised to a stranger, but her friends couldn't understand it. *Wake up, xiao jie, it's 1985! Do you know how backward arranged marriage is? You don't even know him. He could want sex every hour—did you hear about the guy Li Hua married? Well, if you did, you would rethink this plan.*

It was true. She didn't know Zhen Zhiwei, even though she had grown up an hour's walk from his home. Lina had seen Wei only twice in her life. The first time was when she was seven and went with her father to the Zhens' to drop off a set of water pails they had borrowed. She didn't remember anything beyond the vague outline of a tan-skinned boy standing in the yard, whittling away at a tree branch. What she remembered more clearly was her father asking her about him on their way home. *What did you think of him?* She wasn't sure how to respond. *Somebody needs to give him a haircut,* she finally said. Her father laughed. *You'll make a natural wife.*

The second time she saw him was at the silk factory one afternoon when she was thirteen. Playing at the edge of the woods, she glimpsed Zhen Hong coming outside with his two sons. One of them was the younger brother, Qiang, sent over to their house every so often on an errand for his father. She couldn't get a good look at the taller one. He'd turned from her as soon as she'd caught sight of him. Then he'd pulled Qiang's arm and the two took off down the street. It wasn't until the back of his head disappeared from view that Lina realized the other boy must have been Wei.

She would have liked to meet her future husband, but her mother, Jiajia, had forbidden it. Lina's father had made the marriage agreement without her consent, and throughout Lina's preadolescence the issue was a point of tension between the parents, surfacing whenever their own marriage wore thin. Jiajia accused her husband of being too reckless with their daughter's future. She was opposed to limiting Lina's marriage options at so young an age. But as Lina grew older, she sensed that an equal if not greater part of her mother's concern was that she did not like the Zhens. The family was too liberal for her tastes. She didn't trust them.

Jiajia's father had once owned a successful business selling linens, but when the Three-Anti/Five-Anti Campaigns were instituted in the 1950s to punish the financially elite, the company had been taken away from him. The government labeled him a *youpai*—the worst kind of conservative there was—at a time when conservatism and capitalism were one and the same. Jiajia and her father burned all their Western books and records, packed two suitcases full of clothing, bade good-bye to Jiajia's mother's grave, and moved to their new government-assigned home. They'd lost everything, and now they would live like commoners in one dirty room that didn't even have its own kitchen. Jiajia thought her father had gotten off easy in the grand scheme of things. He hadn't been sent to a labor camp like some of his associates, hadn't been beaten in the streets. But the *youpai* label still killed him in the end. The constant taunting from the neighbors and the Red Guard drove him to depression and eventual suicide.

When Jiajia married Fang Lijian, she'd done her best to put her family's past behind her but found it wasn't possible. Her father's *youpai* label followed her to her new husband's post as an associate professor at a small Suzhou university. One day, two years after Lijian had been hired, he was called into the department chair's office, where two of his colleagues were already seated. In the interrogation that followed, they accused him of promoting conservative ideas in his classroom. "What kind of ideas?" Fang Lijian asked. He'd spent his life studying molecular structures. He wouldn't know how to begin talking politics, not even to defend himself against these men. The university's Communist Party representatives scheduled staff meetings where they encouraged colleagues to accuse one another of counterrevolutionary ideas. Better to wrongly accuse someone than to risk the spread of right-wing ideology, especially when it came to dealing with academics, whose positions afforded them intellectual power. Fang Lijian sat through weeks of meetings until it was agreed that his colleagues lacked the evidence to convict him. Instead of being jailed, he was sent to the countryside to be reeducated at a cadre school.

And so Jiajia had a second man in her life taken away from her. She spent the time her husband was gone raising her daughter alone and studying his letters for signs of mental collapse. There were rumors of brainwashing and psychic bullying in camps like the one to which Fang Lijian had been sent. Who knew what else went on in such remote places, far from the public eye? Who knew how long it would be before he was released? She waited and waited. But finally, after the longest year of her life, her husband came back, and to her relief, he was mentally sound. He'd changed, of course. Among other things, he'd made a friend—a Communist Party friend—by the name of Zhen Hong.

At first glance, Zhen Hong was different from Fang Lijian in every way two men could be different. Whereas Fang Lijian was slight and serious, Zhen Hong was built for fieldwork. He had strong, sturdy legs, a commanding voice, and a gregariousness that made him loved by all who knew him. Unlike Lina's father, Zhen Hong hadn't been sent down by the government as punishment for right-wing leanings. He was an unofficial director of the commune, a local farmer who had been identified by the CCP as someone with a knack for managing people. The two men had become close over the months, and when Fang Lijian finished his countryside stint, they both applied to work in Suzhou. A silk factory in their village was hiring, and the two were reassigned to work alongside each other.

If it had just been a typical friendship, Jiajia might have eventually found a way to overlook her political prejudices. But when she discovered that Fang Lijian had promised their child to Zhen Hong's family, any chance of her accepting the Zhens into their lives was gone.

"They're common," Jiajia once said in the heat of an argument. "We send them meat every winter. Isn't that payment enough for your debt? We have to send them our own flesh and blood too?"

"Zhen Hong is as good as my brother," Lijian countered. "And as much as you don't want to admit it, we are postrevolution. Who isn't common now?"

"Postrevolution, shi ba? You're the only liberal I know who goes around arranging marriages."

Every once in a while, Jiajia would bring up the topic of a "debt," and Lijian's mood would darken in a way that was unnatural to his temperament. The few times Lina had asked to hear more, both her parents became close-lipped. For Jiajia, the topic seemed to be something she brought up only for provocation's sake; for Lina's father, it seemed to be a point of shame. Though they would stop arguing when pressed for information, the tension between them took days to completely melt away.

It was never worth prolonging these moments of discomfort, so Lina stopped asking and began piecing together what information she could. From the bits her mother had let slip during their conversations alone, it was clear that her father and Zhen Hong's friendship wasn't the only basis for the arranged marriage. Jiajia told Lina that when she was a baby, life had been hard. Her father had been sent to a labor camp, and for a couple years, their future as a family was uncertain. It was around this time that Zhen Hong had done her father a service that pulled them out of a difficult situation. Although, if you asked *her*, there was such a thing as too much gratitude for a kind deed done. Sometimes you had to take kind deeds for what they were — acts of service that carried no obligation. True kindness demanded no repayment, and in fact the idea of repayment diminished the goodwill in such a gesture. Didn't Lina agree?

Jiajia often revealed more than she realized when preparing dinner, the rhythm of the knife work lulling her into a meditative state suited to honesty. Lina, sitting nearby, shelling peas at seven years old, at twelve, at seventeen, didn't have an answer for her, but she did have the impressionability to remember the things her mother said, word for word. She knew that her mother felt guilty for her own bourgeois pedigree and blamed herself for her husband's time at a labor camp. Zhen Hong, however, had the right kind of background. He came from a long line of farmers and had always had pull with the government officials. After the Cultural Revolution ended, he even joined the Communist Party. It was likely that at some point during their friendship, Zhen Hong had put in a good word for her father. He might even have been the reason Fang Lijian was allowed to come home after just one year of toiling in the fields. Whatever kindness Zhen Hong had done for Fang Lijian was significant enough to turn Fang's cheeks red every time Jiajia brought it up. Lina's heart went out to her father. She knew, even if her mother didn't, that he would never sacrifice her happiness just to repay some debt. But if marrying Wei had the added benefit of absolving Fang Lijian of some shame from his past, that was even more reason for her to do it.

The Zhens seemed to sense Jiajia's condescension and, strangely enough, to accept it. Occasionally, they sent the younger brother over with coal or a bag of fruit, meant as a modest gift. When he showed up at the front door, Lina's mother let him inside without a word. Qiang would set the bag down on the kitchen floor and peer around the room just long enough for Jiajia to grow impatient. Then he would leave through the side door. The entire interaction took less than thirty seconds. Out of respect for Jiajia, the Zhens never sent the betrothed Zhen brother over with packages, and they themselves never stopped by the Fangs' home. But sometimes, if Lina was by herself when she visited the silk factory where her father worked, Zhen Hong would call out to her. Years of sedentary labor had rounded out his shoulders, softened him into a balding, bear-shaped man with crescent eyes. When she came toward him, he'd reach into his pocket and pull out a few peanuts to offer her, still warm from being close to his body.

Lina liked the thought of having Zhen Hong as a father-in-law, and she liked having the security of a future designed just for her. Since her father had begun telling her about Wei when she was a little girl, the idea of him as her husband had grown like the sapling planted outside their home the year she was born. Glimpsed every time she went in and out of the house, it became essential to her concept of self. "Love," her father had once told her, "is not some mysterious force that comes from nowhere. It requires time and commitment, both of which are in your control. See that tree over there? All it needs is light and water. Don't you know the simplest things can be the most magical? Remember: Time and commitment. If you have these two things, you can have any manner of love."

Fang Lijian's perspective on love was different from any she'd heard before. Lina's friends had watched too many American movies and to them, love was a classic car that would come roaring in from nowhere when the time was right, pick you up, and peel away. For all their warnings to her about relinquishing control by marrying a man she didn't know, they seemed to crave the kind of love that made you lose control. They wanted to "fall" in love — that was the American way — whereas the idea of falling anywhere, with anyone, had never once appealed to Lina.

Adults, however, treated marriage as a rite of passage or a way to increase a family's social standing. The men with whom her father played cards were alternately bored and exasperated by their wives. They referred to them as "old hens" and complained about the shrillness of their voices and their loosening skin. But Lina's father was different. When Fang Lijian spoke to Jiajia, it was with respect that bordered on deference. And while Jiajia could be sharp with him at times, her love and respect for Fang Lijian were evident in the way she repeated his thoughts to the other mothers in the neighborhood when he was not around. *Lijian thinks we'll have more rain this season. Lijian thinks we'll come back from the famine in a couple years, not because of the harvest but because of the production in the cities. Lijian's going to town tomorrow to ask around—we'll see what he thinks.* Lina wanted the marital relationship her parents had, and she believed that her father knew best how to attain it.

"How do you know Zhen Zhiwei is the one for me, Baba?" Lina asked him once. It was not that she did not trust his judgment; it was that she was hoping he would admit to having powers of divination. She was fascinated by the idea of fate, that every moment in your life could be planned for you, was just awaiting your arrival.

Jiajia snorted when she heard this. "Indeed. *How*, Baba?"

Fang Lijian's mouth hardened, but he did not otherwise acknowledge his wife. Instead, he turned toward Lina at the table and placed both of his hands on her knees. "Zhen Zhiwei is a bright boy with a good soul," he said. "And the Zhens are a warmhearted family who have raised him well."

While he did not answer Lina's question, she was appeased by his certainty. Fang Lijian rarely insisted on anything that went against Jiajia's wishes, and his stubbornness in this one respect meant that he was sure of the best plan for Lina's future. In her mind, she filled in the details of the rest of her life. She'd marry Wei, move in with the Zhens, and walk across the village to see her parents every day. She'd have many children for her parents to play with to make up for her being an only child.

As the Zhen brothers grew up, they began to develop reputations in the community. Wei was smart, dutiful, and a little bit proud; Qiang was wily, charismatic, and wild. Each was a leader in his own right — Wei of a group of boys who took academics seriously but who were not above skipping school when it was clear that the instructor could not teach them anything new; Qiang of a group of boys who rarely went to school and spent most of their days climbing trees outside the classroom and dropping well-aimed shoes onto the heads of the students beneath them. Every now and then, Lina met girls who went to school with the Zhen brothers, and when she mentioned her arranged marriage, they said, *Zhen Zhiwei? Not bad, you lucky thing.* And she watched their eyes wander away from her to picture him in some light she hadn't yet seen.

When she thought of Wei, she could not come up with anything physically descriptive. She couldn't imagine the way he walked or laughed. But she associated the idea of him with a distinct sense of comfort she'd formed on the long, bored days outside the silk factory, staring at the water. The view from that bank had led her to picture the span of her life stretched out ahead of her, steady as the sea. And while this wasn't an accurate memory of Wei, it was maybe the most accurate memory of who she was as a thirteen-year-old: a girl so sure of her prospects that she wanted them to happen slowly. She wanted to savor it all, piece by piece.

But by seventeen, Lina outgrew this patience. She was bored of her hometown, knew every stone along the lake and every square meter of the woods and the silk factory inside it. The building where her father worked always looked as if it were on the verge of collapse, its walls filled with cracks that climbed almost as high as the ivy. She wanted new vistas, new friends, new teachers. Mostly, she was tired of studying; it felt as though she had been preparing for college for forever.

In the spring of college entrance exams, scoring well was the priority for all Chinese high-school students. Lina and her friends studied for the Gaokao twelve to fourteen hours a day, taking breaks only to walk from class to class, to perform the school-led eye- and neck-muscle exercises, and to eat the food placed in front of them. Every morning, grandmothers across the nation prepared the same breakfast for high-school fourth-years: a bowl of soybean milk served with a stick of fried dough and two hard-boiled eggs; *1-0-0* it read when arranged on a table. A superstitious plea for the test score they all wanted. The score that would determine whether a child attended a good university.

Lina had never liked the taste of eggs. When her grandmother wasn't looking, she fed one of them to the dog. She took her time with the other one, drumming it on the table, trying to make the cracks in the shell as fine as possible. Those ten minutes were often the only minutes in the day when her thoughts weren't directed at memorization, explication, or performing the basic functions needed to live. Breakfast time was when her mind was freshest, and she used it to imagine.

Now that she was older, Lina decided she needed to know more about Wei. He was her sure thing, the one part of her future that wouldn't be influenced by her performance on the Gaokao. Even Jiajia had to admit that, family line aside, Zhen Zhiwei was a good match for her daughter. The community thought him smart and focused. He was handsome enough, too, although Lina had never been one of those boy-crazy girls. She could have done with less.

What she needed more of was information. Because Wei went to a different high school, there was only so much to be gleaned from her classmates, so she came up with a plan. Qiang, the younger Zhen brother, was still sent over to the Fang family with small gifts every so often. Now that the weather was warm, he'd started bringing by bags of oranges and peaches, which he set softly against the kitchen stove. Lina could see into the kitchen from her room, and she watched him whenever he came over, wondering which qualities of his also belonged to his brother. They were only a year apart in age. Did Wei have the same curve to his back, the posture that made Qiang seem as though he was always shouldering a weight against the wind? Was the bridge of his nose quite as high? Lina promised herself that the next time the boy stopped by, she would talk to him and ask him some questions about his brother.

"Zhen Zhiqiang."

The afternoon was bright and hazy. Lina's father had just finished dusting off the roof, and some of this dust had made it through the doors, clouding the distance between Lina and the boy crouched before the stove. He looked up, and though the sun behind him made it hard for her to see his expression, she could tell by the way he froze in place that he was startled to find her in the doorway of the kitchen.

He straightened up. "Lina." He said her name so casually—calling her not xiao jie, not mei, not Fang Lina, but Lina—that she was sure the Zhen household spoke of her often.

"You should have some tea," she said. "Do you want some tea?"

He looked from one end of the kitchen to the other as if searching for an escape route. Then he nodded.

She put the kettle on to boil and removed two tin mugs from the cupboard. At a loss for what to say to him after that, she busied herself by putting away washed dishes and setting out a bowl of watermelon seeds, the way her mother did for guests. When the water was ready, she filled two mugs. He had not moved from where he stood and suddenly seemed to her less like a boy and more like a wolf on its best behavior. She felt odd about asking him to sit down at the table.

Instead, she handed him one of the mugs and led the way out the door to the backyard. Lina sat on the step and Qiang's feet landed next to hers, light as a cat's. Lina considered the questions she wanted to ask him but could not think of any that would come out naturally. It would be awkward to launch straight into discussing Wei, but what else was she supposed to say? Qiang didn't seem the type to engage in small talk.

"You must be tired, carrying that fruit all this way," she finally said.

"Why? It doesn't weigh much. I've carried far heavier. What about the coal I brought last winter?"

"That's true," Lina said.

Qiang shrugged. "I look weaker than I am. Ba's always trying to get more muscle on me. That's why he sends me everywhere with packages. I tell him if he wants me bigger, he should feed me more."

Lina giggled, which seemed to relax Qiang.

"My brother is bigger than me. I guess you know. He was born that way, so there it is. Ba doesn't send Wei anywhere anymore. He's too busy studying for the entrance exams."

"Me too," said Lina. "That's all I've been doing. Which placement is he taking?"

"Science and engineering."

"I'm taking liberal arts."

"Too much studying isn't good for anybody. Wei talks in his sleep, you know. Differential equations and all that." He closed his eyes, leaned his head back, and pretended to snore, muttering numbers loudly on each exhale.

"Huai si le!" Lina laughed, swatting him on the arm. "You should show your brother some respect!"

Qiang opened his eyes wide in mock innocence. "I'm just concerned for his health!"

"Don't worry," Lina said. "It will be you soon enough. You're one year below us, right? What will you test for?"

"The sports university, of course," Qiang said. "I'm not getting all pale and nearsighted. I'm getting exercise. They need young proletariat men like me to continue to march for the revolution." His sarcasm was so unexpected that it made Lina laugh even harder. By this time most of the revolutionary fervor had passed, but it was still unheard of—dangerous, even—to joke about the revolution in public.

Suddenly, Lina felt they were doing something very wrong. She wished she'd looked at the clock before coming outside. She wasn't sure how much longer it would be before her mother came home, and she was anxious about being seen with Qiang. He must have sensed her nervousness. He looked away from her and crouched with his elbows over his knees and one thumb kneading into the base of the other, as though he were trying to crack it. With Qiang to Lina's left, a shadow was cast over her torso. The upper part of her body began to chill while her cheeks warmed in the sun. A few meters away, two chickens fought over something on the ground. Minutes passed, during which one of the neighborhood kids ran down the street yelling a crass version of a nursery rhyme. When he was gone, the silence seemed even riper between them.

"You'd better go," Lina finally said. "My ma's just gone to the market."

As if there were springs attached to his heels, Qiang leaped off the remaining steps to the ground. He started to walk around the side of the house, but before he reached it, he stopped and turned to face her.

"You should eat the oranges first," he said. "The peaches aren't ripe yet."

Without waiting for a response, he disappeared.

After a moment, Lina stood, feeling even more uneasy. She bent to pick up Qiang's full mug of tea. Then she walked out to the brush to dump it, taking care not to look at the bottom of the mug after she did. A few years ago, her great-aunt had taught her how to read omens in tea leaves. Up until then, she hadn't considered the range and abundance of possible bad fortunes in the world—false friendships, mechanical troubles, wasted time, tardiness, financial ruin, broken commitments. As hard as she'd tried to forget the symbols, she had never managed to unlearn what she knew.

6

Wei woke, as he had every day since the phone call from his brother, to the memory of Qiang's voice. On the phone, it had sounded distant and staticky, like he was calling from the grave. *Ge,* Qiang had said, *wo shi Qiang? Neng ting jian wo ma?* Brother, do you recognize me? Do you hear me?

It had been so long since Wei had been addressed as Ge — "Big Brother" — that it took him a moment to be able to answer. *Yes,* he'd said, finally recognizing Qiang's voice. *Can I come see you? Can we meet?*

Wei rolled over and swung his legs off the mattress at the expense of his back. He didn't do well with these soft hotel mattresses, never had. In the bathroom, he took a piss, shook five times for luck. *Strange,* he thought to himself, *the habits that follow you through the years.* Into the shower, then. Bath mat laid down, the spray on. Water pressure set to deafening.

Qiang was alive. *Alive.* And he was coming to visit. This news had been spinning around in his head all week, a distraction that gave him boosts of energy to get through the workday. He still had a brother, which meant that he and Lina still had family left. Would he recognize Qiang? How much had he changed? Wei had his phone number now. He could ask him to text him a picture.

No; ridiculous. Of course he would recognize him. Hadn't Qiang recognized Wei, after all? How ironic that it was *Pitch 360*, in the end, that had brought Qiang to him. Wei laughed softly, shaking his head. He was tempted to nominate Sandrik for a raise. And how like Qiang to so casually call him up after twenty years of silence, announce that he would be coming to visit, and not even stay on the phone long enough to exchange the usual pleasantries.

Since childhood, Qiang had been drawn to extremes. Everything he did, he had to go all the way. He stayed out until nighttime shadows could no longer see him past their parents' bedroom. He skipped so much school that a neighbor had been able to give his kid a free education by sending him there under Qiang's name. The moment an idea sparked in his mind, Qiang had to turn it into action. One of the clearest memories Wei had of his brother was when Qiang was six years old. Their parents had dropped them off at the home of an old woman who took care of the villagers' babies while their parents were working. Usually, Wei was able to keep Qiang out of mischief when his parents weren't home, but the previous week Qiang had almost burned the place down by trying to melt a cooking pot into scrap metal. After that, their parents decided to spend the five mao a week on professional supervision.

The old woman's home was one of the larger ones in the village. A small front living room connected to the kitchen, and through the kitchen's curtained-off doorway was a bare bedroom that contained one large bed, where the babies slept. From the moment the brothers walked in the door, Qiang had that restless look on his face. When he reached to grab at something on the old woman's table, Wei had immediately taken hold of his brother's wrist. *Fang kai wo!* Qiang complained, but as hard as he shook, Wei wouldn't let go. Though only a year older than his brother, Wei had always been far stronger, and he kept hold of Qiang even as the other children approached them to talk and play. The caretaker was busy preparing food for the babies in the back room and Wei knew that the moment his attention was no longer on Qiang, there would be trouble. *I'll hold him until she comes back,* Wei thought. But the old lady took her time, and Wei had gotten tired, and he finally let Qiang loose. For a few minutes, Qiang stalked around the room, rubbing his wrist and scowling—harmless enough. But the next thing Wei knew, there was a chorus of howls coming from the room beyond the kitchen.

Wei and the others rushed through the curtained doorway and collected at the foot of the bed filled with screaming infants.

"Zen me la?" the old woman asked repeatedly, shaking Qiang by the shoulders. "Ni gan shenme le?"

She couldn't get him to talk. He was convulsing with laughter, flushed from his forehead to his fingers. Finally, he brought a hand to his face and pinched his nose. Having been woken from sleep many times with his own nose between his brother's fingers, Wei immediately understood this gesture. Qiang had pinched all the sleeping babies' noses, one by one, until they were awake and crying.

If only he'd stuck to pinching noses. The older Qiang grew, the more alarming his antics became. His preteen years were spent stealing candy from the market and animals from other families' yards, and lying to teachers and officials if he was caught. Qiang's one redeeming quality was that he wasn't a fighter. He enjoyed terrorizing other children so that they chased him, but he was better at running away than he was at fighting. He seemed to think there was more honor in running too. To elude a person took speed and cunning, Qiang had once explained to Wei. To fight meant to hit or be hit, which didn't require much cunning at all.

But once Qiang dropped out of school, that all changed. Nightly dinners began without him and were eaten in silence, the Zhens' ears trained for Qiang's footsteps and the sound of the door opening. As angry as Ma and Ba were when he came home, they always fed him, with Ba delivering ineffectual lectures over cold noodle soup. Then Qiang started coming back with nicks up and down his arms and neck. When they asked him about it—when Ma stripped him and made him lift all four limbs so she could look for hidden damage—he refused to reveal anything. *Get Qiang to talk,* Wei's father had begged him, but Wei didn't know how. He had always been more like a third parent than an older brother to Qiang, and their relationship was further strained by their parents pleading with Qiang to behave more like Wei: to study hard, sit still, stand straight, speak up. During the moments of closeness the brothers did share—playing basketball at the recreational center or fetching water from the local pond—Wei could not figure out a way to start the conversation.

Instead, he followed him. One day after school when Wei was a third-year, he spotted Qiang and his group of friends coming toward him down the road. He ducked behind the nearest tree and waited for them to pass. They did so without noticing him, and after that, the decision to spy on his brother was hardly a decision at all. He followed the boys until they made the next turn in the road. This told Wei that they were going to Zhu Lin, a neighboring village.

But after the boys reached the village center, they kept going. The sun set as they walked, and by the time they stopped, Wei no longer knew where they were. There were trees around them; a clearing. Wei kept within hearing range but made sure to stay out of sight. Soon, he heard other, deeper voices belonging to boys he didn't recognize. They looked to be older than Wei.

"Shouhuo zenme yang a?" one of them said. "Did you get what we asked?" Wei moved closer just in time to see Qiang and his friends step forward. They emptied their pockets, opened their messenger bags, and laid what they had on the ground: coins, cigarettes, and other objects Wei couldn't make out.

There was murmuring and soft laughter from the older boys.

"Not bad," one of them said. "There's hope for our minions yet. Jian Hua, the bag."

The largest of the boys collected items from the ground while the boy who had spoken began to pace the clearing.

"Tingzhe!" Wei shouted. Before he knew what he was doing, he had stepped into the clearing. Now he could see the expressions of his brother and his friends, some of whom seemed surprised to see him, others relieved. But Qiang alone was filled with fury.

"Who is this?" the leader of the older boys asked.

"He's nobody," Qiang replied.

"I'm Qiang's brother. And these things are stolen."

The older boys looked at one another and began to laugh.

"Qiang's your brother, you said?"

Qiang stood from where he had been crouching on the grass. "He's no brother of mine."

Wei was surprised how much the words hurt. Qiang had never rejected him like that before. Or maybe it was his lack of hesitation in doing it that hurt him.

"Look, friend, why don't you leave?" The older boy—the one who had done most of the speaking—looked from Wei to Qiang and seemed genuinely amused. "We could fight you, but honestly, I'm feeling lazy tonight. I'd rather save my energy for a real fight. I've heard of you. You're a smart enough guy. It's four to one. You do the math."

"I'm not leaving without my brother," Wei said.

"Fine by us," the boy said. "Take him."

Wei stared at the boy's face. He looked to be about seventeen or eighteen. A scratch, or a scar, was visible just below his jawline.

"I'm also taking whichever of these things he's responsible for stealing. I can't speak for these other delinquents. They're not my problem."

"You're not taking anything," the boy said. "These things belong to us now."

Wei paused, assessing the situation. "What do you want with them anyway? They're just boys."

"Want with them?" the lead boy asked. "Hao xiao. They're the ones who want to be friends with us. Isn't that right, Qiang?"

Qiang glared at Wei so fiercely he might have set the whole forest on fire. His mouth was as thin as a fishing line.

"Come on," Wei said to him. "Let's go home."

Qiang didn't move until, finally, the older boy said, "Get out of here! And by the way, anybody else's brothers hiding in the bushes? Speak now or get the hell out!"

On the way home, Wei had tried to question Qiang. *Who were those boys? How did you meet them?* But Qiang admitted nothing—he didn't even try to come up with excuses. And that's how Wei's one effort to save his brother put more distance between them than ever. From then on, Qiang's antics only got worse, and it became clear that those boys in the woods were a local gang that had taken him in. They stole from villagers and fought other gangs for fun. They provided Qiang with cigarettes and knives and taught him how to be even stealthier than he already was— for Wei never again had the opportunity to follow Qiang.

The gang itself began disappearing for months at a time, working its way deeper into black society—fighting other gangs, gambling, running up debts, and worse. So when Qiang finally disappeared for good, Wei was upset but not surprised. Deep down, he had always known they would have to let Qiang go. And as hard as he had worked to try to find his brother, he knew that the search was futile. If Qiang didn't want to be found, he wouldn't be. The only way for the Zhens to see him again was to wait for Qiang to change his mind and come back of his own accord.

After Wei and Lina had been living in the U.S. for ten years, there was a freak accident that took all four of their parents' lives. Early one morning in America, they had received a call from China's department of transportation services. The Zhens and Fangs had been traveling from Suzhou to vacation up north when their train had collided with a freight train traveling in the other direction; none of their parents had made it.

There was no time to absorb the shock. Wei and Lina had packed up and taken the next flight out of Philadelphia, arriving just in time to help with the last of the memorial-service arrangements and greet the distraught family and friends. Wei had never told Lina, but he had tried to delay the service as much as possible for a reason. He was giving Qiang more time—time to hear the news, time to process it, time to arrange for his own travel. He knew without a doubt that his brother would be at the service. Black society was well connected. It was impossible that Qiang wouldn't have heard of his parents' accident. But when the day came, Qiang wasn't there. That's when the possibility occurred to Wei: What if his brother was dead?

In the shower, Wei rubbed his eyes with the heavy heels of his hands, trying to clear his thoughts. No good dwelling on the past now. It was time to make a new start with Qiang and try for a better relationship than what they'd had. Wei shut off the water and opened the shower door. He stopped. Had he shampooed? Had he soaped? He had definitely soaped—the bar was sudsy. The shampoo was always the tricky one. He leaned in close to the bottle, looking for water droplets on its surface. There were only a few flecks, which meant that he probably hadn't. He rubbed his fingers into his scalp, held them up to his nose, and sniffed. Couldn't tell. Felt a little greasy. To be safe, he turned the water back on to shampoo again. He could almost feel the nutrients being leached from his hair follicles. This, most likely, was the cause of his hair loss—shampooing twice a day due to distractedness. Even before this business with Qiang, he'd found himself becoming less alert. Work stress collected like sap along the walls of his mind; every problem seemed to stick in his consciousness.

By the time Wei emerged from the shower, he felt moderately awake. He dressed without turning on the closet light, a routine he was able to manage by requesting that Lina buy him dress shirts and pants that matched one another interchangeably. Thus, his wardrobe was filled with light-colored tops and dark-colored bottoms, creating a staid but straightforward personal style. Lina was still sleeping when he crossed the bedroom. While he'd been rising earlier with his mounting workload, she had been getting out of bed later, as though the hours of sleep he left behind had taken up residence in her.

The clubhouse was emptier than usual; there wasn't even a line at the takeaway counter. As Wei walked toward it, the blue-tiled walls of the corridor seemed to move, converging in on him like the barrel of a wave.

"Good morning," Wei said to the attendant.

"Good morning, Boss Zhen." She checked her list. "It doesn't look like I have anything here for you."

"Shi ma? My wife must have forgotten to put in my order last night. Could you fill it for me now while I wait?"

"Sure. Two hard-boiled eggs, yogurt, and a croissant?"

"You got it."

As she left to prepare his breakfast, Wei heard his name being called. He turned around to see David Ming, chief risk management officer for Deutsche Bank, walking toward him. David was dressed in short sleeves and khakis. This could mean one of two things: One, that David was going to skip work today, which was unlikely. Two, that today was not in fact a workday.

"Zhen Zhiwei! Don't tell me you're heading into the office!"

Damn. So it was a weekend. He panicked; this was the second time in two months he'd made a mistake like this. He had to get more sleep.

"I was," he said casually. "But my meeting just got canceled."

"They're working you hard over there. I hope you're taking care of yourself."

Wei shrugged. "Once in a while, you know, I don't mind going in on a weekend. Except it looks like I woke up early for nothing."

"The fact that you can usually sleep in is a good thing. None of the rest of us can wake up past seven anymore." David nodded toward the dining area, where Nicholas Pan and Steve Yao, fellow Chinese-American expats and corporate executives, were already seated with their food. "Anyway, I'll see you over there." He headed for the griddle station.

Wei removed his tie, folded it, and zipped it into the front flap of his briefcase. Saturday—how could it be Saturday? The alarm had gone off. No, it hadn't. He'd woken to the sound of Qiang's voice.

At the coffee bar, he asked for two espresso shots and drank them standing up. Then he ordered his omelet, loaded bread into the toaster, and filled a plate with fruit.

"Get out of here with that healthy stuff," Nicholas said as Wei approached the table. "Our wives are going to come downstairs in a minute and you're about to make us look bad. You know how long it took David to get Peng to let him have pancakes?"

"I only get to eat them once a week," David said with his mouth full. "And you're ruining the experience."

As Wei sat down, the espresso hit him so suddenly that his body felt like a gong. He felt rung.

"Peng told me your brother's coming next week," David said. "You have Expo tickets yet? I can get you fast passes if you need them."

"I'm set, thanks. Actually, a vendor sent a couple more over yesterday. If any of you are interested, I have extras."

"The World Expo is the last place on earth I want to be," Nicholas said. "Crammed into those exhibits with a million other people? No, thank you."

"I was going to have Lina take my brother and Karen during the week, when it's less crowded."

"But it's China's year!" said David. "You don't want to see us outdo every other country there? I heard the U.S. is so in debt at this point that they're funding the American pavilion entirely from corporate donations. That's us." He jabbed his thumb into his chest. "We're paying for the Expo."

"I don't know how it is over at Ford, but we're not being philanthropic about it by any means," Nicholas said.

"Oh, come on. Your company has its logo all over the website! It's one of the biggest sponsors."

"That's not charity, that's advertising. Millions of Chinese are going to see that pavilion. Ask the industry expert. What do you think, Wei? Is the ad space in the pavilion worth it?"

Wei's job at Medora had grown so vague that even his closest friends had trouble understanding it. It was easier for them to remember him by industry rather than by title and for him to pretend to know more about sponsorship price points and outdoor advertising than he really did.

"It depends on the layout and what they end up putting in the space," Wei said. "Could probably make the same amount of money work harder digitally, though."

The men nodded, already losing interest. Nick drew his phone out of his pocket. "My wife is picking me up a watch while she's in Hong Kong. Which of these do you think I should get?"

David leaned over to look at the screen. "Hey, the Batman watch! Limited stock, right?"

"GMT Master Two," Nick said. "I don't know if I like that one. But the one with the blue face is nice." He flipped to a different image and presented it to the group. "I can tell her to pick up extras."

"Yeah? I'll take one."

"Let me see that," Wei said, reaching for the phone.

"Are they all Rolex?" Steve asked. He was the resident watch connoisseur and the only one at the table who had a real collection. Wei had heard from Lina, who had heard from Steve's wife, that Steve had a motorized arm in his bedroom that kept all his watches moving when they were not being worn.

"Oh, don't be a snob," said Nick. "If they're too tacky for you, just say it."

"They're nice. Understated. Go back to the left. That one."

"So two Batmans, one blue. I'm going with blue too. Wei?"

"Blue," Wei said. "And one more for my brother."

He decided, for once, to treat his wallet the way these men treated theirs — like conduits for their imaginations. The thought of Qiang wearing a watch that matched his own made it easier for Wei to picture them starting their relationship over — not as rivals, but as equals. Despite the fact that he was sleep-deprived and didn't know what day it was, despite the fact that he had become middle-aged in the blink of an eye, Wei felt his life was suddenly full of possibility. After all, what he had thought impossible had happened: his brother had decided to come home.

The clubhouse restaurant had begun to fill up with ayis and young children. Five years ago, Wei would never have imagined they'd be hiring their own ayi. Lina used to be the kind of woman who rejected the idea of hired help. She used to have so much energy. She would have taken the task of cooking for four as a challenge. Back in Collegeville, when Wei picked Lina up from the elementary school where she worked, he would see her standing there behind the big metal doors, her eyes fixed on the approaching car. Before it came to a full stop, she would pull the passenger-side door open and toss in her bag. Then she would throw herself into the backseat with Karen, whom she nearly dragged into her lap with excitement. Wei had watched them in the rearview mirror, fascinated by his wife's energy as she chattered the whole way home. How could a person have so much to say to a five-year-old? How could you work with children all day and have enough of that energy left over for your own child? Wei's energy was all drawn from the same inner reserve. After work, he was so tired that he could barely take Karen into his arms. The love was there, of course, but by the end of the day it was dulled.

Lina, however, had an unexpected resilience, an ability to compartmentalize. She could work a ten-hour day in which nothing went right — one kid threw up, another punched her in the gut and called her a Chink—and still, she would spend the evening mastering Western recipes she'd copied from library books. It was like Newton's third law of motion: every action has an equal and opposite reaction. She could take the tiredness and the hate and turn them into acts of love and creation for her family. *Here, taste.* She would hold the spoon out to Wei. *It's sour*, he said, making a face. *Xiang xia ren, ba?* She liked to tease him about his unworldliness. *This is how the Italians eat noodles. I'm trying to teach you some culture.* But when she thought he wasn't looking, she added a spoonful of sugar to the sauce. They ate with chopsticks, the tomato base staining the bamboo a shy red. *Say "linguine,"* Lina told Karen. *"Linguine,"* Karen said, and the word slipped out as easily as the noodles did from the chopsticks held in her stubby fingers. By the time she was six, she could recite the Pledge of Allegiance in under seven seconds. *I pledge allegiance to the flag of the United States of America and to the republic of witches' hands one nation under God indivisible with liberty and justice for all.*

When they first arrived in America, it was Lina who had single-handedly taken on the task of learning the country. On weekends, she turned on the TV and watched shows where white people screamed at one another onstage and chased one another backstage. Then commercials came on. Then black people screamed at one another onstage and chased one another backstage. He had watched Lina squint at the TV, trying to pick up on the essential American thing she wasn't getting. During their earliest years in America, when Wei was still a grad student in Penn's engineering program, Wei and Lina were too poor to afford real entertainment. After dinner, they would pass the time by walking into drugstores to look at all the strange American sundries on display. Lina lingered in the holiday aisles, fingering tinsel or heart-shaped chocolate boxes, choosing just one thing at a time to bring home. It wasn't until later that they realized they had been buying Easter chicks on Valentine's Day and discount Halloween candy on Thanksgiving.

How quickly their understanding of American life had increased after they'd had Karen! Kiddie parties and playdates meant forays into the homes of others, which allowed them to observe up close how they lived. Not the staged moments—holidays over at colleagues' homes, with their perfect gold-rimmed dinnerware and cloth napkins. They saw real behind-the-scenes stuff: knives magnetized above the sink, boxed meals in the fridge, and kids who sometimes climbed into bed with their shoes still on.

Now, in the clubhouse restaurant, Wei sensed his wife coming toward them before he saw her. Lina's carriage was erect, mastlike. She walked in a way that made her seem taller than she was. After saying hello to the other men, she eyed Wei in his suit. "You have a meeting this early?"

"It was canceled." The corner of her left eyebrow tensed—she knew he wasn't telling the truth. But instead of pulling him away from the others to find out what was going on, as she would have done years ago, she simply nodded and opened her handbag.

"Here," she said. "The girl at the takeaway counter said you ordered this." She took a white paper sack out of her bag—his forgotten breakfast—and placed it on the floor next to him.

Things felt off between them these days, but what the problem was he couldn't quite figure out. And so he labeled it a second-tier emergency, pushed it out of his thoughts for now. Lina was making small talk with the rest of the men, nodding in her distant, perfunctory way.

"Sit down," Wei told her, pulling a chair out next to him.

She hesitated, sending a glance toward the booth near the windows where her friends were sitting. The decision to eat with the men caused a minute and fleeting strain on her expression, which only Wei could detect. Then she sank into the seat and picked up where she'd left off in conversation.

7

On Saturdays, most of Sunny's housemates either went in late to work or had the day off. In the early morning, the house was quiet, which meant Sunny could take her time getting ready. She could lie in bed and fool around on her phone while the water was boiling for her breakfast. There was just enough time to eat and drink a cup of tea while playing Happy Farm and responding to the WeChat group that included her mother and sister.

Sunny: How are you feeling, Yanzi?

Yanzi QQ: I'm permanently attached to the couch. I can't move. It makes me nauseous.

Tong Mama: She's fine. Just using the baby as an excuse to be lazy.

Yanzi QQ: How many years has it been since you've been pregnant, Ma???

Tong Mama: I was still harvesting the fields in my eighth month when I was pregnant with you. You're lucky you didn't drop out between my legs.

As much as her mother teased Yanzi about being lazy, Sunny knew that she couldn't be happier that Yanzi was pregnant. In fact, she was willing to bet that her mother had been the one to tell Yanzi to start relaxing, for the good of the baby.

> **Yanzi QQ:** Jie, you need to catch up! You're still only on level sixteen on Happy Farm. Are you even playing anymore?
> **Sunny:** I'm behind! 😒 Help your sister out and donate some resources!
> **Tong Mama:** Your sister is a working woman...she doesn't have so much time like you.

Sunny knew her mother too well not to understand that this was yet another way of shaming her. In Mama's mind, the real, important work was to continue the family line by carrying a child. This was what made a woman a woman; it was work that men could not do. But what would she say if she knew that soon Sunny could be sending home almost twice her usual amount? That was more than what any of her uncles or brothers were making.

> **Yanzi QQ:** Jie, you should get pregnant like me and farm all day! From the couch!
> **Sunny:** How's the real farm doing? Are you leaving all that work up to the boys?
> **Yanzi QQ:** Bunny's boyfriend comes around to help a lot now. I think he's on his best behavior because he's getting ready to propose.
> **Tong Mama:** 😊 Soon it will be her turn to farm from the couch.

She should just accept it; there would be no end to the proposals, the marriages, the children. Last night, Sunny had been thinking so much about Rose's situation that she hadn't given much thought to her own. Being accused meant her job was at risk too. The Zhens might not think she took the bracelet, but management could have its own ideas. Why shouldn't she take the job? Doing so would prove her innocence. She couldn't afford to risk losing income, especially now, with Yanzi's baby on the way.

"What are you still doing here?"

Sunny looked up and was surprised to see Yang Zifei standing before her in a bootleg Bathing Ape T-shirt, the corners of his eyes still crusted over. He plunked his mug of tea down on the table and sat across from Sunny. "Aren't you usually gone by now?" he asked.

"It's Saturday, so the traffic isn't so bad. I can leave a little later. Why are you up so early?"

Yang Zifei was in his midtwenties. He worked during the day as a tree surgeon on the street crew of the Xuhui Landscape Development Company and at night as a server at a club in Hongqiao. Sunny sometimes ran into him when she was leaving the house in the morning and he was just coming home. He shook his head, sending his bright copper hair flopping across his face.

"I couldn't sleep right last night. Rice wine sometimes does that to me. I don't know why. It washes away my worries like a scented bath and I sleep like a baby, but then, *bah!* Slaps me awake three hours later. Nothing is going right for me this week. Did you know someone stole the incense burner I bought for the bathroom?"

"I saw the note you left," Sunny said.

"I thought finally we got a good group going here. Everybody was getting to know each other. I thought I would do something nice for us, de-stink the place a bit. Like you — how you always wash other people's dishes if they've been sitting there too long. That's a nice thing. Anyway, it seems like the two of us are the only ones with the right idea about community living. Everybody else is all for themselves."

He took a loud sip of his tea and pointed to Sunny's phone, which had just lit up with a Happy Farm notification.

"Still playing that one, ah? You should try Heroes of Kung Fu. You need a computer for it, though."

"I have no time for computer games. No money for a computer either."

Yang Zifei shrugged. "Isn't that true for us all. Go to a café."

"Maybe." Sunny spooned the last of her zhou into her mouth and got up to rinse out her dish. "See you later."

"Hey, wait a minute," he said. "There's a café around the corner. I could show you how to play."

Men often wanted to be friends with her; she didn't know why. Maybe it was because she wasn't pretty enough to make them nervous and didn't talk very much. They probably liked that she let them do all the talking. After all this time in the city, Sunny still wasn't sure what the social rules were for making friends or having lovers. She scanned Yang Zifei's carefree posture and naive eyes. He was too young for her, too young to fall into either category.

"The next time I have a day off, I'll let you know, okay?"

"Okay," he said, smirking. "See you never."

By seven o'clock, the sun was already so high that riding fast on her motorbike did little to cool Sunny down. She passed the ginkgo-lined streets, trying not to breathe in too deeply. Beautiful as the little fan-shaped leaves were, the female trees produced berries that in summertime smelled like boiling vomit. In autumn, the green leaves would burn up into constellations of yellow, as if absorbing the last of the summer sun. Though the trees were beautiful—tourists loved Lu Xun Park for the views—Sunny sometimes wished that she could trade them for the simple plane trees that decorated Xuhui District. Their low canopies provided more shade in the summer heat and a subtler sort of beauty. Yang Zifei had once described how he and the rest of the street crew pruned the plane trees twice a year. Once, in March, to remove dead branches, and the second time, in May, to remove the young ones. When Sunny asked him why the young branches needed to be cut off, he told her that they sucked the tree's resources. Took up too much room, used up too much sunlight. *Plus, when typhoon season comes, all that extra weight puts the entire tree in danger of being blown over.*

If only people thought of self-preservation in similar terms. Seemed like nowadays, every baby on the way was good news, regardless of whether the family could support it.

Sunny squinted hard into the wind, trying to keep her eyes protected from the debris that flew in from the streets. She made a mental note to buy goggles from the underground market, no matter how silly it made her feel to wear them. Traffic in Shanghai was too dangerous to be distracted while driving. The last thing she wanted was to leave the earth the way her husband had—dead on the side of the road. She merged onto the expressway between a BMW and a taxi. What kind of car did the Zhens have? Probably a BMW or nicer. Reminded of the job offer again, Sunny felt her heart skip. She leaned in, cut around the luxury car, and sped ahead in the next lane.

At the hotel, the regular security guard was back on duty. Sunny found him sitting at a table in the service hall, inspecting radios and filling out reports. "You have a new schedule," he said, sliding a clipboard in her direction. She flipped to her name and saw that 8202 appeared next to it every morning for the next two weeks. Usually, she and Rose would rotate.

"What happened?"

The guard shrugged. "Lady knows what she wants." When she didn't make a move to leave, he added, "They'd better find that bracelet."

Sunny was already in the elevator when it occurred to her that she hadn't looked for Rose's name on the schedule. What if it wasn't there at all? She pulled her phone out to send a text but could only stare at the blank screen. She wasn't sure how to ask a question like *Have you been fired?* Finally, she settled on *How are you?* Thinly veiled, but the best that she could do.

Outside apartment 8202's service entrance, Sunny rang the bell, knocked on the door five times, per custom, and entered the Zhens' kitchen. The rooms were silent; the family was downstairs at breakfast. Sunny wouldn't make the mistake she'd made yesterday and spend more time than necessary in the same room as Taitai. She'd clean the southern wing of the apartment first.

Boss Zhen's study looked out over the river through a bay window that stretched the length of the room. Along the left side of the wall ran a set of wooden cabinets that held glass trophies and a parade of family photos. In these vacation shots, Karen appeared at all different ages, but Taitai and Boss Zhen looked the same, she with her chin tucked into a practiced smile, one arm around her daughter, he carrying something that ultimately ruined the aesthetics of the shot—his wife's backpack slung over one shoulder, or a map that had been opened and refolded the wrong way. He seemed weighed down by practicality in a way that his wife was not. Although his study was cluttered, his belongings were mostly functional. Along with the cheap notebooks, there were great reams of paper on which large English words appeared on color-ink backgrounds. Twenty words per page, at most, some filled with graphs and images, all binder-clipped together and sitting in the corners of the room beneath little notes that read *Q1, Q2, Q3,* et cetera. On his desk, there was often a banana peel curled up on a dish, empty teacups. Occasionally, a discarded pair of pants could be found draped over the armchair, the belt hanging loose from the loops. Evidence of a hurried existence made him relatable to Sunny; unlike Taitai, Boss Zhen was under pressure from the outside world.

Sunny shook out a pair of pants by its waistband and felt weight in one of its pockets. She reached in and found a stack of business cards held together by a rubber band. The cards were dual-language, one side printed in English, the other Chinese. On the Chinese side was his company's name, MEDORA GROUP, and then, in smaller letters, GENERAL MANAGER, SHANGHAI; VICE PRESIDENT OF STRATEGY, GLOBAL. None of the maids had any idea what this meant, but once, when Rose was ill and Sunny was double-teaming a shift with a stand-in girl, the girl asked him to explain what he did. He'd looked startled. "I'm a problem solver," he had said.

Sunny thought about that statement a lot. Boss Zhen's job didn't sound too different from her own when he put it like that. She couldn't help thinking that if she had been born a city kid, maybe one with more patience for schoolwork, a contender for one of those fancy degrees that hung on Boss's wall, she might have been good at his job too, whatever it was.

Sunny was just a few minutes away from having the master bath cleaned when the front door opened. Within seconds, she heard Karen come down the hall, enter the bedroom, walk through the closet, and stop in the doorway of the bathroom. She grinned at Sunny, then glanced reflexively at the toilet.

The toilet in the master bath was motion-sensing, with a lid that rose whenever someone came near it. It was also self-flushing and self-warming, with little blue lights at the base of the tank that blinked when it was active. A couple years ago, Karen had admitted to Sunny that she and the toilet had an agreement: she would never step foot in the master bathroom if the toilet would never come out of it. There was something about the way it blinked, she had said, that made her sure it could move in other ways too. Although she had since proclaimed herself too old to believe in such things, she still seemed unwilling to take any chances.

"I heard Mom asked you," Karen said. She stood with one hand on her hip, the other holding a paper cup of coffee. "You're going to say yes, right?"

"What are you doing with that coffee?" Sunny said. "That's for grown-ups."

"It's not coffee," she said. "It's a latte. So, are you?" Sometimes, Karen's persistence was cute. Other times, it was rude.

"Let me ask you something," Sunny said. "What does your family do that requires you people to shower three times a day?"

"Swim? Don't change the topic!"

Sunny picked up the towels that had been tossed in the Jacuzzi and added them to the growing pile of laundry inside the closet.

"Daddy thinks you *take initiative*." Karen, changing tactics, had said the last words in English.

"What's *take initiative?*"

She scrunched up her face. "I'm not sure. But he says that all the time about people he wants to hire. Basically, it means you're smart." Sunny thought about this and came to understand the quiet power Boss Zhen had over Taitai and Karen. She, too, warmed in the light of his approval.

Zhen Taitai appeared behind her daughter. She looked relaxed this morning, with her hair pulled back from her face. In one hand, she held a paper cup that matched Karen's.

"Sunny, zao."

"Zao, Taitai." Sunny stood. "I wanted to talk to you about your offer. I've decided to accept."

At these words, Karen let out a squeal. But Zhen Taitai only smiled faintly and put her arm around her daughter.

"I'd like you to start as soon as Monday. Can that be arranged?"

"Yes. What time should I come by?"

"Around eight fifteen. Don't worry about your other shifts—I've already given the manager a heads-up that I've made you an offer."

She tipped the last of her coffee down her throat and set the cup on top of a stack of shoe boxes in the closet.

As Taitai turned to leave, it occurred to Sunny that her new employer had never once entertained the idea that her offer might be refused. She thought of Taitai sitting at her desk with a calculator, figuring out the precise salary that would be too high for Sunny to refuse. When the wave of disgust passed, she picked up Taitai's coffee cup from the stack of shoe boxes. Before throwing it out, she turned it in her hand, marveling at what had just occurred. Despite the messes Taitai left behind, despite her willingness to live amid disorganization, there were some things in her life that the woman had arranged so perfectly.

Sunny's shift ended at noon. There had been no one in the service hall to check her bags, and she wondered if this was an issue with security or another result of Zhen Taitai's orders. Outside, the sun's rays were magnolia white, and Sunny stood still for a moment, waiting for her eyes to adjust and her courage to build. Finally, she opened the text message she'd received from Rose.

My schedule has changed.

Sunny took a deep breath. If that was all, it wasn't too bad. Mine too, she wrote back. Should she tell Rose she had accepted the job? Or would Rose think that was what had caused her schedule change? Her phone buzzed again.

Will you be around the Bund area tomorrow? We can have lunch.

I'll be there, she wrote.

Sunny took a deep breath, got on her scooter, and rode home.

• • •

The Bund did not belong to people like Sunny and Rose. But neither did it belong to the newly rich *fu er dai* or the tourists or even the government. This part of the city had grown into something bigger than just a wide riverbank, its western side fitted with a raised boardwalk. It was the mantelpiece of Shanghai, a place to display the things China had collected from other countries over the years. In the old days, there were European trading houses and banks. After that, there were consulates. Now there were nightclubs and haute couture—Armani, Gucci, Prada. It was a place to buy a luxury handbag and then take it out for a walk along the river.

But lovers still met here, and old Shanghainese families out on weekend strolls. There were vendors selling flying toys, laser pointers, and goopy balls that splattered and stuck to the pavement. You could find paper lanterns here during the midautumn festival, and jasmine garlands woven by old women. The Bund was as inclusive as it was discordant, and that was why Sunny and Rose continued to meet here when they could have met somewhere more convenient.

On that Sunday afternoon, they balanced their thermoses on the metal railing facing the river and unwrapped their lunches. For Sunny, it was pork baozi that she had steamed in the microwave at home that morning. For Rose, it was leftovers from last night's meal, rice fried with sausage and bai cai. Rose had invited Sunny over for dinner a few times, but she had always declined. She imagined that eating someone else's home-cooked meal would bring about the most painful kind of nostalgia—like hearing the Anhui dialect spoken, only to turn around and find that it was neither family nor anyone she knew. Since accepting the position as the Zhen family's ayi, Sunny had been thinking a lot about the risk Rose was now exposed to; she wasn't young anymore. At forty-five, she was certainly hirable but would never be at the top of anyone's list. Sunny comforted herself with this thought: Job or no job, at least Rose wasn't alone. Her husband and sons were there to help bear whatever came her way.

"Was there a security check yesterday when you left?" Sunny asked.

"Yes," Rose said. "It was fine. You know they don't really do anything to you during those checks. They're just a hit to your pride."

"You're tougher than anyone I know," Sunny said. This had always been true, but Sunny told Rose now because she felt she needed to hear it.

"Sunny, ah. I used to be tough and now I'm brittle. You bend me and I break. Suddenly—*pah!* Like that." She clapped her hands together and looked at Sunny. Rose had a small slack of skin underneath her chin that hadn't been there when they first met. Today, her eyes seemed darker than usual, and abruptly, Sunny couldn't hold her gaze anymore. She turned toward the water.

Across the river, Pudong was barely visible. Clear days were getting rarer in Shanghai. Whereas the buildings had once stood beaming bright rays of sunlight off their mirrored faces, now their shapes could barely be made out through the smog. Everything looked the color of tombstones: a light, marbled gray.

It wasn't until Rose also turned to observe the skyline that Sunny allowed herself to understand what she had been trying to ignore: A change had occurred in Rose's voice. A dangerous tone had broken through her usual calm.

"Are you trying to tell me something?" she asked.

When Rose didn't say anything, Sunny knew.

"You didn't."

"I brought it with me. I just need your help putting it back."

"No. Rose, I can't."

"I didn't tell you yesterday, but it's bad. Lilly heard from the hotel manager's son that they're going to let me go." She looked Sunny straight in the eye now, and her expression was almost childlike. It took Sunny a moment to understand that this was what Rose looked like scared.

"You can't put this on me. I'm the only other person accused. Now that the Zhens are off your schedule, I'll be the only one of us who has access to their apartment. How is it going to look if the bracelet reappears now?"

The smile on Rose's face looked impersonal, loosely attached. This was not someone Sunny recognized. Her best friend had suddenly turned into a stranger. From the time they had been accused, not once had it crossed Sunny's mind that Rose might have stolen the bracelet.

"Well, if you can't, you can't," Rose said, squinting across the water in the direction of Lanson Suites. A moment passed. Sunny felt that she should explain herself to Rose but also that there was nothing to explain. If anything, it was Rose's turn to explain.

"Why did you do it?" Sunny finally asked. There was no anger in the question, only curiosity.

"I don't know. It was impulsive. Stupid. I'd had a bad week." Rose shook her head.

"But what were you going to do with it?"

"I didn't think—I just took it. We're machines for them, aren't we? They program *go* and we *go*." She was stirring the contents of her thermos but did not lift her spoon to her lips. Finally, she turned and leaned her back against the railing so that she and Sunny were no longer facing the same direction.

"It's a job like any other," Sunny whispered.

"Boss Zhen has a job too. What makes him sit high in the clouds while we're there mopping at his feet, taking his leftovers out in the trash?" Sunny had never heard her sound like this before. Whenever they complained to each other about work, it was always out of frustration and camaraderie. Never had she sensed any deeper resentment.

"Aiya…It's not about that, really. It's just, there comes a point when you wonder, 'What is there left to lose?' Only my dignity. Ha! Stealing from a fujianü and a lao ban." She shook her head. "At the time, it felt like power."

Rose opened her purse and took out a package wrapped in tissue. "Here," she said, reaching over to stick it into the pocket of Sunny's jeans.

"No. I really—"

"You do what you have to, but I'm giving it to you anyway. I have no use for this."

Sunny could feel the beads being stuffed against her thigh, and then Rose grabbed both her hands so that she couldn't fish them back out of her pocket. "I'd rather leave it to the next generation. May you prosper."

Her tone was bitter, but it was also tinged with relief. Sunny had said no, and now Rose could save herself the effort of hoping.

"You're only a few years older than me," Sunny said.

Rose shook her head. "It's not about age. It's about how much you can stand. The foreigners are one thing, but these Chinese-born...it's sickening to watch them accumulate their handbags and their fancy cars. To clean up after their parties. They're not so much younger than us. We're all Chinese, aren't we? Our parents all grew up under Mao and Deng Xiaoping together. The entire country was poor—together. They act like they weren't raised in a place where for most people, breakfast was watered-down rice, too thin even to be called porridge. They think they're so much better than us because they got schooling and went abroad..." She stopped, took a breath, then continued in a quieter voice. "It's not about age," she repeated. "It's that you've still got strength to deal with this nonsense. I'm on my way out."

Rose dropped Sunny's hands. Then she screwed the lid on her thermos and pulled the plastic bag back up around it. Even though Sunny suspected that Rose had already come to terms with the potential loss of her job, there was something indecent about the way she packed her lunch—like someone getting dressed after failing to seduce. Sunny heard her leave but did not turn. She stayed by the river for another half an hour, finishing her lunch and watching the ferries go by.

8

Three weeks had passed; the exams were over. Soon, the students at Suzhou No. 5 High School would find out where they were going to university, or if they were going to university at all. Lina and her friends sat around the kitchen listening to American music on the shortwave radio. Chixi had just returned from Shanghai, and she taught everyone how to dance disco. They cut slits in their pants legs, stole fabric from their mothers' scrap piles, and sewed flares into the bottoms of the denim. They were ready for disco dances, for college, ready to meet their husbands and start imagining homes of their own. They would have television sets, all of them. They would have tasseled lampshades and jewelry fit for film stars. And they would never forget their parents! Never! They would bring home luxuries from the city, intricate doilies to drape over the side tables.

It was possible that Qiang had come during those three weeks. He might have seen the shadows of the dancing girls and turned back. Not that Lina had been looking for him. She thought he was funny and couldn't help pitying him a little. He had sat there staring so intently at her that she thought his eyes might pop out of their sockets. Before they started talking on the steps, he'd been so still and silent — as if scared — and that was how she knew he liked her.

She enjoyed having an admirer. Other boys had admired her before, but the fact that Qiang was the brother of the boy who would eventually become her husband made the attention feel different. She had often imagined Wei observing her as she grew into the ideal woman. When, for example, she convinced the neighbor boys to spend an afternoon cooking Lao Cong's dinner and stringing his laundry the week his daughter-in-law was sick or when her teachers sometimes stopped her mother at the market to say a few words of praise about Lina, the imaginary Wei was an audience to these achievements.

When she thought of Qiang, Lina wanted to show off too, but in a different way. She wanted him to watch her swim from one end of the creek to the other, as no other girls could do. She wanted him to see the way Chixi had taught her to dance, hips swinging and legs ending in kicks. She wanted him to know that she could get in trouble too. Because she had heard from friends who knew Qiang that he was not merely a troublemaker who skipped class. He was a permanent idler, or worse. *Heard he's dumped his friends. He's part of a gang of older guys now. Who knows where he goes during the day.*

One afternoon, Lina's mother sent her off to the factory with her father's lunch. Lina had barely reached the main road when she heard her name being called. Qiang was coming toward her, his gait more wolf-like than ever.

"Zhen Zhiqiang," she greeted him. "All the other rising seniors are studying for the Gaokao already. What are you up to?"

"I'm sure you've heard I dropped out," he said darkly. Lina blushed. She had heard, but she'd expected him to evade the question.

"Are you working, then?"

"I work at the factory sometimes, delivering textiles. I drive them all the way to the city and once in a while to Shanghai. Have you been to Shanghai?"

She shook her head.

"Oh, you should see it. Everyone's dressed nice."

"Do they wear our silk?"

"The clothing is nicer than what we get around here. You should see Shanghai if you get a chance." He took a cigarette out of his pocket and lit it.

"I have to go now," she said.

"Where?"

"To the factory. Ba forgot his lunch."

"I'll walk with you," he said, and before she could answer, he started off down the street. She stood where she was for a moment, and when he sensed she was not behind him, he stopped. Glanced down at his cigarette. He dropped to a crouch, extinguished the cigarette, returned it to his pocket, and then turned his face up at Lina as if to say, *Now are you coming?*

As they walked, he told her about what it was like inside the upper floors of the factory, where the silkworms were kept on narrow shelves. "Trays and trays of them, with little black bodies that then slowly turn to white," he said. "And they're eating all the time. You can hear them just munching when you walk into that room."

"I don't believe you," she said.

"I guess they don't teach you everything in school."

The road led to a lake on their right and the factory on a hill to their left. Years ago, a few of the factory workers had taken it upon themselves to pave the entrance with stones. The project had been attempted rather halfheartedly and then abandoned, making the climb more difficult than it had been before. The steps were winding, and a few of the stones wobbled beneath their weight. But Lina and Qiang both ascended with a practiced dash; they'd each taken this route so many times that neither needed to think about which stones to avoid. When they reached the top, Qiang hung back.

"I'll come meet you when you're done," he said, squinting against the wind. "I want to show you something."

"Hao ba," Lina agreed and turned to enter the building.

The silk factory had a large, central room on the ground floor where silk was spun into reels. With high ceilings and narrow, paneless windows, the central room was solemn and templelike. Its walls were covered in peeling green paint, but the space was clean, cool even at the height of summer. Workers stood in rows facing the machines, whose familiar hum Lina could hear before the room came into view. Time seemed marked by the clicking of the spinning reels. The men and women standing before their trays were deep in concentration, doing their best to keep up with the silkworm cocoons that shot along the belt every few minutes. At the doorway, a man stopped Lina and asked who she wanted to see. She gave her father's name.

"Fang Lijian!"

From their ranks, one man broke free and hurried over. Although Fang Lijian had been a silk spinner most of Lina's life, Lina still thought of him the way her mother did. He was a university professor displaced during the Cultural Revolution, a man unsuited and overqualified for his current work. Silk spinning had made Fang Lijian more sure-handed, but he still retained the distant, unsteady gaze of an academic. When he reached Lina, he returned her smile, took the lunch box from her, and nodded his thanks to the guard. Within seconds, he was back at his station. He'd have to increase his speed to keep up with the others before the belt moved again.

On this summer afternoon after her exams, Lina was in less of a hurry than her father. She watched the graceful movements of his hands swirling in water, picking up a cocoon, and feeling for the end of its silk thread. At night, when he came home and held his hands against her face, his skin would feel as dry as a walnut. But now, as he held the cocoon up to his eyes, his fingers glimmered with moisture and moved with practiced deftness. Lina raised her face to the slight breeze coming from above. The overhead fans swirled slowly, as if powered by the mood of the room. For the first time, she thought about the fact that she would be away at school for four years and that soon, home—and the village, and the factory—would be places she could access only through memory. She let out the breath she didn't know she'd been holding. Then she turned from the doorway and made her way back down the corridor.

"Lina. Over here."

Lina stopped and looked around at the concrete walls, darker here in the unlit corridor. To her left was a steep stairwell, and Qiang was crouched on one of its steps just higher than her head. He motioned for her to follow. Wordlessly, she mounted the first stair, but as soon as she did, he disappeared to the second floor. She listened to his footsteps and followed them. Higher and higher they went, Lina just barely able to keep up with Qiang's light bounding.

Finally, after what must have been more than ten floors, he stopped. Lina came upon him suddenly—a hard bundle of flesh that almost sent her bouncing backward—and took a moment to get her bearings. Her vision was pulsing from the effort of the climb. When it cleared, there was only darkness. This landing didn't have a window like the others. She couldn't see where Qiang was, though she knew he was near, and suddenly she felt scared of their proximity and the fact that they were alone. Qiang might be her future brother-in-law, but he was still a teenage boy who had dropped out of school. He was still a boy who was rumored to spend his days behind closed doors, in dark places like this one.

"I'm over here," he called, and only then did she realize that he wasn't standing next to her anymore.

Suddenly, light swept into the hall; a door had been opened to her left. Qiang's silhouette moving back and forth made the sun rays dance, and Lina had to hold a hand up to shield her eyes.

"Hurry up," he said. "They feed every hour and a half. I don't know when the workers will get back."

Lina took a breath and walked toward him. Inside the room, it was humid and bright. The sun made it hotter here than it had been in the hallway. Bamboo shelves rose from floor to ceiling, extending almost the entire length of the room. Each shelf space was so narrow—just horizontal slivers of darkness wedged between the latticework side panels—that it was difficult to see what they contained. Qiang walked over to the closest shelf and drew out a large woven tray.

Inside were hundreds of silkworms wriggling on a bed of green leaves. They ranged in size. Some were tiny black specks, some were larger and gray, some so translucent that their bodies appeared to have been tinted green from the leaves. Qiang carried the entire tray out into the aisle and set it on the floor. The two of them got down on their knees to look.

"I told you you could hear them eating," he whispered.

"I don't hear anything." She bent her head to get closer.

"You don't have to do that. It's coming from the entire room. Listen."

That's when Lina realized that what she had mistaken for the sound of a generator was really hundreds of thousands of silkworms nibbling on mulberry leaves.

"*Tian a*...you really can hear it!"

Qiang grinned. He picked up one of the larger silkworms and held it to eye level. Then he handed a mulberry leaf to Lina.

She scooted closer to where he was kneeling. Peering at the insect, she couldn't tell which end of the silkworm was its head, but soon a little brown mouth showed itself. She held the mulberry leaf up to it and the silkworm ate from one side to the other, as far as it could reach. Then it came back around to eat in the opposite direction. Soon, a quarter of the leaf was gone and its bottom edge scalloped with bites.

"It doesn't stop!" Lina said. "Where does all the food go?"

"Where do you think it goes?" Qiang turned the silkworm over in his hand and pointed to its belly, where a dark line showed underneath the flesh, fading as it disappeared into the midsection.

"It already went a little on my hand. Look, there it goes again." The silkworm hung from the edge of Qiang's palm, its body curling and un-curling. Slowly, a drop of liquid ballooned from its rear end. Qiang set the silkworm back down into the tray, where it paused and raised its up-per body in search of the mulberry leaf that had been hovering above its head just a moment before. Finding it gone, it settled down and began searching for a new leaf.

The tray was littered with worms working delicate holes into the greenery. "See those little black spots along the body?" said Qiang. "Those are their nostrils."

Lina laughed. "What do you mean, nostrils?"

"They breathe through them."

"Qie! Those aren't nostrils. You have to have a nose to have nos-trils — "

Qiang suddenly turned his head in a way that made Lina stop talking. In one quick move, he lifted the tray and slid it back into the shelf. Voices were coming from the opposite end of the room.

"Let's go," he whispered.

Back in the corridor, Qiang pulled the door shut behind him. They walked toward the half-lit staircase and descended the steps. This time, Lina counted each landing they reached; there were seven floors in all. When they neared the bottom, Qiang's movements slowed and quieted, and Lina followed his lead. They walked out of the building without see-ing anyone.

That night, Lina could barely sleep. If she listened hard enough, she thought she could hear the silkworms eating and, outside her window, Qiang's footsteps moving through the trees. She pictured the silk-spin-ning room, the fans making their lazy revolutions. She never would have guessed that silkworms lived in the floors above that ceiling! The fac-tory was a place she thought she knew intimately, but really, she had known only that one room where her father worked. How had she never wondered about the rest of it? What else was she missing out on, what forbidden corridors and hidden rooms existed in the places she knew so well?

Now that the entrance exam was over and school was out, her time was her own again. She could explore her hometown as she never had before, and Qiang would be her guide. She'd have to be careful about it, of course. She was sure her parents would disapprove of her spending time with him. But they were gone to work during the day, and there were so many hours to fill before they came home.

Lina looked for Qiang the next day and the day after, but he didn't come by her house. A week passed before they met again. Lina was outside hanging the wash when she noticed him coming down the road. He had that same slow prowl that made it seem as if he were sneaking up on her.

"Hi," she called to him when it was clear he was headed for her house. "What are you doing?"

"I'm making sure you're not getting into trouble," he said, smiling. There was no mistaking it: he was flirting.

"Look who's talking," Lina muttered and went inside, thinking that ignoring him would teach him a lesson. He couldn't talk to her like that. She wasn't a loose girl or one of the miscreant wanderers that he hung out with during the day. And she wasn't somebody who was just waiting for him to come by her house either. *In fact,* she would say to him if asked, *the only reason I'm at home this morning is that Ma had business to attend to this weekend and I've been left in charge of the chores.*

She continued on with her work—the laundry, the cleaning, and then the washing of vegetables so that they would be ready to cook when her mother came home. Through it all, Qiang circled the front and backyard. Finally, Lina gave up ignoring him and went outside to where he was sitting at the edge of the road.

In front of him was a stack of playing cards that he shuffled and separated into piles. She stood over him and waited until he looked up.

"Don't you have any friends?" she asked.

The second Lina said it, she worried that Qiang would think she was flirting back—but instead, he looked very serious.

"My friends are older. They're all working."

What kind of work? Lina wanted to ask but didn't. If he admitted to being associated with a gang, as her friends said he was, she would have to stop talking to him—and she didn't want to stop talking to him.

"Okay, so why don't you work? Aren't you supposed to be delivering materials for the silk factory?"

He motioned to the cards in front of him. "This is me working. I'm practicing. Come here. I'll teach you how to play."

Lina sat down beneath the phoenix tree and watched him split two decks into six stacks, two rows of three.

"These," he said, pointing to two of the stacks in front of her, "and this one," he added, pointing to one of the stacks in front of him, "are yours. The others are mine. The rules are the same as Zheng Shang You, except we go in a circle and control three hands at once. You know how to play Zheng Shang You, right?" She nodded. "Okay, we'll look at our cards first and then you start with the stack to your right."

Lina picked up each hand and organized them by suit. She played her first card, then waited for Qiang, who took his time. He held one fist to his mouth in concentration. Finally, he set all three hands facedown in their starting positions, fanned ever so slightly apart. Whenever it was his turn, he plucked a card from the pile without consulting any of his other hands. After four or five rounds, he stopped the game.

"Hao, I've got it. In this pile," he said, pointing to the one directly in front of Lina, "you've got a joker, a king of hearts, and a couple of useless cards you're trying to get rid of. In this one, a pair of jacks of clubs and a queen of spades. And that last hand has no face cards at all. Just a string of telephone digits. That's the hand that's making you nervous."

She stared at him, astounded.

"You're wrong about the double jacks. One of the jacks is in this hand. How did you do that?"

A grin spread across Qiang's face. "It's partly memorization. Partly reading your responses. I'll get better as we keep playing. Let's go again."

With the cards spread out in piles like this, she recognized the game as one her father and his friends played some nights at their house after dinner. They drank, smoked, and talked as they played, and although they gambled on it, none of them had ever seemed as focused on winning as Qiang was now. He began to stop her fewer and fewer rounds into each game. Every time he stopped her, he correctly named the cards in each of her piles. The way he said, "Hao, ting," once he had everything worked out in his mind was fascinating to watch. All the wild energy went out of his body when he stared at the backs of those cards, trying to decipher what they were. This focus made him seem more mature than he had that day at the silk factory, bounding down those unlit concrete steps.

They played until the reflection of the sun had swum from one side of the lake to the other.

"I should go," Lina finally said, standing. Qiang looked up—she saw herself coming back into focus in his eyes.

"Tomorrow I'll bring a third deck," he said. "We'll make two rows of five."

Lina dusted herself off and walked back to her house. When she was halfway to the gate of the yard, she turned around.

"Think what you could achieve if you spent your time studying books instead of cards!" she called across the road to him. But Qiang just kept shuffling his decks. He either did not hear her or pretended not to.

9

On Monday morning, Sunny walked up to the front gates of Lanson Suites instead of the back.

"They're expecting me in 8202," she said to the guard, then added, "I'm the Zhens' new ayi."

The guard spoke into a mouthpiece, paused to listen, and then motioned her through.

Sunny had been in the lobby only when she was assigned to clean the floors or maintain the seating areas. Each time, she had focused on refilling the fruit basket and straightening the seat cushions as quickly as possible, because the task was an add-on responsibility—she'd still had her regular rooms to clean. Now, as a visitor, Sunny walked through more slowly to take it all in. The space looked like a marble forest, with great stone pillars for trees. Beyond the front desk was a large, abstract painting whose colors matched the Lanson Suites black-and-marigold logo. To the west, past the elevators, a floor-to-ceiling wall fountain sent water misting down into a shallow rectangular pool. Before it stood two armchairs, one couch, and a table shaped to look like the trunk of an ancient tree that had been chopped at its base. Everything smelled of jasmine. Sunny had come to associate the scent of jasmine with Lanson Suites because of the hotel's soaps and shampoos, but in the corners of the lobby, there were live jasmine plants in tall, fat pots, the blooms' starry white faces drifting all the way down to the floor.

One place Sunny had never been was inside of the residents' elevators. The car doors stood open for her, and floor number 20 had already been pushed by the lobby attendant. The interior looked like that of the service elevator, but in place of a padded quilt covering the walls, there was a framed mirror and a little marble shelf displaying a vase of red and coral begonias. By the time the doors opened on the twentieth floor, Sunny felt as though she had walked onto the set of a play. She knew the people whose job it was to wash these floors, scent these halls, and deliver the mail each morning. She was familiar with this production.

A copy of *Shanghai Daily* sat in the silver envelope holder next to each apartment door. Sunny could read only the translated title and the date, but when she removed it from the Zhens' envelope holder, she felt how light it was. It resembled a brochure more than a newspaper. She liked the thought of news items being omitted, things that the government did not want these foreigners to know. Not that the government reported whole truths to the Chinese either, but still.

With the paper held to her chest, Sunny rang the bell.

Pahng, pahng, pahng. Footsteps came to the door. It opened with a heavy whoosh, and Sunny found herself looking at all three Zhens at once: Karen, her face puffy with sleep; Taitai, standing in front of the hall mirror and fastening a string of pearls around her neck; and Boss Zhen, who had been the one to open the door.

"Zao," he greeted her, and he moved aside to let Sunny in.

"Zao."

"We're going to breakfast," Karen said. "Come with us." She took Sunny's hand, and while this did not feel unnatural, it was the first time Karen had ever done it. Sunny saw Taitai watching them in the mirror.

"We'd love for you to eat with us," Taitai said, "but for today, can you stick around to watch the apartment? There's supposed to be someone new coming to clean and we haven't met her yet. I'm going to change our cleaning time to an afternoon slot, but for now…"

"Of course," Sunny said. "I've already eaten anyway."

"Great. There are some things in the fridge if you get hungry. We'll see you in a little while." Taitai gave her hair a final tousle so that it fell back in a perfumed whisper. She smiled at Sunny as she sailed past her.

After the door shut behind them, Sunny stood still, listening to the Zhens leaving. The arrival ping of the elevator sounded and Sunny could hear Karen's voice disappearing between closing doors.

Now was the time.

Sunny removed her shoes and placed them beside the other pairs lined up near the door. Then she headed straight for the master bedroom. Its door was closed. She hesitated just a moment before opening it and stepping inside.

Tired, gray light came in through the windows, giving the room an ethereal glow. Sunny stopped and took in a sharp breath. Taitai's side of the room had never been so neat. The bureau was clear of its usual mess. Used cotton pads had been thrown away, and her bottles of lotions and sprays were standing right side up with their caps on. The floor was immaculate. Sunny doubled over to look beneath the bed. Even the bras and panties that often wound up trapped there seemed to have been put back where they belonged.

Sunny hadn't had an exact plan for how she was going to return the bracelet, but it was clear that she wouldn't be able to do it today. Taitai had searched every inch of the bedroom for the bracelet since Sunny had last been in to clean. To slip it back into this room without anyone realizing she'd done it would be nearly impossible. She sat down on the bed, suddenly feeling the effects of a sleepless night. How foolish of her to believe that she could help Rose. It was as foolish as thinking she had ever had a choice in whether to take this ayi job. As much as Sunny loved

Rose, her first loyalty was to her family. Returning the bracelet would be too big of a risk. Forget five thousand a month; if she was caught with that bracelet, she wouldn't even be able to get her old job back.

From down the hall came the sound of a door opening. Sunny rose and smoothed out the part of the bed she had been sitting on. She was halfway across the living room when she realized that it wasn't the front door that had opened, but the service door.

"Zao!" In walked a maid who used to work in Tower Six of the complex.

"Joyce!"

"I heard you're an ayi now. Congratulations. How's the family? Easy on you?"

"I just started today," Sunny said.

"Na, I'm sure you'll find out soon. You used to have this shift, right? Where should I start?"

"Start in the master bedroom. Sometimes when Taitai comes back from breakfast she goes straight into her room and closes the door and then you can't clean it until she comes out again. It holds everything up." She led Joyce back to the south end of the unit, her heart slowing with every few steps. Sunny opened the door and showed Joyce inside. "It's typically messier than this, so don't get used to it."

Joyce started to pull the covers from the bed and Sunny got on the other end of the mattress to help. When the maid began to protest, Sunny waved her words away. "It will only take a minute between the two of us." Together, they lifted the edges of the mattress. They stripped and tucked and smoothed and creased. They fluffed. Though it had been less than an hour since she'd become an ayi, Sunny performed the quiet, controlled exercise of making a bed with a feeling of loss. She would miss this job, one whose end goal — visual perfection — was both simple and monumental.

Joyce cleared the cups from the nightstands while Sunny took care of the trash. As she kneeled to pull the plastic lining from inside one wastebasket, she found a piece of paper with writing on it. She wouldn't have noticed it if it had not been deliberately placed in the middle of the bin. The Chinese characters were small and self-conscious, so unlike the English words in his notebooks, that it took Sunny a moment to realize that the handwriting was Boss Zhen's.

Miss Sunny,

Thank you for your attention, but this is trash.

Regards,
Zhen Zhiwei

Underneath the note was the pair of silk socks Sunny had rescued twice from the garbage bin.

Her face grew warm. She lifted the socks from the bin and laid them side by side on her thigh. They were deep indigo blue, flawless in material and design. She checked for holes, as she had done the first time she found them in the trash; there was no evidence that they'd been worn. She pictured Boss Zhen sitting in his study composing this note, then folding the socks and placing them in the trash can, taking care to center the note exactly on top. How embarrassing. She wanted to melt into the carpet. He'd probably forgotten that today was the day she was starting as their ayi and that there would be a new housekeeper on duty. Or maybe he didn't know the difference between the two professions. What did it matter to someone as wealthy as he was which of his hired help took out the trash and which was there to watch his kid?

Just like that, Sunny understood Rose's impulse to take the bracelet. How would it feel to encounter the waste of wealth day in and day out for fifteen years, as Rose had done? Fifteen was a lot more than the five years Sunny had worked. She tried to picture herself cleaning houses at age fifty-five, at sixty. What would the job mean to her then? Would it still be something she wanted to hold on to? Her mother's words came back to her. *Now that I'm old, my children take care of me. Who will take care of you when you're old if you're too stubborn for children?*

Sunny could try to convince herself that she'd come to Shanghai because of the higher pay and the pretty building she had once seen on a postcard, but the truth was that she was here because she didn't know where else to go. She dropped the socks and note back into the wastebasket and stood up. Out of habit, she rolled her shoulders to readjust the stiff fabric of her tunic, only to find she was no longer in uniform. How naked she had felt standing in front of the Zhens this morning in a T-shirt and jeans, dressed as herself for the very first time.

Sunny walked out of the bedroom, down the hall, and onto the balcony. A breeze swept up from below and quieted her nerves. Suddenly, she didn't care what happened to her. She looked beyond the other towers of the complex, out at the Huangpu River, one of the oldest landmarks in the city. Nowadays it was home to tourist cruises and government-sanctioned holiday floats, but once its purpose was to carry the cargo sent downstream by laborers, people who built buildings and steered ships and carried wares on their backs. People like Sunny. *What is it, Boss Zhen? What kinds of problems can you solve that I can't?*

And then she had an inspiration.

From her pocket, Sunny removed the bracelet and unwrapped it. The ivory beads were surprisingly light, almost like a child's toy in texture. Up close, she saw there was a little carved pattern of trees or animals, but she didn't pause long enough to determine which before tossing the bracelet from the balcony. For a moment, it disappeared into the glimmer of the water below. Then, with a delicate splash, it was absorbed into the depths of the pool.

Sunny turned to go inside just as Joyce was coming out, watering can in hand.

"The plants look fine," Sunny said. "It's been humid lately. You can give it another day." Joyce nodded and returned to the kitchen, happy to be able to skip a step on her list.

Alone in the living room, Sunny sat down on the couch next to the phone. She picked it up, pressed zero, and waited for the lobby attendant to stop speaking English so that she could ask her question.

"Hello, this is the Zhen family's ayi. They wanted me to call and request a pool cleaning. They were in there swimming yesterday afternoon and overheard a child saying he'd had an accident."

"Oh, yes, we can do that," said the voice on the other end. Sunny recognized her as Clara, a part-timer who had never sent so much as a nod Sunny's way. Her tone on the phone was twice as sweet as it was in person.

"Don't just chlorinate it." Sunny heard herself growing bold. "Taitai wants the whole thing drained and refilled."

"Of course. Will there be anything else?"

"No, that's all."

A pause on the other end as, Sunny imagined, her request was being written down. After she hung up, Sunny took a deep breath, a little giddy at her own cleverness. It would all be handled now—they'd find the bracelet and return it to Taitai, who would think she'd lost it while swimming. Maybe it wasn't too late for Rose to get her job back.

Sunny had never noticed how quiet it was up there on the twentieth floor, so far above the construction. The only sound she could hear was Joyce shuffling about in the kitchen. Her reflex was to stand and help, but she caught herself and sat back. Today, she would allow herself to enjoy the stillness and the peace. Maybe she could get used to this kind of luxury.

10

On the afternoon his brother was due to arrive in Shanghai, Wei sat in the company stockroom on top of a plastic tote loaded with cleaning supplies. Suddenly, the door opened and the office manager walked in.

"Boss Zhen, what are you doing?"

It wasn't until then that Wei noted the pain spreading from his inner wrists to the tops of his shoulders. He had been trying to fit his elbows between the shelves on either side of him so that he could type on his laptop.

"Writing an e-mail."

May didn't move from where she stood with her hand on the doorknob. "Why aren't you at your desk?"

"I just got back from a meeting. They were shooting in front of my office so I came in here to work while they finished." The heat from the laptop had made his knees sweat; Wei set the machine on the ground and massaged his wrists.

"I can tell them to shoot somewhere else," May said, plucking a box of tissues off a shelf. "They're only there because they wanted a background with the company logo."

"I'll be fine," he said, but May seemed reluctant to leave.

"You should probably know that there are people waiting outside your door."

"Is it the TV-show director guy?"

She poked her head out into the hallway. "No. It's just Chris over there now."

"Can you tell him to come in here, please?"

A moment later, Wei's chief of staff appeared in the doorway.

"There you are," Chris said. "Can you come out to Mint Lounge next Friday? We're taking Rumi out for their quarterly event."

"I don't think so," Wei said. "My brother's coming to town."

"The account team told me to beg you. All of their higher-ups are traveling. I said I'd go, but the Rumi people might be offended if you weren't there too."

Chris was in his early thirties, but his demeanor was more suited for someone twice his age. Wei had a soft spot for young men who took themselves too seriously — it was what he was guilty of too. But unlike Wei, Chris wasn't good at the social aspects of the job. He was not a partying kind of guy, and Wei knew that it wasn't the account team that was begging for him but Chris himself.

"We'll see," Wei said. "Maybe just one drink."

"Thank you. Thanks. I'll put it on your calendar." Chris made to leave, and then stopped, perhaps noting the incongruity of his boss sitting in the stockroom, his laptop and a cup of coffee by his feet. "Are you hiding from the cameras?"

When he didn't get an answer, Chris cleared his throat and backed out the door. "Okay, so next Friday," he called. "Don't forget."

•　•　•

Wei entered the apartment to the scent of steaming wanzi and fish stir-fried with ginger and scallions. The last time Lina had made this flounder dish was back in Collegeville, and its smell reminded Wei of the cold nights he'd arrived home after taking Acela Express from New York. There would be a single light on in the kitchen and smoke creeping along the ceiling of the living room. American kitchens weren't designed for wok use, Lina complained. She had tried the American recipes and decided people here didn't know what real cooking was. All that boiling and baking? Those were safe ways of preparing food. Oil was meant to be splattered on walls, the wok lid held in front of your body like a shield. Cooking, she said, was an act of love and creation. Danger should be somewhere in the mix or it didn't count. You had to put yourself on the line; you had to sweat. Chinese cuisine required more energy and a higher flame.

Now, as Wei walked into their kitchen on the other side of the world, he could see the concentration on his wife's face. He stood beside her at the stove, and Lina stopped managing the hissing and steaming in front of her long enough to kiss him on the cheek. Her lips were soft and warm, and between her eyebrows was the V of focus she wore when things were going according to plan.

"Boss Zhen." A voice greeted him from behind. He turned, startled, to find the ayi they had hired standing at the opposite end of the kitchen near the sink, snapping string beans. It was disorienting to see her wearing an apron that matched Lina's.

"Sunny, ni hao."

"You told Little Cao he needs to go directly to the airport to pick up Qiang, right?" Lina asked.

"He knows," Wei said.

"But he forgets."

"He knows," Wei said more softly. He could sense a fight about the driver coming on and he didn't want to argue before his brother showed up. "It smells delicious," he said before leaving the kitchen.

In the darkness of the bedroom, Wei undressed, hung up his shirt and slacks, and put on a pair of drawstring pants and a cotton tee. Only then did he turn on the light to look at himself in the bathroom mirror. Older, yes. That couldn't be helped. He smiled to expose his teeth and watched the lines on either side of his mouth stretch down to his chin. It looked as though he'd been gouged by a pair of claws. Easy on the smiling, then.

Wei had thought a lot about what he would wear for his brother's arrival. He wanted to look as close as possible to Qiang's memory of him as a country boy, which meant dressing casually. No slacks, no ironed shirts, and definitely not the watch he'd bought through Nicholas, which was now locked away in the safe. What had he been thinking, buying one for Qiang? The last thing he wanted was for Qiang to see that he had grown into the type of person his brother had always suspected he'd become, someone who announced his salary by wearing it on his wrist. *Prince Wei.*

The name came back to him with a shudder. Qiang used to taunt him from up high in the trees as Wei passed below with his friends. *Prince Wei! Wangzi! Where are you going? Don't you know you have exams to slay, princesses to impregnate? Do right by your people, give us a smile, give us a wave!* Wei had been a favorite in the community and Qiang never let him forget it. He was at the top of his class, a student who was smart and well rounded, the kind of smart that was easy for parents to appreciate. He was also the son of Zhen Hong, a farmer by birth and staunch supporter of the revolution. Zhen Hong was proof that if a person was humble and hardworking, he might one day have a son who could embody success.

It was hard to represent the collective hopes of a village without wanting to be what everyone else wanted him to be. Despite himself, Wei had acquired a taste for the village praise. Qiang seemed the only one who could see this truth about him, and looking back, Wei realized that was largely what accounted for the distance between them. Qiang's teasing made Wei more self-conscious than he let on. He was embarrassed by his desire to be celebrated, and his brother was a reminder of this ugly need.

There was one occasion in particular that Wei remembered — the summer evening that he met Lina for the first time. He had just been admitted to Fudan University and his parents had decided to throw him a party. Up until then, he had considered marriage in very general terms and given little thought to the girl who was to become his wife. He had trouble imagining himself married. When he thought of the word *wife* he could only picture his mother, and none of the girls he'd met came close to fitting the role his mother played in the Zhen household. The women he knew talked too much and changed their minds too often. They sought others' opinions indiscriminately and didn't think before speaking. He'd told himself that when the time came to marry, if Lina didn't seem like a good fit, he'd simply lay out his reasons for not agreeing to the match. His parents were reasonable people. He'd make them understand.

But then came the moment Lina appeared. He couldn't remember what they had said during that exchange, but it was the first time in a long time that he'd felt unprepared. He'd thought he'd seen everything their small town could offer, had skipped ahead in his mind to the other cities he'd live in, the university he'd attend. And then, in front of him, was this girl with her startling eyes and loosely braided hair, the ends of which she fingered absentmindedly. He had trouble meeting her gaze, but she had no trouble staring at him. It was an act of appraisal. She seemed to be asking, *Do you live up to your reputation?* Wei was immediately drawn to the challenge in that stare, and her strange mix of innocence and maturity made him understand for the first time how a young woman could grow into a wife.

Later that night, he had played basketball with his friends and Qiang while Lina watched from the sidelines. He could feel the heat of her stare the whole time. After the game ended and her parents picked her up,

Qiang finally said what he'd been thinking all night. *Look at you, pretending not to care! I know the only reason you wanted to play basketball tonight is to show off. Otherwise, you'd be back at the party lapping up all that praise.*

Wei had been annoyed with Qiang all through the game—he was a faster, more agile player than Wei, and guarding him that night was more difficult than it usually was. He knew that Qiang was showing off for Lina too. It wasn't uncommon for his brother to pick a pretty girl and follow her around for a while. Considering the way Qiang had been whispering to Lina that night, it looked as though he had made her his next target. But it would be no use to make fun of Qiang. Qiang wasn't vulnerable to embarrassment for the simple reason that he could freely admit to wanting to attract the attention of a certain girl. Unlike Wei, he was not held back by pride.

Wei turned from his brother and spoke to his friends: *You know what? I think I want to keep playing. Let's switch things up. Zhong, I got you this time.* The other boys reorganized themselves. It was as Wei had planned—because a few of their number had already gone home, Qiang became the odd one out. *Sorry, kid,* Wei said. He watched his brother's face grow dark as he understood what Wei had done. For years afterward, Wei would think about that moment and wonder where Qiang had gone after he'd left them that evening. If he had stayed the night of the party, and if Wei had been making more of an effort to include him in his own circle of friends all along, would things have turned out differently? Would Qiang have been adopted by Wei's crowd rather than by a band of miscreants who valued neither honor nor education?

When the door to his bedroom opened, Wei flinched. Lina came in, her face flushed with heat from the kitchen.

"What's wrong?" she asked.

"Nothing."

Lina untied her apron and flung it on the floor. "Are you nervous?"

"A little," Wei admitted.

Lina caught his face between her hands. "He found us. We can stop wondering where he is now and whether he's alive. What could be better than that?"

He knew she was right, but it didn't stop him from feeling that the stakes were higher than ever. Last week, before the adrenaline of Qiang's phone call had worn off, he'd been worried about whether they would recognize each other after so much time apart. Now, he was worried their reunion would remind Qiang of the reasons he'd left in the first place. Wei didn't know how to be the kind of brother Qiang needed. He had never known how to withhold judgment or project the right balance of patience and understanding. What made him think he could do it now?

"Zenme le," Lina said, and she guided his head toward hers for a kiss. Her way of saying, *Stop thinking.* But when she kissed him a second time, and her top lip lingered against his bottom, Wei knew that the kiss wasn't just for his sake but for hers. He reached under her shirt; his fingers met the warmth of her back and ran up the valley of her spine. Lina stripped off her T-shirt and revealed a bra fringed at the top with lace. Giving birth had widened Lina's hips and left her skin rosier than it had been before pregnancy. In her twenties, her skin had been marblelike — beautiful but cold. He preferred her flesh as it felt now. The exaggerated heft of her breasts and swell of her ass seemed more substantial, somehow more human than her body had been when they first married. It almost begged to be touched. She led him over to the bed and sat him on the edge of the mattress. Leaning her weight on one knee, she swung the other over him and pushed down on his chest until he was lying flat. Wei ran the side of his thumb along her thigh.

It wasn't unusual for Lina to want sex suddenly now, but it hadn't always been this way. In the beginning, he had been the one to coax it out of her. On their wedding night, she'd lain faceup, her arms straight on either side of her body, as though she were in a coffin. She'd been uninterested in any form of touch. Looking back, it made sense; this was in the month before they were to leave for America. Of course she would feel distant from him, this man who was about to take her away from her parents. So he didn't push her; he knew instinctively that the only thing he could do was wait. For twenty-three nights, he slept on his side, one arm draped over her stomach. It wasn't until they were in Philadelphia that she let him have her for the first time. And even then, it had taken a while to earn the slow giving-in of her body. But that had made the experience even more precious; he loved discovering her sexuality with her, loved that his touch was transforming her. Even her laughter during sex seemed to come from her entire body. And when they were done, when she lay against him with her thighs still vibrating, he wrapped her up in the bedsheets and held her cocooned while she metamorphosed back into herself.

But it had been years since then, and somewhere along the way Lina had learned how to pleasure herself. Now, when she came toward him wanting sex, her eyes held a look of total control. That he couldn't predict these lustful moods unnerved Wei a little, but what upset him more was that he seemed to have very little to do with their genesis. He was merely filling the void without creating it. Of course, he was grateful for the fact that they still wanted each other (his friends' marriages were falling apart in irreparable ways), but there was something unsettling about it. It was yet another area of his life where he had lost control.

Lina got up, went to the door, locked it, and came back to him. She pulled on the drawstring of his pants, even supported his lower back with one hand as he lifted his bottom so she could slide off his briefs. Then she moved on top of him, her body arched, looking for the spot she was now an expert at finding on her own. Her eyes were half closed, and even the position of her head gave away the fact that she was somewhere far away — somewhere Wei would not be able to get to.

He felt himself starting to shrink. *No way*, he thought. He flipped over so that she was on her back, but when he tried to reenter her, his knee slipped off the edge of the mattress. He fell, barely catching himself with the ball of one foot. A tingle went through his right thigh and calf — the phantom pain of a near injury.

When he looked up at Lina, her eyes were open. He had taken her from wherever she had gone. And hadn't that been what he'd wanted? For her to look at him with the kind of recognition and tenderness that he saw in her face now? But when he was inside her again, the feel of her hands on his back was different. The urgency was gone, replaced by encouragement and love.

He couldn't do it. Encouragement and love were not what he wanted in the moment — they felt too much like pity. She wanted to be somewhere else? Fine. He'd let her go. He'd rather her not see him at all than see him like this, his full weight unsteady on one arm, soft from years of office use. He slid down to the floor, put his head between her legs, and stuck to the things he knew how to do.

• • •

The lamps were off. Light flowed from the closet doorway, pleated with shadows, like a spread dress. Wei shut his eyes again and rolled over onto his back. He was overwarm, sweating. Real sleep was a kind of magic, wasn't it? Lose awareness for a little while and wake to see the world you left at a tilt-shift. In the dark, he refamiliarized himself with the room. The kelp hanging from the bedroom door handle became a shirt of Lina's. The tuft of grass peeking out from behind one leg of a console was a hairbrush. When a blow-dryer came on in the bathroom, Wei sat up. He watched how Lina's silhouette made the shapes on the carpet move.

Finally, he got up and walked to the bathroom, where she was bent over at the waist in a cream-colored slip.

"How long was I asleep?"

"About fifteen minutes," she said. Only that long? He felt cheated. He placed his hands on her hips to pull her toward him, but she straightened up and out of his reach.

"Get dressed. It's almost seven." Lina gave him a chaste pat on the chest and slipped out the door, leaving him alone in the bathroom, inhaling what was left of her shower steam.

Wei took a quick rinse, dressed, and went out to the dining room. He was startled a second time to find the ayi there, bringing out dishes from the kitchen. Secretly, he held this against Lina, the complication of adding another person to the household. His wife was circling the table in a coral-colored dress, touching this dish and that, moving them until they fit together just so. The meal was composed of both home-style dishes and Shanghainese cuisine. At the end of the table was a plate of Chinese broccoli, which must have been one of Sunny's creations, because Wei could not remember Lina ever having made it. But the rest of the food were her recipes. The whitebait soup, starchier than those made by the restaurants back home, was a specialty of Lina's. She had topped it off with fresh cilantro, which looked particularly green beside the shrimp dish. Next to that was chopped lotus filled with sticky rice, its honeyed glaze catching the light from the chandelier. Arrayed around the main dishes were patterned saucers for collecting shrimp shells and flounder bones, and dainty bowls good for only a few mouthfuls of soup. The table was being set in the showy Shanghainese way, which made Wei uncomfortable, but he let it go. Lina was right. Cooking was an act of love and creation, and what better way to show Qiang how much they loved him than by presenting him with a feast? Wei was about to give his compliments when Lina looked up and frowned.

"Why aren't you dressed?"

"I am dressed," he said. "I'm just not dressed up." And then: "Why are *you* dressed up?"

"I'm not," Lina said, more softly, turning her attention back to the dishes. "Put on some real pants, at least."

So she was nervous for Qiang's arrival too. Wei was moved; she hadn't put this much effort into preparing a meal since the last time they'd hosted a lunch for the women in Lanson Suites.

"Where's Karen?" he asked.

"She's downstairs with the Canters. Tutoring the boys."

"She's coming back for dinner, right?"

"She should be here any minute."

This summer, Karen had been spending more time with the Canters, an American family who lived a few floors below them. Since transferring to a boarding school in the States, she'd lost the playmates she'd had in Shanghai and could not afford to be picky about company. The age difference between Karen and the Canter boys made them unlikely friends, but Karen could be persuaded to spend time with them as long as everyone involved considered it tutoring.

Sunny came up from behind him. Her feet made next to no noise as she shuffled past in her slippers, carrying a bottle of Johnnie Walker Blue. When Lina asked Wei who he thought they should hire as an ayi, he had named Sunny because he'd always admired the woman's work ethic. But he hadn't given the question much thought; now that Sunny was here, he decided that she was a little too quiet. He wasn't sure he'd like having her in the house all the time.

"What are you doing?" he asked Lina as she took the whiskey from Sunny. A store of these bottles was kept in the bar to be used as emergency gifts for clients.

"It's a special occasion."

"There are good Chinese liquors in the cabinet. How do you know Qiang drinks scotch?"

"How do you know he doesn't?"

Her hair had been ironed into a dark flag that hung over her face. She picked at the seal on the box.

"I just think it's kind of showy," Wei said quietly.

"You think you're so much better than your brother that you couldn't possibly enjoy the same kind of liquor?"

Perhaps the question was meant to tease, but it came out barbed. The doorbell rang.

"He's early," Lina said with a start. She performed a last visual sweep across the table and said to Sunny, "Start stir-frying the pork." Then she disappeared into the kitchen and Wei was left by himself. He took a breath, walked to the entranceway, and opened the door.

Wei blinked; before him stood one of the uniformed lobby guys. The floral scent of the hallway filled his nose.

"Lao ban, the dry cleaning Taitai dropped off yesterday."

"Oh. Thank you," Wei said. He accepted the clothing and closed the door.

Lina appeared, wiping her hands on her apron, wearing a wide smile.

"Oh," she said when she saw the dry cleaning. She took the clothing from Wei, separated one plastic-covered hanger from the rest, and handed it back to him. "Here, put these on. I don't know that you have any other pants that are freshly ironed."

Rather than argue, Wei returned to his bedroom to change. At least doing so would pass the time.

When the doorbell rang again, he strode toward it more calmly. He dragged one hand through his hair while he opened the door with the other. But this time, it was just Karen standing there, chewing on the ends of her hair.

"What happened to your key?"

"I forgot it," she said, wounded. He was rarely gruff with her, but he couldn't stop himself.

"Well, be more responsible."

"Why does it matter? It's not like no one's home." She sulked off to her room.

Wei shut his eyes briefly, thought about opening the whiskey early.

The sound of Lina's footsteps came from around the corner, then stopped when Karen passed. He saw his wife's reflection in the mirror hanging in the dining room—an unreadable expression appeared on her face. But before he could guess at what it meant, she caught him looking at her and quickly brought her face back to neutral.

"Are you okay?" he asked. He wanted to say *Are we okay?* but didn't. Her eyes landed on his chest and stayed there. The kitchen fan went on and they heard meat hitting the wok with a crackle.

"Taitai," Sunny called, but Lina did not seem to hear.

"The table, the food—everything looks great," Wei said, and Lina returned a faint smile. He reached for her, and for a moment, she leaned her body against his.

"Taitai!"

"What is it?" Lina asked. Sunny's response was inaudible over the stir-fry. "Zenme le?"

Together, she and Wei moved into the kitchen. "I think someone's knocking at the door," Sunny said, nodding toward the service entrance connected to the kitchen.

Lina walked over and wrenched it open. Standing there, wearing the shadows cast by the harsh overhead light of the laundry hall, was Zhen Zhiqiang.

11

"Lina," Qiang said, grinning. She moved back and he stepped inside to set his bag on the floor. Then he turned to Wei. "Ge."

Many synapses fired simultaneously, and suddenly Wei's physical memory of his brother overwhelmed him. He remembered the stifling warmth of Qiang's body against his under winter blankets. The way Qiang smiled over his shoulder as he left a room and his slow, loping walk. And that expression! He'd forgotten how cheerful his brother's demeanor was.

They stepped forward and hugged, then pulled back to look at each other. Wei was surprised to see that the skin on his brother's face was looser. Little lines drawn on by the years. But his smile and the way his eyebrows grew in near-perfect arcs, their ends pointing down toward the mischief in his eyes and mouth, were just as Wei remembered.

"Di," Wei said, "you made it." He pulled Qiang in for another hug, and then the two began laughing. Wei recalled just how deep his brother's laugh was as it vibrated against him. Deep, but not booming.

"Ta ma de," Qiang said. "It's been too many years." He turned toward Lina and hugged her as well. She responded a beat late, laying an arm around his shoulders as he was already pulling away. For a moment, their eyes connected and they shared an embarrassed laugh—perhaps finding a foothold in their past familiarity. Now Qiang faced Sunny, unsure how to address her.

"This is Sunny, our ayi," Wei said. "Actually"—he paused awkwardly—"I don't think we know your Chinese name."

"Sunny is fine," she said with a nod. "Just leave your bag where it is. I'll take it to your room in a minute."

"Karen!" Lina yelled, as the three of them moved into the living room. "Come out here and meet your uncle! Should we have some tea? Or are you all ready to eat?"

Just as they were about to sit down, Karen came in from the hall.

"Wah," Qiang said. "This is your daughter?"

Anyone else would have followed that up with compliments and questions (*She's beautiful! She looks like you! How old is she? She's tall for her age*), but Qiang said nothing. He looked from Wei to Lina to Karen and back again, his face full of genuine wonder. He reached his palm out to her, and to Wei's surprise, Karen went to him and put her hand in his. Karen had always been spoiled with adult attention and was catlike when it came to giving and receiving love. She was interested in winning the affection solely of those who had better things to do than woo her and was rarely receptive to attention so readily given. But now, Qiang stared at her speechlessly for so long that he made her laugh. Without saying a single word, he had charmed her.

"Address your uncle," Lina said, urging Karen to pay her respects.

"Shu shu," she obliged.

They took their seats in the dining room, Lina and Qiang on one side of the table, Wei and Karen on the other. Qiang's eyes traveled from the dishware to the chandelier to the gold-rimmed glasses that Sunny was filling with wine. As closely as Wei looked, he could find no trace of contempt in Qiang's expression—only what might have been awe.

"Zui jin zenme yang a?" Wei asked. In this sentence—*How have things been lately?*—were the echoes of a hundred other times Wei had asked it of business contacts or their wives, people whose personal lives he cared very little about. It felt wrong to hear himself saying it to his brother when he truly wanted to know every detail of where he had been and what he had done all the years he'd been away.

"All right," Qiang answered, spooning tofu and ground pork into his bowl. "Same old. Getting on in years, doing some traveling." He chewed heartily, making no attempt to elaborate and not bothering to return the question. Wei had forgotten the cadence of conversation with Qiang, how one-sided it could be. Qiang felt neither the need to give details nor the pressure of silence. It was refreshing. Qiang's eyes traveled between Karen and the spot above Wei's head on the dining-room wall where Karen's picture hung. Finally, he shook his head and said, "You have a daughter. I still can't believe it."

The school portrait was taken of Karen a few years ago, before she had discovered makeup. She was seated before the type of backdrop favored by school-portrait photographers—a vomity mixture of blues and greens—and she was wearing her Black Tree Academy polo. Her teacher had done Lina and Wei a kindness by pinning Karen's hair back so that her smile came through unobstructed. Her torso was turned from the camera as though in midtickle.

"That one's so old, Dad. You keep promising to take it down." Karen had spoken in English to observe Qiang's reaction—to see if he understood the language. It was her way of assessing how much power she had over this new adult in the room.

"Karen's home for the summer but goes to school in the States," Wei said, bringing the conversation back to Chinese.

"She looks like Lina."

The curious thing about Lina was that you could never tell what would move her. Wei had seen her accept compliments and censures alike with poise. He'd also seen her flustered at an offhand comment, something not necessarily directed toward her but that had still landed someplace tender.

Wei's attention was suddenly captured by a glint of light on Qiang's wrist, and for a few seconds he stared, disbelieving. It was the very same watch he'd just bought for them both. There was that black and blue bevel. It couldn't be real. How could Qiang afford a Rolex?

"So what are you doing for work nowadays?" Wei asked casually. Another pause here in which Wei could not tell whether he had provoked discomfort.

"I'm an entrepreneur," Qiang said. "I work in hospitality."

Wei tried to contain his surprise. He hadn't given much thought to what Qiang could be doing for employment, but he assumed it was something straightforward, like a line cook or a deliveryman. Not something that required, well, *drive*. And where had Qiang learned how to build a business? He hadn't even finished high school.

"You have your own business?" Wei asked.

"Yes," Qiang said. "In hospitality."

"Hen liao bu qi. What kind of hospitality?"

"We're like a travel agency. We book vacations to Macao."

Now Lina and Wei shared a look—Macao was a favorite destination for idlers and men bent on doing business the old-fashioned way: by getting drunk and gambling. The gambling part they knew Qiang was familiar with.

"We provide financial services too. People who book with us can gamble freely without worrying about taking money in and out of the country. They gamble on credit. We sort things out later."

"And I guess your profit is commission-based?" Wei asked.

"Dui," Qiang said. He offered nothing more—just a simple yes. In Wei's experience, it was liars who overexplained. But Qiang wasn't like other people, and Wei was almost certain that his brother's income was not all commission-based.

"It looks like you're doing well," Wei said. "That's a nice-looking watch you have on. Rolex?"

Qiang glanced at his wrist and seemed surprised to find the watch there.

"I have to keep up appearances, you know. If you want rich men to use your service, you need to dress rich." He held eye contact with Wei. Was it his imagination or was there a bit of aggression there? As if he was trying to say *You've made your way and I've made mine.*

"Let me see," Lina said, taking hold of Qiang's wrist. A lock of her hair fell forward, alighting on its reflection in the watch crystal. Lina tilted the watch face this way and that, as though examining the face of a thoroughbred. "Nice," she said finally, giving Qiang's wrist a squeeze and settling back into her seat. Then she looked up at Wei and nodded ever so slightly — yes, it was real.

Dress rich. Qiang's words echoed in Wei's head. He considered his brother's buzz cut and colorfully stitched T-shirt, the faded appearance of his jeans. He had misjudged them, believed them cheap and ill-considered. Qiang had likely spent some time choosing an outfit for this occasion. He'd probably visited a store that he thought modern and trendy, held shirt after shirt in front of him as he looked into the mirror. How different it was to dress rich than it was to dress wealthy. And Qiang hadn't even been able to pull off rich, not really — the hotel staff was proof of that. They'd sent him up by the service elevator, for heaven's sake. They'd thought he was there to fix the sink.

"In fact," Qiang went on, "that's really the main problem we're running into right now. We've made a few trips already with our clients and the setup works. It's totally legal and everybody has a good time. We just need more interest from clients. There are only so many rich businessmen in Kunming, you know?"

He raised his eyes to look at his brother then, and Wei's heart clenched. So this was what Qiang had come for. He wasn't here to make amends or to reconnect with his family. He was here because he wanted Wei's business contacts.

There was something that had been bothering him about Qiang as soon as they'd begun this topic, and Wei now knew what it was. It was the way this speech seemed rehearsed, like he had worked up to this moment in the conversation. Wei had been at enough dinners with vendors to know what a pitch sounded like. He brought his attention back to the table, where everyone seemed to be waiting for him to speak.

"Who's *we?*" he asked, his voice breaking on the first syllable.

"What?" Qiang asked.

"You said *we.* That implies you're working with other people. Who are the other people?"

Admit it, Wei thought. *You're still involved with the gang.* Qiang understood what Wei was asking and didn't know how to answer. Startled by the sudden intensity in his brother's voice, he lowered his gaze and resumed chewing his food. Wei wanted to shout at him, make him get up from the table and look him in the eye. How disrespectful to show up at Wei's house asking him to support his business — the business owned by people he had abandoned his own family for. Wei could neither keep questioning Qiang nor back out of this conversation. Lina and Karen were now looking at Wei as if his head were on fire.

"Colleagues," Qiang finally said. "You wouldn't know them — "

"Wei's in advertising now," Lina interrupted. "Did you know that?"

Qiang shook his head and once again met Wei's eyes. "Weren't you at school for something else? Math. No — " He cast about for the correct subject, and the longer the silence lasted, the more unbearable it seemed. Wei relished his brother's discomfort until he felt a sharp pain pierce the top of his foot. He jerked his leg back, out of reach of Lina's high heel.

"Mechanical engineering," Wei finally said.

"That's right." Qiang smiled, relieved. "Why did you decide to switch?"

"The job prospects were better in software, so I did that after I got my master's and then—well, one thing led to another and I ended up in advertising."

"It's a funny story," Lina said brightly. "After he graduated from Penn, Wei had already signed on for a job with a railway company, but then one day he gets a phone call from a software company asking him to apply for a job as a data analyst. He told them he didn't know anything about analyzing data and that he'd studied mechanical engineering and they said that they were just looking for someone good with numbers—right, Wei? And the salary somehow turned out to be much higher than what the railway company had offered him. So he broke his contract."

"And now you have your own TV show," Qiang finished for him. He said it softly, testing. A flash of shame came over Wei as he thought about his brother seeing him on *Pitch 360*. How must he have looked, mumbling those words of introduction to a roomful of pert twenty-somethings, his face full of makeup? *Of course Wei would want his own TV show*, Qiang had probably thought. *He's always been vain like that.*

Wei chose his words carefully. "We created the show to attract job applicants out of college. I appeared in the first couple episodes just to introduce the pitch challenges, but it was taking up too much of my time. So I asked them to replace me—"

"Dad," Karen cut in. "You promised I could see you shoot."

When Karen had seen the episodes online, she'd called him right away. *Wow*, she'd said. *You're like somebody. You run those guys.* And suddenly, he'd felt proud of what he'd done. Because even though the show was a bad representation of what went on in the advertising world, his daughter had been interested in his career for the first time. It made him wonder if one day she might understand and be proud of the work he did, the way he had once felt about his own father's work.

"I just have to find a good day to bring you in there, honey," he said in English. "Lately I've been so busy."

Qiang didn't seem to notice that he'd been excluded from the conversation. "So what is it that you do for them exactly?"

Wei took a deep breath before beginning to explain. "Back in New York, I was working in strategy, but as general manager for the Shanghai office, it's more business development–related."

"So, sales," Qiang clarified.

"I oversee the big deals," Wei said, "but I also manage the overall direction of the company and its composite parts. We can handle everything from copywriting to market research. We also translate campaign ideas into Chinese and come up with marketing strategies."

Qiang nodded slowly. "You help sell American products to the Chinese. Does it ever happen the opposite way? Do you help the Chinese sell to Americans?"

Lina flinched.

"Well, no," Wei said with a laugh. "I know it sounds a little imperialistic. But Medora is an American company. Our biggest clients are American."

"Of course," Qiang said quickly. "That makes sense."

"But we serve Chinese businesses too," Wei added, trying to lighten his tone. "For example, last year we collaborated with the Ministry of Commerce to create the 'Made with China' campaign."

"Wait, I know that one!" Qiang said. "The one with the iPod and the shoes…"

"That's right."

Last year, the Ministry of Commerce had collaborated with four Chinese trade associations to sponsor a thirty-second commercial. Its goal was to rebrand China's international image by reworking the phrase "Made in China" as "Made *with* China." The commercial opened with a shot of a runner stopping to tie his shoes and a close-up of the inside of the sneaker tongue that read MADE IN CHINA WITH AMERICAN SPORTS TECHNOLOGY. A shot of a family eating breakfast and a close-up on their refrigerator: MADE IN CHINA WITH EUROPEAN STYLING. The back of an iPod: MADE IN CHINA WITH SOFTWARE FROM SILICON VALLEY— and so on.

"It was an interesting approach," Qiang said.

"But?" Wei prodded.

Qiang chewed, thinking. "It's just that China is already seen as a contract country. People don't think China is coming up with any of its own stuff. They think it's just producing other countries'."

Wei nodded but felt his hand tighten around his chopsticks. Usually, he was a master of patience in the face of ignorance—his job all but depended on his ability to appear open and generous toward people with uninformed opinions. And yet.

"Maybe. But the point is that other countries rely heavily on China. At the end of the day, it's the production backbone of so much of what the rest of the world consumes. It's a collaborative effort because Western companies have chosen Chinese business. And China should be recognized for that."

Lina began to say something, but Qiang interrupted.

"I just don't think we can get ahead by pushing this idea that we work for other countries. China should be more like America and try to be recognized for its innovation, not how well we can help Americans make money," Qiang said.

Since when was Qiang concerned about the economic health of the nation?

"You know, it's not always about who is making money off whom. The Chinese have a lot of buying power right now. Because there is so much opportunity here, American companies are making products to suit China. Take Hollywood, for example. They just cast Jay Chou in a blockbuster because they know it will do well in the Chinese box office. When's the last time an Asian man got to play a superhero?"

Qiang began to reply, but Wei barreled on. "What I'm saying is that money isn't the only kind of power that counts. Culture is power too. For so long, cultural conversation has been dominated by the West. But not anymore. And we're helping to make that happen."

"Okay, but who says we need Hollywood? Isn't it better to start our own conversation than respond to what the West is doing? Have you seen any Chinese films lately? The Chinese make great films—they're getting better every year."

"He's right," Karen said. "They're much funnier than American films."

Just as Wei was about to respond, Sunny appeared in the kitchen doorway. "Is anyone's soup cold? I can heat it up for you."

"Yes, please," Lina said, her voice half an octave higher than usual. "Take mine. Wei, you haven't touched yours either. Give it to Sunny to warm up."

Wei leaned back in his seat, allowing Sunny to reach across him. As she did, she broke the men's eye contact, and in this brief interval they gathered themselves.

After a moment, Qiang raised his wineglass. "I'm proud of you, Wei, really. All of this…" He gestured toward the apartment, the food, and his family. "I'm not surprised by any of it. You deserve it. Everything you have, you've earned. You always have." Wei studied his brother's face for resentment or irony but found none. Qiang looked almost remorseful. Taken aback, Wei raised his glass too.

"To homecoming," Qiang said. "I'm glad to have found you again." He turned to Lina, who took up her glass as well.

"To homecoming," she repeated. "We've been in Shanghai for years and it's never felt more like home than it does now, with you here."

They drank.

"What about you?" Qiang asked, turning his attention to Lina. "Are you a historian now or did you get picked up by a software company too?"

Lina's eyes brightened and she gave the barest hint of a smile.

"A historian?" Wei asked, surprised.

"Yes—I remember she studied history," Qiang said.

"Actually, she studied English," Wei said.

"Actually, I studied both." Lina patted her mouth with a napkin and placed it on the table. Karen stopped chewing and looked back and forth among the three other Zhens.

"You did?"

"Yes. I finished my history requirements in the first two years at university. So in my third and fourth years, I studied English."

"Oh," Wei said. "I didn't know that." And he was surprised that Qiang did. He knew that Lina and Qiang had been friends when they were younger, but he'd never quite been able to imagine it. The two had nothing in common.

"I was never going to be able to use the history degree. Learning English was what mattered at the time. But anyway, to answer your question, I became a Chinese-language teacher at a private elementary school."

Qiang was quiet, as if trying to conjure the image of Lina in front of a classroom. "You were always good with the neighborhood children," he said. "Do you still teach here?"

"No."

Something had happened to the balance in the room. Wei felt somehow that he and his wife were being shamed. He was suddenly defensive, and for what? Because he and Lina weren't the same people they had been when Qiang had seen them last? Qiang acted as though he were there to hold them accountable for not becoming the people he'd expected them to become, but it wasn't right. He no longer had any claim over their lives.

"Do you travel at all for work?" Qiang asked his brother.

"I used to travel through China a lot when we first set up the office here. Now I just move between Shanghai and New York. But mostly I stay here."

"New York," Qiang said. "What's that like?"

"It's busier than here, less space. Kind of like Tokyo, but dirtier."

"What about you?" Lina asked. "You said earlier that you travel. Where do you go?"

"Nowhere fancy," Qiang said. "Mostly just within China. Macao for work. I went back to Suzhou a few months ago. Have you two been, since moving back?"

"No," Wei said. "We haven't been since — "

Since the funeral. Wei stopped himself before he finished the sentence, but Qiang knew what he was about to say. Wei couldn't help but feel pleased at his brother's discomfort. He could sense Lina trying to catch his attention across the table, ready to give a warning.

"You said Auntie Pei was the one who tracked down my number," Wei said, changing the subject. "Who else are you still in touch with from the village?"

"Oh, not many people. They're all gone. They left when the silk factory closed down."

"The silk factory is gone?" Lina asked this in what was almost a whisper. She stared at Qiang now as though he'd announced the death of a close relative. Wei hadn't thought about that silk factory in a decade. Both his and Lina's fathers had labored for years inside it, but it had never meant as much to him as it had to Lina. She had spent much of her childhood passing time in the surrounding woods and lake, and from Qiang's expression, it seemed he'd been attached to it as well.

"They closed it down last year," Qiang said. "There was talk of putting up a solar plant on top of it. The building is still there, but they're going to level it soon. This summer for sure."

"Shi ba," Wei said. "Well, maybe we'll plan a trip. Karen's never been to the village. Karen, want to see where Mom and Dad grew up?"

"Not really," she said, and the bluntness of this response made the rest of the family's efforts at politeness seem futile. A moment of silence later, Karen asked, in English, "Is he ever going to stop eating?"

It wasn't until then that Wei noticed Qiang's saucer had become so full of shrimp shells that stray pieces had spilled onto the table. At some point during the meal, Sunny had brought the rice cooker from the kitchen and placed it within Qiang's reach. He now spooned what remained in the pot onto his plate, poured in the last of the fish sauce, and dug into that too.

"Careful of bones in the sauce," Lina said, pleased. Wei was glad that at least in this one aspect, his wife could consider this meal a success.

After dinner, Qiang went out to the balcony for a smoke. Seeing him go, Lina filled two glasses with scotch, handed them to Wei, and pushed him in Qiang's direction. Wei had no choice but to follow him.

Outside, he took the chair closer to the door. Next to the pool below, light quivered against the trunks of the decorative trees. He had a vision of Qiang as a child climbing the young camphor trees that grew near their home and had branches low enough for him to mount.

Qiang pulled out his box of cigarettes, offered one to Wei, and raised his eyebrows in surprise when he accepted.

"You smoke now?"

"On occasion."

Qiang took a drag, then let his arm fall to the side. His fingers curled around the cigarette, and his thumb rested lightly on the filter tip. The remembered sight of his brother's hand in this exact position made Wei's chest seize up; he was filled with the sadness of growing old and the feeling of loss of their younger selves.

"I didn't mean anything by what I said earlier about your job," Qiang said. "I was just surprised by what you do."

"Really." He couldn't manage to keep the sarcasm completely out of his voice.

"I guess all this time, I'd imagined you building rockets or something.

I remember you and Ba would talk about it after dinner, the two of you looking out that single square window like it was the frame of your future."

The mention of their father only made Wei feel more on edge. "We were just dreaming," he said.

"You had the brains for it."

"So did you." They locked eyes. Qiang looked away first, took a sip of his drink, and shook his head. "I was too restless for a lot of things."

Even though Wei had thought the same thing about Qiang only a week before — he was built this way, he was too restless — it sounded far too easy coming out of his brother's mouth.

"He looked at you like you were a better version of him," Qiang continued. "Same good heart, but the brains too. I remember how he used to talk about the future of China like it was something he was handing off to you."

Now it was impossible to miss the bitterness in Qiang's voice. It was true; their father treated the two of them differently. Wei had always felt that his father required more of him and took it personally when Wei did not measure up. Qiang's upbringing, however, was conducted in the manner of an amateur chemistry experiment. He was coddled at times and overly disciplined at others, as if his parents were blindly guessing at the right combination to produce the right kind of reaction. While he did seem to care for his sons equally, Zhen Hong never held Qiang to the same standard as he did Wei.

"I never got involved in that political stuff," Wei said.

At the peak of his career, their father had been a low-ranking party branch secretary. But soon after the Tiananmen Square shootings, Zhen Hong's faith in the revolution broke completely. Wei was in America by then, and when he called his father after the shooting, he was near tears. "That was us," Zhen Hong had said. "We shot those kids."

"That wasn't you, that was them," Wei had said, but his father wasn't listening. Wei should have told him what he really thought: that if the party leadership had been in the hands of men like Zhen Hong, whose compassion for fellow human beings never outweighed his idealism, history might have taken a different turn.

"I always felt like he saw himself as part of the generation that would unify the country and make social progress," Qiang said. "And he saw you as part of the generation that would put China on the map in terms of—well, the rest of the world. Economics. Science. All of that."

There it was again, that tone. As though Qiang were enumerating the ways in which Wei's life had gone offtrack.

"You had something extra," Qiang went on. "This...energy that none of us understood. What a thing it was to watch you, year after year, doing well in school. Forget building rockets. You were the rocket. To us, anyway. They named you well. *Wei*. 'Greatness.' You were destined for it."

Qiang peered up at him, his face shining from the heat or the drink.

"What are you trying to get at with all this remember-when stuff?" Wei asked.

Qiang looked surprised to be taken out of his reverie. "I don't know, I'm just talking. I don't mean anything by it."

"You're talking like no time has passed. It's been twenty years."

"I know," Qiang said.

"Why are you here? I won't be angry. Just tell me why."

A look of confusion spread across Qiang's face. "To see you."

"You're not here for business contacts?"

Qiang's mouth fell open. "That's not—"

"Isn't it?"

Wei tried to read his brother more closely, but there was some brighter emotion in the way—fear, or pure wonder at how quickly their conversation was once again going to shit.

"We've spent all night talking about me. What about you? I want to hear about why things went offtrack for you. Why you left and never came back."

"Hao," Qiang said, shifting in his seat. "That's fair."

"You have no right to make any kind of judgment on my life's work."

"I'm not making any judgments," Qiang said, his voice low. "I'm just trying to get to know the person you've become after twenty years. And don't forget, you left town first."

"I went to *America*," Wei shot back. "I went to school."

"Wah, *America*," Qiang said. "In that case."

"Don't act like it was the same thing. Everyone knew where I was going. I didn't just take off."

"Of course everyone knew where you were going," Qiang said. "It was only a matter of time before you left town. We all knew it. For me, it was the opposite. There would have been no reason for me to leave. That was a frightening thought, hao ma?"

Wei let out a gasp that was almost a laugh. "That's your excuse?"

He could see the tendons on Qiang's neck raised, betraying his effort to keep his voice calm. "No," he said. "It's not an excuse. Just an explanation."

"Let me see if I understand your explanation. You were frightened of living out your days with loving parents in a town that would have supported you had you, for one moment, applied yourself?"

Wei cringed at the word *applied*, felt he was channeling his father. "For years after you left, I thought, *He's confused. He's just a kid.* And then enough years passed that it wasn't possible to give you the benefit of the doubt anymore. After that, I thought you were dead. For some time, I really thought you were dead, because how else could a person — not a kid anymore, an adult — treat his own blood the way you treated yours? Running off with your criminal friends because we mattered so little to you. I always thought you were trying to prove something. When you didn't come back, I thought you must be either dead or heartless. And now I know."

Qiang stared dumbly ahead at the water as though determined not to let Wei's words affect him. "It's more complicated than that."

"Why are you here?" Wei asked again. He realized he was standing now. Looking down at his brother was making him dizzy.

"I missed you," Qiang said without an ounce of feeling in his voice. "I wanted to see you, and I wanted to explain."

"Twenty years is how long you miss someone before you show up at their door, *ah?* What about Ma and Ba? You miss them yet?"

He could feel that he was on the verge of tears. A shadow passed within the apartment; there was someone in the living room. Wei sat down again.

"Fine," he said more softly, jerking the deck chair forward so that he was positioned across from Qiang. "I'm listening. Explain."

A movement in his brother's eyes, like an animal dodging back into the trees. He hated how easy it was for Qiang to present himself as the prey even if he had been the one to hurt others. Wei's instincts told him that the way to get his brother to talk was to seem uninterested and un-aggressive, exactly the opposite of how he was now, hunched over with his hands on his knees. But they were both men; he wouldn't baby him anymore. It was time for Qiang to own up to his mistakes, his turn to step up and speak. He'd give him five more seconds. Four. Three.

Qiang stood abruptly and tossed his lit cigarette over the edge of the balcony. Then he returned to the apartment, shutting the door softly behind him.

12

At the beginning of August, a few weeks after their Gaokao scores came in, the graduating seniors were matched with universities. Lina was accepted by her second-choice school, Chujiao University, in Hubei Province. To get to Hubei, her father said, she would have to take a train west through parts of China that even he had never seen. *Look out the window,* he told her. *It will be a long ride. Sketch the sights for me and send it home in a letter.*

A month before her departure date, Lina was consumed by thoughts of what it would mean to leave behind everything she had ever known. During those summer nights, she and her parents would return to the table after the dishes were washed and put away. Her father would read, her mother would recite a list of the things they still needed to buy for Lina's trip north, and Lina would study the angles of their faces, trying to commit them to memory. Her mother had had a picture of them taken for Lina to bring with her, but neither of her parents photographed well. Jiajia's posture was too stiff, and Fang Lijian's face looked sullen in the grainy shot. Lina didn't want to remember either of them that way; she wanted to remember them just like this—one rambling and the other silent, each member of their little family with nothing much to say to the others because they had spent every day of the past eighteen years in one another's company. When it was time to sleep, they pulled their bed mats from their rooms and arranged them outside on the grass in front of their house. Jiajia brought out a pail of water and poured it in a circle around them to cool the earth and keep out the heat as they slept.

After dark one night, Lina and her family were outdoors laying down their mats when a man came running up the road from the opposite direction of town. Lina thought she recognized the person's figure, and when he got close, she saw that it was Zhen Hong. Her father met his friend at the gate.

"Zenme le? Are you all right?"

As soon as Zhen Hong caught his breath, he lost it again because he broke out in laughter. "I can't believe it," he finally said. "My son. Full marks. Fudan accepted him."

Lina saw the two men stare at one another in disbelief. Fudan University was one of the best schools in the country, and it had accepted Wei.

Fang Lijian pulled his friend into a hug and, though Zhen Hong was much larger, lifted him off his feet. They stumbled and danced together, one pale scholarly frame pressed up against his bulkier best friend, each clapping the other on the back. When they parted, Lina could see that there were tears in Zhen Hong's eyes.

Jiajia rose from where she sat on the mat and walked over to them. When Zhen Hong saw her, he stepped back from her husband, as if he'd been caught stealing.

"Is it true?" Jiajia asked. "Fudan? Everyone says Wei is smart, but…"

She placed her hand over her mouth and let out a little cry of disbelief. "My sincerest congratulations."

Soon, all three of them were talking with excitement. After the Fangs said good-bye to Zhen Hong, Lina's parents exchanged a look, and Lina understood that something momentous had taken place — not only for the Zhen family, but for their own.

Two days later, Lina and her mother were preparing lunch when Jiajia made a declaration. "I think it's maybe time you officially met Wei."

Lina finished rinsing her knife, shook the excess water into a metal bin. "I thought you didn't want me marrying him," she said. But even she knew things had changed. An acceptance from Fudan University meant that Wei was the most eligible prospective son-in-law in the surrounding towns. It would be stupid, Jiajia knew, for Lina to wait for someone better to come along.

Jiajia sighed, handed her daughter a skinned zucchini. "It's clear that boy is going somewhere. Plus, Fudan is in Shanghai. If you marry and settle there, it won't be so far from home."

Lina sliced the vegetable lengthwise and turned the two halves on their sides. "What if I don't want to leave home?"

"Of course you want to leave home," Jiajia said. "What are you going to do in a small town like this? You'll be bored the rest of your life, that's what."

Jiajia often told Lina about the house she used to live in when her father was still in business, how she'd had embroidered jackets to wear and a growing collection of books and records by overseas authors and composers. Even after these items were confiscated by the Red Guard, she'd never stopped thinking of Shanghai as a place that represented freedom and comfort. She'd never admitted it to her husband, but she hadn't wanted Lina to build her life in Suzhou. She'd always wanted her daughter to go to Shanghai, and in the past twelve hours, Wei had become a part of this dream rather than a hindrance.

"When would we marry?" Lina asked.

"Oh, not for some time. Right after college. That's always best."

Lina did not respond. Everything was coming at her too quickly. The thought of Wei as her future husband was one thing, but she was not ready for courtship. These past weeks with Qiang had shown her that what she really wanted was more time to herself—time to discover the world.

A few days later, the Zhen family threw a celebration. Lina and her parents walked the two and a half miles over to the Zhens' home carrying a bag of peanuts and a whole melon. By the time they got there, the three of them were sweaty and breathless. Zhen Hong saw them and ran over, took the food from their hands, and yelled for his wife to bring over slices of fresh-cut watermelon. "Here," he said, pushing a wedge into each person's hands. "You must be thirsty."

As Lina bit into her slice, she surveyed the yard. Neighbors had brought their own kitchen tables to place out on the lawn, and all the tables were covered with food. Wei's mother must have saved her ration coupons for weeks, or else the neighbors had chipped in; it was the most decadent spread Lina had ever seen. There was red-braised pork belly, lion's-head meatballs in cabbage soup, mapo tofu, and deep-fried spring rolls. Music was coming from inside their house as well as from a portable radio that had been set out in the yard, so there were two songs playing at once. Lina saw teenagers wandering in and out of the house, but none that she knew—they were all from the school Wei attended. Her parents might have felt similarly out of place, because after eating their watermelon slices, they strayed back to the edges of the group.

Lina turned to follow them, but as she did she walked right into Zhen Zhiwei.

"Hello," she said. She was so startled that she managed this greeting quite casually. This was as close as they'd ever been to each other. He was very good-looking, she decided. He had a straight, strong nose that gave way to sharp, determined eyes. Unlike the other boys at the party in their cotton shirts and pants, he was dressed in a khaki-colored Mao suit, which was why earlier she had mistaken him for an adult.

"Hello," he replied, wiping a sheen of moisture off his forehead with the back of his hand. His skin was tanned and rosy, as though he'd spent every sunlit hour since the end of the exams outside. The jacket fit him well. Its double pockets accentuated the breadth of his shoulders, and the clean lines of the tunic made him look dignified.

The next few seconds passed in silence as they studied each other.

Finally, she said, meekly, "Congratulations on Fudan."

"Thank you." His voice was deeper than Qiang's.

"So. Where's your brother?" She didn't know what else to say.

"He's not home yet. I don't know where he is."

Lina remembered that as far as Wei knew, she wasn't acquainted with his brother at all. She nodded, doing her best to act as though she had only been asking to be polite.

"I bet your parents are really happy—"

"We're going to play basketball later"—a pause before he continued—"over by the school. It's very close to our house. You can come play if you want."

"Oh," she said. "I don't know. Maybe I'll watch."

"Okay."

"Okay," she said. She broke eye contact and gestured toward the food. "I'm going to get something to eat first."

"Right. It's late. You should eat."

Lina turned toward the dinner spread, and Wei walked back to his friends.

It was dark when Qiang finally showed up to the party. No one acknowledged him and he acknowledged no one except for a nod at his brother. He took up a bowl and began filling it with what was left of the food. If he knew that Lina was there, he didn't let on. After a while, Wei walked over and whispered in his ear, and they both looked over at her.

"Ba," she said to her father. "The Zhen brothers are going to play basketball at school. It's just down the road. They've invited me."

"It's dark out," he said, but Lina's mother put her hand on his arm.

"There are lights on the court. We passed it on the way here, remember? Let her go."

He shared a long look with his wife. "All right. As long as you stay with Wei. Don't wander away."

There were nine boys who started off toward the school. Lina was the only girl. She hung back, falling naturally in step with Qiang. From time to time, a few of the other boys turned their heads in their direction.

"They're all looking at me," she whispered to Qiang. "Like they're trying to see if I'm good enough for your brother."

"You're good enough," Qiang said. "And besides, they're not looking at you. They're looking at me."

"Why would they be looking at you?"

"I don't know. They don't like me."

She waited for him to go on, but she also knew him well enough by now to realize that he hated talking about himself. The rumors she heard about him had gotten more serious. One day, Lina and Qiang had been playing outside the silk factory when one of her father's colleagues waved her over for a private word. *You stay away from that kid,* Wang Shushu said. *Zhen Zhiqiang is wild. It might be hard to believe because the other brother is such a success, but make no mistake. One of my friend's boys was part of Qiang's group last year. He said they got mixed up with a band of criminals who had them doing all kinds of things to initiate them into their gang. Stealing crops, livestock, money, you name it. They had them fight each other for entertainment. Most of the boys got scared off quick. All except that one.*

Lina didn't know whether to believe the rumors about Qiang, but if she had heard them, then surely Wei's friends had too. Their fathers had probably warned him the same way Wang Shushu had warned her. *Rumors are just rumors*, she told herself. *Qiang would never hurt me.*

The road was wide and the voices of the boys up ahead echoed so that their whispers seemed to come from the trees. Lina inhaled the summer-green Suzhou smell, a scent so intoxicating that every year she begged her parents to let her sleep outside even after the air had picked up a chill. Ahead, the paved court next to the school glowed a dull yellow. Once they all could see where they were going, the boy holding the ball began dribbling it, and Lina became nervous again.

When they got to the court, she sat a few steps from the road. The game was three-on-three, with Qiang and Wei guarding each other. They were well matched but had different styles of playing. Qiang was quick, unpredictable, and better on defense; he managed to steal the ball more often than anyone else. Wei was not as light on his feet as his brother, but he had better aim. Lina didn't know much about basketball, but she could tell that Wei was in tune with the game in a way that the others weren't. The ball didn't stay long in his hands before he passed it off to a team member, and his feet never wasted a step.

After about an hour, they took a break. Qiang came over and sat next to Lina while the other boys kept to the far side of the court. Wei alone remained in front of the basket, sending the ball through the net again and again.

"Look at him show off," Qiang said. "Are you impressed?"

"No," Lina said, and Qiang laughed.

"He's like that with everything. Obsessive." He'd probably meant for it to sound dismissive, but he couldn't hide the awe in his voice. "My parents think he's naturally good at everything he does, but he's not. He just can't let go of anything until it's perfect. It's not about winning. Winning isn't enough for him. It's like he isn't even playing against other people. He's playing against the game."

"That's how you are too," Lina said.

"What do you mean?"

"When you're playing cards—it's like I'm not there. It's like you're playing against the game."

Qiang's expression softened as he registered the compliment, but he shook his head.

"If I told you that of the two of us, I was the normal one, would you believe me?"

After every shot, Wei retrieved the ball and returned to the same place on the court, his head bowed, each dribble a decision. When he released the ball, his knees bent at the same angle, his arms true as the needle of a compass. Years later, at a public recreation center in Collegeville, Wei would show Lina how to distribute her weight evenly on her feet and arc the ball through the air so that it became an extension of her body. "Again," he said after she made her first basket. "You want it to go in like a whisper, not a shout." By that time, she often knew him better than he knew himself; she admired him but could also see his limitations. Wei was a man for whom there would always be a ball, a basket, a court. His self-worth was defined by his ability to figure out the best way to play a game. But ask him why basketball, why that recreational center in America and not China, why he was with Lina and not another woman—one he had chosen for himself instead of one assigned to him by his parents—and his answers were vague. *Because I love you. Because it feels right.* For most of her life, Lina liked being with a man who answered her own uncertainty with stubbornness and simplicity. For Wei, *Because I love you* was reason enough not to question the life they had together and the one they had left behind. And because he treated their relationship as something solid, she had been able to have faith in it too. The aunties from back home had been right: dependability was the best trait a husband could have. It wasn't until she grew older that Lina began to wonder if Wei's focus on the concrete questions—*How much money should we set aside for Karen's education? At what age should we aim to retire?* — wasn't a way to avoid thinking about the questions he didn't know how to answer.

But on the night of Wei's celebration party, Wei's focus and perfectionism were still alien to Lina, and to a teenager, alien was attractive. She had lied to Qiang. She was impressed.

"So are you saying that he's not as smart as everyone thinks he is?" she asked him.

Qiang considered this. "No," he decided. "He is."

Wei called to his brother, indicating that the game was about to resume. When Qiang stepped onto the court, Wei made as if to pass the ball to him but withheld it for a moment — just long enough for Qiang to understand the question Wei didn't want to ask out loud: *What are you doing over there with her?* Qiang received the ball and took his place on the court, ignoring his brother's glare. Shortly afterward, Lina's parents came up the road to retrieve her. She dusted herself off, called good-bye to the boys, and retreated to the darkness and comfort of her parents' company. On the way home, she walked between the two of them, holding their hands in her own, hoping for silence — boys gave a person a lot to think about.

Lina didn't see Wei again for the rest of the summer. He'd been admitted to an honors program at Fudan University that started in June, and within a few weeks, he'd packed up and left for Shanghai. But Qiang still showed up at her house each day with playing cards and promises of fun to be had at the lake.

They kept clear of the roadside and the silk factory, and weeks passed without the two of them running into anyone they knew. The closer they grew, the harder it was for Lina to ignore her friends' warnings about Qiang. She was frightened by the way he dodged her questions. She was scared, too, of the scar tissue on his abdomen and back that were visible every time they went swimming. One day, when Qiang took off his shoes and socks and stripped down to his shorts to wade into the water, a small knife fell out of his shoe. It wasn't a kitchen knife. It wasn't like any knife Lina had ever seen. This one had a small, curved blade with a marbled handle. A leather case fell out with it.

Qiang kicked the knife and its case beneath his pile of clothes before Lina could get a closer look. "Why do you have that?" she asked. He paused so long before answering that Lina thought he wasn't going to.

"I steal chickens," he said. "It's better to cut the wire than climb the coop."

"Where did you get it?" she asked, but by then he had already jumped into the lake.

She had learned that if she wanted answers from him, she had to surprise him into giving them. An hour later, when they were lying on the ground, drying off in the sun, she asked him, "So, where is it that you go to fight?"

Qiang didn't say anything for a long time. When a fly landed on his chin, he let it crawl over to the left side of his face.

"Do you think I'm going to tell your parents?" she asked. "Or is it that you think I'm too delicate to hear about it?"

"I don't get in fights," he said quietly. "I haven't for about a year now."

"Then why do you have those scars?"

"Those are old scars from when I was initiated. Now they don't want me fighting anymore — I only gamble."

"You gamble?" Lina sat up. Water dripped from the ends of her hair and patterned the dirt between them.

"I play cards. Like the games I play with you, except I play with older people for money. The brothers set it up." Qiang finally looked at Lina. "We don't even really have to steal now, because I make so much money."

"I don't understand," Lina said. "Who are you gambling with?"

"People from other towns, people just passing through..." He twisted at the waist and propped his head up on his elbow. "If you really want to know, I can show you. Come with me tonight."

She'd never seen his eyes so wide. "No way," Lina said. "My parents don't even like it when I go to someone else's house for dinner."

"That's okay, because they won't know. On weekdays we play when everyone else is asleep."

"You want me to sneak out?"

"Your parents both work long hours. They'll be snoring. No one's going to know the difference."

She thought about running around in the dark and felt her cheeks begin to flush. "No."

Qiang lay back down and they both stared up at the sky. "Look, think about it. If not tomorrow, another night. What about the night before you leave for school? Staying up all night is the best way to make sure you can sleep soundly on the train up to Hubei. And if your parents find out—which they won't—there's not much they can do to punish you, is there?"

Of course, Qiang would think only in terms of getting in trouble. Lina was more concerned about how anxious her parents would feel if they found out. They would spend the next four years wondering if she was in Hubei making bad choices. How awful it would be to discover, on the last night of your daughter's childhood, that she wasn't the type of person you'd raised her to be at all.

Then again, she was just a few weeks away from being free from her parents' protection; soon she would need to make every choice on her own. She had only a few more years before she would be married and, after that, a mother herself. If she was ever going to break rules, now was the time. How would it feel to see the town from Qiang's perspective, a world that was invisible to everyone else? She thought of that day at the silk factory, how it had felt to fly down the unlit steps as they escaped the room with the worms. It had been frightening but also exhilarating to risk being chased and think that she might be found out.

"Hao ba," Lina agreed. "On the last night. I'll come with you."

• • •

The next two weeks passed quickly. Lina's train ticket was purchased and tucked into the inner pocket of her luggage; rolls of cash were zipped into the lining of her jacket. Plastic bags of watermelon seeds were packed along with mantou, dried sausages, and tea eggs, all to eat on the train. The single trunk Lina planned to bring with her sat near the front door, filled to its corners with clothing, books, and miscellaneous items added by her parents. One would remove something the other had put in, thinking it not important enough to take up precious space, and later, when Lina arrived at school, she would find that she had her grandmother's silk shawl but only one sweater for the winter, and a lonely volume three of *Eastern Life Sciences*.

On the night before her departure, Lina was so filled with emotion that she could barely swallow her rice at dinner, let alone appreciate the taste of the fish her mother had cooked for the occasion. She acknowledged her parents' chatter without looking them in the eye because she knew if she did, she would cry. And then, halfway through her meal, when it was impossible for her to field any more questions with mumbled utterances, she cried anyway.

At first, her parents looked at each other helplessly. Then Fang Lijian turned in his seat so that he was directly facing his daughter. He grabbed the two front legs of her chair and pulled her closer to him, as he used to do when she was little. She was surprised to find he was still strong enough to move her weight like this. With his left hand, he picked up her right one, which was still holding on to the chopsticks she'd been using. "Look at the position of your fingers on these kuaizi," he said. "Remember what this means?"

She was holding them as she always did, fingers high up, near the thick end of the bamboo. She remembered the old saying her parents had taught her, about how the distance between the tips of the chopsticks and the beginning of one's grip indicated how far a person would travel in life. She started sobbing harder. "It means I'm going to end up far away from home," she wailed.

Lina's mother hit her husband lightly on the arm, a rebuke, but he ignored it.

"Right. It means that to do what you were put here to do, you will need to travel far. But look at this, Lina." He picked up his own chopsticks and motioned for his wife to do the same. Both sets of fingers had natural positions close to the middle.

"Your ma and I aren't going anywhere," he said. He lifted his free hand up to her face and stroked her cheek with his walnut-shell fingers. "You'll always know where to find us. We'll be right here waiting for you to come back." And right then, Lina believed it—that her parents would always be the center of her world, that she would do whatever it took to come back to them. This was yet another way in which marrying Wei would pay off—if he could find a job in Shanghai that made decent money, maybe one day they could afford to move her parents there too.

Later, Lina lay on her mat, her face dry and stiff from crying. The evening had worn her out. She felt numb, which was lucky, considering that what she was about to do required her nerves to be as dulled as possible. It must have been nearing one a.m. by the time her parents' breathing slowed to a dreamlike cadence. Lina opened her eyes and looked around. A stroke of luck; both had turned away from her in their sleep. *I'm just going to the bathroom,* she planned to say if they woke. Lina slipped into her shoes, stepped down the path to the gate, and c rossed the road.

She found Qiang waiting between the two trees that they had played cards beneath that first summer day. She couldn't see his face but recognized him by the shape of his hair, the way the back of it stood up and waved in the breeze. They walked soundlessly along the shore of the lake away from town, keeping to the dark swath of space between the water and the wan light coming from the roadside.

"Where are we going?" Lina finally asked when she thought there was no chance of their conversation being overheard.

"To a friend's house," Qiang said. "It's not far. He lives closer to you than he does to me."

Lina hadn't known where the gambling would take place, but she'd expected it to be somewhere more exotic than a person's house. They turned away from the lake, walked through the trees, and came out on a bigger, longer road. Ten minutes later, they stopped in front of a farmhouse. From the outside, it looked like any other farmhouse except for the fact that it had two floors.

"We'll go around the side," Qiang said.

The moment they stepped onto the property, a dog began to bark. Lina felt an impulse to take Qiang's hand but held back. She wished he would say something to her before they went inside, just so she could hear his voice. The only other noise was the grass being crushed beneath their feet. The house was lit from within, and the closer they got to it, the longer their shadows stretched. They passed a well and a few feed buckets next to it with dried slop stuck to the tin. They passed a coop full of hens sleeping with their necks tucked into their bodies. Then they were at the door.

The windows on the property were curtained off with peach-and-tan-colored cloth. Through the side door, all they could see was the faint outline of a kitchen. The walls were thin; Lina heard low voices and the scraping of chairs coming from another room. Qiang stepped forward to knock and then back again to stand next to Lina. There was a swish of a curtain to their right, and a moment later, the door opened. Standing in front of them was a boy who looked not much older than the two of them. He glanced at Lina first, then at Qiang.

"Who is she?"

"A friend," Qiang said. A twinge of annoyance crossed the other boy's face, but he stepped aside to let them enter.

The kitchen was empty of people but filled with garbage. The hearth was littered with dishes and glass bottles, the floor with vegetable peels. At first, Lina thought she spotted maggots, but when she looked more closely, she found they were only cigarette butts.

"Lina," Qiang called to her. "Stay with me."

They followed the other boy down a hallway, approaching the sounds of voices. The room they eventually entered was lowly lit. Four men sat at a card table, and the boy who had let them in perched on a couch nearby. A few others were standing around chatting, but they all stopped talking when Qiang and Lina walked in.

"Brother Gao, I'm here," Qiang announced, speaking to the man seated farthest from where they stood. He was the only one who hadn't looked up from what he was doing. He was shirtless, in his thirties, and shuffling a deck of cards. It wasn't until he had squared his stack away and plucked his cigarette from his lips that he raised his head.

"Who's this?" he asked.

"A friend."

"A friend?" The man laughed. He looked around at the others in the room. "Little pissy kid thinks he's allowed to invite friends. What's your name?" he asked, addressing Lina.

For a moment, her heart stopped.

"Relax, I'm just trying to be friendly," he said, softening the tone of his voice. "Miss, thank you for joining us this evening, but your friend Zhen Zhiqiang has improperly invited you to a business meeting. My associate Jian Hua will take you home." He gestured toward one of the others seated, a thick man with a strong brow. Jian Hua rose, brushing the remains of melon seed shells off his lap. He walked to the corner of the room and stood behind Lina, who felt rather than saw his presence.

"No," Lina said. "I—"

"She won't be comfortable with him. I'll walk her home," Qiang said quickly.

The shirtless man's eyebrows went up. "*Tian a,* who knew our bright little Qiang was such a gentleman? It's too bad, because we've kept Mr. Sheng and Mr. Ling waiting long enough already." At this, he gestured to the two other people seated at the table. One was small and neat with a square face and hair graying at the temples. The other had long hair that he wore tied up in string.

The shirtless leader got up and gestured to his chair. "Sit," he said.

"Brother Gao, Mr. Sheng, Mr. Lin," Qiang said, addressing each of the players in turn. "I apologize for the inconvenience. I will see my friend home—it'll take no more than ten minutes. I'll be back right away."

"Think of the impression you're making," Brother Gao said. The softer his voice grew, the more annoyed he sounded. "The girl will be fine. You're acting like Jian Hua isn't a good guy. Is that what you're saying, Brother Qiang?"

Qiang blinked. "I know Jian Hua is a good guy. The problem is, my friend has no reason to trust that Jian Hua is a good guy."

The man with the long hair spoke up. "I don't know why it's got to be so complicated. Who cares if the girl stays?"

Brother Gao sighed and scratched his head. "Jian Hua," he said. "Please, can you ask your sister to come down here?" As Jian Hua left the room, Brother Gao clapped his hands on his thighs as if trying to revive the convivial mood of the room. "Hao! You're right, let's not complicate things. Enough waiting, let's play."

Lina watched Qiang move to the other side of the table and take Brother Gao's vacated seat. He seemed so young, suddenly—as young as that day she'd offered him tea in her kitchen. These were not his friends, she realized. They were his bosses. Qiang looked at her for a long moment, then turned his attention to the cards that were being dealt to him.

Two other men moved to stand behind Qiang, and the rest took positions behind Mr. Sheng and Mr. Ling. Lina was left by herself near the door. A few moments later, she felt a hand touch her shoulder. She turned to face the big man called Jian Hua. "Miss," he said. "Come with me." Something about his voice put her immediately at ease, and she wished she'd allowed him to take her back to begin with. She didn't like this feeling of not knowing what was about to happen.

Out in the hallway, there was a girl about Lina's age waiting at the foot of the stairs. "This is my sister Jian Yun," Jian Hua said. "We call her Cloudy. She'll keep you company while we play our game. Okay?"

The girl who stood before her had deep-set eyes and her hair in two braids, like Lina's.

"Come on," she said, taking Lina lightly by the wrist.

Lina had no choice but to follow the girl up the stairs. It was dark at the top of the landing except for a pinkish-yellow glow coming from a room down the hall.

Stepping into that room was like entering a conch shell, or an ear canal. The walls were painted the color of warm flesh. A white wooden desk stood by one window. Long lace curtains trailed down from either side of the window's pleated valance. Lina thought of the curtains in the kitchen, how cheap they looked in comparison to the ones in this room. The rest of what she had seen in the house was sparse and utilitarian, like all the other homes in town. Cloudy's room was something out of a magazine.

The bed had a headboard with a column on either side of it, the tops of which were shaped to look like Western chess pieces. The bed was un-made and the pillows scattered on the floor. Cloudy picked them up and threw them onto the bed, then motioned for Lina to sit down.

"Wah," Lina said, bouncing on it a little. "Your bed matches your name."

"It's this mattress my brother got for me from Hong Kong. Soft, right?" Cloudy moved some magazines aside and sat cross-legged facing Lina.

The pillows were even softer than the mattress; Cloudy explained that they were filled with goose down. She propped one against the wall, leaned back, and sighed.

"Why do they call you Cloudy?" Lina asked.

"They think I have a bad temper. I don't, I just give them what they don't expect. Somebody has to keep those boys in line."

Now that Lina could see her more clearly, she suspected Cloudy was older than her by a couple of years. Or maybe it was just that she seemed more mature, the way she was leaning back with her ankles crossed. For Cloudy, it seemed perfectly normal to be awake at two in the morning talking to a girl she'd just met. Lina wanted to know if she was in school but thought it impolite to ask.

"Where are your parents?" she asked instead.

"They haven't been around in a while. My brothers take care of me."

"You mean Jian Hua?"

"And Brother Gao, even though he's really my cousin."

Lina nodded and looked around at the room some more. On the wall to the left of the desk was a collage of magazine cutouts of movie stars from the forties and fifties. Lina admired their smooth helmet haircuts and bright lips. Cloudy had a mouth like the girls in these magazines — small in width, but as full as her eyes. Cloudy leaned over to peer into the mirror on her nightstand and took up a tube of lipstick. She smeared a rich red hue onto her lips.

"What are you doing here?" she asked Lina mid-application, as though it was the first time the thought had occurred to her. "What's your name?"

"I'm Lina," she said. "I'm a friend of Qiang's. I guess I just came to watch the game."

"Qiang." Cloudy's smile disappeared. She narrowed her eyes and cocked her head at Lina as if trying to see into the back of her skull. Then she pressed her sorghum lips together to make the lipstick more even, and her mouth, drawn inward like that, made her look annoyed. Lina suddenly saw her as her family must — someone whose attractiveness depended on her mood. Cloudy leaned back against the wall to study Lina from a better perspective.

"Do you know—are you friends with Qiang?" Lina asked.

"Sure, I'm friends with Qiang. I see him all the time. Sometimes when they finish early, I go down to talk to him and he tries to tell me where he keeps all those numbers in his head. That's his special thing, you know?"

"He's pretty good at card games."

Just as quickly as Cloudy had distanced herself from Lina, she pulled close again. "He's the best at card games. I can't even keep track of all the money they've made. People come from three or four towns over to play with us. I think Qiang should get to keep more of it, but Brother Gao gets annoyed if I say anything. Because managing the money is his special thing. Everybody around here has to keep their eye on their own special thing, Brother Gao says, because otherwise it becomes a big mess. So we don't like anybody who is an extra, you know?"

Here, she gave Lina a meaningful look. Just as Lina wondered if Cloudy meant to say that Lina was the one who was extra, she smiled, her teeth brilliant against her lips.

"What's your special thing?" Lina asked.

"I already told you," Cloudy said. "I take care of them. I keep everybody in line."

She reached over to the nightstand and chose another tube of lipstick. Then she unscrewed it and leaned in to dab at Lina's mouth.

"It doesn't sound like much, but it's not easy keeping the peace. Brother Gao wants us to go to bigger cities. He says there's more money there. 'Nobody wants to come out here to some nongmin town,' he says. 'Everybody wants to go to Hainan or Yunnan, where the underground gambling is established.' He says we could have a real business then, instead of living here in this old house just getting by. But Jian Hua doesn't want to leave. He doesn't like the idea of not having a home. You know what I tell him, though? We're a family, and as long as we stick together, home is wherever we go."

It hadn't occurred to Lina that Qiang might be leaving town too. The thought of it made her feel lonely, though she didn't know why—she wouldn't be around to miss him anyway.

Cloudy handed Lina the mirror. She saw her own thin lips outlined in a glossy strawberry red.

"I look…American," she said.

"You do! You look like an American teenager. Now we just have to get your hair curled."

"Can you do that too?" Lina asked.

"Not here," Cloudy said. "You get it done in the city." She unfastened the ties on her pigtails and combed her hair through her fingers to show Lina. "See how the ends are curly? That's from when I permed it."

Lina touched her hair. The ends were stiff, like sheep's wool.

"Do you work at the silk factory with Qiang?" Lina pictured them driving off to Shanghai with the windows down, packages of raw silk tied to the cargo bed, Cloudy's lightly curled hair blowing across his face.

Cloudy frowned. "You think I'm a laborer?"

"No," said Lina, although she didn't know what to think.

Cloudy returned the lipsticks to the nightstand, got into bed next to Lina, and turned off the lamp on the bedside table.

"You can sleep with me," she said in a small voice. Though it was too hot for bedsheets, Lina got underneath them and pulled them up to her chin. She lay faceup like that until she wasn't aware of anything anymore.

Sometime later, Lina heard the creak of a door handle and opened her eyes to see Jian Hua's pancake-shaped face looming above her in the half-light. She sat up too quickly and made Cloudy turn in her sleep.

"We're finished," Jian Hua said, and he left the room. Qiang took his place in the doorway.

"Qiang!" Lina whispered as she eased herself out of bed. She wanted to hug him but instead shooed him away from the room, stepped out, and closed the door behind her.

He was flushed and happy. "Everything okay?" he asked. When she nodded, he held a finger to his lips and motioned for her to follow him out of the house. As they descended the stairs, she felt a rush of relief. The tendons along Qiang's neck jumped with each step he took, and she was reminded of the day they had fled the silk factory and run down the stone path that led from the factory to the lake, the way the muscles in his neck had moved in the dappled light beneath the trees. She had thought then how much more fun her childhood would have been if she'd had Qiang for company. Would she have turned out differently if they had become friends earlier? Would she have found herself sitting at a card table one day too?

As they passed the room where the game had taken place, Lina peered into it. There was only Brother Gao seated there now, surrounded by empty glasses and ashtrays. He was splitting piles of money and didn't look up as they walked by. In the kitchen, the boy who had let them into the house was sweeping the floor, but he didn't turn around to see Qiang and Lina leave.

"What time is it?" Lina asked Qiang after they were back outside in the cool air. Night was lifting. Blackness had turned to blue and then become tinged with violet. Now that they were walking, Lina could feel herself waking up, and it stirred a kind of longing she wasn't expecting and had never known before.

"It's five," Qiang said. "Are you all right? What's on your mouth?"

Lina wiped her lips with the back of her hand. "Lipstick," she said. "I should get this off before I go back home."

As they made their way down the road, Qiang recapped the game for Lina. He told her he'd gotten so good at cards that it was no longer a question of whether he would win. His friends often made side bets on the game: Which visitor would be angry enough to throw the table? How long would it take for one of them to accuse Qiang of cheating?

"Cloudy says they come from other towns to play you because of your reputation," said Lina. "Why do they come if they know they're going to lose?"

"Because they don't think they will. They hear that I'm a sixteen-year-old and they want to put me in my place. So they're ready to bet enormous sums on the chance that I'll lose. They walk in and see the place looking run-down, unclean, and think we're all just a bunch of spoiled teenagers. So it's easy to take their money." His voice had become so smug that Lina found herself wanting to deflate his ego.

"How much of it do you get to keep?" she asked.

Qiang paused at this. "Enough."

"From what Cloudy says, it seems those out-of-towners are not the only ones being taken advantage of in that house."

"What do you know?" His voice had hardened, turning the question into a challenge.

They walked in silence until they crossed the main road.

"Wait a minute," Lina said. "I can't go home like this." She led the way through the trees and to the lake. Lina crouched near the water so that she could reach it with her fingers and did her best to scrub the wax off her lips. Then she patted her chin dry with her sleeve. "Is it all off?"

Qiang leaned in close to stare at her mouth. "I don't know," he said. "It's hard to tell." She could see the line of sweat along his brow and feel his breath on her neck. Lina stepped back and turned toward the lake, willing her heart to slow. From the corner of her eye, she saw Qiang turn too, so that they were standing side by side. "In a few hours you'll be on a train," he said. "Who knows when I might see you again."

"I'll be back before long."

"But I might not be here anymore."

When she turned to look at him, she saw that he was holding something out to her. A bracelet lay there in his palm, looking bright against the blueness of the water and woods that surrounded them.

"It's a going-away present," he said. "I got it last week from a guy and his wife who came to play. He works in imports, said he'd just gotten back from a trip to Africa. Africa, can you imagine? I don't remember the name of the country. Anyway, his friend comes to our table regularly, and he brought this guy — you should have seen the kind of jewelry he was wearing. Elephant tusks around his neck and the pattern of his shirt was... *tian a!* We don't have those textiles here. He said he'd been all over the world. I told Brother Gao I would rather have something from abroad than money. I said I'd like something for a girl, a friend of mine who was leaving. So for my cut, we played for one of the bracelets on the wife's arms. It's made of ivory, can you tell?"

As Qiang spoke, Lina turned the beads over in her fingers. She'd never seen ivory before. It was light, the color of milk. Every other bead had been carved into the shape of an animal — an elephant, a lion, a tiger, a monkey. They were separated by smaller round beads of ivory that were polished so smooth that they gleamed, even in the low light of morning.

"This is beautiful," Lina managed to say. Qiang looked so happy and proud that he almost seemed to become a different person.

"I might not be here when you get back," Qiang said, "because I'm going to work for Brother Gao from now on, and that means I'll be traveling. But one day, when we're older, when you have your degree and Wei has his, we'll meet again. And then the three of us can travel together. We'll go to Africa. And Spain, and America. You know where I want to go most? The United Kingdom. I want to touch the queen's hat. Wouldn't that be funny?"

He was rambling because she was crying. The moment Lina felt the tears come back, she understood that her parents had not been the only people for whom she was crying. She would miss Qiang too. And she would worry about him. All summer she had felt the restlessness in him and dreaded where all that energy would go. She had long suspected that it wasn't anywhere good or safe, and on that night she'd seen for herself the direction in which it was moving. Lina threw her arms around Qiang's neck and he held her uncertainly until her breathing slowed.

"Be good," she said. "Promise."

By now, dawn had almost reached the shores of the lake and Lina knew it was time to leave. When she let go of him, he was grinning in his usual mischievous way.

"Does this mean you don't think I'm a pest anymore?"

She laughed and hugged him again. "You have been a good friend to me this summer." She felt his hand curl around the base of her neck as he spoke into her hair.

"Brother," he said. "One day I'll be a brother to you."

13

Lina hadn't slept well since Qiang's arrival at Lanson Suites. During the days she felt electrified, her body carrying such voltage that she was afraid of touching anything—of pouring tea, of braiding her daughter's hair—afraid she would give herself away. Even walking out to the living room in the morning to find Qiang's slippers left beneath the coffee table or seeing his razor at the edge of the sink in the guest bathroom, its blades tinged with rust at either end, felt like major events.

When he'd walked through the kitchen door that first night, Lina was taken by surprise. She hadn't expected him to remain the mischievous sixteen-year-old boy from her memories by the lake or the sullen nineteen-year-old who had attended her wedding, but she certainly hadn't expected him to look so pedestrian. His bright T-shirt and faded jeans made him appear both older and younger than his real age.

Then she started to notice the ways in which he'd changed for the better. A length of stubble running up the jaw; the heightened angles of his cheeks. Near his left eye was a bone-colored scar that hadn't been there when he was a teenager. It was too wide for a knife cut and too long to be a burn mark. What had happened there? Lina tried to read the topography of Qiang's body secretly, but it was becoming harder to look away from him.

He watched her too. She'd seen his eyes follow her in the reflection of the clubhouse's glass doors as she'd gotten up to refill her plate. Whenever Qiang studied Karen's face, Lina imagined that he was looking for traces of herself in her daughter.

All week Lina had waited for him to tell her why he'd come. Each time they were alone — standing in front of a museum exhibit or waiting for the bill to arrive at a restaurant — she imagined him leaning forward and beginning the conversation. *Here I am,* he might say. *I've come back for you.* But each of these moments passed unfilled, and Lina began to doubt her initial certainty that he had come to Shanghai to see her. After all, it wasn't likely that a man would hold on to the idea of a woman for twenty years. And yet, hadn't she held on to her idea of him all this time? Qiang had come to Shanghai alone. If he had had a wife, surely he would have brought her.

If he *had* come to see Lina, it was likely that the fight between the brothers that first night scared Qiang off. She wasn't sure what exactly had happened between them, only that when he and Wei had returned from the balcony, something was different. Lina's first thought was that Qiang had confessed to Wei about their relationship. But no — that wasn't it. Wei's anger wasn't directed at her. When she asked him what had happened, he said only that nothing had changed: Qiang was still as selfish and unaware as ever, someone who believed he could pass in and out of people's lives as it suited him.

Wei had been working late for days in a row, sometimes meeting the rest of the family for lunch out in Puxi but otherwise not coming home until long after dinner. The coldness that he'd shown toward Qiang since that first night made Lina afraid that Qiang would leave early. Whenever she passed by the guest room, she peered inside and noted how tidy he kept it, which seemed at odds with the rusty razor and the abandoned slippers in the living room. He made his own bed before the maid showed up and kept his duffel by the door, as if he might take off any moment. She tried to make excuses on Wei's behalf. *He's been in a horrible mood for weeks. He's so overworked.*

This morning when she woke up, she could see patchwork light coming in past the half-parted curtains and landing at the foot of her bed. Beyond, Wei stood at the window, adjusting a tie around his neck. He was usually gone by the time she got up, and she wasn't sure whether she had woken up early today or if he was running late. Wei looked over at her and squinted. There was that forehead wrinkle again, the expression of uncertainty that had been passed down to Karen. How strange, she thought, that what you looked for in a mate could change so drastically as you aged. In earlier years of their marriage, she had been attracted to Wei's strength. Now she was more moved by his vulnerability—in the rare instances he let it show.

"Good morning," she said, flinging off the bedcovers but not getting up. As Wei fastened his cuff links, his eyes followed the line of her bare legs. Then he reached out and grasped her foot for a squeeze. "I'm late," he said and walked to the bathroom.

Lina lay in bed for a few moments longer, then got up to part the curtains the rest of the way, expanding the view to the full width of their bedroom. Having new maids replace Sunny and Rose meant that their room had changed. Lina's makeup was lined up across the length of the mirror on her bureau, her hairbrush set to the left rather than the right. If circumstances were different, Lina might have taught the new maids what went where, showed them how to place the towels the way Sunny used to—a few centimeters farther from the shower so that when one was plucked from the pile, the rest didn't come tumbling down. But now she didn't bother. These small changes to their living space seemed to foreshadow some larger, lasting change, one that Lina would not be able to control. She followed her husband into the bathroom.

"What's on the schedule for today?" he asked, patting on aftershave.

"I don't know," Lina said. "Probably something low-key. I need to stop by the wet market in the morning and the Shangri-La after lunch. In the afternoon, I was thinking of taking Qiang to Yu Gardens. I mean, it's always crowded, but I thought if we—"

"Sounds good." This was a new habit of his, cutting people off. The other women at Lanson had shared tales of their own husbands' egos expanding to fit their titles, but Wei wasn't like that. Even as Medora's profits increased and he gained more attention in the news, Wei showed little interest in fancy cars and restaurants. But here's where he had changed: He now expected people to run on his schedule. When he felt that something wasn't worth his time, he rushed it along. Sometimes Lina felt like a program he was watching on the DVR that, every once in a while, he fast-forwarded.

"Are you sure you don't want to come meet us for lunch?" Lina tried again. "Bear the burden of conversation with your brother for a little while?"

"I can't," he said. "I have a twelve-thirty meeting."

She watched him fuss with his tie.

"You have to spend time with him. You can't keep avoiding him."

"I have work to do, Lina. I'm not just saying that."

She watched his face in the mirror, his distracted irritation, and wondered what had happened to his generosity. When they lived in America, he had once helped the Chinese cashier at their local grocery store file his taxes. On winter mornings, he used to run around the bedroom with her clothing draped around his neck so that her clothes would be warm by the time she put them on. Now she couldn't get his attention long enough to make plans for lunch.

"Whatever it is between the two of you is not worth it," Lina said.

"Qiang's come all this way. He's asking for you to forgive him." It wasn't a conversation she'd meant to have with him now, but she wasn't sure she would get another opportunity.

"You don't have to tell me that," he said. "I'll handle it."

How to make a person understand that family members were not things to be handled? That people were not problems, and the thing to fear wasn't whatever his brother had done in the past or whatever urgent meeting he had waiting for him at the office. It was right there between them. It was what she might do to their marriage today, or tomorrow.

"Are you coming back for dinner?"

"I don't know," Wei said, administering the final touches to his hair.

"When will you know?" She knew she was pushing him. She could see him losing patience.

"I'm not sure yet. I'll check in with you around five."

Lina gave a dry laugh. "Sure, check in with me. While you're at it, why don't you set up a time for my midyear review?"

She hadn't meant her words to come out as caustically as they did. But it had worked—when she met Wei's eyes in the mirror, it was clear that she finally had his attention.

"I just have to get through this week," Wei said quietly. And then, with a touch of condescension, "On Friday, I'm all yours."

"Gold star for effective planning. On Friday, you can cross two things off the list at once: the Expo and family time."

He looked at her in surprise. "I don't even want to go to the Expo," he said.

"You speak to me like I work for you. You can't even tell the difference between your family and your office staff. It's *your* brother who's here. Not mine. You should be 'checking in' with *him*. I'm not your go-between."

Wei closed his eyes. "I didn't mean it like that. I talk a certain way at work and I bring it home. I know I shouldn't."

Before when they used to fight, they'd both flare up like this and finish feeling spent, emptied. Like sex, it had been an act of letting go and bringing themselves to the same plane. Nowadays when they fought, Wei kept his cool. It was as though he no longer wanted to win, only to outlast her.

"You're not the only person in this family, you know. I think you like to pretend that everything you do is for us—late hours, whatever. It isn't. You're the sole reason we're here. You're the reason your kid goes to school halfway across the world—"

"You knew how demanding this job was." Wei lifted his hand as if to make a point, then let it drop to his side. "We agreed to come here together. Every step of the way, we agreed."

"You're doing it again," Lina said. "You're talking about our marriage like it's a contract."

"It is a contract." His eyes flashed, and for a moment she wondered if he meant the words as a warning. He'd seen Lina flirt with men before, out of boredom—the male waitstaff, friends at Lanson Suites. Harmless flirting, but she knew it bothered Wei. With Qiang, the attraction was neither playful nor harmless, and she was pretty sure she'd kept her feelings hidden. But it was still possible that Wei had picked up on it. Lina cast about for a way to change the subject.

"After Qiang pointed out that photo of Karen in the dining room, I counted how many days we've spent with her since it was taken. Summer break plus winter break is about ninety days. Ninety days a year for four years."

His face clouded over; she had gone too far.

"I don't know what to say."

She hadn't been trying to hurt him. All she was looking for was some acknowledgment that things were not fine. *I'm sorry,* she wanted to say. *I'm sorry for everything.* And here was the thing: If she did say it, if she did confess to everything—to needling him to fulfill her own need for attention, blaming him for everything that felt wrong in their lives, resenting him for working, even lusting after his brother—he would forgive her. The forgiveness wouldn't come easily, but it would still come, and too quickly for Lina's liking. It bothered Lina that it wouldn't occur to Wei to behave any other way. His need to forgive was greater than his need to understand. He would rather move past pain by shutting it out than by determining its source.

She wanted to protect him, but she couldn't protect them both at the same time. She thought about apologizing but didn't out of dread of their choreographed reconciliation—her cheek on his chest, his hand stroking her back in a way that seemed so infuriatingly *perfunctory* to her, though of course he never meant it that way. In the end, she just looked up and said, "Suan le. You should go."

Wei stood there for a blundering moment, smoothing his tie. Then, not knowing what else to do, he left the room.

The fight left Lina rattled. She sent Sunny, Karen, and Qiang down to breakfast without her and paced around the bedroom. By the time she composed herself and went downstairs, Qiang was the only one sitting at the booth. Lina readied herself and joined him.

"Zao," she said, bidding him good morning as casually as she could manage.

"Zao." When he saw her face, his smile recalibrated. "Sunny and Karen left with Little Cao already. They had a movie to see. He's coming back to pick up the two of us afterward."

"Oh. Sorry…I got caught up."

"They said they were closing up the buffet. I saved some food for you." He pushed a plate of melon balls in her direction. He had also collected a plate of eggs, mantou, and a small dish of condensed milk. It touched her to think of him choosing food just for her.

"How have you been sleeping?" she asked as she signaled the waiter. "Are you comfortable here?"

"I am," he said.

"Really? The mattresses aren't too soft? They order them from this European company…"

"I have a Western mattress at home," he said. "I'm used to it."

"Oh." She had imagined his bed at home to be an entirely different sort — a simple Chinese cot on the floor of a room in his Kunming apartment. She could see him lying on it in midafternoon, his hands behind his head, looking out a window. But what she had imagined — his carefree posture, his simple tastes — was only a memory of him at the lake superimposed over present-day circumstances.

A waitress brought over Lina's latte and for a few moments the three of them were occupied with rearranging plates on the table to make room for the cup and saucer.

When they were alone again, Qiang reached over and placed his hand on top of Lina's. She thought she could feel his heart beating through his palm, but that wasn't possible, was it? The skin at the tips of his fingers looked rough and callused, as if it would catch on the tablecloth if he moved too quickly. Lina slid her hand out from beneath his and tucked it under the table.

"Are you all right?" Qiang asked.

"Yes. Fine."

It was enviable, the way men shamelessly went after what they wanted. What did Qiang care that they were in public? He would touch her like that if he wanted to. Women were the ones left to exercise caution, to pretend things were fine when they were not.

"So, I meant to ask you the other night…" He still looked concerned, and she feared he would say something about Wei or Karen, something that would push her to tears. "Out of everywhere you've traveled, what's been your favorite place?"

Lina was so relieved, she almost laughed. "Copenhagen."

"Why?"

Why? It was simply where she imagined herself whenever she thought of peace and happiness. "People seem relaxed there. The air's clean, they ride bikes around the city, there are parks everywhere…"

"It sounds kind of dull," Qiang said, and she couldn't tell if he was joking.

"It's a nice place to visit."

"When did you go?"

How funny it was that their roles had switched. Now Lina was the one who knew more about the world, having traveled so much with Wei. But most of those trips had been related to his work, and she often felt that the experiences had been crafted for their benefit. The winter they had gone to Kenya for the Medora Group yearly management retreat, they had left the hotel resort exactly twice, once to go to a tourists' market and the second time to go on safari. In the African desert, they had been shuttled around by a driver and an English-speaking tour guide who'd spent half the trip snapping photos of them against the vermilion sunset. At the end of the safari, he'd tried to sell the photos to them at twenty bucks apiece.

And so she didn't feel like a real traveler. Everything—from the catered food to the all-day pool passes—lacked the feeling of true exploration. It was embarrassing to know that her wandering, after all, had meant nothing more than a series of tidy choices: dessert set A or dessert set B?

Had she been a little more like Qiang, maybe she would have seen less traditional options, something other than what was directly in front of her. From the very beginning, she could have chosen to marry neither Qiang nor Wei. She could have stayed in Wuhan and tried her luck as a linguist or earned a graduate degree in history and one day taught a subject of interest to her. She could barely remember which career paths had excited her back then. Surely, it would have been easier to imagine a different outcome for herself at that age than it was now, when half her life had already been lived.

"Lina," Qiang said. "Come on. You should eat."

She had mashed most of her honeydew into a pulpy mess.

"To tell you the truth, I can't remember which year we went to Copenhagen. In fact, I'm only pretty sure that it was me who went and not some other woman who lives in this building. We all go to the same places anyway, you know, share the same pictures. It's my favorite spot and I don't remember if we got there by plane or cruise ship, and like I said, if you want to get really technical about it, I can't be entirely sure it was me at all."

Qiang had stopped chewing. If he was concerned about her before, he was downright alarmed now. The lines in his forehead twitched like an EKG.

Wasted opportunity. That's what her life had become—a series of wasted opportunities. And here she was, complaining about her own poor choices to a person who had barely left the country. *Rein it in*, Lina told herself.

"When I was in college, I picked up this book by a Frenchwoman, Simone de Beauvoir. At a funny old bookshop by the university. The book was called *The Second Sex*."

"I remember," Qiang said. "You wrote about it in a letter once."

Had she written to him about it? That moment in the bookshop felt so vivid that at times she thought it must have happened in a recurring dream.

"It was a whole volume of essays about being a woman and I didn't understand any of it. So I translated it from English to Chinese, hoping that would help. I spent months working on that book, and afterward, I reread it in Chinese and still didn't understand most of what was said. But I do remember one line from the text. 'A person is not born a woman, but rather becomes one…' Something like that. It was eye-opening to me at the time, the idea that gender is not something you're born with but a set of social rules you're born into. You can choose to follow them or not. Knowing that there was a difference made the whole world seem more difficult and interesting and full of possibility."

Qiang nodded for her to go on, but Lina did not trust where this train of thought was leading.

"I think I forgot that feeling. And that's why I feel so old. I feel as though anyone could have lived my life; it's just me that happens to be here. Or in Copenhagen. Or in America."

She laughed now, blinking away tears. "You're not like me," she said to Qiang. "You wouldn't understand."

"No," he said softly. "You're not like anyone else."

"I didn't mean to get sad and grumpy. Finding that book...I brought up that story because it's a very nice memory for me. It makes me remember what it feels like to be young."

"To want to learn?" Qiang asked.

"Not only to learn but to be astounded. To read about the world and want to be a part of it. To work to understand someone else's ideas with the help of two languages and to feel as though you have nothing to lose but time." She remembered the back cover of that book and how the author had looked out from a photo, unsmiling, with a stare so sharp it gave Lina chills. Lina had bought the book on that stare alone.

"And to fall in love with something because of the mystery of it."

"It's true," Qiang said. "That is exactly how it feels to be young." He took her hand again and squeezed it. This time she didn't pull away.

She had been talking about the book but saw that he had heard it differently. He thought she was talking about the two of them and what they had shared when they were young.

"But it isn't just the mystery of it," Qiang said. "There's a reason you're drawn to whatever it is, or whoever it is, you're falling for. They have something you're missing. So you're drawn not only to them but to the part of yourself that is incomplete. It's like...feeling more whole around them. Even if feeling more whole means that everyone else thinks it's wrong." His focus had shifted from Lina; he looked as if he were watching a scene play out that she could not see.

So he *was* here for her. He was tired of feeling incomplete, and that's why he had come to find her again. Lina's mind flashed forward to a life with Qiang in it, the one she'd been imagining when she hired Sunny for the summer. He would live in Shanghai and she could see him during the day while Wei was at work. He would be part of the family again; she would have a best friend. Without the eyes of their parents and Wei monitoring them, the time they had together would be theirs alone. *Tian a*, it could never happen. And yet, wasn't there a way to make it work?

Qiang smiled at her and reached over to pick up the mantou. He dipped it in the condensed milk and held it out to her. Lina didn't normally eat the stuff, but she took it from him now. Her throat was still tight and the bread was dry going down, but she barely noticed.

"You feel better?" he asked.

"Yes," she replied. "I feel just fine."

14

The Zhens' driver was a large man with no visible neck. Sunny had seen him in the parking lot before, smoking with the other drivers while they waited for their charges. On her first day as an ayi, she had recognized him by the bright red T-shirt he often wore, which made him look even bigger thitean he was. *We need a new driver,* she'd heard Taitai joke. *The one we've got makes our car look small.* Each time Little Cao pulled the Mercedes up outside the lobby, a muted, dull thumping of C-pop could be heard coming from the vehicle. As soon as the car came to a stop, he would turn it off and get out to greet them.

The expression on his face was the same as the one on the Buddha charm Little Cao kept hanging from the rearview mirror. They both had oversize earlobes and jolly, loose jowls. Taitai sent Sunny and Karen on daily excursions to the movies or the shops, and Sunny sat directly behind the driver, so she spent a lot of time watching the Buddha swing back and forth as if it were moving to the rhythm of Little Cao's rambling. Little Cao wasn't young, despite his insistence on being called "Little." But his energy was youthful and curious; it was as if everything he set his gaze on, he was seeing and appreciating for the first time.

"You don't say much," he told Sunny the afternoon they circled Yu

Gardens, waiting for Taitai and Qiang to finish buying dumplings. The rush-hour traffic had clogged the tourist site, making it hard not only to find parking but also for the car to move more than a meter a minute. It had been hot out, but now the sun was just an orange throb in the antique pavilions that made up the bazaar. Karen was asleep, her head in Sunny's lap.

"What is there to say?" Sunny asked, surprised. Little Cao was a circular conversationalist. He talked aloud about the same few topics — his brother, who owned a factory in Tianjin that made German products; the superiority of German craftsmanship and ingenuity; and the difficulty he had learning to use his new cell phone. He hadn't made it clear until this moment that he expected her to participate in the conversation.

"I've never met an ayi with nothing to say. Where are you from?"

"Anhui." She didn't need to ask where he was from; she had heard him banter with parking attendants in Shanghainese. After living in the city for years, its dialect still fascinated her more than any Western language. Like all Chinese dialects, it had Mandarin roots, the precisely shaped words gutted and flattened to make room for lower tones and looser tongues. Shanghainese sounded lewd to Sunny's ear. Its words for "thank you" resembled the Mandarin for "go wild."

"Did you come out here alone?" he asked.

This was a way of finding out if a person was married. Sunny met Little Cao's eyes in the rearview mirror and scanned his face for that kind of interest. All she got back was the same ready smile. If she went by that smile, she'd have to assume he would be happy to marry anyone — Taitai, the traffic guard, a Pekingese pup they'd seen on the street.

"Yes," she said. "I came out years ago. Now I'm out over in Hongkou District."

"Group living?"

"Yes."

"This is a good gig, I bet. How much do you make?"

"Five thousand a month for the summer."

Little Cao made a noise through his teeth. "That much and you're still living with the rest of the ant tribe? I know people like you. You break your back sending money home and meanwhile you can't get a good night's sleep because a bunch of college graduates are fucking in the bed next to you. Am I right?" He cackled and winked at her. "You've got to take care of you. If your body starts breaking down, who is going to provide for Mom and Dad? Who's going to upgrade their TV to a sixty-four-inch, right?"

"I just started," she said. "This is better than anything I've ever had. I'm still getting used to it."

"All right, all right. What do you do for fun?"

She almost laughed. "I don't have time for fun."

"I mean, what do you do with your friends?"

She hadn't heard from Rose in days. It was all she could do not to go down to the service hall and ask after her. "I don't have any friends."

"Qie! No time for friends, no time for fun. Let me tell you what happens to people like you. Either you get burned out and go back to where you came from or you hang on here, miserable from day to day, thinking it's all for the greater good of the family. Can't last like that. If you ask me, the best thing a person can do is live for himself. Work for your family, live for you. Send some of that money home, but spend some too."

With these last words, he lifted his palm and let it drop on the steering wheel. The car horn released a loud blare, and Karen lifted her head from Sunny's lap.

"What happened?"

"Nothing," Sunny said. "We're here. We just have to find parking."

Karen sat up, squinted out the window. "I want to get out now."

"Your mom and uncle are coming out soon."

"No. I'm bored, I want to get out."

Sunny hesitated. Her instinct told her that she and Karen should not get out of the car. It was clear from that first dinner that there was awkwardness within the Zhen family. Boss Zhen and his brother were not close—and it wasn't just because many years had passed since they'd seen each other. On the night of Qiang's arrival, when Sunny stood at the kitchen counter eating her dinner, she hadn't been able to concentrate on the meal. The stop-and-go cadence of conversation in the next room set her on edge. When she had at last peeked in to check on them, Karen was leaning forward in her seat, for once paying attention to the adult conversation. Taitai's jaw was set, her eyes locked on her husband, who had grown so red in the face, Sunny thought he might have had too much to drink. Qiang was the only one she hadn't been able to read. He'd been sitting with his back to her and he'd kept his voice low throughout the meal. But since then, she'd noticed that he and Taitai had warmed up to each other. While Wei was at work, the two of them spent hours drinking tea on the balcony, their postures secretive. Whatever was going on between them, Sunny would rather not know.

"Come on!"

"You've been awake five seconds," Sunny said, stalling.

"I want to find my mom." Karen's voice tightened into a whine. Sunny finally relented and cut a glance at Little Cao in the rearview mirror. *You're responsible for this,* her look said, and she followed Karen out of the car.

Little Cao had dropped them at the entrance closest to the pearl market. Sunny knew the outskirts of the bazaar well but hadn't entered the main thoroughfare in some time. She let Karen lead the way through the crowd, past shops selling women's stockings, household items, seasonal decor, and more. At the craft bazaar, vendors held their mouths too close to bullhorns, shouting advertising deals in rhyming couplets. Some had recorded their own voices and played their ads on staticky sound systems. A few artisans carried handmade pieces, but most other wares were mass-produced and shipped in from neighboring factory towns.

The main attraction in Yu Gardens, other than the gardens themselves, was the dumpling house. It was located down a narrow alleyway among stores that sold novelty items like silk-embroidered wall hangings, framed portraits of Mao, and signature stamps engraved on imitation jade. Sunny had never seen the line for soup dumplings less than ten meters long and today was no different. Foreigners shifted from one foot to the other, weighed down by their long-lens cameras and shopping bags full of pearl jewelry. Near the pickup window was a trash bin in which an old Chinese lady rummaged for discarded dumplings. Every time she found one, she bit open the doughy skin, freed the meatball, and popped it urgently into her mouth. Sunny watched a white man lift his camera to his face, think better of it, and recap the lens.

"There they are," Karen said. She pointed to the front of the line. It took a while for Sunny to realize that the woman standing with her feet together, her hands in the back pockets of her trousers, and her head thrown back in childish glee was Zhen Taitai. Qiang, his body angled away from hers, was giving her a grin and a sideways look. Sunny had glanced at them twice without recognizing them, and that was because she had seen something she wasn't expecting—something she shouldn't have seen. But it was too late to turn away. Karen was already running toward them.

"Mom!"

Taitai turned, startled. When she saw Karen, a flicker of fear crossed her face. Then she narrowed her eyes and scanned the crowd for Sunny.

"Karen woke up and wanted to join you," Sunny said as she approached.

"But we're almost done here. If you had called, I could have told you that."

In the week that Sunny had worked for Taitai, she'd come to realize that her authoritative attitude was a front. In practice, she was eager to turn most of the daily decision-making over to Sunny. Aside from the feast Taitai had made on the night Qiang arrived, she had shown no interest in planning meals or making grocery lists and had nothing to say about what Sunny and Karen did with their days. This didn't mean that Sunny was any less intimidated by Taitai. There was always the fear that at any moment she could snap out of her distraction and say something cutting and critical. Now she had.

But something had changed for Sunny, seeing Taitai with her head thrown back like that. It was suddenly clear that she was just as vulnerable as everyone else. Human enough to be flirting with her husband's brother. Sunny wasn't exactly surprised—she'd suspected romantic feelings between them, and yet she hadn't wanted to believe it. It seemed too sordid and banal an affair for the Zhen family, who had a reputation at Lanson for being classy. Now that her suspicions were confirmed, she couldn't help but see other things too, like the way Taitai took every opportunity to put Karen's body between hers and Qiang's.

"Zhi dao le," she replied. "Next time I will call."

But Taitai was no longer paying attention to her. She was fussing over Karen, smoothing back her hair and tucking away a tag that was poking out of her shirt. The line had moved forward and now they found themselves at the takeaway window.

"Four boxes—half pork, half chicken," Lina said, reaching into her pocketbook for her wallet. Sunny heard her phone chime and opened her purse too.

Message (1) from Rose: I should probably tell you that I was let go.

There wasn't anything more—just that single sentence.

"I'll be back," Sunny said to Taitai and Qiang. "I need to find a bathroom."

Without waiting for a response, she walked off toward the center of the gardens, her hand still in her pocketbook, closed around the phone.

As soon as she was out of view of the dumpling line, she placed a call to Rose.

"I'm fine," Rose said, picking up on the first ring.

"When did this happen?"

"Two days ago."

The closer Sunny got to the middle of Yu Gardens, the louder it became; she turned and headed east instead. "Two days ago? Why didn't you tell me sooner? What are you going to do?"

"I don't know," Rose said. "I've started to look around. But it's kind of nice waking up late—I'm already used to not having anywhere to go." A dry laugh escaped her throat.

Sunny had been trying not to think about the foolish thing she'd done to try to save Rose's job. Each morning when walking across the lobby on the way to the elevators, Sunny had stopped to peer out the glass back door of the reception area, toward the infinity pool. Each morning, it appeared the same as always, black and white marble glistening beneath flowing water. When she'd asked at the front desk if it had been drained and refilled, the lobby attendant on duty recognized her as a former employee of the hotel and had been frank with her. Did Sunny know how often children pee in pools? All the time. They had a filtration system in place for that, and chlorination. They drained the pool water once in midsummer and once in early September. Whatever Sunny had been told on the phone the day she'd requested the cleaning was probably one of the false promises they often made to keep residents happy. So Sunny had stopped hoping for that bright yellow plastic sign that announced closure for cleaning and looked every morning only out of habit. Once, she had even gone out into the courtyard to get closer to the pool, trying to see into its depths. Was the bracelet lying on the stone floor of the deep end, invisible to the eye? Had someone found it and taken it instead of turning it in? Why hadn't she considered these outcomes?

"Jian gui," she said to Rose now. "I can't believe it really happened."

Rose's silence was long enough to make Sunny worry she had lost her signal.

"Listen. I shouldn't have asked you to take the bracelet back," Rose finally said. "That was my burden, not yours."

A paper-kite vendor came down the alley, ringing a bell as he passed, drowning out many of Rose's words. Sunny ducked into another alley, pressing the phone harder to her ear. "Suan le," she said. "Don't worry about it. I don't want you to ever think you can't ask me for help. I'll keep my ears open to see if there are any opportunities. There are new hotels every day, seems like. I'm sure you'll find something."

It was difficult to imagine Rose in a uniform different from Lanson Suites' black and khaki.

"Well." Rose sighed. "I'll miss you. I guess I wasn't going to see you anymore anyway, now that you're working for the Zhens. How have they been treating you?"

She was trying to change the subject. Rose was unused to being the vulnerable one in the friendship. For years, she had been the one to advise and take care of Sunny, and now that the roles were reversed, neither of them knew how to behave.

"Fine," Sunny admitted.

"Where are you?"

"In Yu Gardens."

"You're with them now? Get off the phone. We'll talk later."

"Let's get lunch next weekend, okay?" Sunny could hear the desperation in her voice. "My treat." In that moment, she feared Rose would say no. The restrained tone of their conversation seemed to indicate things were now different between them.

"Ms. Big Spender, ah?" Rose laughed. "I have to warn you—I eat more now that I'm unemployed."

"Eat as much as you want," Sunny said, relieved. "We'll see a movie after."

"Hao ba."

There was a moment of silence in which they both seemed to be figuring out how to end the conversation. "Go back to work," Rose finally said again, and she hung up.

Later, on the car ride home to Lanson Suites, Sunny watched Taitai sleep in the backseat, Karen wedged between them. When they entered the tunnel running beneath the Huangpu, orange slices of light crossed Taitai's face, showing the hollows beneath her cheekbones. It should have been easy to hate this woman, who was so blind to another's ruin. What was a bracelet compared to a livelihood? Here she was, asleep in the middle of the day, while Rose and her husband were trying to figure out how to make up half their income.

But Sunny didn't feel much anger toward Taitai. The things that made her insufferable—her mood swings, her privilege—Sunny was used to. Over the years, she and Rose had learned how to work around women like her. They had collected secrets about them, information that confirmed how unreasonable or wasteful or vapid they were. Having less wealth than the residents of Lanson Suites had allowed Sunny to feel morally superior, and *that* was why she could work for them—the knowledge that she was better than the people she served. She had thought Rose shared the same belief. But Rose's stealing that bracelet was as good as admitting that these women's belongings had power over her, that their wealth was worth exactly what they wanted it to be worth.

• • •

The man whom Sunny had been set up with had asked her to meet him in Hongqiao at an Internet café. The ride over on her motorbike was a long one, and she was glad. She loved highways. Crossing the overpass with the wind on her shoulders made her stop thinking and start seeing. All of Shanghai was reduced to a spray of glitter on either side. Above her head stretched another overpass; its underbelly carried twin tracks of neon light that changed from blue to green to red as it ran from one side of the river to the other. Sometimes in the Lanson Suites clubhouse, Sunny looked around at the silver serving trays with lids like astronaut helmets and the floor-to-ceiling windows that curved up from the ground and felt as though she had arrived at some point in the distant future. Other times, far along the outskirts of Puxi, she felt as though she'd been transported to the past. The streets there were closer to one another and the shops filled with items that might have been sitting beneath the counter for five or ten years: battery-operated radios, Nokia cell phones, and compact discs, their cheap inserts faded from the sun. But as she rode the overpass now, Sunny liked to imagine that this view was the best representation of Shanghai as it was in the present: charged and ever-growing, its colors changing as it expanded.

The Internet café was in the trendy but affordable part of Hongqiao, in an alley between a massage parlor and a seafood restaurant. Sunny parked, removed her sleeve guards, and placed them in the compartment underneath the seat of her bike. Then she slung her purse across her body and tugged at the back of her shirt so that it wouldn't bunch. She looked up to see that the café didn't have doors, just strips of green plastic hanging from the entryway. Sunny walked up the steps, parted the plastic curtains, and stepped inside.

It was a smoke-filled space, dark but for the rows of computer screens and blinking arcade consoles that lined one wall of the room. The back of the café opened out into a shopping mall, and a bank of windows revealed evening shoppers strolling past. Sunny scanned the booths along the windows and knew immediately whom she had come to meet.

The man looked to be in his late thirties. He had too much scalp and a noticeable overbite but seemed all right otherwise. Strong brow, good skin. When their eyes met, the quality of his expression changed from apprehension to—not disappointment, but what? Surprise? She approached the booth and sat down across from him.

"Are you Sunny?" he asked.

"Yes."

"I'm Li Jun. I was about to order a beer. Should I make it a pitcher?"

"All right."

She removed her pocketbook and placed it next to her in the booth. There was a moment's silence while he studied the menu and Sunny looked around the room. It was filled with teenagers seated in front of computer screens, their heads bowed under the weight of oversize headphones. When Rose said that Li Jun wanted to meet at an Internet café, Sunny had interpreted his suggestion as an attempt to make the setup feel casual. Now she reassessed the situation. She watched the way he stared at the menu without reading it and wondered if they were there because this was his place, the place where he felt most comfortable.

He looked up again and smiled. "The chicken wings are good."

When the server came over, Li Jun ordered the wings and a pitcher of Tsingtao. Then he took a breath and looked at each of Sunny's features one by one, as though he couldn't decide which part of her to speak to.

"Did you just get off work?" he asked.

"Yes."

"It's pretty late."

"Some days are longer than others."

"I've always thought that women who clean homes for a living are hard workers by nature."

"I'm an ayi now," she said. "For a Chinese-American family in Pudong."

"Ayis clean too, don't they?"

"Not where this family lives. It's a serviced apartment, so they have staff there to clean. It's where Rose works too."

"Rose?"

It took Sunny a beat to remember Rose's Chinese name. When she said it, Li Jun nodded—*Dui, dui*—and Sunny wondered if he knew about Rose losing her job. Probably not—it wasn't exactly the kind of news her husband would be eager to tell his friend. But Sunny felt an urge to discuss it with Li Jun, if only to initiate a real conversation. Small talk could be so uncomfortable.

"And this family—are they good to you?"

"So far, yes," Sunny said. "I didn't know what I was getting into, but the work isn't bad. I just take their kid around town, to the movies or the mall or the park. It's funny. The housemaid job kept me pretty busy and I didn't get out much. But I've been working for this family four days and in that time I think I've seen more of Shanghai than I have in the past few years. And tomorrow we're going to the Expo."

"Lucky you!" Li Jun said. "I've been trying to find a time to go myself. It's not so easy, you know? You've got to devote at least a day to it, and even then I've heard there's so many people that you can't see more than a couple pavilions. But you—it's your job to go! How great is that?"

He was nice. He was making an effort. And it did feel good to have someone help celebrate the only perk of the job Sunny was really looking forward to. By this time tomorrow, it would matter less that she'd never get to leave China—the rest of the world would have come to her.

"What do you do for work?" Sunny asked. Li Jun relaxed then, as people do when coming into their conversational comfort zone.

"I run a DVD outfit. We buy movies from all over, burn them to discs, subtitle them in Hangzhou, and bring them here to sell during the week. I have a shop on Hengshan Lu." This was his major selling point, he knew. His eyes widened to take in her reaction.

"Wah, not bad." Sunny nodded. "Rent out there must be expensive. I guess your business is doing well?"

"It's okay," he said. "We had a few good years, but now everyone's watching movies online. Used to be that new releases would bring in twelve times more than the classic titles, but now most of them are just breaking even. Get a new James Bond movie, the Transformers, or something like that, and we can gross. But some of the other ones are just flops for us."

She had to admit it was attractive, the fluidity with which he said this. He was clearly a considered, driven person. Li Jun became lost in thought, absentmindedly running his thumbnail along the table edge between the wood composite and its glass top. He inspected the gunk he found there, flicked it into his lap.

Sunny looked out the window into the mall. Every so often, a person would catch her eye and, in passing, turn his or her head to observe the man across from her. Did she and Li Jun look like a couple? She couldn't really imagine walking hand in hand with anyone the way these evening strollers did. She wondered how many of them were in relationships bound by love, not just marriage. How would it feel to put one person above all others, to have one person to whom you owe nothing — no family ties — one person that you have chosen? Impossible, it seemed to her. But it did happen. Here she and Li Jun were, trying to make it happen.

"Maybe you should stop selling to young people," she said to him.

"What?"

"That rent on Hengshan Lu is too expensive. Sell them out here in Hongqiao during the day instead of to drunk people coming out of bars at night. Make classic movies, stuff old people will like."

"Old people."

"Shi a, old people don't know how to watch movies online."

Li Jun started laughing, then looked at her with heightened interest. "You know, that's not a bad idea. You study business or something?"

"No." Did he think she'd gone to college? Would it be dishonest not to correct this assumption from the beginning? "Like I said, I'm an ayi."

"I know," Li Jun said softly. "It was just a joke. I just meant — that was a good point you brought up. I hadn't thought of it."

Two plates of chicken wings appeared in front of them, still covered in plastic wrap. The café had made no attempt to disguise the fact that the food was premade, and Sunny was okay with that. Li Jun poured beer into their glasses, held his up to gan bei. They clinked, and he continued to watch her, even as he lifted his beer to his lips.

They kept talking as they drank—about their families, their rent, the food they missed from home. He was from a village just outside of Fuyang, the youngest son of parents that, like Sunny's, had barely survived the Great Leap Forward famine. Growing up, they'd both seen their parents count grains of rice in their palms. It did something to you, witnessing the tail end of poverty. It didn't necessarily change your ethics or your discipline, but it did make you more careful. You became someone who took stock of all your available resources, who held on to details longer than most people might. Sunny matched him glass for glass. Once the pitcher was finished, Li Jun stood up.

"Want to keep me company outside for a smoke?"

In March, the city's ban on smoking in public had been expanded to include Internet cafés, but the law was almost universally ignored, especially in out-of-the-way places like this one. Sunny mentally ticked a box in his favor. Rule-following was a good sign.

Outside, they found a spot in the shadows of the steps leading up to the café. He pulled a pack of Double Happiness out of his pocket, and just like that, Sunny felt closer to him. Her father smoked that brand. As did half of China, but still.

Li Jun took one and held the box out to Sunny. Smoking wasn't ladylike, but Sunny accepted one for something to do. He pulled a lighter out of his pocket, and a flame bloomed between them. She leaned in, watched the tip of her cigarette catch and curl, and then released a jet of orange smoke. It changed from orange to blue to purple, reflecting the colors of the neon sign in the window of the seafood restaurant. Li Jun was beside her, and she could see only his profile. His head was bald and smooth except for a half-circle of hair that went from above his ears to the back of his head. He turned the lighter in his hand once, then twice, before returning it to his pocket.

"So," he said slowly. "I would like to be straight with you. I like you. You're smart and a hard worker. I am nobody's dream man, but I have some good qualities—qualities I think you'd appreciate. I'm good at finding opportunities. I'm efficient." He paused here, as though he'd lost his train of thought. But when he spoke again, his voice was sharp with intent, his words sounding almost practiced.

"Neither of us is young and I would not like to waste time. I don't want to try to take this further if there is no road for us in that direction. So. What do you think? Am I acceptable?" He didn't look at her and didn't try to lighten his words with irony.

The pitcher had done its work on Sunny. It was like she was seeing the events take place from two points of view: from where she was, crouched beside Li Jun, staring into the foreign recesses of his ear, and from across the street, where she watched two people conversing in the dark, their knees turned slightly toward each other. A scene from a movie, she thought. How many women had he made this proposal to? And what was she to say?

The easy answer was yes. He was more than acceptable. This was a good man. She felt the goodness leap from him. This was a man who had a home to share and who could run a business. If only he had not asked her so soon. If only he had let her tally points for and against him until her mind was distracted long enough for her heart to decide. But hadn't it already? She looked down at her cigarette and recalled how she had taken it without thought of the impression it might give to him. Didn't that mean something about her natural inclinations—that she didn't care what he thought of her? But what a trivial thing for a person to consider. Who did she think she was, a woman with no personal prospects looking for something as impractical as love? If her mother had been there, she would have told her to use her head. The heart was the most senseless organ there was—yet the most essential. No wonder people were doomed to be fools from the beginning.

"I have lived alone for so long," she heard herself say. "I've become used to it. Maybe too used to it."

A lesser man would have pressed her on the issue, but Li Jun caught her meaning right away. He was still for a moment, and then he nodded dreamily, as if to some sound track she couldn't hear. The halo of color around his silhouette went yellow, green, blue, and the movement of his head was locked in a visual echoing effect. She could see him—from up close, and then from far away—stuck in this scene, playing a role he had played many times. She wondered what upsets life had shown him, and for a moment she regretted that she had not taken the opportunity to know him for a little while longer. But he had asked her to be straight with him, and she had.

15

Oh, freedom! Within months of entering Chujiao University, Lina couldn't imagine how she had ever felt content in the little village that was her hometown. In her letters to Qiang, she tried to explain how much more fun it was to be a college student than a high-school student. He would have liked the school grounds, made up of low-slung boxy buildings almost swallowed up by the surrounding trees. It was said that a boy could climb from the roof of his dormitory onto one of the nearby redwoods and jump from tree to tree until he landed atop the girls' lodgings. No one the students knew had succeeded in this yet, although a few attempts had been made. What the girls received instead were crudely whittled arrows that sailed through windows, private messages tied to their tail ends. Messages, of course, that turned out to be anything but private. As soon as an arrow made its twittering entrance, there was a wild scramble for that piece of folded paper. But the moment it was seized, the room settled into controlled anticipation. The others made way for the victor to stand atop a dormitory chair and read aloud the name of the addressee and the details of the date requested—a cup of tea at the school cafeteria or a short walk around the campus grounds. Following this was a round of cheering and hollering from the girls who already had boyfriends and exaggerated teasing from the ones hoping to hide their disappointment. Secretly, everyone wanted to hear her own name read aloud.

How unfair, these girls must have thought, that the name on the slip of paper was so often Lina's. Lina, who never took any of these young men seriously. Lina, who was pretty but not the prettiest; smart, but not the smartest; and nowhere near the most capable of making a home. Look at the way she left her pants rumpled in a heap at the end of her bed! Look at the way she kicked her shoes off so carelessly that she had to get on her knees to retrieve them from beneath the bunk!

Maybe it was because Lina was already betrothed that she felt comfortable around the other sex. She knew instinctively how to make boys laugh and tell her their secrets. Although she kissed a few, she never went any further than that. But she made them feel as though she had. She had heard from one of the other girls that the boys considered her kind of charm "intimate." They also thought that she was a bit of a tease, to act so reservedly when she practically flaunted herself in her bell-bottoms and high heels and the lipstick that she wore when she went off campus.

Lina knew that her way of winning hearts was a little cruel. A little cruelty suited her. Meeting Cloudy that day in the gambling house had struck something in Lina. It made her want to know how it would feel to be someone men found daring instead of precious. Cloudy's sophistication came from the fact that she had seen more of the world than Lina and was willing to be changed by it. The way she described their gang family's dynamics showed that she had her own ideas about how things should be run, and the others respected her for it. Cloudy was not a person bound by convention, and Lina decided she didn't want to be either.

These other girls at school assumed that attractiveness had everything to do with sweetness and docility. Lina was starting to learn that it wasn't enough to give men what they wanted. You had to give them what they didn't expect. But even as she shocked the girls with some of the things she said (*Oh, let them look in the windows! They see us naked in their dreams anyway*), Lina knew she was a fraud. Her whole attitude was adopted, an experiment in modernity. She could pretend to be as loose, fashionable, and freethinking as she wanted, but only because it was so easy to appear the opposite of what young, marriageable women were supposed to be when you had a fiancé waiting for you back home.

Fall turned to winter. There were seven students in each dorm room, and every morning, one of the seven would rise earlier than the others, dress in multiple layers, and walk to the dispensary to fetch five gallons of water for the dorm mates to share. If a girl had a sweetheart, she and her beau would sync their shifts so that they could complete their duties together. He would carry his five gallons of water in one hand and her five in the other, and she would tuck her hand into the woolen nest of his pocket as they walked the fifty meters back to the dorms. Whenever Lina woke early, she watched these couples come and go down the snow-covered paths and felt very lonely.

What she was doing with Qiang — sending letters every week — might be crossing the line, but she couldn't bring herself to stop. Early on, she had written to Wei too, but his responses felt too formal, too composed for her to develop any kind of honest communication with him. Qiang's letters were never forthcoming (she suspected that there was a lot about his life he wasn't saying), but they were full of details that teased her imagination.

Lina,

Fall comes easy. We live four to a room — Brother Gao, Jian Hua, Cloudy, and me. It won't be that way for long, Brother Gao says. He has relatives coming and we are building a family here in Beijing — one that will expand to other cities so that wherever we go in the future, we will have a home. But for now, it's just the four of us. We work for the restaurant below our quarters, a big canteen-style eatery where Cloudy does the cleaning and the rest of us man the cook stations. My favorite job is roasting the locusts that we skewer and serve daily. You should see them jumping in their bags when they come in from delivery. Sometimes I hold the bag up to my ear to hear them speaking to one another. I imagine them saying their last words. Do you remember the day I showed you the silkworms at the factory? I miss those worms more than I miss my family—is that strange? I wish I could show you everything I see here too. After work, we explore the city. It's full of lights, even late at night. Some parts of the city are so bright, you forget there's even a moon.

I think of your letters often and sometimes when I serve a customer, I like to imagine that it's one of your professors or new friends. I take my pretending so far that I give them free treats— some sticky rice or a small bowl of hong dou soup. My way of sending love to you.

The four of us are lucky that we've got a room together, and it's warm above the kitchens. It might be worth it to stay here through winter. For now, send letters to the address below.

Yours,
Qiang

Was she in love with Qiang? For the other girls at school, the idea of love was tied to marriage in a way that made the whole thing seem as rich and pure as a piece of European chocolate. They could not imagine how confused Lina felt about the matter. None of them had ever been promised to the most eligible boy in her hometown. None of them had ever woken up with the voice of that boy's brother echoing in her head.

Qiang hadn't come back to Suzhou during any of the summers she was home from school. In his letters, he always claimed to be tied up with "business in the north," and Lina knew better than to ask too many questions. Although they had never spoken about it, Qiang knew not to write her at home, and so there were long summer months when they did not exchange any news. But Lina could not separate him from thoughts of summer any more than she could separate summer from the sun, or the lake, or the heat. During school breaks, Lina spent time with her high-school friends and dined at the Zhens' home. Afterward, she went on walks along the river with Wei.

"Lily-face!" Wei called out whenever he saw her. Once, she had worn the flower in her hair and Wei had poked fun at her by saying that it was almost as big as her face. Every now and then he would wrinkle his nose in pretend distaste and claim that the ghost of the lily was still there, that the flower had liked her so much its smell stayed with her always. Wei could be playful, but that didn't hide how serious he was by nature. She had never met someone so grounded and ambitious at the same time. During these summers of courtship, he had spoken about their future together, and she was impressed by the way he had the details of their life planned. He knew how much an apartment would cost in Shanghai. He knew the average salary levels in different cities. And he spoke about the possibility of living and working abroad in concrete terms. There were programs that funded students like him, and loans available. These conversations were in a different league than Qiang's offhand dreams of traveling to Africa and the UK.

While Lina could not quite imagine herself sharing a life with Wei, she felt flattered to be included in the plans of this local celebrity. He spoke about the world as though he could control it the way he did a basketball game with his friends, and that made Lina feel secure with him — so secure that she let him kiss her. Because the summers were long and Lina felt curious about sex, it had gone even further than that. There was some clandestine fumbling in the dark, propelled on her part by, if not lust, then a lust for lust. "Lily-face," Wei whispered into her neck. "You smell even better up close."

In her final year, Lina became more focused on schoolwork. She had registered for English as a second major, which fit her new image of herself as a world citizen. Deng Xiaoping had just opened China's doors to economic trade, and Lina associated the ability to speak English with the ability to walk through those doors. By the time she came across *The Second Sex*, at a bookshop, she was ready to have a hand in the things that would happen to her, to live a life less planned out than her own. After all, *One is not born, but rather becomes, a woman.*

For the first time, Lina considered the possibility that her match with Wei wasn't her best option. Not because she wanted to marry Qiang, but because she wanted time and space to claim these decisions as her own. Even Mao himself had said, "Women hold up half the sky." Before getting married, she wanted at the very least to travel, as Qiang had, and to furnish her inner world with memories to last her the rest of her life. She meant to talk the matter over with her father each trip home, but had always found some excuse to put it off. And then, one day in the spring of her last year at school, she received a letter from home.

Lina,

I wonder if Wei has written you the good news. He applied to the prestigious University of Pennsylvania for graduate studies in mechanical engineering, beginning this fall. Last week, he found out he was accepted with a full scholarship and stipend. The university will be supporting him to live and study in America for the entire length of this program.

Lina's heart lifted—how long would it take to complete a graduate program? Perhaps it would be years before he came back, years when she might be able to travel or stay in Hubei or move to Suzhou to work on her own. She read on.

We have never spoken in any concrete terms about your marriage or future with Zhen Zhiwei. It's time now that we do. Your mother and I feel it would be best for the two of you to marry this summer and for you to move to America with Wei.

His opportunity is perfectly suited to your own studies. Not only is the scholarship enough to support the both of you, but the school offers education to the spouses of grad students. If you go with Wei, it is likely that you also will be able to pursue a master's degree, free of charge. Your education in English will be even more useful to you in America than it would be to you here. If you thrive and build a life there, we will be so happy for your success. If you decide to come back to settle, what you will have gained both in terms of language skills and worldviews will be incomparable to others in your position. These plans are sudden, of course, and we would hate to be separated from you for an indeterminate length of time. But it is also an op-portunity too great to be hoped for. When these sorts of opportunities present themselves, it is not up to us to say no.

Please write Wei your congratulations. We are planning for a July wedding and look forward to your arrival in a few short months.

With love and pride,
Ba

Lina stared at the words. Marriage. America. It shouldn't have come as a surprise, and yet it did.

How could two things that represented such different experiences—one a limitation, the other an adventure—be wrapped up in one? Lina reread the letter and set out to write a response to her father, but the words wouldn't come. She tried to write to Wei instead, as her father had suggested, and while this seemed straightforward enough, she found she couldn't do that either. How could she congratulate him on his scholarship without also addressing their plans for marriage and expressing excitement for it—excitement she didn't feel?

The person she finally wrote to was Qiang, and her note consisted of a single line: *Are you coming home this summer?*

And then, long before she was ready, her time at university was over. Bags packed, hands held and squeezed, and one last walk around the department corridors, the English majors yelling, *Good-bye! Good luck!* to one another in their new Continental accents. It seemed like just yesterday that she'd boarded the train that smelled of grease, sweat, and urine to go to Hubei for the first time. When she climbed aboard that final summer to return to Suzhou, she was already used to the odor, and as the train started to move toward home, she wondered if even this was a thing she'd come to miss.

On the night before her wedding, Lina lay in her childhood bed, staring at the familiar shapes of the branches outside her window. During sleepless moments in her youth, she had watched the shadows of these branches grow or retract, depending on the time of day. With night now thickly upon their village, she could barely make out the tree her father had planted years ago, with its split-neck trunk growing in opposite directions. Summer wasn't nearly over yet, but the humidity had begun to dry up and cool air was already sweeping down the country, working its way through the open window next to her bed.

Lina turned on her side and looked around the room in the dark. During the months when she was at school, her mother had kept her desk and bed covered with a thin floral sheet. Each time she came home for summer break, she unveiled the furniture by flinging the cover off, sending dust particles swirling in the sunlight. As they settled, and as she took in the parts of her room that had been blurred in her memory of home, she would be overcome with memories of her childhood—especially those of the summer by the lake with Qiang before university began.

She liked Wei. She could imagine loving him too, for all the reasons she knew were important, but which she had only been able to appreciate so far in an abstract way—his intelligence, for example, and his determination. Sometimes, at school, she had missed his kind, questioning face. Plus, you didn't say no to America. What if her feelings for Qiang were only temporary? Would she shed them once she left Suzhou, the way she had left her docility behind when she went off to college? There were moments when she wished she could fast-forward through the wedding, their departure from home, and their move to America to arrive at a place where she could belong fully to Wei. If a life with him was to be her fate, she wanted to skip the hard parts.

Except she had seen Qiang. A week ago, she heard from Zhen Hong that his younger son was coming back to town for the wedding, and the next day, there he was, sitting across the dinner table. She couldn't stop her face from turning red and her collar from sticking to the back of her neck. The two said nothing to each other, and when it came time to gan bei, she was even hesitant to touch her glass up against his.

He looked different. His face was angular, more watchful, his skin a shade darker than she'd expected it to be. His letters had made it seem as though he and his friends worked indoors all day at restaurants, retail stores, or warehouses, and their real lives happened at night. That was when they went out to explore the city, but what they did precisely, Lina didn't know. Gambling, she suspected, was the least of it. Qiang had written to her about his business prospects in other cities, but he did not elaborate on what he considered "business." He didn't spend much time describing his present life, and yet he wrote pages and pages about the places he planned to go.

It wasn't just that he looked different; he *was* different. He no longer belonged to their little suburb of Suzhou. He was mannered, for one thing. Deferential. At dinner, he had gone so far as to spoon shrimp into everyone's bowl. From the looks on the Zhens' faces, Lina wasn't the only one surprised by his behavior. After four years, it was Qiang who seemed like the newest addition to the Zhen family home, not her.

Lina sighed and got up from her bed. Barefoot, she crossed the room and walked down the hall, feeling the coolness of the dirt floors against her feet. She had intended just to walk to her parents' bedroom and stand outside their door for a moment, thinking their proximity would calm her. But as she passed the kitchen, Lina happened to turn her head. She almost jumped.

In the dark was a cloudlike apparition; at first, she thought it was a ghost. And then she smelled the cigarette smoke. She moved closer to the window until she could see where it was coming from. Just outside the kitchen door, Qiang was sitting with his back to the house. He hadn't seen her looking, and Lina took the chance to study the changes in his face that she had been able only to catch glimpses of during dinner. His jawline had grown sharper. Viewing him in profile, she saw his nose had acquired a small bump halfway down the bone. Five or six cigarette butts were littered by his feet, which meant he'd been sitting there for some time.

Lina left the window and moved toward the door. Qiang must have heard her approach the moment before she opened it, because he was no longer on the steps.

"You scared me," he said, stepping out of the shadows.

She shut the door behind her.

"What are you doing here?"

"I guess I—I came to say good-bye," he said.

But if he had come to say good-bye to her, he would have come to her window. *He's not here to say good-bye to me*, she realized. He was here to say good-bye to this stoop, the place where they'd had their first conversation.

"I'm not going anywhere yet," Lina said.

"Yes, but it feels like I'm giving you up."

Lina's chest tightened as she looked at him. The face he had grown into was unfamiliar and somehow more familiar—as if deep down, she'd always known this was the face he was meant to have.

"You never said anything before."

Qiang bowed his head and rested both hands on his hips, looking down at the ground. He kicked the butt of a cigarette with his foot. This was as close as they had ever come to admitting that their feelings for each other went beyond friendship.

"What good would it have done? I know what you're going to say—" He stopped Lina before she could respond. "What good does it do now to say it? But you knew, right?"

The look he gave her was pleading, almost desperate. If she told him yes, she would be admitting responsibility too. If, years from now, she was still unable to forget him, it would be her fault just as much as it was his that things had not worked out. But wouldn't it have been her fault in any case? She did not want to give him an answer.

"I'm not a match for you," he said, resigned.

"Then why are you here?"

"Because," he said, "when I saw you yesterday—when you came to our house, I looked at the way the two of you sat next to each other, and for the first time I thought, *Maybe he's not a match for her either*."

If Qiang could see it too, it must be true. Just like that, Lina's last bit of hope for falling in love with Wei disappeared.

"Is he?" Qiang asked when she didn't respond.

"My father thinks so."

She almost cringed as she said it. Deferring to the opinion of her father? It was as though she had not changed at all during those four years away at college. *One is not born, but rather becomes . . .* She couldn't even finish the sentence in her head.

"I have prepared for this marriage my entire life, and it still feels too soon," Lina said.

His eyes were still, his mouth ajar. She wanted to touch him — to lay a hand on his, just once, in a way that wasn't sisterlike. His nose was running, and he used the back of his hand to wipe the snot away. When the hand came back down to rest by his side, she took it. They looked at each other for the thin edge of a second. And then they kissed.

It was soft, and sweeter than she'd thought it would be. It lifted the tension in her heart and sent it coursing through her blood to the outermost reaches of her body. It was the warmest feeling she had ever had. When it was over, she pressed her head into his neck, and he wrapped his arms around her shoulders. A lifetime passed. No time passed at all. The minutes bloomed like a flower, closed back up into a fist. She knew then that it was love, because what else could have such a multiplying effect? The whole world had opened up around them in duplicate. She felt the breeze on her shins, but the rest of her was numb with pleasure, and she wondered if she was standing up by herself or if he was holding her upright.

"Well?" she whispered. "Aren't you going to ask me not to marry him?"

Qiang pulled back from her, and she felt her weight shift back onto her feet. He opened his mouth to speak, but nothing came out. And that's when she knew something was wrong. He wasn't trying to come up with his answer. He knew his answer. He was just putting off saying what he needed to say.

"No," Qiang said. "Because even if you don't marry Wei, our parents will never let you marry me."

"But what about what I want? I have a say in this."

"Tell me the truth. Would you be happy with me?"

"Yes," she said. With that one word, she felt relief flow from his body into hers. He closed his eyes for a moment and then opened them again, as if to make sure she really was there.

"If that's the case, will you come with me?"

"Come where?" Lina asked, but she knew that he meant *everywhere*. He was inviting her to join him and the rest of his ragtag family in their nomadic lifestyle. She remembered the sights he'd described in his letters to her and pictured herself writing the same kinds of letters back to her family. She remembered his promise of traveling with her and Wei one day. *We'll go to Africa. And Spain, and America.* Maybe they could still travel together, but at the end of the night, instead of returning to Wei's bed, she would return to Qiang's.

"Yes," Lina said.

They stood smiling at each other, astonished at the possibility of this: a revision of the ways they'd thought their lives might happen.

"Then that's what we'll do. We'll run away and not tell anyone. I'll talk to Brother Gao about—"

"Wait a minute," Lina said. "No. I could never do that to my parents."

Qiang stepped back from her. "But that's the only way! We'll come back in a few years, and by then there will be nothing they can do about it. They'll have to recognize us as married."

She shook her head. "You're not making sense."

"You'll be safe, I promise—if that's what you're worried about. I don't have any business in the darker end of things. I don't fight anymore. I promise you—"

"Stop, please. If we do this, we have to do it my way. I can't go with you without my parents' consent. This isn't like sneaking off in the middle of the night and coming home before morning. Just let me talk to them. I can change their minds."

"No," Qiang said. "That's not going to work."

"Qiang." Lina started to laugh. "Listen to you! Sometimes I wonder how someone so smart…think about it. Running off with me and not telling your parents—could you do that to them? To your brother? You plan to take me with you and leave them behind? Provide for me and not for them in their old age? What kind of son would you be then?"

Qiang pressed his lips together and looked down at his feet, away from her. That's when she remembered that this man was not anything like Zhen Zhiwei. He was not a person whose strengths lay in planning ahead. Lina was asking a lot from someone who lived according to no strict schedule, who wanted to go where the next gust of inspiration took him. In a moment, he could change his mind. She took his face in both her hands and made him look at her. "We'll be okay," she said. "The hard part will be over once you tell your parents and I tell mine. I'm going to talk to my dad first thing in the morning, and you have to do the same. Hao ma?"

He stared at her, the whites of his eyes shining blue against the lightening sky. He looked terrified.

"It's the only way," she said.

Finally, she felt his head move—a nod. She kissed him one more time, and then let go. She turned to go back into the house.

When the door was shut behind her, she leaned up against the wood, breathing in deeply. She thought, *I want to remember this moment. The touch of it, the smell of it. This is the moment when the rest of my life is about to start.* Finally, she moved to the window again to see if he had gone and found he hadn't. He was still standing there, looking toward the door she'd shut.

16

By the time Wei woke up, Lina was already out of bed. In her place was a towel still damp from freshly washed hair. On the floor, a tangle of tops and skirts that had been considered and tossed aside. He heard her voice on the phone in the next room; it held the breezy tone she used when she was not in the mood to talk but did not want to be rude. "No, not yet, Susan...Yes, not bad...We're doing the Expo today. I'm not sure when, but you'll see me soon enough...All right. Tell them I said hi."

She came back into the room and closed the door. "You're up," she said, seeing Wei. "Sorry, did I wake you?"

She had been out with Qiang when Wei got home the previous evening. He'd been ready to make up with her, but she didn't get in bed with him until midnight. By then he was too tired to attempt the delicate act of apology. He was surprised, now, to hear her speak to him as though the argument had never happened.

"Was that Susan?" he asked.

"Yes. *Tian a*, that woman drives me insane. You know she's only calling because she's bored. She seems to think everyone else's life's purpose is to keep her entertained."

Wei sat up and reached for his glasses. "If you want to spend time with your friends, I'm sure Qiang won't mind being left alone for an afternoon."

Lina walked over to the window to part the curtains. "Please. I hate that woman. I put up with her because I like the others. I'm sure she feels the same way about me."

"No," Wei said, reaching for her. "They're probably a sad bunch down there without you. Probably ran out of things to talk about." He caught her around the thighs and tried to pull her onto his lap but found he had overestimated the extent to which he'd been forgiven. Lina twisted away. "Don't wrinkle," she said, adjusting her blouse. "I just ironed."

Well, that was all right. He would spend the day making things right with her. He would even do his best to smooth things over with his brother, whom he still did not trust but whom he knew he must welcome into their lives—for both Lina's sake and his own.

The five of them, ready for breakfast and waiting for the elevator, were dressed as though they were heading in five different directions. Sunny was the only one who looked prepared for the Expo. Beneath her plastic sun visor, her face was ghosted with sunscreen. She carried a backpack that had a bottle of water in every side pocket, and her body tilted forward against its weight. Karen looked as though she were on the way to a rock concert, her face obscured by turquoise cat's-eye sunglasses. The hem of her frayed tank top just barely grazed the tops of her shorts. Wei, out of weekend habit, had put on a golfing polo, and Lina was dressed as if for a fancy brunch. Qiang was wearing the same jeans and T-shirt he'd worn the day before. Despite the contrast in their attire, Wei noticed a similarity between his brother and wife. They both had the spent, airy quality of people who had enjoyed themselves too much the night before. People who had the luxury to linger for hours in front of the TV, a bag of sunflower seeds split between them. Why hadn't he seen it before? Qiang and Lina were both entitled and had never doubted for a moment they'd be taken care of. They were the kinds of people who blamed others for the things that went wrong in their own lives. He envied them that; he had always been the opposite sort, the type to believe that he was personally responsible for everything.

In search of solidarity, Wei laid his hand on Karen's shoulder. She raised her glasses to look up at him, grazing his stomach with the back of her head. He loved her best like this, when her thoughts and actions still carried the weight of sleep. When afternoon came, there was music and makeup and sometimes she'd come tearing in and out of his study like a wild raccoon. Wei smoothed the hair on the top of Karen's head. It had long ago lost its baby softness. Each time Wei picked up her ponytail, he felt surprised by its thickness and weight. This was her mother's hair. How could such a thin neck hold it up? It made Wei want to hit the brakes on life. Hair like that—it demanded a kind of responsibility he wasn't ready to let his daughter have.

Wei suspected that he wasn't parenting correctly, but the thought of figuring out the correct method was too overwhelming. It made him feel the way he did every time he read the news—helpless in the face of things that were moving too fast for him to understand, let alone react to. Sometimes he felt as though she were the one managing him— "managing up," as they called it at work. When someone lower on the totem pole did this, it was a good thing, a sign of ambition and competence. At home, it was probably something closer to manipulation. But he liked being watched by his daughter like this. Parents around the world studied their children for potential, teased out their talents, patched up the weak spots in their minds and souls, compared them to their peers. Did children evaluate their parents like this—not for potential, but for achievements? Unlike the previous generations, whose collective growth had been stunted by the Japanese occupation and the civil war, the members of his generation had left China for *education*, not for gold or railroad jobs or other false promises of wealth. Chinese nationals of his age could claim that they had done it on their own, and there was so much to come. They were still at the peaks of their lives.

"Dad," Karen said sweetly as the elevator dinged open, "you have white hairs growing in your nose."

"Hush," Wei said, and he nudged her inside.

They had only just sat down to breakfast when Wei's phone rang.

"Hey," he said uncertainly, stepping away from their table. Chris never called when Wei took the day off unless he had to. The idea that he could not handle any given situation by himself was a hit to the man's pride.

"Hey. Rumi just pulled out."

"Pulled out of what?"

"The show. They were supposed to be the sponsor for the *Pitch* challenge this week but they sent me an e-mail saying they don't want to be on the show."

Wei felt his scattered thoughts align like iron filings around a magnet.

"What? Why?"

To be featured was free publicity. Rumi Electronics was one of Medora's biggest Asian clients, and no client had ever turned down free publicity before.

"They didn't say. It could be nothing, but I thought you should know. Plus, well…the film crew is coming in a few hours and we don't have anything to shoot."

Chris was not going to ask him straight out to come in — it was implied. If the show didn't have a sponsor, Wei would have to call in a favor somewhere. And knowing the show's director, there would be several other questions that would need to be answered before the day's filming could continue.

"We could cancel," Chris said. "Or I could try to figure something else out."

"No," Wei said. "Let me think about what to do on the way over."

As he hung up, his brain branched off to work on three problems at once: how to handle the precarious relationship with Rumi Electronics, whether there were any other clients he could talk into being on the show on short notice, and how he would break the news to Lina that he had to go to work.

"Listen," he said once he returned to the breakfast table. "I'm going to need to meet you at the Expo. I just have to stop by the office first."

Lina set her spoon down, but her face did not seem to register his words.

"One of our sponsors just dropped out," Wei explained. "They're filming today without a concept for the episode."

Karen sat up. "They're filming today?"

"This is Qiang's last weekend," Lina said. "He's leaving on Monday."

"I know, but there's nothing I can do about it."

He could tell by her silence—the way she let his last words linger, that admission of impotence—that she knew he was telling the truth but that she was still going to punish him for it.

"It's all right, Lina," Qiang said.

"I'll try to make it later in the day," Wei said. "If I can finish up this afternoon, I'll meet you all before dinner."

But Lina had decided the conversation was over and returned to her poached egg. She cut a divot into its side, speared the freed piece of egg white with her fork, and pressed the flat edge of her knife against the rest of the egg so that the yolk bled free. All five of them watched as it flooded her plate.

"Well," Karen said suddenly. "If Dad doesn't have to go, I shouldn't have to go." She pursed her lips, behind which lurked a smile.

"You're going," said Wei and Lina at the same time.

"Why?"

"Because it's important," Wei said.

"Why?"

He wanted to make a point about national pride, about progress, about China finally being the country that all the others looked to as a land of wealth and opportunity. Tell her that this was their chance to play host, to show off and celebrate their heritage by putting on the grandest pavilion of all the sixty-some pavilions at this year's World's Fair. But he also knew that saying these things would not help his case with Lina.

"Don't you want to see the Italian pavilion?" he asked instead. "I heard they have a Prada handbag exhibit."

"And I've heard the Spain pavilion has a thirty-foot robot baby that talks and moves like a real one," Sunny put in.

Wei felt a pang of sadness for Sunny. Of course she was eager to go. She had probably already told her friends and family that she would be attending the World Expo. He'd read in the news that there were some folks from the countryside who had spent their life savings on a trip to Shanghai to attend the event.

"See?" Lina said. "Even Ayi wants to go."

Karen groaned and slid down in her seat until half of her body was hidden beneath the table. "What do I want to see a baby for? I've already been to Italy, and Prada's right down the street. It's too hot outside. I want to go to work with you."

She blinked at Wei and widened her eyes. *Managing up,* he thought again. He couldn't bring himself to look at Lina.

"Fine," Lina said finally. "Stay home. Or go with Dad, whatever. Come on, Qiang, let's go. The driver's waiting."

She gathered her purse and stood, her breakfast uneaten. There was a moment of silence while Qiang finished spooning yogurt into his mouth. Then he rose too and cleared his throat.

"See you later," he said, and the two of them left the booth.

Wei was prepared for the derailed TV episode to have caused a commotion in his office. But he was not prepared for the commotion to have spilled out into the lobby. The usual polish and serenity of Plaza 66 was lost to the chattering of the contestants loitering in the reception area. A white backdrop had been set up, as had the umbrella reflectors, but most of the film crew were gathered along the windows, flirting with makeup artists.

"Hi," Chris said, appearing from behind Wei. He sounded more relaxed than he had on the phone. "We had nothing else to do, so we're shooting publicity photos down here. Dash wanted natural light. I think the lobby people are about to kick us out."

"Hi!" Karen stepped in front of Wei and extended her hand. "Chris, right? I know your name from the e-mails — Dad always has them open on his computer. I liked your vacation pictures. Are you on the show too?"

"Ah..." Chris took her hand limply.

"Chris, this is my daughter, Karen. And this is our ayi, Sunny. Did you get my e-mail? Did the abstract make sense?"

"Yeah," Chris said. "I found a couple of junior copywriters hanging around with nothing to do so I gave it to them. They're coming up with a new script."

"Good, good."

"Dad!" Karen pointed behind him. "That guy looks just like you. I've seen him on the show but in person he's even more like you. Can I get a picture with him?"

"Can you get a — " Wei turned to see his on-screen self standing several meters away in front of the plaza's glass elevators. But before Wei could answer, Dash appeared next to him.

"Boss Zhen!" His bleached hair was gel-free today and swept across his forehead in feathery wisps. "Is this your little girl?"

He turned to Karen and smiled down at her. "Hello, beauty, I'm called Dash."

"Dash is the show's director," Wei explained.

As quickly as she'd decided she liked Chris, Karen assessed Dash's blond hair, Chinese face, and Man U jersey and shrank from him. "Can I get a picture with the guy who plays my dad?"

"Listen to that American English!" Dash laughed. "I should cast her in something. Would you like to be on TV?"

Now he had her attention. "For what?"

"For what?" he imitated, rounding out the r like an American. "There are lots of things. Lots of possibilities for American-born Chinese. Stand over there, beauty, let me think about it. I've got to talk to your dad." Karen backed away and wandered over to Sunny.

"She's got your eyes, Boss," Dash said. "Great kid. Look, I know you said you wanted limited involvement in the show, but there are some thematic matters only us foreigners understand, eh? I want to go over today's concept before we begin. There are some things I have in mind…"

Wei had always been proud of the fact that once he set his mind to something, focus came naturally. It was only a matter of clicking into gear. Once he did that, the rest was easy—the conferences, the reports, the snap decisions and sudden inspirations. He moved through sales meetings like he was playing the lead role in a campy musical, each number a song and dance designed to support the narrative he had prepared for his clients. But today, he couldn't turn down noise the way he was usually able to. Beneath Dash's chatter and Chris's questions, he heard Lina's voice from their fight the night before. *You like to pretend that everything you do is for us,* she had said.

When the commotion finally subsided and filming began, Wei shut himself in his office. He stood before the window and peered down at Nanjing West Road, not seeing the people, only the road and the buildings beyond. It had never crossed his mind, who he was doing it *for*. He had to admit that he derived pleasure from solving little emergencies like the one he'd faced today. But he also knew that it was just another way of doing what he'd been doing since high school—performing exercises to test his power and potential. But he was a grown man; it was a little late for potential.

As a poster boy for the Communist Party, his father had never entertained the idea of working for the individual; it was always for the country. He believed that to truly promote hard work, equality, and stability, it was best to take individual gain out of the equation. But on the day Wei had gotten the Penn fellowship, his father had taken him by the shoulders and said, laughing, "Wo ye jiu shi ge nongmin." *I am just a farmer.* It was the only time Wei had ever heard him speak modestly about the power of the proletariat. It was also the only time Wei had ever heard his father speak of himself in connection to Wei's achievements, and that was how he knew Zhen Hong was prouder than he'd ever been. He understood his father's words to mean *If even I can raise a son like you, a son invited to study abroad, what can't our country accomplish?* For the son of a farmer to succeed academically was a win for the common man; for him to be invited to study mechanical engineering in America was also a win for China. He could still remember the words his father made him recite from Mao's Little Red Book, an address to China's youth: *The world is yours, as well as ours, but in the last analysis, it is yours. You young people, full of vigor and vitality, are in the bloom of life, like the sun at eight or nine in the morning. Our hope is placed on you.*

America! The ultimate symbol of wealth and achievement. Back then, some of the older cadres were still skeptical of Western education, afraid that their children would come home infected with capitalist and imperialist thoughts, but most parents in the country wished their own children would have a chance to go abroad. What would they have said if they'd known that in fifteen years, China would be the biggest foreign holder of U.S. Treasury bonds? And how could Wei have known just how powerful America's pull really was? He would graduate and get a job and have a child and not go home — not once — before the call came, ten years later, notifying them of their parents' deaths. He was thirty-two years old; those ten years were almost a third of his life. Ten years of his relationship with his parents carried out on an international calling plan.

He hadn't always wanted to leave China. Once, Wei had just wanted to do something that mattered for humanity — build planes, maybe, or work in astronautics. Take China to the moon and back with better technology than the Americans and the Russians had. He imagined that his life's work would be to reach other planets. That would have been something his father would have considered progress. What had Wei done instead with his fancy degree? He had handed out some jobs. Created a reality-TV show. Helped bring American industry to China, which wasn't much of a contribution if you considered how much the U.S. made off Chinese buying power. Qiang was right. He had spent the past two years studying Chinese herd mentality in the marketplace, its susceptibility to established Western brands, and then he'd gone ahead and placed companies like Nike, Coach, and KFC leagues ahead of every domestic competitor. Deep down, Wei wondered if his homecoming wasn't a way of paying his respects to his mother country, as he had wanted it to be, but an act of betrayal. Had he turned into the imperialist the old revolutionaries had feared their children would become?

In leaving home, Wei felt as though he had acquired a debt. He felt he owed the country something, and he wasn't sure how to repay it. The China he'd found upon his return was not the same one that he had left. Economic reform over the past few years had been successful, but Wei feared that China was getting too rich too fast and that the new policies had set the country up for volatility. There were underground blogs where people were being vocal about the government, but Wei didn't know where to find them. The only way he knew to get real, uncensored news and opinions was to jump the Chinese firewall by switching on a VPN that was routed to a server in the States. But the thought of stealing Internet from America in order to understand what was happening in China made him feel even more like an outsider.

Instead, he found himself scrolling through ChinaSmack, an English-language website featuring news stories that showed the frightening psyche of modern China without pointing any fingers at the government. In those thin morning hours when he couldn't sleep, Wei read article after article: "A Beggar That Netizens Named Brother Sharp Becomes Internet Fashion Sensation." "Foxconn Employees Jump Off Buildings to Protest Low Pay." "Microsoft China's President Discovered to Have Faked His Diploma." "Man Sells Kidney to Buy iPhone." "Boyfriend Commits Suicide After a Six-Hour Shopping Trip by Jumping Off Fourth Floor of a Mall." "Man Sues Wife for Lying About Having Had Plastic Surgery."

Who were these people, and what had the years done to them? Had the moral fabric of their nation been so eroded by political upheaval that it had simply ceased to exist? Wei studied the lao bai xing captured in the background of these pictures, onlookers who could have been his uncles or cousins or aunts. It was still only a small percentage of the population that had money to spare, but still—lao bai xing could be rich now too. If he held the right property, for instance, an ex-farmer could wear fur and eat three-hundred-yuan softshell crabs and buy a Porsche with Swarovski crystals embedded around the logo. Some of the more educated types could go abroad and buy property in San Francisco and New York City. They could send their kids to NYU, to Berkeley, to the University of Michigan, and this younger generation would live in luxury apartments, walk to classes wearing designer backpacks, and have thousands a month in the bank for expenses.

This was not a nation that had lived up to its promise. His father would have wanted better for them all. The nation was finally getting its turn. The yuan was growing. The whole world was watching China as it turned into the powerhouse it had always had the potential to be. "Meet the Middle Class," one of the website's headlines read, and there they were: a group of thirty-somethings standing in line for the new iPhone. Hundreds of people held captive by their portable screens. The few that faced the camera did so with uncertainty, as though somewhere in their past, they had inflicted damage they could neither name nor quite forget.

• • •

The sky had grown dark. Wei knew without having to check the time that it was too late to join Lina and Qiang for dinner, and although failing to show up would mean another mark against him, he felt relieved. Most of his employees had left for the day. It occurred to him that he hadn't eaten lunch; in Conference Room South, someone had ordered food, and a few empty Styrofoam boxes lay open, out of view of the cameras. When he stepped farther into the room, he found Karen and Sunny huddled in the corner, asleep. "Time to go," he said softly. Karen opened her eyes and raised her head from Sunny's shoulder. As he extended a hand to lift her, he noticed that her cheeks were an unnatural shade of pink. Was she ill? Had he left them alone for too long? Just as he pressed his hand to her forehead, Sunny woke too, and he saw that her cheeks matched Karen's in color. They were fine; they had only gotten into the makeup artist's cosmetics.

It was nearing nine o'clock when they arrived home, so Sunny cooked a quick meal she knew how to make with the limited ingredients in the refrigerator: noodle soup with tomatoes, egg, ground pork, and cilantro. But when Sunny placed it in front of Karen, she complained of a stomachache and went to lie down in her room. Sunny was about to remove the bowl from the table when Wei stopped her.

"What are you planning on eating?" he asked.

"The same thing as you, Boss," she said.

"Well, why don't you sit down?"

Sunny hesitated but then untied her apron, draped it over the back of the dining chair, and sat across from him. Wei watched her dress her soup with the condiments sitting on the table between them — sesame oil, chili flakes, and soy sauce.

"You like it spicy," he said. "Almost as spicy as I do."

She nodded.

"How come you don't cook any spicy dishes?"

"Taitai says Karen has a weak stomach."

The woman had a talent for ending conversations quickly without being impolite. She was private, to say the least. That morning when she'd tried to convince Karen to go to the Expo was the only time Wei had ever seen her betray emotion.

"I didn't mean to keep you so late. If I had known Karen wasn't going to eat, I would have just picked up something quick for myself. Or we could have gone out — "

"It's no problem," Sunny said. "She'll be hungry later. It will be good to have something in the house."

"A shame about the Expo," Wei said. "We still have those tickets. Maybe later in the month we'll find a time for the three of us to go."

She reddened. "Too many people there on Friday anyway."

Had he embarrassed her by showing that he knew how much she wanted to see it? It was hard to tell when she refused to look him in the eye.

"How do you like it here with us? Are you comfortable?"

"Yes," she said. "It's better than I thought it would be." Then she shook her head quickly. "I mean the work as an ayi in general. Not working for you."

"You've never worked as an ayi before?"

"No."

"Why not? You're good at it."

"I'm good at housekeeping too."

The confidence with which she said this surprised them both. Boss Zhen was impressed. Few young women in China claimed their own worth so readily. Part of what Lina and Karen liked about Sunny was that they could relax around her, but she had the opposite effect on Wei. He felt he had to rise to the occasion, and that was because she was a fellow perfectionist, someone used to holding herself to a higher standard than those around her did. He felt the need to win her respect.

Outside the elevator that morning, he had thought Lina and Qiang entitled. But wasn't he just as guilty of that? Here was a woman with so much potential, one whose capabilities outstripped her circumstances by a long mile. Compared to her, Wei had had every opportunity, and yet he'd never known what it meant to be satisfied, to curb his expectations. He didn't know how it felt not to always think he deserved more.

"What do your parents do?"

"They farm a little. Sell produce."

"Xin ku a. That's a lot for older folks to manage."

"They do all right. I've got uncles who are out working too. My parents will retire soon."

It struck him that she'd known his family for years now, but he'd had no information about her background until tonight.

"Do you have any family here?"

"No. That's the main reason I send so much of it home. It's just me, so I live simply. Most of the money I save up, I use for taking trips back."

"Your parents are lucky to have you. Not all children think that way."

"Most do."

Was that true? Did Chinese youth have such small imaginations? Or was it that they were not as coldhearted as he was?

"After moving to America, I let ten years go by before I came back to visit," Wei said. "And when I did, it was only because there'd been a train accident. Both my parents and Lina's died very suddenly."

He hadn't planned to tell her this, and yet it felt imperative that this woman—this relative stranger—know exactly what kind of person he was.

She stared at him. "That's horrible," she finally said.

"I know. I bet you can't even imagine not seeing your family for ten years."

"I meant the accident," Sunny said. "I'm sure your parents understood how hard it was for you to travel back."

Who knew how much longer he would have stayed away if the accident hadn't happened? At first they'd put it off because they had loans to pay, and then it was because Wei had gotten busy with work. He had told himself that waiting meant saving more money to send to his parents. He liked the idea of them receiving a big wad of cash and thinking how successful their son had become in America. But if he was honest with himself, the money stood for more than his pride. The more he made, the easier he'd be able to justify his career switch from engineering to marketing. *This is what I sent you to America for?* he could almost hear his father saying. *To do work you can barely explain?*

Wei was no better, no less selfish or cowardly, than Qiang had been, and ultimately their parents had died with neither son by their side.

He shook his head. "All I meant to say was that your parents are lucky to have you."

Sunny laughed uneasily. "I don't think they feel that way."

"Why not?"

"Because I'm not normal."

He waited for her to go on.

"I don't want what other women want. I don't want to get married, I don't want to have a baby. Really, I should have been a son." She made a clucking noise with her mouth and shook her head. "I'm the firstborn, you know. They wanted their first child to be a son. And I've done everything a good son would have done—gone out, made money—except I'm not male. Isn't that funny?"

"You don't want to have kids?" Wei asked. The moment Sunny's face changed, Wei knew he had said the wrong thing. He worried that she would clam up again, but it seemed some long-held grievance had broken loose inside her.

"My cousin was pregnant a few years ago. Everyone was pleased when we found out. Her husband's family had all these superstitions around the birth. They chose the luckiest name, looked up the luckiest day to have the baby. That day turned out to be ten days before the baby was supposed to be due. The next suitable day was a month after that. So they wanted to take the baby out early, under the knife."

"A cesarean," Wei said.

"Yes. My cousin was terrified. We were all terrified. I couldn't imagine what a procedure like that would be like. Later, I found out that the doctor had asked for a hundred yuan extra for anesthesia, and she didn't have the money. She didn't want to ask her in-laws for it. My mother wanted to give it to her, but our family couldn't come up with it fast enough. So we put her under the knife with nothing but a washcloth between her teeth. She had a fever for three days afterward."

The horror Wei felt must have been clear on his face, because Sunny didn't finish the story.

"Now my sister is pregnant and I'm supposed to be happy for her. We have more money than my cousin's family did, but still. My mother says it's silly to be nervous about it. Giving birth is a natural thing for a woman to experience. I guess she's right, but it isn't just giving birth that makes me scared to stay. It will always feel too small for me to be in that town. I can't help feeling that I got lucky by never getting pregnant. I don't want to bring a child up in a world with those kinds of old rules. I had an opportunity. So I came here."

Sunny looked to be about thirty—her parents must be around fifty, Wei guessed. They were younger than his own parents would have been, and yet their beliefs—or the beliefs their community shared—were more backward than he'd expected.

"Do you like it here?" he asked. "Is it better?"

"It's better because I can make more of my own choices," she said. "But that's about the only thing better about it." The rims of her eyes had reddened, and she sniffed fiercely.

He didn't know what else to say. He wanted to erase the pain on this woman's face, but he didn't understand it enough to even try. If Lina were here, she would know what to do. How presumptuous he'd been to think he understood Sunny, to feel they had something in common.

The broth in Wei's soup had gone cold, but he wasn't hungry anyway. He dropped his napkin on the table and sighed.

"Let me warm that up for you," Sunny said.

"I meant to tell you earlier, there are always people at my office asking for referrals for good ayis. Why don't you leave your number with me? I'll pass it along. Just to make sure you have something…long term."

Sunny sat back in her seat. "Taitai has already offered to help me find another family to work for once this summer is over—"

But Wei was determined. "Hold on. Let me get something to write with."

He was grateful for the chance to escape to his study, which he entered without turning on the lamp. In the moonlight, Wei found paper and pen. Just as he was about to leave, he noticed the envelope full of cash Lina had set aside for Sunny's first week of work. Lina had been planning to give it to her on Sunday, but Wei decided on the spot to pay her early.

Wei came into the dining room just as Sunny did, carrying his reheated bowl of soup. She set it on the table and wiped her hands on her apron before accepting the money, pen, and paper. "Thank you," she said, and she wrote down her phone number in large, blocky print. Then she handed the paper to him and folded her hands in her lap.

"Let me call Little Cao to take you home," he said, seeing that she had finished her food.

"That's all right. I've got my motorbike."

"It's late. Leave it here. I'll tell him to pick you up tomorrow morning too."

Sunny rose again and started to clear the table, but Wei waved her off. "Please. I'll take care of it. See you tomorrow."

Finally, the woman nodded and collected her things. Then she was gone, and Wei was left with the rest of the night before him.

17

Lina had chosen to wear a silk blouse dyed cherry-tangerine, a color so rich that it made the fabric look textureless. It was cut to the length of a tunic but designed to fit like the top half of a traditional qipao. The Hong Kong clothier Shanghai Tang made modern takes on Chinese classics, and that was just how Lina wanted to be seen, modern but classic, as she stood with one hand held across her brow, taking in the expanse of the Expo grounds.

It wasn't until she leaned over the railing of the Expo's raised entranceway that she stopped picturing herself and started seeing the crowd. There were thousands of people below—shuttle buses driving off to pavilions beyond view, elderly visitors wearing visors in wheelchairs, and children holding spray bottles topped with spinning Styrofoam fans. Beside Lina, Qiang opened his map and laid it against the railing so they could trace a route. "Are we starting with the UK pavilion?"

"If that's the one you want to see the most, then yes, we should go there first."

The absence of the rest of the family never felt so significant as when they were in a throng of strangers. It felt as though there was nothing preventing them from being carried off by the crowd, from choosing to become strangers themselves. Lina watched sweat collect at Qiang's temple and slip down around the back of his ear.

When it became clear that neither Wei nor Karen was coming to the Expo, Lina knew that she could make no excuses—today was the day she would have the conversation with Qiang. Qiang, too, seemed to sense that something was coming to a head, and this mutual knowledge made them shy around each other. More than once that morning, he'd averted his eyes as soon as she caught him looking over at her.

Lina wished he would help her out a little. She wished he could overcome whatever fear or guilt Wei had instilled in him that first night on the balcony and remember that he had an obligation to her too. All those years ago, he had let his loyalty to Wei determine the course of the rest of their lives. Though he'd come all this way to finally reconnect with her, he seemed in danger of repeating the same mistake again.

As they boarded a crowded shuttle bus headed in the direction of the UK pavilion, Lina found herself pushed up against him. At close range, he had the sweet, peppery smell of scallions snapped at their roots. At even closer range, he smelled like Wei. The familiarity of this caught Lina off guard, and she tried to back away, but there was no space to back into; for a moment, they struggled against each other. He maneuvered his arm around her head so that he could grasp the overhead handle, and in this new position, Lina found herself staring into the face of his watch. Where had he gotten such a thing, and why did it excite her so much to wonder about it?

"So many goddamn people. Fan si le," Qiang muttered. She could hear the damage that cigarettes had done to his vocal cords over the years. Each time the bus made a turn, it took all her focus to swing her weight the other way.

As the bus picked up speed, their attention turned to the pavilions outside: Lithuania, Spain, Poland, Turkey, Namibia. They varied in shape, size, color, and materials. Some resembled museums, others adventure-park rides, others transportation hubs or UFOs. Lina thought back to that day by the lake when Qiang predicted that they would travel together. *We'll go to Africa. And Spain, and America. You know where I want to go most? The United Kingdom. I want to touch the queen's hat. Wouldn't that be funny?* Who could have imagined that they would find themselves touring the world like this? She almost laughed aloud. It was ridiculous but true; they were acting out the life they would have had together in the simulacrum of the Expo grounds.

At their destination, they stepped out into the unobstructed glare of the morning. The sun felt so loud, it stood in for conversation. They walked down the newly paved pedestrian pathways and soon arrived at the UK pavilion, a structure so gray and spiked that it looked like a porcupine stuffed into a box. The Seed Cathedral, it was called. Each spike was a fiber-optic rod that jutted out from the center and moved in the wind; the combined effect was of a dandelion gone to seed. The rods housed different species of seeds at their interior ends, representing the United Kingdom's commitment to the environment.

"I don't see the end of the queue," Qiang said. "Do you?"

A line of people wrapped around the side of the pavilion and continued past the Polish exhibit, then disappeared down another roadway in the opposite direction of where they had come.

"*Tian a.* Let's go up front and ask them how long the wait will be."

At the pavilion entrance was a scrawny Chinese youth wearing a white UK Pav polo, a headset, and a battery pack clipped to his waist.

"Excuse me, how long is the wait at this point?" Lina asked.

"About four or five hours," he said.

"Four or five—how can that be? How is anyone supposed to see more than one exhibit if they all have a four- or five-hour wait time?"

"They aren't all this long," he said, squaring his shoulders and lifting his head proudly. "The UK pavilion is popular. We've been interviewed by CCTV five separate times. I think that's the most of any pavilion."

"Look," Lina said in a low voice, trying for flattery. "You're the guy at the front, so I'm guessing you're the one in charge. We're willing to make it worth your while." She opened her purse.

"No, no, I can't do that." He eyed her bag nervously.

"One thousand yuan," Lina said, but the attendant pretended not to hear. He was looking around to be sure no one else had seen her gesture.

"Come on, Lina, let's go." Qiang pulled on her arm, but she held her ground.

"What do you say, young man?"

Still, he didn't look her in the eye. Finally, he wiped his brow and muscled some brightness into his tone. "At the Polish exhibit the wait is only two or three hours!"

"That was a good effort," Qiang said as he led Lina away. "But it was never going to work. You can't ask the guy in front. They put him there for two reasons. One, he speaks the best English. That means his parents are rich enough to send him to a good school and get him tutoring. Two, he doesn't take bribes."

They had started back toward the bus stop, but Qiang now motioned for her to follow him around to the far side of the pavilion. The Seed Cathedral had a rear door that opened onto a raised platform where visitors stopped for a final photo. Viewed from just the right angle, the pattern of the Union Jack could be seen in the fiber-optic rods. Past this, the guests exited through a ramp that led back into the park.

"We want someone with low responsibility," said Qiang. "Someone who got this job because a family member knew someone, not because he did well on the interview." He nodded toward one of the staff members stationed at the corner of the raised platform, a man about twenty years of age. He was pudgier than the first, and his hair was cut in the style of a J-rocker. His head was lowered, so his eyes were covered by his bangs. This, they discovered as they came closer, was because he was looking at the cell phone he held surreptitiously at thigh height.

"Him."

The word sent a thrill through Lina's neck and arms, igniting a part of her that had been dormant for years—the need for something to *happen*. When she approached, the young man looked up right away. He knew immediately what she was after. They had exchanged barely a few words before he agreed to the thousand-yuan price—half now, half later.

"I can only do it when we're close to closing," he said. "Meet me here at ten thirty. You'll have only half an hour, but it's not big in there. It will be enough time to see everything."

"Thank you," Lina said. She had recently adopted the habit of carrying around bank envelopes full of cash expressly for this purpose. She opened one of them now and counted out five hundred RMB. Then she bent down to wedge the cash beneath the base of a crowd-control stanchion near the security guard's feet.

Although they had spent almost every waking hour together since Qiang's arrival, Lina had not been able to forget that he was just a visitor in her life. But now, as they turned away from the security guard, she felt she had just experienced what it might be like to be a permanent fixture in Qiang's world—how it must feel to be his wife.

They spent the next hour walking through the joint-Africa pavilion— a long rectangular construct, the outside of which was painted to resemble an African sunset. Inside were individual stalls where taxidermied animals were on display alongside blown-up, mounted photos of indigenous plant species, basket-weaving techniques, and more. Lina and Qiang sampled Ugandan coffee and then walked over to see Lucy, the 3.2-million-year-old skeleton of a female hominid found in Ethiopia.

"There she is, the one who's traveled farthest to get here," Qiang said.

"Through centuries," Lina agreed.

"It feels a little like we've traveled through time too, doesn't it?" he asked.

Now, she told herself. *Ask him now.* This reference to the past was as close to an opening as she would get. But when she looked up at him, he was reading the exhibit's placard, as though he hadn't said anything out of the ordinary. She changed her mind, and they walked on.

The middle of the pavilion was made up of nothing more than a marketplace of wares. Vendors sold leather wallets, braided bracelets, pins, magnets, and enameled keychains. Lina had doubts about the origins of these trinkets — she would not be surprised if they were to turn a corner to find Expo interns picking MADE IN CHINA stickers off the merchandise. She tried a different opening.

"Do you remember that ivory bracelet you gave me?"

"Of course!" Qiang said, his eyes regaining their childlike twinkle. Lina had seen him share a look like that only with Karen, and she was encouraged by it. "Do you still have it?"

"No. It was stolen from me recently. One of the maids took it."

"Wah…shi ba. That's a shame. I would have liked to see it."

Lina must have appeared visibly pained, because Qiang said quickly, "But now look at you. You have everything. I bet if you wore a different bracelet every day, it would take a year to get through your jewelry box, am I right?"

These words only hurt her further. Here she was, trying to connect with him, and he insisted on making her out to be just some rich man's wife. It dishonored the history of their friendship and the hungry way they had tried to understand each other as children. A humid gust of wind moved through the pavilion's open doors, and Lina could feel her hair lift from the base of her neck.

"Come on," she said. "Take out that map again. Let's figure out where to go next."

Because they knew most of the afternoon would be spent outside waiting in lines, Lina and Qiang chose to queue up outside pavilions with interesting exteriors. The Polish exhibit, for example, was made of plywood and perforated in a pattern of a folk-art design to resemble traditional Polish paper cutouts. It was so finely done that the structure seemed light enough to be carried off by the wind. Inside the Ireland pavilion, they walked through corridors full of LED lights, one of which was designed to re-create the experience of being caught in an Irish rainstorm. The American exhibit looked like a cross between an airport and a car dealership. It had big gray walls both inside and out, doors made for giants, and frigid air-conditioning. Lina and Qiang sat through a brief video of President Obama and ethnically diverse citizens saying hello in different languages. After that, in true American-theme-park fashion, they were shown a 4-D animation of a girl planting a flower, complete with a "rain shower" that left their shoulders and cheeks damp with mist manufactured from an unseen source overhead. After the video, they were hustled through a roomful of advertisements for the corporations that had paid for the exhibit. All in all, Lina told Qiang, it was the most accurate representation of America that she had ever seen.

The temperature had dropped with the sun, and now there was even a light breeze that moved across the Expo grounds. Just like that, the entire day had passed. Soon they would be getting in the car to go home, and Lina was still no closer to addressing the unsaid. Each opportunity that went by had made it more difficult to raise the topic. Besides, what if the conversation ended with him asking her to be with him? Did she trust herself to say no? Having Qiang here in the flesh instead of in her mind meant that he had to exist in the same world as Wei and Karen. The separation between desire and consequence that Lina had thus far been able to maintain would disappear. To do anything with Qiang other than exactly what they were doing—which was nothing—would jeopardize her life with her family, and that was out of the question. Maybe it was too late for explanations. Maybe the better thing to do in this case was to let the matter go and take Qiang's visit at face value: a long-lost brother reentering their lives. No more, no less.

The crowd had thinned a little, but it still took a while to get back to the UK pavilion. When it finally came into view, they found that each rod of the Seed Cathedral was aglow, and the entire structure looked even more psychedelic than it had in the light of day.

Their co-conspirator at the British pavilion must have seen them coming, because by the time they approached, he was already shaking his head.

"I said ten thirty. It's ten forty-three. I was going to let you in through the back entrance, but now they have someone stationed there to make sure that no one who leaves goes back in. They've stopped letting people through the front altogether."

"Can't you talk to the other guards?" Qiang asked.

The guard shook his head. "The British have strict policies. I can't risk it."

"Boss, please. We have Expo tickets only for today—it's the only day we can see it. And we've already paid you."

"I'm sorry," he said. "If it were anyone but Jeremy standing there." He gestured toward the double back doors, where the man who had originally been guarding the front entrance was now stationed.

Lina was unwilling to leave but didn't know what else there was to say. She wanted to kick herself for not keeping a closer eye on the time.

"Where do those stairs lead?" Qiang suddenly asked, pointing to a barely visible stairwell at the perimeter of the site.

"That's the staff entrance."

"Mind if we use it?"

The guard tossed his hair out of his eyes, considering.

"It's pretty high traffic down there. You'll probably get tossed out as soon as you open the door."

"We'll take our chances."

The man looked from Qiang to Lina and back to Qiang. Then he acquiesced with a nod of his head. "Fine with me, but I don't know you. Welcome to the UK pavilion. Huan ying nin." With a laugh, he stepped back to let them through.

The stairwell was so completely shrouded in the shadow of the Seed Cathedral that it was a mystery how Qiang had even spotted it. Lina followed him, keeping one hand on the banister and stepping as carefully and lightly as her shoes would allow. At the very bottom he paused, waiting for her to catch up. "Are you ready?" he asked.

A situation like this was exactly the sort of thing Lina sometimes imagined when alone in her room at Lanson Suites. Trespassing in the name of adventure, slipping into the kind of life that marriage to Wei had not allowed. But now, as she stared over Qiang's shoulder, watching his hand on that doorknob as he waited—for what, she didn't know; probably some signal discernible only to a miscreant's sixth sense—she was suddenly embarrassed to find herself there next to him. What they were doing struck her as foolish.

Qiang opened the door.

The corridor they entered was lit on either side with blue runners that spanned the length of the floor. The only open door they passed revealed an employee break room filled with lockers, notice boards, and a few folding tables. They could hear music and people speaking to one another in Chinese coming from deep within the pavilion. When they got to the end of the hallway, they stopped and listened. A few women were in the next room, counting off the end-of-day administration duties.

"It sounds like one big room in there—an open-plan office space or something. We're just going to have to walk past like we know where we're going."

"Wait!" Lina said. "I don't like this. Let's go back."

"Mei wenti. Just follow me."

"I'm not joking. Come on."

"It's not a big deal. They're office workers, they won't care or even notice."

"Qiang."

"Lina." His eyes had that steely, reckless look she remembered from when they were young.

If you don't jump in the lake, I'll push you in.

If you do, I'll kill you.

You'll have to catch me first.

Before either of them could say anything more, the door through which they'd come opened. From where they stood halfway down the hall, they could see the man with the J-rocker hair come through, calling to someone over his shoulder. Lina felt a hand on her arm, and the next thing she knew, she was being pulled into a darkened room.

Room was a generous description; it was more likely a storage closet. When she took a step back, her heel met the edge of something squat and heavy. She careened backward and caught herself with one hand, knocking something hollow-sounding onto the floor.

"Are you okay?" Qiang whispered. He yanked her to her feet.

"You're crazy!" Lina felt around for her handbag, which she had dropped in the process of trying to catch herself.

"Stop moving, will you? You're going to knock something else over."

"I'm getting out of here."

"No, *xu*, wait. I hear people. Just wait a little bit."

They both fell silent and listened; they could hear footsteps passing both in front of the room and coming down a far set of stairs. From the right wall of the storage closet came the sound of lockers being opened and shut. They waited. Lina could not tell how far Qiang was from her but could feel the heat coming from his body. This was as alone as they had ever been, aside from that last night by the lake. If he turned toward her now, there was no telling what she might do. Lina felt prickles along the back of her neck.

"Ni hai hao ba?" Qiang whispered. "You're breathing funny."

"There's not enough air." She realized then how shallow her breath had become.

"Hao le, hao le, just hold on. Sit down here—"

"No, it's too hot. I—"

"Wait—"

But Lina had already wrenched the door open and flung herself into the corridor. She felt her knees hit the floor. Through her gasping, she listened for the sound of someone coming toward them, but no one did. The dull flashes that had been clouding her vision disappeared as the blue lines of light along the floor came into view, seeming brighter than they had before. There were no other sources of light, and aside from the faint humming of a fan or refrigerator, there was silence.

"That must have been the last person," said Qiang. "It's past eleven."

To the right, an exit sign glowed. To the left, a cavern of black. They looked at each other and then laughed in disbelief. Qiang extended a hand to Lina and helped her off the ground. They headed deeper into the pavilion, past the office space, and stopped in front of a room lit with a rich scarlet glow.

"*Tian a!*" Qiang said. "The British like their luxury, a!" They peered into a lounge with plush seating and a fully stocked bar backed by red glass tiles.

"I don't think this room is for employees," Lina said. "It's probably for special guests or sponsors."

"And troublemakers like us. What'll it be, miss?" Qiang asked, ducking behind the bar.

"Gin, I think."

Lina sat down on the couch and ran her fingertips along the leather and over the brass studs that lined the arms. She watched Qiang search the bar, opening cabinets and pulling out drawers. He came back with two drinks and put one of them in her hand.

"The labels were all in English," he said by way of apology. "I picked the one that looked most expensive."

Holding their drinks, they went back out to the office area and then ascended the stairs. Qiang stopped before he even reached the landing, and when Lina came up behind him, she saw why. Fifteen-meter-high walls were covered floor to ceiling with glittering nodes of light. As they walked closer, the illumination shifted, causing some parts of the walls to shine more brightly than others. The Seed Cathedral appeared to be inhaling and exhaling. Up close, they saw that the walls were not walls at all but thousands of acrylic rods. Encapsulated at the end of each one was a different species of seed, backlit by the light funneling down the entire length of the rod. Together, they created a pixelated viewing effect, a "wall" made of undulating planes of light. Lina felt as though she had walked into the diamond-lined stomach of a whale.

"Fiber optics," she explained to Qiang. "They're powered by LED lights at the other end. During the day, the LEDs are off and the room is lit by natural sunlight instead."

"Are the seeds all different?" he asked.

"Shi a, all sixty thousand species. There's a seed bank in Britain that stores different varieties of seeds from all over the world so that they will never become extinct."

They walked around the room looking at spiky seeds, furry seeds, seeds the length of an eyelash and some as big as walnuts. She watched Qiang in profile. The lambent light played across his features as he circled the room. As she walked under the fiber optics, the anxiety she had felt from being alone with him was replaced by delirium. Or maybe that was from the drink.

"What I love is that they're made to mix with the world," Lina said. "Some seeds have wings so they can be disseminated by the wind. Some are small enough to be swallowed by birds and carried far away."

"How convenient," Qiang said. "If only humans were designed that way. Traveling would be a lot easier."

But they aren't, Lina wanted to say. *Humans are designed to stay in each other's lives, not to float around unattached. They are designed for families, for commitment, for—* but she wasn't even able to finish her thought before she remembered her own family, and her stomach tightened.

He raised his drink. "To our lucky explorations," he said.

Their glasses made a tinny, dry sound when they met.

"You know what I just realized? The first night you came, when we drank that wine—that was the first time I had a drink with you. Your face was red as a lantern. I don't think I would have guessed that would happen. Your brother's face doesn't get red."

He grinned. "You're wrong. We drank together at your wedding."

At the word *wedding*, Lina was jolted out of her giddiness.

"You barely count as having come to our wedding," she said softly. "After that first gan bei, your seat at the main table stayed empty. I looked around for you and saw you over by the door talking to the aunties. The next time I looked, you were gone."

She hadn't forgotten a thing, not the octangular room, the restaurant's red and gold velvet wall hangings, the fish appetizers their families couldn't afford, their parents beaming across the table at one another in celebration of their own lives joining along with their children's lives. At one point, Wei had been bending forward in his seat to play with one of the neighborhood toddlers, so only the top of his head was visible. Overlooking, as always, what was immediately in front of him—the fact that Lina's attention was elsewhere. She sat there as numb as she'd felt the entire day. The images of the others seemed to revolve around her while her eyes were anchored across the restaurant. It was centripetal, the way the rest of the night spun around the one moment she remembered the most clearly: the sliver of blue sky coming through the front doors as Qiang opened them and slipped through. Had he only looked back, she thought. Had he looked back at her just then, things might have been different.

That morning, she had gone to her father. It was Fang Lijian's habit to take a long walk every Saturday from his home to an adjacent town and back again. On the day of her wedding, he was surprised to see Lina up so early. *Ba, let me walk with you. I have something to say.* His face betrayed excitement; he was expecting her to share good news, some new detail in her and Wei's plans for America, perhaps. And that's why she could not make eye contact with him while she talked. She did her best to tell him what had happened to her in the time between graduating high school and coming home from college. She tried to explain without quite knowing herself how she had fallen in love with Qiang. He listened quietly without interruption and after she was finished, there was a minute in which he did not speak. Only then did she look into his face.

It was worse than what she'd imagined. He looked not only disappointed but also full of sorrow and shame. That's when Lina felt her own resentment flare up. What claim did he have on her life like this? What right did he have to be ashamed of her? She hadn't done anything wrong; the only thing she was guilty of was changing her mind. *I don't care if you agree,* she finally said. *My life is not yours to direct as you please.* But none of this needed saying; Lina knew it as soon as she saw her father bow his head. *And Qiang—he wants this too?* he asked.

She'd thought he would be angry; she hadn't expected this air of defeat. He seemed tired right down to his joints. *More than anything,* she told him. *This is what we both want more than anything.*

By then, they were well past the borders of their own town and heading toward the Zhens'. *You're right,* Fang Lijian finally said. *Your life is not mine. You have the freedom to do as you please, and the worst thing I could do is take that freedom away—I understand that more than you know. I will talk it over with Zhen Hong.* He looked straight ahead down the road, as if determined to face whatever hardship lay at the end of it. Lina suddenly knew that what she had set in motion was bigger than just herself and Qiang and Wei, bigger than her father's hopes for her happiness. That's when she remembered the debt her parents had once argued over when they discussed her marriage and her future.

How much do you owe Zhen Hong Shushu? she asked her father then. *What was the debt? Can't it be repaid if I marry Qiang instead?*

Fang Lijian gave her a sad smile. *That's my business, not yours.*

And suddenly they were outside the Zhens' home and Lina was sitting on a tree stump by the side of the road, picking at a scab on her ankle, waiting. Waiting. Ten minutes passed, then twenty. She was almost numb with fear and excitement when she saw her father come out of their home. *Is it done?* she wanted to know. *Is it over?* Instead of a straight answer, Fang Lijian had wrapped his arms around her in a hug. *Oh, Lina,* he said—his voice was tender and sad, but in his embrace she felt only relief. *You're confused, xingan. You're nervous, that's all.* And that's how Lina came to know that Qiang had not said a word to his family about her. It was as though she had dreamed the previous evening, as though the most important night of her life had happened in her sleep.

"Jie, you're not mad, are you?" Qiang asked. "You know how I dislike family gatherings."

Here he was, twenty years later, pretending as though none of this had happened. "Especially weddings," Qiang added. "I almost didn't go to my own wedding."

Lina felt her tongue go dry in her mouth.

"You're married?"

"Yes," Qiang said, surprised at her surprise.

Lina struggled to form her next words.

"You've been with us for days now and you haven't mentioned a wife. Do you have kids? *Tian a,* you have kids."

"No, no kids."

"Where is your wife now?"

"Home in Kunming."

He was married. She didn't know why she had dismissed the possibility before.

"Why didn't she come with you?"

"I wanted to come alone."

She felt weightless, as if she had been catapulted into space. Had she imagined everything that had happened between them in the past week? The way he watched her, their sensitivity to each other's movements in a room—those physical communications that had seemed so loud to her, so full of need. She'd felt sure that his wants and doubts matched hers and that when Karen sat between them in the backseat of the car, Lina wasn't the only one to wonder what her daughter might have looked like if Qiang had been the father.

"Who is she?" she asked.

"Her name is Jian Yun. You met her once before."

"Cloudy."

"That's right," he said, surprised.

Lina expelled a little breath that was almost a laugh. "So you've got a gangster wife too. I should have guessed."

Cloudy, with her bright lips and darting eyes. The girl whose image had haunted Lina through her college years, whom she'd tried to emulate, as if becoming more like Cloudy would bring her closer to Qiang.

Lina had had no reason to assume that he would still be in love with her. It had pleased her, all these years, to think that he had not followed through on telling his family about them for both of their sakes, not just his own. But what if he hadn't been genuine that night before the wedding? What if he'd never planned to leave with her at all? Qiang was staring past her shoulder at the wall of seeds, avoiding her eyes.

"I never understood how you got away with the things you did when you were younger. Everybody in that family just let you do what you wanted. In and out the door, gone all night. It's truly amazing that you and Wei could have come from the same family—"

"What do you want me to say, Lina?" he said, his voice rising. "That I wish it had been you I married? Hao. I wish it had been you."

The whites of his eyes shone. She hadn't imagined it—he still felt something. But this wasn't how it was supposed to go. He had finally said the very thing she had been waiting years to hear, and she didn't feel any better. In fact, she hated him for saying it.

"What right do you have to tell me that now? You have never taken a shred of responsibility for anything in your entire life. And now you're an old man. I hope you can live with that." She knew she was about to cry. She knew she should stop talking but she couldn't. "We had a deal. You were going to talk to your parents and I was going to talk to mine. What happened between then and the wedding? Tell me that, at least."

She remembered being pressed up against Wei's chest in those first cold Philadelphia months thinking about liminality—about that small span of time in which a threshold has yet to be crossed, when a person is readying himself for change, and any number of events can alter who he becomes. Maybe Qiang had woken up the day of the wedding, and instead of the first things he saw being his own hands, his own face in the mirror, he saw his mother placing a bowl of porridge next to his bed. Maybe the previous night, instead of going straight home, he had stopped to have a word with Brother Gao, and the man had filled his head anew with dreams about Shanghai. Maybe he had meant to speak to his parents, and the difference was that Lina had been willing to break her parents' hearts for the first time in her life, while Qiang, in the end, had decided he could not break his parents' hearts again.

But now the question had come out before she was ready to hear the answer, and she regretted it the moment it left her mouth. She didn't think she could stand it if he said what she feared. *I didn't love you enough* was the answer she'd spent all these years dreading. *It wasn't any one deciding factor. I just didn't love you enough for it to be worth it.*

Watching him standing there, his lips parted with no words coming out, Lina despised him for the power he had over her. She hated how much potential there still was for her to be hurt.

"I've never been good at giving answers," Qiang finally said. "But you deserve one. That's the least of what you deserve."

"Never mind," she said. "Just forget it."

Here was the other thing: The more she relied on him to tell her why he'd left her all those years ago, the more power his absence would have over her. He was married. She'd pictured him missing her all these years, but he'd moved on. She'd heard everything she needed to. "Are we done here?"

He stepped toward her, but she held up her hand. "I don't want to talk about this. I can't talk to you right now. Please. Let's just go."

As if on cue, the LED lights went out, patch by patch, like fireworks dying overhead. Soon, all that was lit was the red *ru kou* sign marking the exit doors. Lina walked toward it, her hands extended to avoid bumping into the walls of seeds. She could see the red gleam of the sign reflecting off the metal bar of the cathedral's doors, anticipated its cool touch on her fingers. When she finally reached it, she leaned her full weight forward and pushed.

She pushed again.

18

Sunny sat in the lower level of the lobby with her week's salary held tight in her hand. *Luosuo si le.* What had come over her? The job was taking a toll, that was certain. Twelve hours a day with the Zhens for five days in a row, and suddenly she was confessing her life's struggles to her employer. She had even brought up childbirth! *Tian a,* Boss Zhen probably thought she was looking for pity—no wonder he'd paid her early. She shoved the envelope of cash into her purse without counting it.

I think I'm good at knowing whom to trust, Taitai had said when she hired Sunny. How naive Sunny had been. She thought Taitai had chosen her because she wouldn't spread gossip about their family around Lanson Suites when what she had really been hired for was to help the adults keep their secrets from one another—to give Taitai the opportunity to flirt with Qiang in private and Boss Zhen the freedom to return to his work without having to admit that he was doing it to avoid his brother. There was so much in the household that went unsaid, hidden resentments and pleas for attention coloring their conversations as falsely as a bad accent. It made her miss her own family even more. They had their problems, but at least they were honest about them. At least they wanted to spend time together. Day after day, she watched the Zhens navigate conversations as they would a minefield. It made Sunny so anxious that she wasn't sure how much longer she could last with them. Was this what she'd risked Rose's job for?

Some mornings, Karen would lay her head in Sunny's lap and complain of uneasy dreams. In those moments, Sunny would feel something close to hatred for the kid's parents. But when she let herself see them for who they were, she felt for them too. As she'd left the apartment that night, she'd caught sight of Boss Zhen, alone in the living room, glancing around as if unsure what to do with himself next. How in need of protection he'd seemed then.

In her years of working as a housekeeper, she'd witnessed the dissolution of more than one marriage. For all his intelligence, Boss Zhen was a little out of touch with reality—he didn't seem to know he was on the verge of being cuckolded. It was the busiest career men, the stoic and implacable ones, who had the most difficulty when their personal lives were disrupted. She hoped he would work things out with Taitai. Boss Zhen wasn't the sort to live well alone.

It should have been easy to hate Taitai, but that was impossible too. The woman walked around the apartment in a white silk robe, hungering to be noticed. Sunny knew that there was nothing worse than feeling useless in a household, especially if your presence had once been so necessary. She remembered how it had felt to move back home after her husband's death, how she, too, had invented ways to make herself useful. It was heartbreaking to watch Taitai convince herself that the family cared how the apartment was decorated, or where they went to dinner, or what she wore to lunch.

Headlights swept across the lobby as the Mercedes came down the parking-lot ramp and pulled up outside the door. Inside the car, Little Cao lowered the music and greeted her with a nod. As she sank into the leather seats, she wondered if this was how Boss Zhen felt at the end of a workday—a sense of conflict rather than completion.

"So," Little Cao said, eyeing her in the rearview. "Are you going to tell me what you're worried about?"

"What do you mean?"

"I've been a driver for a long time. I know exactly what it sounds like when someone gets into the car in a bad mood."

The last thing she felt like doing was humoring him, and yet she couldn't ignore him completely.

"I don't know what you're talking about. I'm not in any kind of mood."

Little Cao sighed. "Okay, don't tell me. Sui ni bian. Drivers and ayis are supposed to be friends, you know. You're not cleaning rooms with the other housekeepers anymore. Who are you going to talk to if not me?"

If the Zhens' secrets were now her secrets too, Sunny was reluctant to trust Little Cao. She didn't know what kind of relationship he had with the other drivers or what secrets they shared about the families they worked for.

"I had a friend who was fired," Sunny said instead. "Taitai accused her of stealing her jewelry."

Little Cao sighed and rubbed the back of his neck. "There's nothing you can do about that. Happens all the time. These employers—they expect it to happen. See, I have a theory. Human beings, right? We're all takers. Doesn't matter how much we've already got. We'll take anyway."

"I don't believe that," Sunny said. "We don't all do this. I don't."

"I'm not saying *you* do. But those of us who do, it doesn't make us bad people. We give too. There's as much pleasure in that as there is in the taking. But the trick is to take small things regularly. Everybody takes small things all the time. Kickbacks for doing business, a little bit of embezzlement, whatever. That's why China is not like those other countries where people are taking each other's lives. We've got enough corruption built in to allow for some taking. So I take when I can. You should take when you can. Now, I don't know if your friend did it or not, but maybe she should have. That way, when she's eventually screwed, there will be no regrets. Am I right?"

Sunny considered this and gave a nervous laugh. "You're the most philosophical driver I've ever met."

"I'm probably the only driver you've ever met. I speak for my profession when I say we spend a lot of time waiting for people to come out of houses and restaurants and bars, so it gives a person time to think."

Twice that week he'd taken Qiang and Taitai out to eat alone while Sunny had stayed home with Karen. What if he had seen something happen between them? It was possible, she supposed, that he could know more about the Zhens' marriage problems than she did. After all, he'd been working for them for years.

"You said you take things," Sunny said after a moment. "What do you take?"

Little Cao giggled. "Bet you can't guess. It doesn't cost anything. I'll give you a hint: the thing I take is in this car right now."

Sunny looked around the sedan's cream interior—the tucked leather, the dashboard with its exaggerated gauges and dials, Little Cao's eyes in the rearview mirror shining like black tapioca. There was nothing extraneous in this car. Just the day's newspaper folded into the back pocket of the front seat, a box of tissues on the rear deck, and Little Cao's canteen of tea.

"I don't know," Sunny said. "What is it?"

He stuck his hand into a cup holder and flung something into Sunny's lap—a stack of business cards bound together by a rubber band. Sunny recognized them as the ones from Boss Zhen's study. "You steal his business cards?"

Little Cao raised a finger and wagged it in the air. "Flash one of these and you can get a table at any of the best clubs on credit. I keep a suit jacket in the trunk. See? I tell you my secrets too. Now we're even."

Sunny turned the stack over in her hands, remembering the day she pulled them from Boss Zhen's trouser pocket. Even then she had sensed they were more than just pieces of card stock with his contact information on them. How much more, she didn't know.

"What I told you isn't really a secret," Sunny said. "The whole hotel knows."

"Can't you see I'm trying to build a relationship? Maybe you won't tell me a real secret today. But now you're more likely to tell me one tomorrow, shi ba?" He wiggled his eyebrows at her and Sunny couldn't help but smile back at him.

"You should come out with me sometime. See a Shanghai unlike any Shanghai you've ever seen before."

"I'm not really the partying type."

"Who says you have to be a type to party? Once I took my great-aunt out to a karaoke bar. She drank my friends under the table while singing 'The Bird Afar'...and with perfect pitch! *My dreams were once...*"

The rest of the lyrics trailed through Sunny's mind. *My dreams were once clear / Old hopes now weighed down with fear / I would have flown oceans for you / When you wanted me near...* She had always wondered how that love ballad had become a popular drinking song. It wasn't just melancholic, it was downright depressing. Wang Jian used to sing it to himself in the shower, and each time, his voice had startled her. It rang out confidently, articulate in pain. *Could it be that one star has changed its course? / Have time's wings grown weary in flight?...* In those moments, she'd wondered if her husband had once been in love. Maybe she was wrong to assume that he had died before really living. It was possible he had experienced all kinds of heartbreak and happiness before marrying Sunny. For the first time, she regretted not having gotten to know her husband properly. It might have been her one shot at understanding another person intimately, and having him understand her. She had been too stubborn to try.

"I need to pick up Taitai and Qiang from the Expo site first and drop them off at the French concession before I take you home," Little Cao said.

Sunny looked out the window. By now, they had exited the highway and landed in a stream of traffic. Black-on-black Audis and Mercedes made up the unofficial fleet of corporate vehicles whose drivers chauffeured the upper-level management. When getting picked up by Little Cao, Sunny and Taitai often had to squint to read the license plates to identify their own. The make and model were not enough to differentiate it from the others.

The radio clock read 12:15. "I thought the Expo closed at midnight."

He dismissed her words with a wave of his hand. "The lines getting out of that place will be just as bad as the ones to get in."

His phone, lying in the beverage holder, rang, and an image of Taitai popped up on the screen. Underneath it were the words BOSS LADY. The photo had been taken from the driver's seat of the car while Taitai was in the back, checking her lipstick. In it, her eyes were half closed and she was baring her teeth in a scowl.

Little Cao picked up the call with his usual joviality.

"Hello?" He listened for a beat. "Ah? Zhen de?" His eyebrows nearly took flight from his face, leaving the rest of his features in pure glee. "Zenme hui, ne?"

"What happened?" Sunny asked, but he ignored her and leaned forward in his seat, affecting a tone of concern.

"Wah...hao, hao. No problem, leave it to me. We'll have you out in no time." He ended the call, tossed the phone onto the passenger seat, and turned around to face Sunny. "Well, miss, it seems that an opportunity has arisen. Zhen Taitai and Qiang have — hee-hee! — have gotten themselves locked into one of the pavilions."

Sunny's stomach tightened. "What do you mean, locked in?"

"She didn't elaborate. All I know is they are locked inside. I'm supposed to tell someone to get them out."

Sunny remembered how Taitai had looked with her head thrown back in flirtatious glee at Yu Gardens. Standing in front of Qiang in that moment, she seemed to have transformed into someone else entirely. Who, Sunny did not know, but what if the person she had become had locked herself in there with Qiang on purpose?

"Supposed to?"

"Aiya, don't worry," Little Cao said. "We'll drop by the Expo first. I promise I will do my very best to free our dear employer. But it might take some time. Things don't always go as smoothly as a person would hope. What if the Expo people are hard to get hold of? What if they're not very cooperative when I ask them to unlock the pavilion? What if it takes quite a few hours—enough for two or three drinks, at the very least—for them to send someone out there to unlock the place?"

"*Wo de tian a*," Sunny muttered. "You'd better send me home first. I don't want to get involved in this."

"Oh, come on, have a little fun," Little Cao said. "This is a sign from the heavens! Nothing is going to happen to them for a couple hours. They're locked away as safe as any of those prized exhibits, and *we*—we will be Zhen Taitai and Mr. Qiang for the night, living large on Boss's tab. Wouldn't that be fun? Anyway, you don't have a choice. I'm doing this for your own good. We're going out."

His expression, however—the way he looked at her out of the corner of his eye—implied that she did have a choice. Once again, Sunny wondered how much Little Cao knew. Did he suspect that, although Lina and Qiang were trapped in the pavilion, they weren't trying very hard to leave? That they'd called Little Cao for rescue rather than Boss Zhen because they thought he might take his time?

"Let me ask you something," Sunny said carefully. "What do you think about the fact that Taitai and Qiang spend so much time alone together?"

Little Cao's eyes twinkled. "Now we're getting somewhere. This is the sort of gossip I'm talking about." But when he looked in the rearview mirror and saw how serious Sunny's expression was, he stopped smiling. "Don't worry. I don't think it's like that. Taitai is too uppity for a guy like Qiang."

"I don't know," Sunny said. "I think you underestimate her."

Little Cao winced and rubbed the back of his head.

"Maybe you're right. These taitai dou wu liao. No idea how to spend their free time so they look for trouble. I'm not saying a person shouldn't get into trouble. Heaven knows I get into trouble constantly. The difference is, I don't *look* for trouble. That's when problems come—when you have everything so the only thing left to want is trouble."

"Stealing Boss's business cards, pretending you're him, running up his bar tab. You don't call that looking for trouble?"

"I call that the perks of the job," he said. "It all gets written off anyway. He doesn't know the difference."

She had a sudden recollection of Boss Zhen coming toward her in his slippers, holding pen and paper in one hand, the stack of bills in the other. The moment he'd offered them to her, he'd looked happier than he had all week. He probably thought that with that one gesture, he was solving all her problems. Other people's problems always seemed simpler than one's own.

Maybe she was being too sensitive. A steady stream of income was not nothing. Her job was to make sure the family members were fed and clothed appropriately, not to manage their emotional lives. Whatever they did to hurt each other was not her business.

"So? What will it be?"

Little Cao's eyes were extra-round as he stared at her, waiting for her answer.

Suan le. What she did in her time off was not the Zhens' business either. Tonight, she would find it tough to go to sleep. Maybe a drink or
two would help.

"Hao ba," she said finally. "I'll go with you. But if we get in trouble, I'm
telling them you took me against my will."

19

After Sunny left for the night, Wei collected the remnants of his dinner and brought them into the kitchen. He hadn't washed dishes since they lived in America and had forgotten how enjoyable it could be, cleaning utensils one by one until they shone and returning the plates to the rack, bright and blank.

It wasn't until his phone rang from the dining room that he realized he hadn't called Lina to let her know he wouldn't be able to make it to dinner, and now it was too late. Abandoning the dishes, he went out to retrieve it. There was her name on the screen. He prepared himself for an upbraiding and then answered.

"Hi."

"Hi," Lina said. Immediately, Wei sensed there was something wrong. There was no noise in the background. And Lina, for some reason, didn't sound angry.

"I don't want you to worry, but we're going to be late. We got ourselves locked in one of the Expo sites." There was a breathless quality to her voice.

"What?"

"We're in the UK pavilion and they've locked all the doors. We got locked in here by accident."

"By accident," he repeated. "How?"

"It's hard to explain. I'll tell you later. But we've been out all day and our phone batteries are about to die so I just wanted to let you know."

Wei could still taste the soup at the back of his throat, and it suddenly made him feel sick. "I'm coming over there."

"No, you shouldn't—just stay with Karen. I already called Little Cao. He's going to get hold of someone who can get us out."

He wanted to reach through the phone and grab her.

"Where is the UK pavilion? Which entrance is it? I'll meet Little Cao there."

"No," Lina said. "It's too late. I don't know how long it will take, and there's nothing you can do anyway. Stay home and get Karen to bed on time."

"Are you sure?" was all he could ask.

"Yes."

"But maybe—"

"Really, we're fine. We'll be home in a few hours. Just go to bed."

There came the sound of a bang. "What was that?"

"Qiang's trying one of the doors again," she said.

This was all his fault. *He* should have been there with Lina, not Qiang. Better yet, he should have been the one to take Qiang to see the Expo instead of Lina. Neither of these realizations was as painful as the recognition that in her time of need, his wife had called their driver for help before she called him.

"I'm sorry about dinner," he said.

"It's all right, Wei, really." Lina's tone softened. "We'll talk about it later. See you at home."

After she ended the call, Wei stared at his blank screen. Then, feeling helpless, he dialed Little Cao.

"Boss!" It was noisy, wherever Little Cao was. Besides that, he was a shouter. Wei put distance between his ear and the phone.

"Where are you?" Wei asked. "Lina just called me. Are you at the Expo site?"

"I'm just about to call one of the supervisors now," Little Cao said. "We'll get them out, don't worry! I'll keep you posted!" He hung up before Wei could respond.

Down the hall, the sound of a door creaking. Footsteps like the slow patter of rain. Karen stepped into the dining room, blinking at the bright overhead light.

"Where's Mom?" she asked.

•   •   •

Neither Karen nor Wei knew how to work the microwave. It did *look* like a normal microwave, with all the expected options and numbered buttons, but they couldn't get it to start. The digital display continued to show them promising things: HEAT, INPUT TIME, SET. But nothing.

"*Dad*," Karen said, after several minutes. Wei was always surprised by how, in a single word, Karen could express an entire range of complaints. "Let's call Mom again."

"We can't," Wei said. "Mom's phone is out of battery."

He'd said nothing to Karen about why Lina wasn't home yet. On top of her stomachache, she had been in a mood ever since returning from his office. Wei could not bring himself to make things worse with the news that her mother was locked inside a building.

"Look, this is what we'll do," he said. He opened cabinets and drawers until he found a pot, which he used to warm the soup. He also scrounged up a bit of leftover paigu — Karen's favorite — stuck it in the wok, and fired up the stove. But as the kitchen filled with the smell of sweet pork, Karen's mood only worsened. She leaned against the refrigerator with her arms crossed, staring down at her dad's feet.

When everything was ready, Wei carried the food out to the dining-room table and watched his daughter eat. Her mouth worked its way neatly around the bone—something she must have been taught in boarding school—and as she chewed, her fingers swept lazily across the surface of her phone. Here was the unexpected theme of his day: sitting at the dining table with cagey women, trying to get them to talk.

"How's the tutoring going with the Canter boys?" Wei asked.

"Fine. Not much I can do about them being stupid, but otherwise it's going okay." She sighed and looked up. "My friend Valerie from school wants to know if I can change my ticket."

"What ticket?"

"Her family said I can stay with them if I come back to the U.S. in August instead of September. I said I'd ask you."

Of course she was asking *him*. There was no way Lina would ever agree to anything like this.

"You've been here only a couple weeks. You want to go back already?"

Karen shrugged. Wei tried to read his daughter's face more carefully, but when she met his gaze again, he had the disconcerting feeling that she was reading him right back. "Let's talk about it when Mom gets home."

"Fine," Karen said, and she bent over her screen once more.

Without warning, a teardrop slid down her nose and hit the surface of the phone. She rubbed it away with the heel of her hand, then sniffed. Before Wei could figure out how to ask her what was wrong, she raised her face to him and said, rather vindictively, "I got my period."

A few seconds passed, during which they only looked at each other. Karen's nose and lips had swollen to a dull pink glow.

"Oh. Do you—do you know what to do?" Wei asked.

"Sort of, yeah." But she continued to stare at him, as though awaiting a directive.

"Okay. Okay, xingan. Hang on."

Despite himself, Wei was relieved. He could not be expected to handle this kind of emergency, which meant this was not a job at which he could fail. He wouldn't call Lina and waste her precious battery. He briefly considered calling Sunny but decided against it. The woman had already spent so many of her waking hours dealing with their family. He couldn't hijack her sleep now too.

Wei walked into the master bath and opened the drawers beneath the sink Lina used. Since he didn't really know what he was looking for, it took a while for him to spot the cardboard box of tampons, each one individually wrapped like an expensive dessert. Tampons weren't widely sold in China, and on each of Wei's business trips back west, he had been tasked with filling entire shopping baskets with Playtex Sport. He plucked one out of the box, took a breath, and returned to the kitchen.

Karen was still sitting in her chair but no longer touching her food. "I should have gone with them to the Expo," she said miserably.

"Here." Wei held the tampon out to her, but Karen just looked at it.

"Is that all you could find?"

"What?"

"Never mind. I'll just wait until Mom comes home."

"Okay." Best to be agreeable. "Okay, that's fine. How do you feel?"

"I don't know."

"Do you want to watch a movie?"

She shook her head.

"Do you want some painkillers?"

"No."

Wei went to her. To his surprise, she returned his hug, and he placed his hand on her back, feeling her ribs rise and fall with the delicacy of an underwater creature. How simple she felt as a physical being in his arms and how complicated she had become. Wei rubbed her shoulders, the way he had when she was young, until her breathing evened out. They stayed in that position—she sitting, he crouched with his arms around her—until he felt his knees would pop, and even then he didn't let go.

If this was the only comfort he could offer, then this was what he would offer.

"You know, I miss you when you're away," he said into her hair. "I barely get to see you, and you want to leave so soon."

"Then move back," she replied.

Back. Wei realized now that Karen still thought of the U.S. as home, whereas he had shed that idea long ago. How had he never noticed that? Was that what accounted for the distance between them? Her tone of voice was a mix of longing and defensiveness and pretending like it didn't matter to her as much as it must. He wanted so much for her right then, not least of which was to live by her side. Had he gone about it all wrong? Did he spend too much time thinking about the best thing for her future and not enough time thinking about what was best for her now? In the years she had been away at Black Tree, she had grown abstract to him. *I have a daughter,* he said to colleagues when they asked if he had kids. He kept her pictures on his desk at his office. On business trips, he picked up knickknacks that he left on her bedroom bureau to collect dust until her next visit home. Had he ever seen her open the little painted box from St. Petersburg, or wear the hair bows from Paris, or use the package of stickers from Japan? He couldn't remember—he couldn't be sure. It occurred to him then that he had no idea what she wanted or why she wanted what she did. He had never sat looking out a window with her, sussing out her dreams, as his own father had with him. Nor had he ever lain awake listening for her to come home, as his ba had for Qiang. If he, too, were to die suddenly, how well would he survive in her memory?

"Okay," Karen said, pulling back from him. "I guess I'll try the tampon."

"Great," Wei said, breathing heavily now from the effort of his crouch. "Who needs Mom?"

Karen opened the box of Playtex, glanced briefly at the instructions that came with it, and then flung it aside and announced that she was just going to figure out how to do it herself.

Several minutes later, when she still hadn't come out of the bathroom, Wei called to her from the hallway. "Everything okay?"

"Go away."

"Are you sure you don't want to look at the instructions?" He had spent the last few minutes trying to read them himself, although the paper was about five shades too pink for his aging eyes.

"No, the diagrams are scary."

The diagrams *were* scary. Wei did not like the names used to describe the parts of the tampon. He didn't think words like *barrel* and *plunger* were very friendly-sounding to young women doing this for the first time. There was also something seedy about *contoured tip* and *finger grip*. Furthermore, with the string hanging out from the end, the device in the diagram looked like a very large, very aggressive sperm.

"I can explain it to you if you want. I'll read the instructions aloud, you don't have to—"

"Please don't do that."

"But if you don't know how, I don't think it's a good idea to—"

"Dad!" Silence, and then a sigh. "I'll read the instructions. Just— shove it under the door. And then go away."

Wei refolded the glossy paper and got on one knee. Carefully, he fed it through the crack under the door.

On the other side, he heard paper rustling, a few seconds of silence, then the sink going on and off again. He rose to his feet and waited, supporting himself with one fist against the bathroom door. Suddenly, he was reminded of the way he'd felt the night Lina gave birth to Karen. It had taken so many years for them to conceive that when it finally happened, it was almost as though they were living another couple's lives. When Lina got pregnant, he'd felt tender toward her in a very new way, but the biggest change was how she was toward him. He couldn't explain it except to say that she had opened up. She began to need him in a way that made him feel irreplaceable and singly responsible for her every moment of every day. At night, instead of rolling apart from him midsleep, she'd held his arms around her in a tight embrace. Her body had gotten big. Her waistline expanded, and the smell of her changed. She'd felt more solid to the touch, and it wasn't because of the baby alone. Holding his hands there in position around her felt so inclusionary. It was like she was inviting him to experience whatever was happening between her and the baby, things that he never could have imagined he'd be able to feel.

Then came the day of the birth. In the span of time between her water breaking and beginning to have contractions, Lina had stopped talking to him. While he called the doctor, gathered essentials, and repacked her prepacked bag, she'd sat against the cold concrete of their bedroom wall with her eyes closed, as if awaiting some kind of judgment. Her silence during that time had seemed like punishment to him, like an exclusion, though he knew she couldn't have meant it that way.

That kind of silence still made him nervous. There was the thought that he was somehow messing up without doing anything. He walked up the hall and back down it. Finally, the door opened and Karen stood there looking—he thought—very normal. She avoided his eyes, busied herself with folding the sheet of instructions in her hand, then handed it back to him. How absurd he felt accepting it, as though he were some authority on menstruation. And yet, how happy.

"How'd it go?"

She shifted her weight from one leg to the other. "Fine."

"How do you feel?"

"I feel okay."

"Good!" As he gestured with his hands, the instructional insert flew from his fingers and landed on the floor between them. He bent to retrieve it, and when he straightened up, he caught the end of a smirk on his daughter's face.

"Can we still watch a movie?" she asked.

"Yeah."

"Can you not work while we watch the movie?"

"Okay."

"Okay," she said. "Then you get to pick what we watch."

He would have been tickled by this display of generosity had she not sounded sincerely grateful. Karen was clearly aware that what had occurred to her body that night fell outside the scope of her father's abilities and understanding. Through her own discomfort, she had been able to recognize his and take care of him in her own way.

On the couch that night, Wei spent a good portion of the movie looking not at the screen, but into the mirrored walls of the display cases next to it. The TV cast a pallid glow on Karen's face and Wei realized then how her features had changed over the past couple of years. The slope of her nose had risen and sharpened, and her eyes had acquired the kind of magnetism he recognized in Lina. With their glances alone, both women had the ability to pull a person close or keep him at a distance according to their will. There was less of Wei in Karen now and more of his wife. From here on out, Wei would have to work to understand his daughter, whereas she would instinctively know what to do with him.

20

Strobe lights. Fish tanks. Leather banquettes lining outdoor bars on the Bund. Women high-heeled so they stood taller than the men. *The too-beautiful ones are hired to be here,* Little Cao whispered to Sunny as they stood in line. *They're part of the decor.* When it was their turn at the front, Little Cao leaned in to the host and gave the name of Boss Zhen's company in surprisingly unaccented English. *Medora Group*—they were the only two English words that Sunny had ever heard Little Cao say, but she thought he'd said them well.

The first club was a dark, austere lounge with very few Chinese clients. Overhead, paper fans dropped from the ceiling on fishing lines. On the full-length glass-topped bar, a trio of bare-legged women in short qipaos moved from side to side in a languid choreographed dance, their expressions bored and implacable. The crowd was outfitted demurely, the women in boatneck dresses and the men in suits. They paid little attention to the bar-top show, but Sunny couldn't stop watching. After a few minutes, Little Cao handed her a bright blue drink. It tasted like its color more than it did like any flavor Sunny could discern. She followed Little Cao to the club's exterior deck, where a knot of guests were drinking champagne. The city behind them was decadently dressed, its lights like diamonds stitched down the front of a black silk suit.

"This is where Boss takes his fanciest business associates. They come here when they're celebrating a deal. What do you think? I bet you never thought you'd end up someplace like this!" Little Cao opened his arms and took a step back as if to make room for the splendor of the occasion.

"It's beautiful," Sunny said.

"It's hard to believe none of that was there ten years ago. I've got nephews older than those buildings over in Pudong. My sister's husband's family had an apartment right where the Expo site is now. Government had to move them out. Their new place is nice."

He set his drink on the railing, took a pack of cigarettes from his pocket, and ran his finger over the filter tips as if struggling to choose one. "What's sad is that her kid doesn't have a childhood. I mean, a place to come back to. A place where he grew up as a child. It will all have to be up here for him," he said, tapping his head.

That's where I keep my childhood, Sunny was tempted to say, but she knew things were different for her.

As she watched him smoke, something clicked in her head. "You're college-educated."

A smile tugged up around his cigarette. "True. I went to college a long time ago."

Earlier, at the Expo, when Little Cao had spoken with the overnight guards, his language had suddenly become formal and erudite. *Do you know who I am?* That was the question Little Cao had asked without forming the words. He was playing Boss Zhen, and it had worked well enough. He had convinced the guards to call the Expo officials as well as the police commissioner, and when none of them picked up their phones, he'd instructed the guards to keep calling every half hour. He had left his own phone number with the weary and resigned look of a business traveler who had missed his connecting flight. *Give me a call when you finally get through,* he'd said before walking away. Seeing Little Cao manipulate the guards like this made Sunny wonder about the ways he was manipulating the Zhens. Around Boss Zhen and Taitai, there was no hint of the shrewdness he'd shown tonight. In fact, he was the opposite — cheerful to a fault and oblivious to their criticisms of him. Was he playing a dumbed-down caricature of himself whenever they were around? Was it possible that, like Sunny, he approached his job with the same instinct to hide who he was?

"How did you end up a driver?" she asked him now.

"I went to college for only two years. My parents got sick. I'd just gotten married. The only thing to do was to start working, and driving was the best option at the time."

"That's too bad," Sunny said.

"Mei you, it's fine. Turned out for the best. I'm not cut out for an office job anyway — or any kind of nine-to-five job, really. I'm not a worker like Boss Zhen. To be honest, I'm a bit like Taitai. A dreamer. Driving around lets me think my thoughts. It's really an okay outcome. What about you? What did you do before you cleaned homes?"

"I helped out around the house, tended the family business."

"Why'd you come out here?"

She'd been asked this question countless times by now. Why didn't answering it ever feel any easier?

"There wasn't space for me at home anymore. I was married and my husband passed, but I wasn't close to his family. I didn't belong there or at home anymore, so now I'm here."

Little Cao frowned. "You ever think about marrying again?"

"Sure," Sunny said. "I don't know."

"A single woman living in *qunzu* and sending money home —"

Sunny hiked her voice up so it was high and cackling. "A single woman working in the city, it doesn't seem right. What are you going to do when you get old? Who's going to take care of *you?*"

Little Cao grinned at the impersonation. "Who's that? Your mother?"

Sunny nodded. "My question is, why does everyone think getting married will solve everything?"

"I don't think that. I just think, you know, things are harder to bear alone."

Next to them, a woman squealed and sent a martini glass tumbling off the side of the balcony. It was followed by a delicate shatter down below and the echoing laughter of men. The city still seemed like a movie set to Sunny, even after all this time. She and Little Cao had driven here by way of the overpass. From there, they'd had a full view of the Expo's electric landscape of pavilions, closed for the night, but still filled with colored lights. She thought of Taitai again, trapped in one of those buildings. Did she ever get tired of the brightness and excess? Or did years of playing a leading lady make a person stop noticing how artificial the world around her was?

"I don't know what I'm doing," Sunny finally said. "Today Boss Zhen offered to help me find a permanent ayi position and I couldn't be happy about it. I kept thinking about what it would mean to stay here forever and I couldn't stand the thought of working for a family with no end date in sight."

"Why?" Little Cao asked. "Because you don't want to be an ayi or because you don't want to live here?"

"I don't know. I miss home, but I don't think I could live there for good."

Everything Sunny wanted seemed impossible for her to have: the comfort of a family without losing herself to their needs, a feeling of stability without the requirement of marriage, and love—if she was lucky enough—in whatever form it came.

"Of course you couldn't! You make five grand a month and you're living in group housing. You don't like making friends. You're set on working here without living here—" Little Cao shook his head. "Not everybody who moves here from the countryside can figure out a way to stay. Sometimes not even people who grew up here can. But you have. You have an opportunity to build a life for yourself here if you want. But you can't do it when your heart is half there and half here. You've lived here five years and you've never been out to a proper bar before."

He was right. Rose had worked for half her adult life only to be shunted aside. Sunny, however, had been handed the ayi opportunity after just a few years of being in Shanghai. She knew she should be more grateful.

"You should give Shanghai a real try. Take whatever Boss Zhen can get you. It doesn't have to be forever. You save the money, maybe later take a secretarial class or something. You're still young. Who knows? You could end up working in an office."

At Medora earlier that day, Sunny had studied the rows of desks filled with young men and women typing on computers. Could it really be possible to have a job like that, one where — as Rose had put it — it would be someone else's responsibility to take her leftovers out in the trash? Was it work she would even enjoy? Little Cao was staring at her, waiting for some kind of acknowledgment of what he had said, some indication that she would take his advice.

"Don't drink that too fast," he said, motioning to her half-empty glass. "The night's just started."

The second club they went to was located on the fifth floor of a shopping mall. Its interior resembled a large amphitheater, complete with a high dome and U-shaped seating. Suspended from the ceiling of the uppermost level were large, glittering balls that reflected colored light. The dancers here were dressed in blue satin and performed on a stage that stretched from one end of the venue out into the center of the dance floors. Middle-aged men sat on couches, absorbed by the glow of their cell phones.

It was much louder here than it had been in the first club, and Little Cao had to shout to be heard. "Boss Zhen rarely comes here himself. Sometimes he sends me to take his younger associates here with clients who like a wilder lifestyle. Usually *before* the deals are made. Alcohol helps, zhi dao ba. Girls help." An attendant led them to a booth with a low table and handed them a menu and a flashlight. Little Cao ordered drinks and snacks, which arrived on the shoulders of waiters or held high over their heads above the crowd—trays of fruit and popcorn and bottles of baijiu. Soon after, three or four businessmen came to their booth and greeted Little Cao. It wasn't until they sat down that Sunny recognized their faces from Lanson Suites. But she hadn't glimpsed these men behind newspapers in the breakfast room or down in the gym. She'd seen them smoking in the parking lot, bending to inspect the wheels of one another's cars, and, on cold days, sipping hot tea from their canteens as they stood talking in a circle. They were drivers. Drivers in suits.

Her first instinct was to leave. She didn't want to be seen here with Little Cao by others who worked at the hotel. She didn't want to risk all the other maids finding out and thinking that her new job had changed her, that she had been taken in by this lavish lifestyle. She especially didn't want to risk the Zhens finding out. But the other drivers drew her into their circle so quickly and earnestly that it was impossible not to give in to their warmth. Bottles of Chivas were brought out with a stack of glasses and chilled cartons of oolong tea. The man closest to her poured the whiskey and Little Cao mixed in the tea. As Sunny sipped her drink, she started really listening to the music. American songs—that was expected. What surprised her was how the others in the club, even the Chinese nationals, all seemed to know the words.

"What's the song saying?" she asked Little Cao.

He stopped singing long enough to shake his head and say, "Not a clue!"

After that, her thoughts started to get a little slippery. She remembered the men getting more comfortable with her, calling her *mei*. They seemed to like the novelty of having a woman around and took the opportunity to make spectacles of themselves and one another. *Mei, see this scar right here? Ask him how he got that. Go ahead, ask him!*

Later, they sat four to a cab. How these drivers roared with laughter when there was someone else hired to drive! They cheered as they piled in, jostled and smacked one another playfully on the cheeks. They haggled for cigarettes with street vendors through the open windows of the car, stopped for sustenance at a FamilyMart, and, during a moment of extreme exuberance, lobbed a half-eaten tea egg at an apartment building.

The third venue was a lounge called Baby Gold. It was hosting a costume party, but Sunny couldn't get a feel for the theme of the costumes. Women walked by in slashed leather and wigs. Men had on wide-brimmed hats and shirts open at the collar. Cigarette smoke filled the air, and at first Sunny didn't notice the decor. But after they were seated, she saw that the lounge was designed to look like a million decks of cards had exploded inside it. Embedded in the translucent floor were cards scattered faceup to achieve a dizzying effect. The bar's countertop displayed the majestic queen of hearts, flanked on either side by a jack of diamonds. Above the crowd stood performers in stilts, and in the middle of the dance floor was a ten-foot-high martini glass filled with hard candies wrapped in cellophane. Standing — well, half dancing and half stomping — around inside the glass was a very small man. A very, very small man, dressed in leather to match the women's outfits.

"I can't imagine Taitai and Boss Zhen here," Sunny said to Little Cao. They watched the little man unwrap a lollipop and stick it into his mouth.

"Well, not *here*, exactly. This place...you wouldn't bring a client here."

Sunny realized what the main difference was between this place and the other two. The clientele was almost entirely Chinese.

"That's right," Little Cao said. "We're away from all the hotel bars now. New establishments trying to rise up, make a name for themselves. When we go out, it's important to end the night somewhere like this. Spend our own money in a place that's never heard the name Medora Group. That way we don't forget what it means to really be Shanghainese, right? That this is ours. It was ours long before those foreign bastards got here." He was a cheery drunk, his eyes sparkling. "Anyways, we'll get a call from those Expo guys any minute. Time to go soon. But I just wanted to show you what Shanghai is like outside of those luxury high-rises. Thought you'd want to see it."

He sat back in his seat to give Sunny a wider view of the room. A peal of laughter came from the table next to theirs, where two couples were playing liar's dice. Sunny was surprised to see the game set up here, in this fancy club. An unexpected reminder of home. She noticed then that there was a stack of leather playing cups and dice at their own table too.

"This place is my favorite so far," Sunny said to Little Cao.

"Shi ma? Mine too."

"How are your bluffing skills?" Sunny nodded toward the playing cups and the five dice sitting in a row on a tray, waiting to be thrown.

"Not bad." Little Cao winked. "When there's money involved."

"I'll take that bet," Sunny said.

An hour later, after Sunny had relieved three drivers of all the cash in their pockets, she wandered out onto the smoking deck, looking for a breeze. Here, a few blocks west of the Bund, Lanson Suites was barely noticeable, its thin neon-yellow lighting outshone by larger digital displays facing the river. Sunny had sobered enough to feel a gentle throbbing sensation at the back of her head. She picked up an abandoned glass left at the edge of a table, swirled the last drops of liquid around its bottom, and set it down again. Then she looked out toward Pudong, thinking how expansive the city always seemed, especially tonight.

A man was staring at her. He was leaning up against the same railing as she, a thin crop of hair circling a shiny bald spot. Li Jun! He must have been standing there all along. When he saw that she had seen him, he smiled and came toward her.

"Shi ni a," she said. *It's you.*

"Shi de." He must have had a few himself, because his movements were no longer as jolty and unsure as they had been on their first date. He didn't show any memory of their uncomfortable parting. He just looked genuinely happy to see her.

"Hai hao ba? I never would have expected to see you here. Do you go out a lot?" he asked.

"No," she said. "This is my first time, really. In Shanghai, I mean."

"I don't either. One of my friends invited us out to celebrate a new job…" He waved his hand behind him to indicate a general affiliation with the club-goers inside. "Ah, are you with…anyone?"

"Oh, no," she said. "I mean, yes. Just some friends from work."

Li Jun took this as an invitation to step closer.

"From Lanson Suites," he said.

"That's right."

His eyes moved across her face. "You know, I thought about what you said at dinner. I think you're right about my shop—the rent on Hengshan Lu might not be worth it. There are new developments cropping up in Tang Zhen and plenty of expat families moving in. They don't know how to use the Chinese net yet, and the English-speaking ones can't navigate Chinese sites anyway, so the business prospects for me might be better. I'm not ready to give up the Hengshan store, but rent out in Tang Zhen isn't too bad. I think I might start another branch over there, just to see how it does."

He caught himself rambling and held his fist up to his mouth, cleared his throat.

"That's great," Sunny said. "Congratulations."

"Thank you. I mean it. Thank you. I don't think I would have ever thought about the problem that way. That I should aim for a different kind of customer, that is."

"Sometimes it's easier for an outsider to see a problem for what it is."

"It's strange how fast these plans have grown since the idea took root. I've already lined up some places to check out."

Relaxed now, he was smiling. For a moment, Sunny couldn't believe it was the same man. Tonight, when they were no longer evaluating each other as candidly as they had the previous night, he was sparking her imagination.

"Listen," Li Jun said, "I'm glad to have run into you. I thought I might not see you again. I wanted to tell you: I was too forward last night. It was too soon. There should be romance, right? We could take it slow." When he saw her hesitation, he shook his head. "That's okay! I don't mean—I just mean maybe we could be friends. And then we can see where it goes. You know, I have a strong feeling about you. I think you're a very capable woman."

"Thank you," she said.

"Wah, I'm talking too much. Don't listen to me. I've had some drinks. Can I buy you another one? Let's just see each other again. No pressure."

Sunny laughed. "Yes," she said. "Let's be friends." She held her hand out to him, and when he took it, he didn't let go. Something about the night, or the alcohol, made her curious enough to take another step into this unfamiliar territory.

"Did I tell you that I used to be married?" Sunny asked.

"No, but Rose did." Sunny wondered what else Rose had said when she described her. *I know a woman. She's in her thirties, married once, no children. Strong build, no great beauty, but honest and hardworking.* What kind of man would Li Jun have been to want to meet her? Maybe—just maybe—a man meant for her.

"I was married to my first husband before I was ready," Sunny continued. "Something about our conversation last night reminded me of that feeling. Of being forced into…an arrangement I'm not ready for."

Li Jun nodded.

"I don't know that I'm ready, even now, for a second marriage. One thing I do know is that I don't want to repeat the experience of marrying someone for practicality's sake. I know that might sound foolish to you, but that's how I feel."

"I understand completely."

"So, yes, you're right. You asked me for an answer too soon. But I also refused you too soon."

At this, he looked up, a hint of hope in his eyes.

"What about dinner?" he asked. "Just as friends."

Sunny smiled. "All right."

"Next week, I have some business over by where you work. Lanson Suites, right? Afterward, I'll wait for you to get off. We can eat at one of those nice hotels. Like the Shangri-La!" He laughed at himself and shook his head again. "Okay, maybe not the Shangri-La. I don't want you to get the impression that I am wealthy. But maybe someplace along the water?" He had begun to perspire, but she was laughing, and Sunny thought, *This could be okay, maybe even good.* She drew her phone from her pocket.

"Here," she said. "I don't think we've exchanged numbers."

Her own voice sounded off to her. Soft, even flirtatious. Was she capable of flirtation? Apparently. It made some sense, what Little Cao had said about her working here without living here and leaving half her heart at home. If it was difficult to take the leap to pursue a career opportunity, it was even harder to do it for love. Who knew how many ways she was saying no to possibilities of love without knowing it? It felt right to act out of character tonight, to agree to Li Jun the way she had agreed to come out with Little Cao.

As if conjured by Sunny's thoughts, the Zhens' driver opened the door to the smoking deck and stepped outside. He appeared to be searching for her, and once he caught sight of her standing with Li Jun, his eyebrows shot up. He backed away, knees lifted high in an exaggerated gesture of retreat. She couldn't help but laugh, and Li Jun turned around to spot Little Cao just before he disappeared.

"I think that's my cue to go," Sunny said.

Li Jun nodded. "Next week, then. I'm going to text you to remind you."

"I'll remember."

After Sunny stepped through the doors and into the club, she turned around for one last look at Li Jun and saw him facing the water again, elbows out, torso leaning forward. She felt at peace, watching him. It was a little like the way she felt when she finished cleaning a room—like she had done some small good, made things, if not better, at least more manageable for the moment.

21

"Qiang?"

"I'm here."

Lina sat cross-legged on the floor and leaned against the metal door. She felt curiously removed from the situation. The sensation of being trapped had turned itself inside out, and now there was a freedom that came from not being able to see the confines of the room or exactly where Qiang was sitting.

"How long has it been?"

"Thirty-eight minutes."

Although the air-conditioning had been turned off, the floor was cool, and Lina felt chilled. She pulled her knees up to her chin and wrapped her arms around her legs.

"It seems like yesterday we were teenagers sitting by the lake like this with nothing to do," Qiang said.

Lina stiffened. "We're not teenagers anymore."

"Well, I know that."

She drummed her head back against the door, lightly at first, and then audibly. It was easier to be flippant with him than angry at herself. She was the one who had forgotten they weren't teenagers. What was she doing, paying off a guard to sneak them into a place like this?

The UK pavilion had four possible exits. Aside from the one in the Seed Cathedral, there was the side door through which they had come, a door off the VIP room, and the back door, which led to the exit ramp. All four were locked. After trying each one and the main entrance twice, Lina had released a string of southern swearwords that she hadn't known were still in her vocabulary. Qiang, however, had taken it all as a matter of course. He'd inspected the main door's lock and hinges one last time, given a confused and impressed *Eh* when they'd proved resistant to his manipulations, and finally settled down on the ground to await rescue.

"Tell me about the funeral," Qiang suddenly said, breaking the silence. "What was it like?"

Maybe it was the darkness of the cathedral that did it, but scenes from the week following their parents' deaths came to Lina more vividly than they ever had before. The experience had been dreamlike, in the way that terrible things in dreams don't seem so terrible, and trivial, normal events can seem worse than they should. Lina remembered booking flights and packing both hers and Wei's clothing with the calm, purposeful air of someone going on a business trip. The plane ride hadn't been easy with a fourteen-month-old, but perhaps she should have been grateful for the challenge and distraction of keeping Karen quiet, fed, and asleep. It wasn't until they landed in Shanghai for a transfer flight that Lina felt the panic start to set in. There were people pushing to get off the plane, loudspeakers announcing flight-change information, a legless man on a rolling wooden platform pushing himself down the aisles of the gate as he begged for coins, the frightening set of Wei's jaw, and the crying child in her arms. She couldn't handle it — she had thrust Karen at Wei and gone on a long walk around the airport by herself, trying to breathe right again.

The next day, Wei had arranged for someone to watch the baby while they attended the service alone. Not having Karen in her arms somehow left Lina feeling even more bereft and she'd sobbed through the entire ceremony, making a spectacle of herself in front of hundreds of people she didn't know. She didn't remember the procession at all, just the stiffness of Wei's suit jacket, into which she'd kept her face pressed, inhaling the scent of public transport, shoe polish, and sweat. Afterward, she and Wei were led to the crematorium and storage facility where their parents' ashes were kept. The building didn't look so different from the school where Lina worked. It had been recently built and still smelled of paint varnish. The interior felt commercial, impersonal. The hallways echoed beneath their feet. The cremation urns were stored in little square lockers, rows of which stretched from floor to ceiling. Each locker had a name, a birth and death date, and a small photograph of the deceased attached to the locker door. They'd looked for his parents first, and then hers, and found that although their forms had been processed at the same time, the two couples' urns were located in different aisles. Out of all the terrible things, that one felt like the final kick in the gut.

"It was what you would expect," Lina said. "There were a lot of people there. The whole silk factory showed up, seemed like. And some of your dad's friends from Yunnan had heard. They came up."

She could hear the rustling fabric of his jeans as he got more comfortable.

"I heard too, at the time. I wanted to come down but I couldn't."

Couldn't—or wouldn't? He would have been gone ten years by then. He had kept tabs on them for that long without ever seeing them.

"They were your parents," she said.

"You don't understand. That was '99. I was wanted."

"Ha!" The single syllable echoed along the floors of the cathedral. "It's not like you haven't escaped the law before."

"No," Qiang said. "Not the law, Lina. I was wanted by other gangs. *Tian a*, if it had been a matter of just turning myself in…"

Lina and Wei had spent most of that funeral trip in the tea lounge of the hotel, Wei trying to stay on top of his work and Lina staring out the window at the minimal foot traffic. They had chosen a hotel halfway between their hometown and the city center. After dark, they'd taken walks in the direction of the village until the number of street lamps along the roads started to diminish. Then they turned around and walked back. Neither of them brought up the fact that Qiang wasn't there. Lina was so overcome with grief that she remembered it only as a shadow of a thought, but Wei must have felt differently. His own brother, after all. She should have asked Wei about it. Why hadn't she taken care of him in the ways that he had taken care of her?

"By that point, I'd made such a name for myself gambling that half the gangs in Beijing wanted me dead and the other half wanted me playing for their tables. Brother Gao hired three guys just to protect me, you understand? Cloudy and I, we never slept without people we knew outside our door. If they'd found out anything about my family, that would have made it too easy for them. I would have been putting you in danger. I knew you and Wei would be going back to America after the funeral, but I couldn't risk it."

She hated that the mention of him and Cloudy together stung. Lina wondered what the woman looked like now—if she still seemed so stylish and bold, or if being part of *hei shehui* had made her less resilient. And what would Lina be like now if things had worked out the way she'd wanted them to when she was twenty-two?

"The last time we spoke, when you came to my house that night, you said that if I was to go with you I'd be safe. That wouldn't have been true, would it?"

Qiang sighed. "I don't know, Lina. I don't know what choices I might have made if you had been with me. My whole life would be different, wouldn't it? I didn't lie to you about the fighting—I never fought. I never wanted to and Brother Gao wouldn't have let me anyway. I made too much money to be risked."

She pictured Qiang and Cloudy huddled up in a casino suite, a passel of hotel shopping bags cluttered around the foot of their bed and three men with concealed weapons strolling around outside their door.

"So that's what you've been doing all these years? Playing for money?"

"No. Once we had enough money, there were other operational things we could do. There was a group of guys working for us whose job it was to settle disputes between other black-society operations. So our business was mostly managing them. We ran gambling dens because by then we had enough money to pay off cops. Brother Gao, he eventually went off and did his own thing—drug trafficking, prostitution. Me and Cloudy and Jian Hua, though—we never got into anything like that. For a while, we just laid low. But it takes some time for your name to fall off the radar."

Lina and Wei had spent more than twenty years wondering where Qiang was and what he'd been doing, but now that she had the information, she could not make sense of it. Underground factions, gambling halls, paying off cops—it all sounded like a pitch for a crime movie.

"You couldn't have let us know? Sent some kind of word that you were okay?"

"Send word back to my family that I was involved in a gang? Yeah, that really would have put them at ease." How petulant he sounded. This was not a side of Qiang that Lina had ever seen before. Wei had told her about the spats Qiang had gotten into with their father, but she had never quite been able to imagine them until now.

"We're not stupid. We knew what you were doing, what you were involved in. Maybe not the specifics, but we knew you were part of black society. We thought you might have been dead. Even when you were years gone, Wei would wake up sometimes in the night, and he'd turn over, and his expression—I knew he was thinking about you. I could tell."

"I know you both think badly of me, okay? I know. That's because I *am* bad. I misled you, I hurt my family...I was wrong. I own up to it."

His words came out in a rush, so different from the usual unhurried quality of his speech. She could tell that saying them had afforded him some relief. How disgusting. What good was admitting you were wrong when there was nothing to be done about it and the only thing left to be had was forgiveness?

And yet, so much of what she loved about Qiang was his willingness to be wrong. Wei was never wrong. Every moment in her husband's life was anticipated and optimized. He prided himself on his control over his surroundings, whereas Qiang seemed desperate for his surroundings to effect some change on him. Wei would never have put himself in a position to say *I wish I had ended up with you*. Wei was the type of man who would have made it happen.

"What was America like?" Qiang asked.

The want in his voice was so clear. Wasn't it natural for him to have spent years wondering about them too? The word that came to mind when she thought about life with Wei was *grounded*. Against all odds, the two of them had been able to establish roots on the other side of the world. But Lina knew that wasn't what Qiang was asking. He wanted to know whether she had come to love Wei after all. *Do you think you'll be happy with him?*

"It was happy," she finally said. A lump rose in her throat. "A solid, steady kind of happy—the sort of happy nobody talks about because they don't think about it unless they're asked."

"Well," he replied after a moment, "it's a good thing I asked."

Even though she couldn't see him, she could imagine his posture exactly, the way his arms were looped loosely around his knees and the heavy drop of his head.

"I think we should talk about it," Qiang said suddenly. "How I never fulfilled my end of the bargain."

She wished she could see his face. She'd waited so long to have this conversation, and she felt robbed of the sight of him.

"I regret leaving Suzhou. I came here to tell both of you that I was wrong for leaving. But I don't regret not telling my father about us like I said I would. That would have been the worst way to betray our families."

Ba, let me walk with you, she had said the morning of the wedding. *I have something to say.* She had knowingly let her father down, and she had done it for Qiang. It was one of the last times she would see him.

"All you ever did was cause your family pain. You think marrying me would have been the worst thing you could have done? You've always made the selfish, impulsive choice. So why the sudden moral high ground? Why is it that when it came to the two of us, you suddenly developed a conscience?"

He exhaled as though he had been holding his breath, waiting for her to ask just that question. But when he answered, all he said was "It was never supposed to be me."

So, silence — Qiang's favorite card to play. The image in her mind had only grown clearer with time: young Qiang lying beside the lake, turning his body so that all she could see was the damp gleam of his ribs, the wet, crumpled fabric on his hips. By his boot, a small curved knife. *Why do you have that?* He'd paused then as he paused now, deciding how much of himself to reveal. It was always on his terms, this opacity. She hated that she still felt such a need for his answers. She didn't want to need him at all.

But now there was no denying that silence was the weaker move. He knew this. She hoped he also knew how despicable she had come to find him, how lacking. He had to answer.

"If I'm going to tell this story," he finally said, "I have to start from the very beginning. What do you say to another drink?"

She'd say he was stalling. But the truth was, she felt she ought to prepare herself too.

"All right," she answered.

Lina heard his footsteps approaching, and then Qiang's hand appeared out of the darkness. Lina allowed herself to be helped to a standing position. Together they walked the perimeter of the cathedral, arms outstretched to feel for the wall of seeds, searching for the way back downstairs. The red light of the VIP lounge was a shock to her retinas, and they both squinted as they reentered the room. On Lina's way to the couch, she caught a glimpse of herself in the mirrored walls and was ashamed of the thin tunic she wore. It was cut too closely to her body. How desperately she played at youth.

Qiang had approached the bar as solemnly as he would an operating table. She watched as he poured each drink carefully and brought them over to the couch.

"Hao de," he said. "Here goes."

22

It begins the way many stories begin: A young man leaves home. He is twenty-two, a professor of chemistry, his glasses flimsy, hair cropped close to his head. Like many other intellectuals of the time, he has been singled out by the party as one who could use reeducating, and so he has left his young wife and newborn child behind in Suzhou. With him is a canvas bag filled with the barest of essentials: linen pants, twill work shirts, heavy winter clothing, and an extra blanket. He boards a train bound west and notes that he is the only one who looks out of place at the cadre school, the only one who has brought a book with him. In three months, he will find the pages of his book missing. By then it will not occur to him to ask who has used it for kindling. The tenets of group living will have become as mindless to him as the first steps he takes in the morning—from his hay mattress to the coal stove to the outhouse at the back of the grounds. Come winter, he will be the one to remove the cover of the book and wedge it into a chink in the window, an effort to keep in heat.

It wasn't an easy transition for Fang, this countryside life. Never before had he carried wood on his back, slept in a room with twenty other men, or studied socialist thought until the words beat against his dreams. Never had he seen a dead woman dragged out of the dormitory by her feet. *Illness,* the dormitory leader said when asked for the woman's cause of death. *But she was fine yesterday!* someone shouted. *No.* The dorm leader tapped her temple. *Not the kind of illness you can see.*

There were terrors that Fang Lijian could not begin to understand. What he did know was that thinking was going to get him in trouble, any way you looked at it. Say your thoughts out loud and you'd be punished by the government. Keep them to yourself and they'd kill you from the inside. He resolved to think as little as possible and to focus on the tasks he was given.

At the end of six months, Fang Lijian felt as if he had lived half his life in the countryside. He was surprised to find that he didn't mind the work itself, even liked the way his muscles had risen into sluglike shapes along his back, the smell of smoked tea leaves, and the novelty of this community and their sun-driven routines. It was simpler, more primal. He had almost forgotten he was there against his will. *What you learn here,* the camp leader said, *is all you will ever need to know.* The hunger for information, which had once led him to become an academic, was now fed by the stories of the other men. Fang Lijian liked listening to the farmhands talk, though he said little himself.

He was particularly taken by a man named Zhen Hong. Earnest and outgoing, Zhen Hong could spend the entire afternoon telling the rest of them about their country — tales of hard work, camaraderie, and nationhood, all featuring common and capable men of the cause.

Fang was no stranger to revolutionary fervor. He had grown up in the fifties, after all. He had memorized the necessary slogans, performed the necessary self-criticisms. Knew that in the eyes of the government, his mind did not belong to him. And yet, in Shanghai, he had been privileged. He had an office in which to hide and did not see the violence of the land reforms in the countryside. Government, to him, meant paranoid men in uniform waving around written directives in an effort to suppress feudalist ideals.

During those afternoons in the fields, Zhen Hong created a different perspective. He spoke about public good, about how every man in China had a place in effecting it. He wanted to help the CCP protect the country in a way that their ancestors had not been able to. *We can't be the country other countries stomp all over anymore,* he said. *We've got to get healthy as a nation. Pull ourselves together, centralize. Maybe not every program or campaign has proven successful, but think of the greater good: We have a system in place. We have grounds for improvement.*

Aside from being a cadre-school director, Zhen had also been a district leader during the Great Leap Forward, and the campaign's failure had intensified the humility and seriousness to which he was already predisposed. This was the part of him that Fang responded to most, for it was the part that existed in himself. Their differences in background and demeanor only made their commonalities stand out, and although Fang didn't say much in the fields (he was a slow worker and privately believed that this afforded him less right to speak), Zhen Hong saw it too. They grew close. After sundown, Fang was in the habit of stopping by Zhen's home to pass the time in conversation or a game of Go. When he looked in on Zhen and his wife, they seemed to him like the future incarnate. If only all of China was made of such hope and drive! Zhen Hong had never been properly educated, and yet he was the smartest man Fang knew. There had to be some validity to the CCP's methods — reeducation, it seemed to him, actually worked.

The days were like a single note played over and over again, but because they were so similar, they blended into one comforting hum. That was how, in the countryside, time could stretch and shrink at once. Everything was shared in the labor camp, and soon the stories of their families back home became communal too. Every man there had someone he had left behind. Bent over fieldwork, their faces reflecting the luminous green of the tea leaves they harvested, they told stories that rose to the same tone and pitch. Their sentiments evened out. Marital indifference and resentments disappeared for some, and for the lucky few who had it good back home, something was lost in the telling of their wives and children. Their memories lost sharpness. The idea of missing became bigger than the missing itself. Aside from the weekly letters that Fang Lijian received from his wife (updates on the baby, news of the neighborhood gossip), his family was excluded from the world of the tea farm. His thoughts of them became what he reached for rather than what reached for him.

A young woman came into Fang's range of vision so subtly he didn't know he was looking at her until he couldn't look away. Her name was Yuzi. She had full cheeks that ended in a sharp little chin. She wore her hair in two braids at the top of her head and worked with quick hands and had an even quicker tongue. Yuzi had a child who was just a few months old at the time, barely a bulge of a boy strapped to her back in the Yunnan heat. Because of the way she wore her hair, from a distance mother and son looked like an ant carrying its cargo between the rows of tea bushes. As the story went, Yuzi's husband had been a government official on his way out of Mao's favor. Two weeks before Fang's arrival, he had disappeared. No one knew for sure where he'd gone, but most guessed he'd escaped to Macao.

By the time Fang Lijian got to the tea farm, Yuzi had already won the compassion of the other cadre-school members, and it was only natural for Fang to feel tender toward her too. He found himself dishing out extra pork for the infant during mealtimes and then lingering to watch the boy's mother chew it up and transfer it, bit by bit, into her son's mouth. Unlike the rest of the workers, Fang Lijian was mesmerized not by the woman's misfortune, but by the woman herself.

The more time they spent together, the more the rest of the community began to look in the opposite direction. It was out of politeness, not disapproval. They were relieved that someone was taking care of her.

They must have known that Fang was married, but this was during a time when none of them knew what the country had in store for them. Some of their loved ones had been sent to labor camps worse than theirs, and many of them had disappeared, never to be heard from again. The rules by which they'd lived their old lives seemed too distant from the lives they lived now.

Fang allowed this new, rusticated version of himself to grow close to Yuzi—in the fields, at meals, and, eventually, at night among the tea plants, where they lay naked together, their bodies against the cool earth. He felt as though he were drowning, and every morning he woke thinking about her, the line between dreaming and waking so thin he could still feel her skin against his. He smelled the scent of her on his skin all day; imagined or real, he could not be sure. He couldn't escape her. For a time, he felt there must be something wrong with him. This feeling wasn't love, because he'd felt love before. He loved his wife, and he loved his daughter. What he felt for Yuzi could only be described as a sickness.

Fang Lijian looked forward to winter, when the harvesting would come to a close and he could spend as much time as possible with Yuzi. He pictured them taking the baby for a walk through the rows of tea leaves, the sky low and thick with clouds. But that winter, Yuzi developed a cough that bloomed into tuberculosis. They moved her to a hut by herself, and she insisted that the baby stay with Fang Lijian while she recovered.

Spending time away from Yuzi created the space Fang needed to see the situation in a more objective manner. Now when he looked into the boy's eyes, he no longer saw just Yuzi's features. What he saw in front of him—in his round eyes, in the uncertain wave of his arms—was vulnerability in its purest form. It reminded him of his own family, the wife and daughter he had left in Shanghai. In that respect, he was not so different from Yuzi's runaway husband. In that respect, maybe he was worse. When Zhen Hong came by to check on his friend and his friend's young charge, he could see multiple strains of desperation on Fang's face: his fear and love for Yuzi, the shock of being responsible for the baby, and the guilt of having betrayed his own family.

Meanwhile, Yuzi's health worsened. The blood she coughed up could no longer be contained in the rags that, despite constantly being washed and wrung out, would not lose their metallic smell. During nights at home with the baby, Fang Lijian set about hammering an old tin basin into a bean-shaped receptacle to fit around Yuzi's neck. This way, the fluid could be emptied, quickly and cleanly, into a pit in the courtyard and covered up by dirt.

As Yuzi worsened, she began to grow desperate and slowly lose control of her mind. She asked after her son constantly and fell silent only when she heard the sound of children's feet or their shouts coming through the cracks in the window. Then she would lift her head to look outside — imagining, perhaps, her son's future passing her by.

She died on the day of the first frost. The camp leader had her buried in an unused plot of land a forty-minute walk from where the tea bushes grew. It was far enough, they calculated, that there would be no way for the sickness to contaminate the crops. Fang Lijian refused Zhen Hong's offers to help carry the boy to the burial ground. He kept his arm folded under Yuzi's son's bottom and his other hand on his back as they made the funeral march. The two were chest to chest, and Fang could feel the little boy's heart beating against his own, his short fingers closing tighter around the back of his neck as they went. Along the way, Fang Lijian began to cry, but after days of crying for Yuzi, his tears were no longer for her. Now he was crying for himself. He was crying for the heart of his young wife and the ridicule they'd face when he brought home someone else's son. In the final days before Yuzi's death, Fang had acted on impulse: he had promised her he would look after the boy, raise him until he could go out on his own.

Unlike Fang Lijian, Zhen Hong had foreseen this difficult situation.

He knew that Yuzi would ask Fang and that Fang would not be able to say no. Zhen Hong and his wife were protective of Fang. Never had they imagined they would see a chemistry professor working in the fields, and they viewed him as a physical embodiment of the progress the nation was making. But as much as he supported the idea of equality, Zhen Hong could never see Fang as a true equal. No matter how much time he spent in the fields, Fang could not rid himself of the delicate motion of his wrists as he picked the tea leaves. His eyes still had that strained quality whenever he tried to look farther than middle distance. The Zhens could not bear the thought of Fang bringing home the child; they feared it would ruin his life. Sometime during Yuzi's quarantine, the couple had come to a decision. Now, as the funeral procession neared that unused plot of land, Zhen Hong introduced the idea.

"Fang Lijian," he said. "Give the child to me. Menghua and I will raise him as our own."

Fang stared at Zhen until the words sank in, and then he lowered his head.

"Don't joke around."

"I'm not joking. I mean it."

"This has nothing to do with you."

"Brother, stop a moment." Zhen put a hand on his friend's arm and they stepped to the side of the road, letting the procession move on past them.

"A child born in the fields should be raised in the fields."

"He is not your charge," Fang said. "It's too much to ask."

"A boy is always a useful hand. Plus, we've got one already. It's not much more work to raise two than it is to raise one, and he'll have a brother to keep him company."

"It's another mouth to feed," Fang said.

"Think about what's best for the boy. Menghua is still making milk. We could provide more than you could. What will your wife say when you come home with another woman's son? How will she believe it isn't yours?"

Fang Lijian did not have an answer to this. He wanted badly to take the offer. He felt as though he were finally waking from a dream that had kept him captive these six months. The more lucidly he saw his old life as he'd left it, the more he feared.

"Why are you doing this?" he asked, desperate with hope.

"Because I love you," Zhen Hong said. "You are like a brother, and I will not see you fall."

Fang Lijian looked into Zhen Hong's crescent eyes. It was the first time anyone had ever expressed love for him so plainly and unexpectedly. At that moment, Fang Lijian understood how liberal and forward-thinking Zhen Hong truly was. He felt humbled to be standing in front of this man whose frame of mind was so clear, whose actions were driven directly by his ideals and desires, whose life was simple because he refused to complicate it. Was that what liberalism was really about?

"I have a daughter," Fang said. "She is almost your son's age exactly. I will do this if we match her with him."

Zhen Hong laughed. "A farm boy and the daughter of a scholar? It wouldn't be right."

"Brother," Fang Lijian said with a smile. "I thought you were all about progress. If we are meant to be family, let's be a true family."

Zhen Hong thought about this for a moment, and then he nodded, a smile forming at the corners of his lips. "That would make me very happy."

"Let's shake on it." Fang Lijian extracted his arm from beneath the boy's bottom and held out his hand. Zhen Hong took it and squeezed, noting how callused Fang's skin had become since the first months that he knew him. And then Zhen Hong reached for the boy.

The child made no sound when being transferred from one man to another. Already, he had acquired the detached expression of an orphan.

It was a look that in his teenage years would be interpreted by his teachers to mean mischief. By the time the two men rejoined the crowd and the boy witnessed his mother being lowered into the ground, he had changed families twice. He would change once more before he reached the age of eighteen.

23

"You," Lina whispered. "You're the boy."

She half expected Qiang to tell her she'd understood the story wrong, but he only took a deep breath and leaned forward, steeling himself against her reaction.

"This is—this is all impossible. My father would never cheat on my mother."

But even as she said the words, she doubted them. Her mind back-tracked, trying to fit everything into place: the veiled arguments between her parents about a debt, her mother's refusal to speak to Qiang each time he came to their house.

But how could her father have been capable of it? Those summer nights when the three of them slept outside on bamboo mats, she'd woken to find him wrapped around her mother, as close as a wisteria vine. Lina had always thought of her parents' relationship as a paragon of marriage, and to this day she could remember her father's voice in her head: *Love is not some mysterious force that comes from nowhere...Don't you know the simplest things can be the most magical? Remember: Time and commitment. If you have these two things, you can have any manner of love.* She had lived her entire life by his ideas of what it meant to love.

"I know you were close with your father," Qiang said. "That's part of why I didn't want to tell you. I didn't want it to change your memory of him."

Between where they stood at opposite ends of the bar were uncapped bottles of liquor. Qiang had taken a swig from each one as he neared the conclusion of his story. He seemed to want to punish himself as much as he wanted to get drunk. Lina stared at him now, his expression stoic but unnerved.

"How could it not?" she asked. "He always spoke of marriage as a sacrament. If what you're saying is true, then that was all a lie."

Qiang shook his head. "He made a mistake."

She remembered the look on her father's face when she admitted her feelings for Qiang—it was as though his spirit had broken. And no wonder. Choosing Qiang over Wei would have meant undoing years of his own penance.

"I always thought my parents' love was the strongest of anyone's in our town. I was proud of it. I wanted what they had."

"This doesn't mean it wasn't. Maybe it was as strong as it was because of it."

"Because he *cheated* on her?"

The sight of her mother's back, one shoulder tensed as she worked the kitchen knife.

"No, because she forgave him."

Poor woman. To continue to love her husband as much as she had after all that must have been the work of a lifetime. And there she had been, thinking Jiajia's dislike of the Zhens was political.

So Qiang had done the right thing after all. It would have been impossible for him to marry Lina. As selfish as Lina was capable of being, she could never have allowed her mother to look into the face of her son-in-law and see the face of her husband's mistress.

Qiang abandoned the liquor bottles and came to stand beside her.

"Your ba loved you," he said. "And he did his best by you and your mother." He lifted his hands as though he meant to lay them on her shoulders, but then thought better of it. "I did a lot of growing up in the years after you left for America. I used to think that being orphaned meant I was short of the kind of love a person deserved. I would deliver fruit to your family, and your father would look at me in this particular way—with a certain kind of love, yes, but mixed with other things: longing, regret, and shame."

Lina had always thought that Qiang was sent to her house because the Zhens didn't want to upset her mother by sending Wei. Now she saw an ulterior motive. Her father must have wanted to see Qiang. He must have still cared, despite the reminder of shame Qiang brought with him.

"In my mind, I somehow convinced myself that if your father had taken me in, things would have turned out differently. He loved my mother, and I thought that meant I'd have a chance of him loving me. Really, though, I'd known pure love all along. I'd known it from Zhen Hong, my true father, and Menghua, my second mother. To take in a child and give love so willingly like that, with no obligation—isn't that the most generous love of all? I didn't see that at the time. All I saw was the love that was withheld from me. Love I thought I was entitled to. Your father's love. And, later, your love. There is so much love that we throw away so easily for not understanding it. So don't do that. Don't find a way to doubt him."

He was close to her now, and she could smell the alcohol on his breath.

"Why do we do that?" he asked, his voice climbing. "Why do our minds fixate on the kinds of love we're not getting instead of the kinds of love we are? We expect it to be the thing we want it to be. And we're blind to every other form of it." His collar was wet with perspiration.

"I don't know," Lina said. Forty-three years old and her entire life now seemed a mystery. How could she have idealized her parents' love?

How could she not have sensed her father's betrayal beneath it all, his contrition?

"You know, I spent a lot of time when I was growing up wishing I was Wei. Hating him for being what I wasn't."

"And now?"

"Now I don't. I don't know why. I guess I've been me for too long. I wouldn't know what to do with...all that."

He rolled his shoulders as though shrugging off whatever it was about his brother that threatened to make them the same.

"Wouldn't know what to do with what?" Lina asked. "A career? A family? To you these things probably mean nothing."

"No, I didn't mean—" He rubbed his face and shook his head. "I'm not the kind of man Wei is."

"No. You're not." Her voice was low and full of contempt. "You've told the story as though you were there," she said. "Those details—how do you know these things? Did you talk about them with my dad?"

Qiang shook his head. "Zhen Hong told me. Once I knew the truth, I wanted the particulars of the story. I wanted to know who my real ma was, and I guess he didn't feel right withholding that from me. The parts of the story I don't know, I've filled in with my own imagination. I've had a lot of time to think about it. Can you imagine? I spent that whole summer we were together thinking about that story. But even before that, it was never far from my mind."

"When did you find out? That you were...that you weren't biologically..."

"Young. Maybe eleven or twelve years old. I came home one day after doing something against my father's wishes—I can't remember what it was, but it was something that made him decide to tell me. It was the only way he felt he could get my attention, I think. To say that I wasn't his real son. I think he regretted it afterward, because it had the opposite effect. I started to use it as an excuse to misbehave. I guess I was sure that a day would come when he'd kick me out of the house, and I wanted it to happen sooner rather than later. I wanted to get it over with."

An orphan. Lina recalled Qiang at the Zhen family dinner table after he'd come back from Beijing. How clearly he had seemed set apart from the rest of them. He had surprised everyone by serving his parents, and filling their teacups every few minutes. Had he been mocking them by playing the part of the good son? Oh, Qiang. It was one thing to grow up feeling like a foreigner in your family, another to have that foreignness confirmed. Zhen Hong had likely told him that story to threaten disownment, not realizing that simply by telling him, he had already done it.

"After I left home and ran off with Brother Gao, I thought about that year in the countryside even more. Maybe I've filled in some places with my own imagination, but the important facts are there. Trust me, if I could reimagine that story in a way—" He interrupted himself with a laugh that ended in a sigh.

"Is that why you left home when Wei and I went to university? Because you wanted to distance yourself?"

"That was why I left the first time."

"And the second time? After our wedding?"

"The second time it was because I was in love with you."

Ai shang ni le. In Chinese, the verb associated with romantic love was "to rise." It was proof that Americans had a better understanding of its true nature, or else that romance existed only for the young and naive.

"And Wei never knew?"

"No," Qiang said. "Did he ever know about—you know—us?"

"No."

He nodded; she could see he was relieved.

"I asked my father about you," Lina said. "On the day of the wedding, I asked him if it could be you instead. I said I'd still be marrying into the Zhen family. He would still be repaying his friend's kindness—"

She understood suddenly, just as the words were coming from his mouth.

"And of course it wasn't true," Qiang said, "because…aiya, because I *was* the debt. And you were the repayment."

He paused, giving the words the gravity they deserved. One look at his face told her that he expected them to effect some change in her, that understanding the situation fully would convince her to forgive him. But as the truth became clear, she only grew angrier. He had known all along that they could never be together and still he had let her fall in love with him. He had allowed her to hope. Finally, she was able to see what her husband saw: that Qiang was selfish by nature. How had she overlooked this essential part of who he was?

"If you had explained things to me years ago, maybe I wouldn't have spent so long wondering what happened between us."

Qiang lowered his eyes. She could see disappointment take over his body, could feel his instinct to pull away. "You're right. I should have said it then."

"And now?" she asked before it was too late. "Why did you get in touch now?"

Qiang shook his head. "For years, I tried to forget about you, and Wei, and my parents. I thought if I never saw you again, I could start over. Go my own way. When I lived at home I felt caged. After I left, for the first few years, that feeling went away. But slowly, I felt the cage drop down on me again. It only got worse when my parents died. I realized that it wasn't good enough to have physically escaped our village—that you and Wei and my parents were a part of me, and I couldn't escape from myself.

"A few years ago, I decided I wanted to see you and Wei again, but I was afraid. Afraid you'd be angry, afraid my own jealousies for my brother would rear up again. I looked you up when you were in America. I had Wei's e-mail address through his company's website but I never used it. Then one day, I saw Wei on TV, and that's how I knew you were back. I took it as a sign that it was time."

So he was selfish and a coward too.

"Lina, I'm sorry—"

She shook her head. "I know. It's over now. Thank you for telling me."

The muscles in her back pulled at the base of her spine. She had been standing all day and her shoes bit at the heels of her feet. The desire to be home and in her own bed came over her so swiftly that she almost lost her balance. Lina took off her shoes and walked barefoot to where Qiang was already sitting on the couch, his head in his hands. The leather of the couch tugged at the skin on her thighs, then gave as she scooted back. The charge between them was gone—he was just a man sitting next to her on a couch. She wasn't angry anymore. She felt pity for him, but only distantly.

"Does Wei know you're adopted?" she asked after a while.

"No," he said. "I think I would have known if he knew. My greatest fear used to be that he would find out. It was so clear to me back then that he was their real son and that I wasn't. Sometimes I thought he must have been incredibly oblivious not to have known. But why would he have reason to suspect if our parents hadn't said anything? Every time I messed up I thought Ba was on the verge of kicking me out. If Wei had known too, I think that would have been too much for me. But now I want him to know. I have been trying to find a time to tell him. Our parents are gone now and I'm all he has left besides you and Karen, and I want to be a good brother to him even if I wasn't before. I will never have the chance to be a good son to my parents. That I will always regret."

He was crying freely now. She wanted to say something to comfort him but there seemed to be nothing left to say. Instead, she placed her hand on his back and waited for him to regain control. Finally, he wiped his face with the palm of one hand, swallowed, and sighed softly. He lifted his arm around her and pressed her to his chest. It was warm and unfamiliar, and her body could not help responding with a light tingle.

But then the feeling passed; she closed her eyes. In time, their breathing slowed, became almost one.

•   •   •

And then morning. Beneath closed lids was a dawning of color—a bright light being waved in front of her. Suddenly, Little Cao's face came into view. He extinguished the flashlight function on his cell phone and smiled. Beside him were three Expo guards, backlit by the red glow of the bar. One held a broom, another a clipboard, and the last a walkie-talkie. Beyond were four policemen, their expressions ranging from awe to annoyance. Lina followed their gaze to the uncapped bottles of liquor still sitting on the bar, the drained glasses on the countertop, and Qiang snoring lightly beside her. She shook him by the wrist. When he opened his eyes and saw the policemen before them, he bolted upright. A sheepish smile crossed his face.

"What is this?" One of the policemen took a step toward the bar and lifted an empty bottle. When he looked up, his upper lip was pulled into an expression of disgust. With his other hand, he pointed a finger at Little Cao and shook it emphatically. "This," he said, "this is too much."

"Now, wait a minute—"

"This is destruction of property!" He switched his flashlight on and waved it in the direction of Lina and Qiang. "This is a breach of security!"

"It's a breach of *their* security," Little Cao countered. "Two Expo attendees try to visit one of the most popular attractions at the Expo and they get *stuck* in there."

"They're drunk," the officer said wildly.

"We're not." Lina stood and slipped on her shoes as discreetly as possible. "We were just looking at the Seed Cathedral and the lights went out. We didn't mean to get trapped. And then we got bored waiting so we came down here…"

She smoothed her blouse and watched the officer recalibrate his opinion of her as he took in her outfit, her perfect Mandarin accent.

"This is Zhen Taitai," Little Cao said. "She lives in Lujiazui. In Lanson Suites."

"Ni hao." Lina extended her hand palm-down toward the officer. He let it hang there a fraction of a second before he shook it. Then he craned his neck to look behind her.

"And who is that?"

"That's my brother-in-law," Lina said. "He came from Kunming to see the Expo." She wished Qiang would wipe that stupid smile off his face. "Thank you for coming to rescue us. We'll pay for all the liquor. We've been here for hours. All we want to do is go home."

The officer drummed the flashlight on his thigh, deliberating. "Jian gui," he finally said. "Get their information and let them go. Then we can all go back to bed."

Lina and Qiang gave their names and addresses to the policemen, and they all climbed up the winding stairs into the Seed Cathedral. Though it was still early, each of the cathedral's fibers had caught its share of sun and sent pinpoints of light pulsing along the curved walls. The door to the site was propped open, and out stretched the Expo grounds, draped in the shadows of early morning. It had been a long time since she'd been awake this early. Aside from those first jetlagged days in China, she'd never seen a sunrise from the windows of their apartment in Lanson Suites. Not like she had every day in Collegeville, when she got ready for school just as the sun's first rays were pricking through the dense tree leaves in their backyard. Summer mornings in Collegeville were wet, dewy. Nothing like the dry heat moving across the Expo grounds.

On the way to the car, Little Cao rambled on about how difficult it had been to reach anyone of consequence at the Expo, the idiocy of the people he'd dealt with, and how it had taken hours to get hold of a UK pavilion representative with the key to the exhibit. But aside from his chatter, the streets were silent and empty. No bikes on the paths, no directives shouted from storefronts, no peddlers with their piles of hair clips and three-pack socks spread out on tarps. It was too early even for the vendors to be out selling baozi. This was not a Shanghai she had ever known, and Lina looked around, bewildered, as though she were arriving here for the first time.

During the ride home, Lina kept her face turned toward the window. The cityscape must have been completely transformed since Qiang had seen it in his teens, coming to Shanghai to deliver silks. *You're almost unrecognizable,* he'd said to her a few days ago at Yu Gardens as they waited in line for soup dumplings. When was the last time someone had looked at her as closely as he was looking then? *That's funny,* she'd thought. *With you around, I recognize myself again.* But he was only a reminder of her younger self, nothing more. Still, his coming was proof that after all this time, there was still a chance to make amends—not only with him, but with the person she used to be. It frightened her, the ease with which she could arrive in a place without any obvious intention. And yet she could no longer blame her unhappiness on Qiang or Wei. It was no good imagining the other choices she might have made. Dreams of a life lived differently were just that—dreams. No more real than Qiang showing up as a solution to her sadness, just an excuse not to think about the here and now. Lina had a home, and a child, and a husband who did not always know what was best for the family. He needed her help now just as much as he had when they had first moved to America. Somewhere within Lina was the woman who had learned how to make the unfamiliar familiar and build a home out of an environment she did not understand. She would call forth that woman, starting today.

In Lanson Suites, Lina and Qiang rode the elevator up to the twentieth floor in silence. Qiang's T-shirt was wrinkled, his jaw bruise-green with a day's growth of beard. Lina had fixed her hair in the car, but her makeup was a lost cause. The eyeliner had dissipated in the heat, leaving only gray shadows below her tired eyes. She wondered how the two of them would look to others if the car were to stop on floors along the way. Did they seem like lovers? If so, they must look stiff and tired, a whiff of failure about them. And yet, Lina was satisfied. She felt like she had stepped out into the world for the first time in a very long time.

The apartment was silent when they walked through the door, the furniture bathed in the rose and blue light of dawn. When she turned to look back at Qiang, he shrugged, his crooked smile returning easily to his face.

"Are you going to talk to Wei?" she asked him. "You know...about everything you told me?"

"I will," he said. "I'll tell him today."

She nodded, studying the angles on his face, the curve of his back as he turned toward her. This was good-bye. After they parted she would no longer be able to think of him as a lost love or a missed opportunity. He would become a brother to her, as he was meant to be from the beginning. She grasped his hand and squeezed. He returned the pressure and then bowed his head in a show of respect. Finally, they parted and turned down their separate hallways.

In the bedroom, Wei lay fully dressed, curled on top of the bed with his back to the door. Lina stripped off her top, dropped her skirt, and embraced him from behind, pressing up against him like an answer to a question.

He stirred when he felt her weight on him and raised his head to look out the window. The sun had begun to rise over the river.

"What happened?" he asked, squinting at her. "Did you just get home?"

"Yes."

"Why did it take so long?"

"They couldn't find anyone with a key." Lina went on to describe the entire adventure—the guard who would not be bribed and then the guard who would, their VIP-lounge drink raid, Qiang digging through the contents of office desk drawers searching for hairpins with which to pick the lock from the inside.

"I should have known," Wei said, chuckling. "Same old Qiang, right?"

"Yeah." In her tiredness, she forgot for a moment that she was lying on her own bed and instead felt the leather couch beneath her, Qiang warm by her side.

Then she saw her husband watching her. All the humor had gone from his face. She wondered if some part of him knew—if his avoidance of her and Qiang this past week wasn't due to his work but was a way of protecting himself from the knowledge of it. Wei's arm suddenly felt like deadweight across her chest. She imagined him sinking into the bed with each exhale, imagined herself pulling him from its depths.

Had her father felt this kind of guilt when he came home to her mother after his year away? *Remember: Time and commitment. If you have these two things, you can have any manner of love.* All these years, she'd thought he'd been teaching her how to find love. Maybe what he'd really been teaching her was that the hard part wasn't finding love. It was keeping it.

"Actually, I don't think Qiang is the same," she said, running her fingers along Wei's arm. "I really think he's different now. He wants to talk to you later today. You should hear him out." She could feel the muscles in his forearm twitch at her touch. "It's not your fault he ran away."

"I know," he said. "But I keep thinking about my dad's life. Since Qiang's homecoming I've been worrying about all the ways I might have let down my ba because of what I did or didn't do with my life. But I know he would have wanted Qiang back with us."

For the first time, Lina forced herself to imagine, realistically, what it would be like to have Qiang in their family again. They'd take trips to Kunming. They'd meet Cloudy.

"He's married," she said. "Did you know that?"

"No—really?"

"Yes. To a girl from our hometown."

Wei turned so that he was facing the ceiling. "Wah. Maybe he really has changed. Do they have kids?"

"No."

"I wonder why."

She and Wei had never talked about whether they wanted children. Never—not even during the time they had trouble conceiving—had they considered the possibility that they would not one day be parents. But Qiang and Cloudy had grown up with a better understanding of the ways parents could fail their children.

"I think Karen should be educated here," Lina said.

In a burst of clarity, she got up on one elbow and stared at Wei. "I want to be the one raising her. She's an international child, and I think that's what's going to give her an advantage later on in life—the ability to move between cultures, speak two languages. There's a better chance of that happening here than in the U.S."

Lina's parents had wanted her to dream big in both love and life. She had succeeded by taking a chance on America but failed by not making it back before they died. There was time to prevent her child from repeating her own mistakes. It was Lina's job to raise Karen to be a woman who was not only loving but also resilient and independent. A woman who would have a stronger relationship to whatever combination of people and places she eventually came to consider her home.

"You might be right," Wei said finally. "I think that would make her happy. For now, at least. By the way, Karen got her period."

"What?"

"I taught her how to use a tampon."

"You *what?*"

"Father-daughter project."

He was, after all, a man capable of surprising her.

"Oh, Wei. I should have been here."

"It was fine. We did okay. I think she was just nervous."

Lina lay back down. "A pad would have been easier," she said after some thought.

"Ah?"

"A pad. A maxi-pad. You just peel and stick. They're in one of those bottom drawers over there."

"Oh," he said, disappointed. That was Wei—if the job wasn't done in the best way possible, he considered it a complete failure.

The curtains hadn't been drawn the night before, and now the sun was brimming past their edges. Lina shut her eyes. Its warmth was a welcome-home.

24

Little Cao arrived just before noon, by which time Sunny had been awake for hours. Despite the alcohol in her bloodstream — or perhaps because of it — she had woken suddenly at five thirty, mind clear as a chute. For the next few hours, she'd drifted in and out of sleep until she could stay in bed no longer. She got up and showered, ate breakfast, and packed her bag for work, the same as she had almost every day for the past five years.

"Good morning, mei nü," Little Cao said when she got into the car. "How do you feel?"

Even after showering, Sunny was worried that she smelled faintly of the whiskey that she had hardly been able to taste, let alone smell, the night before.

"Oh, I'm all right. It's been a while since I've had that much to drink, but I've felt worse."

When she'd woken that morning, her memory of the previous night seemed too strange to be true. She reached for her purse and found that it was stuffed with cash. Besides the money Boss Zhen had given her, she had the ten-, twenty-, and hundred-yuan bills she'd won from the drivers at liar's dice. She felt like the scholar in that folktale, the one who dreamed of a hundred white knights telling him where to find treasure in his own backyard. Here it was, as improbable as myth. Sunny had looked around for a good place to stash it all, but nowhere in her room seemed safe enough. She had returned the lot of it to her purse, thinking that the next time she went with Taitai to City Shop, she would stop by an ICB and deposit the money.

"Cao," she said. "I wanted to ask you something. What's a good, inexpensive area to live in that's not too far from the city center?"

"Well, I live in Hongqiao. Why? Are you thinking of moving?"

"Maybe," Sunny said. "It might be time for me to live somewhere a little less depressing."

He grinned at her. "You thinking of living alone or with roommates?"

"Well, I don't really know anyone I could room with," she said. "I guess I could ask around Lanson Suites, see if the other housekeepers need someone."

"I'll ask around too," said Little Cao, looking a little smug.

He was right, after all. It was time to invest in herself and in her life here, time to make plans for her own future. If moving to Shanghai meant that Sunny had chosen a life of uncertainty, she didn't regret it. She only needed to think harder about how to make it work.

It was comforting to know that a permanent ayi job could lead to other options. Rose had worked her whole life as a housekeeper only to discover one day that she couldn't stand it anymore. That might have been Sunny one day too — it might still be. Just yesterday she'd been reminded of how arbitrarily the Zhens wielded their power — how they had decided, with no more than a moment's debate, that Sunny and Karen would not attend the Expo. She was disgusted with herself for having been so let down and for wanting to go so much. But it wasn't wrong to want to go. One day, she'd like to be able to buy things like Expo tickets for herself. If that day never came, it would still be nice to have other kinds of comforts. Something closer to what Rose had, perhaps. Not just a place to live, but a real home in the city.

"What happened with Taitai and Qiang?" Sunny asked suddenly. She had been so absorbed in thoughts of her own life that she only now remembered that Taitai and Qiang had been trapped in the Expo. "Did you bail them out finally?"

Little Cao gave a belly laugh. "You should have seen them lying there on the couches of the VIP room in the British pavilion. Empty glasses littered everywhere, like they'd had a party. The looks on their faces as guilty as if they were teenagers who had snuck into a love motel. You were right about the two of them after all."

Sunny dreaded the day ahead of her. When she got to Lanson Suites, she'd assess the situation. If tensions were high when she arrived, she would suggest taking Karen out for a drive or to the movies. Give the adults room to sort things out among themselves. It was only lately that she realized how much she had relied on the calm of her housekeeping job. And that was another reason moving to her own place would be good for her. If she had a space to come home to, maybe she would last longer as an ayi.

It was twelve thirty when Sunny arrived at the apartment, but the household was just waking up. Karen came out first, dressed in a two-piece swimsuit and wearing heart-shaped sunglasses on top of her head.

"Morning," she said, flopping down on the couch next to Sunny.

"Going swimming?"

"Later, I think." She wiggled forward and nestled her head in Sunny's lap.

"How are you feeling?" Sunny asked.

"Better."

Sunny tugged a blanket off the back of the couch and draped it over Karen's exposed midsection.

Next, Qiang came in from smoking on the balcony. Sunny searched his expression for an indication as to what had happened between him and Taitai the night before but could not tell anything. After a brief hello, he disappeared into his room.

Sunny had just finished reheating yesterday's leftovers for a light lunch when Taitai came out of her room. Like Karen, she was dressed to swim.

"Zao," Sunny greeted her. "I warmed up some food — the others have already eaten."

"That's all right," Taitai said. "I had a little too much to drink last night. I'll just eat some yogurt. It should be better for my stomach."

She whisked past Sunny to stand before the refrigerator.

"How was the Expo?"

"All right. We didn't even try to see the China exhibit, the line was so long. But the Irish, the English…overstayed our welcome at the English one a bit. Got home pretty late." She tucked a strand of hair behind her ear and mixed her yogurt, just as if it were any old weekend morning. How skilled she was at the simple act of omission. No wonder she was able to keep Boss Zhen in the dark.

"Oh, before I forget." Taitai motioned for Sunny to follow her into the living room. She ducked behind the dry bar, rummaged through one of its cabinets, and lifted out a small shopping bag.

"Here," she said, presenting it to Sunny. "I picked this up for you. We do a lot of swimming in this family."

Inside, beneath a few layers of tissue, was soft red material. A swimsuit. Sunny felt her face grow hot. She didn't mind accepting Taitai's hand-me-down purses or taking home the leftover food from the Zhens' kitchen, but this suit had been bought specifically for her. It was too personal a gift. She held the bag back out to Taitai.

"It's very kind, but not necessary. I've got a friend I can borrow from. I'll bring a suit tomorrow."

"Aiya," Taitai said. "You should have your own suit, and since it's part of your job, I should provide it. It's the way things should be." Without waiting for a response, she disappeared into the hall. "I'm going to get my things, and then we'll go down together."

So Sunny was left holding the small square shopping bag while Taitai roused her husband from his study and Karen from the couch. "Come, come, get changed!" Taitai called to Wei. "It's going to get too crowded down there if we wait any longer."

Despite herself, Sunny experienced a rush of pleasure in lifting the light, woven handle of the bag between her fingers.

In the pool-house changing room, she hung the suit from a hook on the bathroom stall door to admire it. It was a cherry-colored one-piece, as bright as the ones Sunny had seen on the Olympic swimmers on TV. NIKE, the tags said, and after twisting the suit this way and that, Sunny decided that she couldn't tell the difference between the real thing and any number of fake Nike merchandise they sold beneath People's Square or at the Shanghai Technology Market. There was no doubt, though, that this one was real. The small paper bag it came in had even been marked with a logo.

Sunny ripped the tags off with her hands. Then she took off her clothing, parted the suit by the shoulder straps, and stepped into it. Here, maybe, was where the real thing was better than the fake, because as she pulled it up over her hips, the fabric seemed to know just how far to stretch. When she was dressed, she came out of the stall to stand in front of the mirror. The suit fit perfectly, but the brightness of it was a little alarming. Sunny pictured the other maids watching her from up above and wondered if she looked like a taitai.

Outside, Qiang, Wei, and Karen were seated at the far end of the pool, where they had managed to claim three deck chairs clustered together.

Taitai was already in the water doing circular laps despite the pool being crowded with families. She darted past them beneath the water, coming up for air only when she was halfway around. When she saw Sunny walking toward the Zhens, she stopped.

"How does it fit?" Lina asked, shielding her eyes against the sun.

"It fits." She wished that Taitai hadn't yelled loud enough for the other sunbathers to turn and look at her.

"Sunny, can you swim?" Karen asked.

"Ayis can do everything, remember?"

Karen grinned. "Then let's go in!"

"You go first. I'll be there in a minute."

Karen got up, abandoning her magazine and leaving wet patches on the fabric where her body had been. Sunny sat at the end of her chair and watched the girl race around to the deep end of the pool and take a running jump. In the next chair over, Boss Zhen cleared his throat and held out the magazine he was reading to Qiang. He pointed to an article, muttered something about rising apartment prices, and shook his head. It was the closest Sunny had seen them since the first moment they were reunited in the kitchen. Even if the air had not yet cleared between them, she sensed that the magazine was something of a peace offering.

Sunny's skin felt hot beneath her palms. She reached for the bottle of sunscreen standing at the foot of Boss Zhen's chair and coated her shoulders, legs, face, neck, and feet. All greased up, she headed over to the steps of the pool and lowered herself into the chill, back first. The coldness was transformative. She ducked her head under at the final step and, when she resurfaced, pushed off the wall of the pool so that she was floating on her back. The water broke over her chest, not as frigid as it had felt before. Above, a thin layer of clouds moved across the sky. With both ears below the surface of the water, Sunny attuned herself to the pulse of the pool and the movements of those around her. And then Taitai drifted into view.

Sunny righted herself, sending water streaming from her hairline down into her eyes.

"Refreshing, right?" Taitai was leaning against the pool's stone lip, watching her.

"Very." Sunny swam over, and together they clung to the wall and faced the shallow end of the pool, where Karen was calling for Qiang to get in. He left his conversation with Wei and crouched at the edge of the platform that extended over the rim, fingers grazing its surface. A bright plastic ball floated by; he grabbed it, tested its air pressure beneath his fingers, then palmed it beneath the water. When he pulled away, the ball shot up into the air. It landed with a light bounce on Karen's head and the two of them laughed.

"He's good with her," Sunny said after a moment.

Taitai glanced at her quickly and Sunny wondered if she could read it all in her face — if she could see that Sunny knew what had happened between the two of them the previous night. Was it her imagination or did Taitai's eyes fill before she blinked and looked away?

"Are you married?" Taitai asked after a moment.

"No," Sunny said. "I was."

"That's a shame," Taitai replied. "Although maybe not. Marriage tends to make the years speed by. How old are you, thirty-something?"

"Almost thirty-five."

"I can't remember much of what's happened to me between age thirty-five and now. Well, besides raising Karen."

"That's something," Sunny said. "That's a lot."

Taitai raised her eyebrows as if to agree. Just then, Karen climbed out of the pool and headed toward them. Her legs glimmered and left a trail of water droplets along the concrete. As she leaned over the two of them, Sunny could feel the coolness of the girl's body cutting through the heat, and the water flying off the ends of her hair.

"I'm getting hungry," Taitai said, squinting up at her daughter. "I should have listened to Sunny and eaten something. Want to come to the club with me?"

"I was going to lie out," Karen said. "Thirty more minutes."

It pained Sunny to see the girl bake her body. Most Chinese did everything they could to stay out of the sun, but the Zhens were always trying to find ways to be in it.

"Fine," Taitai said. "I'll ask Daddy."

But the men were deep in conversation again, and Taitai changed her mind.

"If they come looking for me, tell them I'm inside, all right?"

After Taitai left for the clubhouse and Karen went back to sunning herself, Sunny was alone in the deep end except for a few other ayis and their charges. She gestured hello to them as she made her way to the side of the pool hidden in the shadow of the acacia trees. At first, she'd been drawn there only by the promise of shade, but once she saw the metal frame of the skimmer grille, she knew what she was looking for. Sunny grazed up against the dark stone of the pool, unhooked the grille, and slid her hand inside. At first, all she felt was rectangular smoothness. But when she reached in a little farther, she felt a depression. Leaves, debris — this must be the filter basket. What else? Her fingers met something hard and pebbled. She rolled it between her fingers to make sure it was the shape and size she remembered. Then she pulled it out of the chute and examined it, holding it below the water.

It was just as Sunny remembered: lightly but intricately carved, like a child's bracelet. She slipped it over her hand and dropped her arm to one side. The ivory beads, almost weightless in water, settled around the base of her thumb. It was so unlike any of the other jewelry Taitai wore that it must have seemed to Rose like a castoff from her collection. No wonder she had taken it, thinking it would go unmissed.

Sunny squinted up at Tower Eight and counted the floors, from the first all the way up to the twentieth. She imagined herself as she had looked that day, leaning over the balcony, tossing the bracelet into the water. How clever she'd thought she was being then, throwing it away as though everyone's problems started and ended with the bracelet. The truth was more complicated than that. These objects of luxury they handled — how easy it was to fill them with meaning, to let them represent what you did or didn't have. How difficult, in fact, to know what you wanted in the first place.

ACKNOWLEDGMENTS

This novel began in the fiction workshop of the MFA Program at the University of Wisconsin-Madison and received much support and guidance from the community there. My gratitude goes out to professors Danielle Evans, Jesse Lee Kercheval, and Judith Claire Mitchell, who gave me a home in the Midwest. Thank you to my cohort-family, Piyali Bhattacharya, Hanna Halperin-Goldstein, Christian Holt, Will Kelly, Walter B. Thompson (honorary member), and especially Jackson Tobin, who read both the first draft and the last. I owe you all the beers and chicken chipotle wraps City Bar has to offer.

My agent, Rebecca Gradinger, shaped this story enormously by finding me when she did and asking just the right questions. I am lucky to have such a thorough, wise reader and strong advocate. Luckier still that she comes backed by a group of smart women: Melissa Chinchillo, Grainne Fox, and Veronica Goldstein at Fletcher & Company.

Thank you to Judy Clain for her unending enthusiasm and generosity toward this book. The entire team at Little, Brown — Alexandra Hoopes, Lena Little, Ashley Marudas, Craig Young, Sabrina Callahan, Reagan Arthur, Tracy Roe, Jayne Yaffe Kemp, and Lucy Kim — went above and beyond in making a new author feel welcome and delivering my novel into the world.

At NYU, I am indebted to Marcelle Clements and Emma Claire

Sweeney for showing me what it means to take this work seriously. I also want to thank my grade school reading and writing teachers, Julie DiGiacomo, Susan Rothbard, and Frederica Glucksman. They saw in me an early love of language and held me accountable to it.

Several people were valuable resources when it came to researching this book. Thanks to Quan Chen for his knowledge of Suzhou and its surrounding villages in the 1980s; to my uncle, Lingyi Tan, for information on Chinese crime; and to Dylan-Lee Smith for his knowledge of the Expo grounds and the layout of the UK Pavilion. Any deviances from fact on these accounts are due to my own errors and imagination. To Eva: Thank you for the stories. You are an inspiration.

To everyone who has reached out to me in support of this book and every reader who has picked it up, your time and attention mean the world to me. Special thanks to my oldest friends and readers, who have been cheering me on for years: Alex and Susie Yang, Vinay Daryani, Ada Zhang, Maggie Chong, Christina Herbach, Angela Wu, Bena Cheung, Lilly Chen, Mengyi Luo, Annie Yoon, Jimmy Shi, Chloe Krug Benjamin, Joe Koplowitz, Ali Cuan, and Dizheng Du.

To Stephen Hogsten—for following me on this journey, for your love and infinite faith, I am humbled and deeply grateful. No one packs the contents of two apartments into a hatchback quite like you do.

This book has been a group effort by my tiny, fierce, and loving family, particularly the ones who raised me. My grandparents, Rennian Yang and Mingru Tan, taught me that the best kind of storyteller is a compassionate one. My parents, Lingshi and Lorna Tan, read multiple drafts of this novel and facilitated interviews in Chinese. More importantly, they showed me how to live adventurously, think independently, and love boundlessly. My voice is rooted in our home, wherever that home may be. Thanks, Mom and Dad, for proving that the safest path isn't always the one worth traveling. As immigrants twice over, you knew how to dream big. And then you taught me how to do it.

QUESTIONS AND TOPICS
FOR DISCUSSION

1. What promises—spoken and unspoken—have the characters made to one another, to themselves, and to the countries they feel allegiance to?

2. How do the characters' expectations drive or limit their actions?

3. Why is the story set in Shanghai? How does the physical and cultural landscape serve as context for the lives of the characters?

4. How do Lina's and Wei's relationships to China and America change over time?

5. What is Sunny's relationship to her hometown, and how does it evolve throughout the novel?

6. What are the ways in which each of the characters assumes the role of caretaker? Do their roles and responsibilities shift throughout the novel?

7. Lina feels that she may have limited herself by choosing to marry rather than to pursue a postcollegiate plan. Do you think she regrets her decision?

8. What do you think Lina's and Wei's hopes are for Karen's future?

9. How has Sunny's perception of her own identity and abilities evolved by the end of the novel?

10. "There's a reason you're drawn to whatever it is, or whoever it is, you're falling for," says Qiang on page 185. "They have something you're missing." Lina believes he is talking about her. Do you agree?